RUN, CLARISSA, RUN

Rachel Eliason

ISBN: 0988573016
ISBN-13: 978-0988573017

ACKNOWLEDGMENTS

SRS, Nanowrimo and writing software

November is national novel writer's month. It has something only a novel writer hyped up on way too much coffee could possibly conceive, Nanowrimo. Started back in 1999 by 21 bay area writers, Nanowrimo was a challenge, write a novel in a month. The philosophy behind Nanowrimo is to get rid of the internal editor by writing very quickly. Nanowrimo has grown over the years from those 21 writers to literally thousands all over the world. There are group write-ins, weekly pep talks from Nanowrimo.org and much more.

I did my first Nanowrimo in 2009. I already had several rough drafts of novels under my belt by then, but writing a novel in a month proved too much with other aspect of life going on. I made it to about 25,000 words into my novel and gave up.

In 2010 I skipped Nanonwrimo because I had something a little more important going on, for me personally at least. In October of that year I flew to Thailand to have SRS (Sexual Reassignment Surgery). While laid up in a hotel room in Thailand I spend an inordinate amount of time on my laptop. I surfed the net, wrote in my journal, wrote a blog and wrote articles for a local LGBT paper.

I got caught up in a thread on one forum about writing software. I had never used any software to design or layout novels prior to this. I felt that, like most books on how to write a novel, such programs were little more than distractions, ways of not writing. Too many would be writers spend too much of their time reading about writing, talking about writing and thinking about writing but not actually writing. However, wanting to have an informed opinion on the subject I downloaded several free writing programs to test.

One was Storybook and it's become my favorite tool. I created a test file to see what the system could do. What would I write about? The first thing I had thought when I woke up in the recovery room after my SRS was, why hadn't I done this sooner? After all the anxiety and doubt, once I made the leap I couldn't help but wonder why I hadn't realized years ago this was what I needed to do.

So I created a fictitious fifteen year old transgender character that somehow knew they must transition and somehow manages this act. But how would a fifteen-year-old have that kind of money? How would they convince a surgeon to take their case? What would drive them?

As I asked and answered these questions new characters and subplots emerged. As I entered the characters and subplots in the program, new ideas for scenes came to me. In a matter of three weeks "test file" became "the runaway." I had drafted a complete novel in a fraction of the time it usually took me.

Then I began writing and an even greater magic unfolded for me. Knowing each scene, each coming step there were no awkward places, no stops while I thought through the next step. I just wrote. In December of 2010 I had my own personal Nanonwrimo. In three and a half weeks I wrote a 60,000 word novel.

I began drafting other novels using this software and I loved it. However the final piece of magic came a couple months later, when I came back and re-read The Runaway. It was a rough draft, but far less rough than my others. It needed far less work in my opinion and seemed far more worth putting the work into. The Runaway draft one became Run, Clarissa, Run draft two, then three, four, five and six. Now as the two year anniversary of my SRS rolls around it comes to you as a completed novel. I hope you enjoy reading it as much I enjoyed writing it.

Chapte _ _ _ _ _ _ _ _ _ _ _ 1

Chapter Two _ _ _ _ _ _ 8

Chapter Three _ _ _ _ _ _ _ _ _ _ 22

Chapter Four _ _ _ _ _ _ _ _ _ _ 33

Chapter Five _ _ _ _ _ _ 46

Chapter Six _ _ _ _ _ _ 54

Chapter Seven _ _ _ _ _ _ _ _ _ _ 67

Chapter Eight _ _ _ _ _ _ 87

Chapter Nine _ _ _ _ _ _ 97

Chapter Ten _ _ _ _ _ _ 108

Chapter Eleven _ _ _ _ _ _ 123

Chapter Twelve _ _ _ _ _ _ 137

Chapter Thirteen _ _ _ _ _ _ 145

Chapter Fourteen _ _ _ _ _ _ _ _ 162

Chapter Fifteen _ _ _ _ _ _ 172
* * *

Chapter Sixteen 187

Chapter Seventeen 204

Chapter Eighteen 217

Chapter Nineteen 245

Chapter Twenty 257

Chapter Twenty-One 280

CHAPTER ONE

Clark sat up, enveloped in darkness, the echoes of his scream still in his ears. His jaws gaped as he gulped for air. Sweat ran from his brow. He panted, as though he had just finished a long run.

Slowly the world came into focus. The vague light coming through the small window of his basement room dissolved the inky blackness into a gray-scale world. He heard a sound above him, his mother's footsteps.

He lay back on his bed and waited. The grayness grew to include a line of white under his door as his mom turned on the basement light outside his room. Then the light pierced his eyes as she opened the door a crack.

"You okay, hon?"

"Yes, Mom," he replied wearily, "just a nightmare,"

"Again?"

"Yes."

"Anything I can do?"

"No." It was a resigned rebuttal. Clark rolled away from the door.

There had been a time when he would have called her closer, let her hold him until he felt safe again. There had been a time when they would have discussed the dream. That seemed a long time ago now.

His mom waited a few minutes and then sighed wearily. The light vanished.

After he was sure his mom was gone for good he got up and turned on his light. On the far wall Lady Gaga stared at him. The bottom of the poster bore in black felt tip the cryptic message, "don't get your hopes up."

Clark had added these words himself as a message to both his mother and himself. To his mother it said, "Don't think this one poster of this one beautiful women means your youngest son is going to suddenly become a normal boy with normal interests." For Clark, it was a bitter reminder. You can wish all you want but don't think you are going to wake up one morning and be a beautiful woman like that.

Clark sank down and curled up on the floor, staring up at the poster. *I should just kill myself,* he thought morosely, *get it over with.* Life wasn't going to get any better.

I shouldn't think that way. It was wrong. Besides it was so clichè; Emo kid takes life under Lady Gaga poster. What a depressing headline.

He went to his vanity. No, he reminded himself bitterly, his grandmother's vanity. It had ended up in his room because there was no where else to put it, not because he had said repeatedly he wanted it.

He reached into the lower left drawer. He pushed aside the junior high yearbook and assorted newspaper clippings about his dad. Underneath was a small compact, some eyeliner, three tubes of lipstick, two bottles of nail polish, and a bottle of polish remover. He selected the eyeliner and looked into the mirror.

This was the only thing to soothe him after the dream. Sleep would come again, but not for awhile. Hopefully it would come before morning, when he had to get up for school. And hopefully it would bring the other dream this time.

There were two dreams that ruled Clark's life. The first had been with him for a long while. He first remembered having it when he was four. They had been staying on his uncle's farm, back when his dad was still alive.

His aunt had asked him in the morning if he slept well.

"Yeah," he had replied. "I had the best dream ever."

"What was it?" His aunt had asked.

"I was old," he began (To a four-year-old, every adult was old), "and I was a woman!"

This proclamation was greeted by howls of laughter, good natured from his aunt, less so from his brother, his uncle and, as much as it pained him to think about it, from his father.

"What else?" His aunt had asked.

He merely shrugged, put off by the reaction he was receiving. Not that there was anything more to the dream. He was grown up and he was a woman. The dream had grown in the tiniest details over the years. He was in his thirties or forties, not old old but clearly adult. He was in his house, sitting and thinking. He - no, she - was thinking about how she had been a boy once. There was nothing else, no plot. No reason why this one dream should hold such happiness for him.

But it did. It sustained him for many years. It told him that whatever he endured now, it was just now. Someday things would be better. He didn't understand the why or the how. He just knew. When his mom had taken him shopping for school clothes and refused to buy him a single outfit that he chose, because they came from the wrong side of aisle, he endured it. When his father had forbidden the six-year-old from buying any more Barbie dolls, it had been hard but okay. When he was caught red handed with his mother's lipstick; always the dream saved him.

Clark paused to look at his reflection. The dream had saved him for many years but not any more. It couldn't save him, it was only a dream. When he was about fourteen he had come to fully realize that he was not going to some how magically grow up and be a woman. He was a boy and he would remain so as long as he lived.

It was about then the other dream came. This one had more action but no more plot or meaning. He was being shoved into a bank vault. He could never see the faces of those doing the shoving but he could feel the struggle like it was a real visceral experience. He woke sweating and sore from trying to fight them off. They would wrestle between the desks and counters of the bank as he was dragged inexorably towards the vault. Always he would wake before they got there. But he still knew somehow, intuitively, that if they got him there they would close the door and it would be blackness forever.

#####

"But mom, I need it for school" His brother's voice grated on Clark's tired ears. At school and around his friends, Jeremy took great pains to speak in a deep slow voice. But around mom he let a nasal whine creep in.

"I just don't know if I can afford it right now," his mother replied.

"You want me to do well in school, don't you?" Jeremy had their mom on the ropes and he knew it. She wanted both her sons to do their best. Jeremy wanted a new laptop.

"Are you sure it's broken?" She asked.

"Yes, I keep telling you, yes." He whined again. "It will barely boot. I can't get anything to run in less than ten minutes! And even then it barely works. I can't get the Internet at all."

"It's probably a virus," Clark put in sagely.

Their mother moaned. "I put Norton on it just a couple of months ago. Fine, let me check the bank account. And maybe next weekend when we are in Des Moines we can look around."

"I want a Mac book this time." Jeremy put in, instantly mollified.

Their mom shot Jeremy the don't-push-your-luck stare and he shut up. Clark knew his brother would have to settle for whatever was on sale at Walmart or Best Buy. But at least he had a computer of his own. Clark had to share the desktop with mom. He wasn't sure which was worse, having to sit in the living room to surf the net or having his mom read and comment on what he was doing.

Clark had been angling for his own laptop for some time. Now he would be waiting once again. There was no way they could afford two laptops. And it was not like he had his brother's pull. Jeremy was a star athlete and a good student beside. He got the first laptop, an HP thinkpad, for a 4.0 grade point average last year. Despite scoring well on all the aptitude tests he was given, Clark barely pulled a C average. Besides, unlike his brother, he required therapy just to function and therapy wasn't cheap.

Jeremy had finished his third frozen waffle and downed his orange juice in one gulp. He got up from the table. Clark toyed with his first frozen waffle, half eaten on his plate. He thought about saying something smart about how much his brother ate compared to him but he decided against antagonizing Jeremy right now. Instead he said, "hey, Jer, maybe I could have your old computer." He shrugged, "Maybe I can get it sort of working you know."

Jeremy gave him a skeptical look. Then he shrugged. "Whatever. But I am telling you, it's broke."

#####

Shelley Pirella's dark blond hair fell across her face. She tossed it over one shoulder and bent down again. Her arm fished the drier, manually turning the drum to make sure everything was out.

Her hand came out with a pair of white panties with bright pink dots on them. She looked them blankly for a long time. She didn't recognize them.

She crumpled the offending panties into her fist. She could almost imagine slamming her fist into her husband's face. Tears threatened to overwhelm her but she held them back. She felt a strong urge to throw something, preferably at him.

She bit that back too. It wouldn't do any good and she would only have to clean it up anyway. She had thrown things at him the first time. She had threatened to leave. Threatened a lot of things she didn't do. Now she just sighed.

Leaving was not an option. It wasn't money, she was a nursing supervisor at a busy hospital. It wasn't the kids, though she told herself often enough that she stayed because she wanted the girls to have a father, even if it was a lying cheating father. At least he was good with the twins. He wasn't abusive like her own father had been.

Shelley Pirella was a good Catholic woman. She came from a long line of good Catholic women. When asked why she never left her abusive alcoholic husband, her mother merely pointed to the crucifix on the wall. Shelley had surrounded herself with other good Catholic women. When Marilee had left her husband two years ago, her clique had broke ties with her "to show her the err of her ways." Shelley still missed Marilee from time to time but she was resolute in her beliefs too.

That didn't mean there weren't other ways to show her anger, to make him pay. But first things first, she needed a new babysitter.

#####

"All of those virus cleaning sites are scams" Jeremy said authoritatively as the brothers walked into school that morning. He had been insisting that the laptop was beyond repair the entire way to school. One big reason was crystal clear; he had told Clark in no uncertain terms he was not to even try fixing the laptop before the weekend. If by some chance he succeeded it would remove any reason for mom to buy a new one. Clark readily agreed to the condition, he wasn't about to fix the computer only to have Jeremy claim it back.

"Most of the sites are," Clark allowed, "but not all..."

He was blinded by pain as he hit the nearest locker. His head spun.

"Faggot," he heard from the retreating back. The bully's name was John. He was one of several jocks that routinely used that word for Clark and almost as routinely body slammed him into the wall or the nearest locker.

"Fucker," Clark muttered at the retreating back. Looking the other way, towards his brother's retreating back he uttered one more "fucker." He didn't know what he expected. His brother was civil enough at home and on the way to or from school. He could even be okay at school but he had made his position clear a long time ago about this sort of thing.

"I can only do so much," he had told Clark. (Clark couldn't recall what Jeremy had ever done but let it slide.) "If you can't start butching it up a bit, I can't help you." It was his brother's theory that bullying was nature's way of telling you to suck it up and take it like a man. He never harassed Clark himself but he never raised a finger to stop anyone else from doing so, not even his own friends.

With a sigh Clark recovered his fallen books and shook out his hair. He knew his shoulder length blond hair was a big bone of contention. The jocks had threatened more than once to hold him down and shave it off. He had in turn made it clear that he would fight tooth and nail if it came to that. So far nobody had made good on their promise.

Which was just as well, because he knew there were several teachers that wouldn't intervene either. He had had plenty of talks with the principal about his hair and it was no less a bone of contention there. Clark carefully kept it trimmed a few millimeters above the shoulder, and away from being expelled for violating the school dress code. That most of the girls in this small-town school had hair longer than shoulder length didn't matter apparently. As always, that was different.

CHAPTER TWO

"Mommy, is that a boy or a girl?" Britney asked.

"Britney!" Shelley gasped. At four years old, the girls asked all sorts of silly questions but this was going too far.

The twin sisters were in the front of the car-shaped shopping cart. Britney, in the passenger side had stuck her head out and looked back to her mother, who was inspecting bottles of pasta sauce, to ask her question. While she shushed the girls she followed the line of her daughter's thumb down the aisle.

At the far end of the aisle was a skinny teenager with shoulder length blond hair. They wore a white, gender neutral T-shirt and blue jeans. Shelley couldn't help but have the same question in her mind. Boy or girl?

The teenager grabbed a bag of pasta and disappeared around the corner. Shelley shook her head dismissing the kid and returning to her sauce selection. Tony was raised in an Italian American home that took pasta seriously. Springing a new pasta sauce on her husband was a major decision.

"Mom?" It was Britney's sister Holly this time, from the other side of the cart.

"What?"

"Was it a boy or a girl?"

"I don't know," she replied absentmindedly, selecting a bottle and putting it in the cart.

Two aisles later Shelley rounded a corner to come face to face with a woman she knew, vaguely. They greeted each cordially, each trying to place the other. The woman appeared to be in her forties, about Shelley's age. They had similar names too, didn't they?

Yes.

"Kelly?" She said brightly, "Kelly Holden?"

"That's right." The woman responded.

Tony had served briefly with Kelly's husband. They hadn't been close but Shelley and Kelly were both auxiliary members and had met at functions for army wives, especially during the early days of Afghanistan when their husbands were away. She remembered that Kelly had lost her husband, a helicopter pilot.

"How are you doing?" Shelley said.

"Fine and you?" Kelly answered.

"Can't complain." Visions of white panties with pink spots circled her vision, but she shoved them down.

"Mom, do you want this?" A voice asked.

Shelley turned. It was the teenager again. She, Shelley decided, was holding Woman's day magazine. The cover article read, "The Home Spa: how to replace most store-bought cleansers with products you already own".

"Look at these recipes," the girl continued pointing to the holiday section in the lower right corner. "You were saying the other day we should do something different for Thanksgiving this year, since it's just the three of us. How about Cornish Game Hens?"

Kelly took the magazine and said, "Shelley, this is my youngest son Clark." The 'son' had a peculiar emphasis, as if she had heard the 'is that boy or a girl' question.

Maybe she had. Looking at the teenager again she could see that it was indeed a boy but with the shoulder length hair layered the way it was and the conspicuously neutral clothing it was a close call. It wasn't even just that, there was something about the way he stood, with his weight on one leg so that the opposite hip stuck out or the way he put both hands in his back pockets and waited on his mother's verdict, that could only be described as feminine.

"Who's going to cook these Cornish Game Hens?" Kelly was flipping through the magazine, looking for the recipe.

"I will," Clark responded. "It looks easy enough," To Shelley he explained, "I like to cook."

It was then that Britney decided to pipe in with, "are you a boy or a girl?"

"Britney!"

"Umm, I'm a boy." Clark didn't seem put out the question, in fact he seemed less than sure of the answer himself.

"Boys don't cook" Holly put in.

"They eat." Clark responded. "Why shouldn't they cook?"

The girls didn't have an answer to that. "What do you girls like to eat?" Clark bent over the cart and started talking to them. They giggled nervously and both began rambling at once, as they often did when strange adults showed them any attention.

Shelley and Kelly exchanged pleasantries while Clark talked to the girls about donuts, which were the girls current favorite food. Kelly put the magazine in the cart without thinking about it.

After a couple of minutes there was nothing left to say, so they passed on with vague promises to 'stay in touch'.

"He was nice" one of the girl's commented as they went on. Shelley snorted but didn't answer. She would have to remember to pray for Kelly, for her dead husband and for her overtly flaming son. If he was not a homosexual (he was awfully young and besides there weren't any homosexuals in this small town, part of why she lived here) he was certainly a candidate.

She knew very little about homosexuality but some guy had spoken at their church a few years back. It was, he had said, a lifestyle. Every gay person had a coming out story, a story about how they were first introduced to the lifestyle. In this story, he had explained, was the key to understanding the stereotypes about gay people. They (meaning the homosexuals) looked for outsiders, kids that didn't fit in. They were the most vulnerable, vulnerable to some gay who showed them positive attention.

She spied them later in her shopping, in the shampoo aisle. He was holding a bottle of Herbal Essence, she a generic brand and they appeared to be arguing. Slowly a plan was forming in her mind. He most certainly not gay, he was so young and it was such a small town that there wasn't a gay presence here. But he was certainly somebody who would be vulnerable to the lifestyle. Keeping him off the streets, and away from those influences would almost be a good deed; the girls would be quite safe and Tony (she smirked as she thought it) well he didn't need the temptation either. Maybe she could prevent two sins with one act.

#####

"Whatch'ya got there?" Ben snatched the book out of Clark's hand before he could stop him. He was much bigger than Clark. This was a small Iowa school with barely sixty-some kids in his class and less than three hundred in all four grades combined. The cliques were well established and rarely violated. As a jock, the boy was one of the kings of the school. Clark on the other hand, didn't have enough status to hang out with the geeks. It seemed like the only time anyone even noticed him was when they needed a punching bag.

"Windows for Dummies? They got it half right." Ben laughed. Clark scowled. He was smarter than this kid but he was smart enough to keep his mouth shut too. Ben was on the defensive line, six feet and a heavily muscled. Clark was one of the few sophomores that didn't call him 'sir' but he wasn't about to push his luck.

"Maybe you should check out, faggots for dummies," Ben kept on. Clark's face burned but he kept his mouth shut. "But I guess you're already an expert on being a fag. Look what your kid brother has got," Ben told Jeremy as he came up. Jeremy never stood up for Clark but at least most of the kids toned it down in his presence.

Jeremy took the book and shrugged, handing it back to Clark. "Yeah, he thinks he can fix my old laptop. He's a f-ing genius you know."

Ben laughed and went on his way while the two brothers left the school and headed for Jeremy's car. Well, they both thought of it as his car. Mom considered it 'the second car' because it was rightfully hers. It was just too much for their single mom to also play chauffeur. So Jeremy got the second car as long as he let his kid brother tag along.

They also both had clear and opposite ideas about what would happen in the spring when Clark could drive. Jeremy had said he intended to take the car when he went to college. Clark didn't doubt he'd try. Clark would stand up for his own right to drive and to keep the car. Not that he had much hope. He was already bracing himself to be riding the bus again.

"Just remember," Jeremy cautioned, "don't you dare fix the laptop before tomorrow." For all of his disparaging statements, Jeremy had been in on many of the family discussions about Clark's performance at school and the numerous aptitude tests Clark had taken and excelled at. He knew that while genius might be a stretch, it wasn't a big one. He was afraid that Clark might actually succeed.

#####

"Are you boys ready yet?" Their mom was wandering through the kitchen as she said it, purse in hand.

"Almost," Clark said, pushing his plate away, "Just got to clean up." He started towards the bathroom.

"Your *boy* is ready." Jeremy drawled out slowly, barely even looking up from the copy of Men's health he was reading at the table opposite Clark.

Clark flipped his brother off without stopping. Neither of the brothers were in any hurry. Mom would spend at least the next half an hour running around doing last minute chores, berating the boys about not being ready. It was an old pattern.

Clark brushed his hair and looked in the mirror until his mom's voice had reached a feverish pitch. When he came back into the living room he saw that Jeremy had taken the hint too and was getting his letter jacket out of the closet.

"No, no," Mom said flatly. "It's going to be really cold today. Wear your winter coat."

Jeremy shrugged and put the letter jacket back. He pulled out a black leather jacket. Clark reached around for his winter coat, a tan leather jacket with a line of fringe around the bottom.

A blast of cold air hit him as his mom opened the door. "Come on, we don't want to be late." Mom said.

"We have plenty of time before Clark's appointment, mom," Jeremy said as he followed her out the door.

He was looking forward to today, at least after he got through with therapy. He didn't like this new therapist but he was better than the last one. Today he would have therapy followed by the new therapy group. Then mom and Jeremy would pick him up and they would go out for lunch and then shopping. Jeremy's new laptop would take the majority of the time, attention and money but Clark could still wander the mall and window shop. It beat sitting around his room in Grundy Center, a town too small to have its own mall.

#####

"How are you doing, kiddo?" Dr. Carlton, no Philip, always sounded so cheerful. He had insisted that Clark call him by name, instead of the formal title. Clark in turn had insisted that Philip not use the term 'buddy' in his presence. That term always grated on his ears. Maybe it was because too many of dad's old buddies and mom's new boyfriends, all the men who tried to play surrogate father to Clark, liked to call him "little buddy".

"Fine," Clark replied. And waited. This is what he hated about therapy. The therapist always tried to get him to talk and he had little to say. The result was long awkward silences.

"School going okay so far this fall?" Phillip asked.

"Yeah, fine."

"Still getting picked on?"

He thought about getting shoved into the locker on Monday, the word faggot, about a dozen incidents since then. The boy who squealed every time Clark entered the locker room for gym class, "oh no, a girl in the boy's locker room." Yes, he was still being picked on. Why talk about it? He had talked and talked, what good had come of it? "Yeah," and after a long pause, "about the same, you know."

"Hmm. You and mom getting along?"

"Yeah, we're fine."

"Jeremy?"

Clark shrugged. "Same."

"How did you like the group last time?"

This was the pivotal moment in this session Clark had been dreading the question.

"It was okay." He said.

"Just okay?" Phillip asked.

"I am not gay."

"We've discussed this before," Philip said. Philip was gay. He had said so himself. Besides he had a picture of himself with his partner, Eric, on his desk.

"I know," Clark jumped in, "it's just, well, like that group." It had been a gay youth group that Philip had suggested might be helpful. "I don't have a problem with them, I really don't. But I don't fit in there either. I can't explain it, I just don't. I am not like them." Clark continued.

"What is it about them you don't like?"

He knew what Philip was trying to imply. Philip thought he was gay, that he had some sort of "internalized homophobia" and couldn't accept himself as a gay kid. It was a logical thought, Clark conceded, but he didn't think of himself as gay. It wasn't that he had anything against gay people and it didn't mean he hated himself.

"It's not that I don't like them, I am just not like them." He persisted.

"How are they?" Phillip asked.

"I don't know, they are just, you know, boys."

"And you?"

"We've discussed this before," was all Clark would say.

"Randy?"

Randy was the reason that Clark didn't like therapy. Part of the reason anyway. His mom had taken him to see Dr. Edgerton two years ago, when he was barely fourteen. It hadn't gone well. At least Dr. Edgerton had never called him buddy or kiddo and Clark had never learned his first name. But Dr. Edgerton hadn't had a clue about Clark either.

"Why are you here?" Dr. Edgerton had asked.

"Because," Clark's voice had dripped with sarcasm, "I didn't know that fourteen-year-old boys weren't supposed to cry because they aren't girls."

Dr. Edgerton's solution was that he didn't have enough "gender appropriate" male role models so he was set up with another boy, Randy, who was also in the doctor's practice. Randy had anger management issues and under normal circumstances would have been exactly the kind of boy to torment or beat Clark. Instead they had somehow become friends, at least for a while.

They shared similar tastes in music and Clark had even visited Randy's home a few of times. They had gone to Randy's room and listened to music and talked. Randy had slowly opened up to Clark and most likely had benefited as Dr. Edgerton had planned. Then one day Randy had kissed Clark, taking him totally off guard.

A big part of him said it wasn't him. He hadn't started it. A smaller part said he didn't object either. It had gone on for several weeks then Randy started to want to do more. Clark didn't so he told his mom what was going on, and then under her orders, he told Dr. Edgerton.

That had ended the friendship with Randy. Luckily, he was from several towns away, so he didn't have to see him at school. When Dr. Edgerton had suggested someone else, that ended the sessions with him. Mom was finally convinced he was a quack who couldn't help her son.

Enter Dr. Philip Carlton. Philip was definitely an improvement over Dr. Edgerton. Clark could handle being accused of being gay once a month. He got that several times a day at school.

"I liked the kids okay." He went on describing the youth group, "but the way they talk about being gay, makes me all the surer I am not. They are so..." he groped for the right word, "Sexual."

Philip gave a good-natured laugh. "How do you expect them to talk about their sexuality?"

"I don't know. Look I don't deny the whole Randy thing. I don't deny that I am sometimes attracted to guys but it's not the same as those boys."

"Sometimes attracted to guys," Phillip echoed gently, "but

definitely not gay?"

"It's just different for me." Clark shot back angrily.

"Different how?"

"I just," Clark fumbled for the words, "It's, I don't know, it's not sexual, not like those guys talk anyway. It's more...romantic."

"So if you love the boy, it's not gay?" Phillip obviously was not understanding or accepting the difference.

"No, I mean I don't think about having sex with boys." Clark knew he was not explaining himself well. The problem was that he had no clue how to explain what he felt, other than it was not like how those boys in the group talked.

"Girls?" Phillip inquired mildly.

"No," Clark said sullenly.

Phillip shrugged dismissively. "Fine, you don't have to be anything. And it's certainly not my place to tell you how to identify yourself. The real reason I wanted you to attend the group was because the harassment you face at school is a lot like what many in the group go through. Did it help to talk about that?"

Clark nodded slightly, glad to change the subject. "Yeah, I mean it's kind of depressing to think every school is the same, that there are bullies there too. But it was good to talk about it. Back home everyone just acts like if I would "tone it down" somehow the bullies wouldn't target me. Those kids understood. You can't stop who you are. It's impossible."

"So do you want to stay for the group again?"

Clark surprised himself by answering, "yeah."

"Good. Few formalities and then we'll head over, it's about time anyway. Drugs or alcohol?" Phillip asked.

"No."

"Suicidal thoughts?"

After a long pause Clark responded, "Sometimes, but I can contract." Contracting, Clark had learned early on in therapy meant that he agreed he would not attempt suicide without talking to a professional first. He had also learned that if you weren't able to "contract for safety" they would start talking nut ward and he did not want that.

"Okay then," Phillip said, "let's call it a day."

"Hey!" The voice caught Clark as he started to pull on his jacket. A brightly dressed boy came rushing up to Clark. He swished as he ran, one arm up, wrist limp. He wore black sneakers that he had painted with swirls of neon fabric paint, jeans, a polo T-shirt and long scarf against the cold. He was pulling on a long woolly brown coat as he rushed up.

It wouldn't take a rocket scientist to figure out we both just got out of the gay youth group, Clark thought wryly; Mr. Effeminate, and Mr. feminine. Still Marcus had seemed nice enough in the last two group sessions.

"Wicked group today," Marcus said, "in large part thanks to you."

"Glad to be of help," Clark replied dryly. He had opened up today and told his story, about his first therapist and about Randy.

"That was f-ed up," Marcus went on, "and set up by your therapist."

"Yeah," Clark said, "it was pretty screwed up."

"You from around here?" Marcus was pulling a cell phone from the pocket of his thick brown woolly coat and started typing.

"Grundy Center, up north," Clark replied.

"Wicked awesome!" Marcus chirped and extended his hand out, "Eldora. We are practically neighbors."

Clark smiled too.

"This is awesome. Now I am not the only gay in rural Iowa. We should totally exchange numbers," Marcus went on.

Clark agreed happily even though he didn't think of himself as gay and even though he didn't have a cell phone. It was nice to know there was someone within a thirty-minute drive of home that didn't care he was a freak. He heard a honk and knew that Mom was waiting with Jeremy in tow.

He could only guess at Jeremy's reaction but he didn't care. He quickly rattled off their home number while Marcus typed it in to his phone. On the second honk, he waved good-bye and ran for the car.

"Who was that?" His mother asked as he got in.

"Another kid from the group," he said. "Lives up our way. Marcus."

"What are they running a group for fairies?" His brother laughed. Clark winced. He hadn't told his brother that he was in a group for gay kids. He got teased enough without that information out.

"Jeremy!" his mom scolded. "I'm sure he's a good kid." She asked Clark. "McDonald's okay?" Clark nodded. This wasn't the day for arguing. A cheap meal now meant more cash in mom's wallet later, when they were shopping.

"You guys ready?" Mom said as she approached them in the mall later. They both nodded. They had spent the last half hour or so pointedly ignoring each other but now they came together next to her. Mom had dropped them at the mall two hours ago, to each go their own way while she did the same.

Mom had two small bags, one from Payless shoes and the other from JC Penny's. Clark had a small bag marked B. Dalton's, the book store. It was an early William Gibson novel he hadn't read. It had been on clearance, which left enough out of the twenty that mom gave him for the second bag, the one from Claire's that was tucked deep in his pocket.

Jeremy had no bags, only his new Acer Aspire One netbook. They had bought it at Best Buy before coming to the mall. It had not been his choice. He had his eye on a Mac book. He had played with the Mac book while Clark toyed with the Ipads. Their mother had inspected every laptop and netbook in the place. Money was tight, she told them. With that dire (and common) predictor Jeremy had after quite a bit of quiet pleading been forced to settle for the small netbook.

He had spent most of his twenty at the food court. He had spent most of the time there too, using the mall's Wi-fi to test out his new computer. "Not too shabby for a little machine," he had told Clark confidentially. To mom his only comment was, "it's already almost dead, crappy battery life."

Clark and Jeremy had spoken briefly when they arrived at the rendezvous site. Then they had sat several feet apart and waited. Jeremy wanted enough distance to deny that Clark was his brother and Clark increasingly felt the same way. Clark had tried to read but it was hard to concentrate. His mind kept slipping back to his pocket, to the bracelet, clip on ear rings and nail polish. He wanted to pull them out and look at them again, but he knew he couldn't. Not until he got home and was alone in his room.

"Should we grab something from the food court for on the way home?" Mom asked.

"Aww Mom" Jeremy whined, "can't we go somewhere nice. Like Olive Garden?"

Now that he had his computer, Jeremy saw no reason to continue to go along so readily with frugality.

"I don't think we can really afford it."

"I don't mind Subway." Clark said.

Mom's phone went off and while she fished in her purse to look for it Jeremy mouthed the words 'suck up' towards Clark. Clark made a face and stuck his tongue out.

"This is Kelly Holden," Mom said. "Can I help you?"

Their mom moved away to talk and the boys stood awkwardly together.

"Buy any make up?" Jeremy sneered under his breath.

Not wanting him to guess that he was correct Clark shot back, "look up any porn?"

The brewing fight was broken by their mother's return. "Yeah, maybe. I'll talk to him about it over supper and have him contact you if he's interested." She hung up and turned to the boys. "That was strange," she said.

"What did they want me to do?" Jeremy asked assuming the call was about him.

"It was Shelley Pirella," Mom replied, turning to Clark, "the woman from the grocery store."

"Who?" Clark asked.

"Someone I knew years ago, we ran into her in the grocery store. The woman with the twin girls. They wanted to know... you talked to them, while I talked to her..."

Jeremy looked incredulous to find he was not the center of attention. "What did she want?" He asked, just to be part of the conversation.

"She said you were really good with the girls and they need a new babysitter. Thought maybe you'd be interested. She works evening shift at one of the hospitals in town here and her husband works late. The girls are in day care until four pm. It would be just three hours until he gets off and home, maybe three days a week. I told her I would tell you and you could think about it."

It was a strange call. He had baby sat for cousins and what not, but never as a business. He had sort of assumed that most of the locals wouldn't want him around their children. Maybe he'd been wrong.

But did he want to baby sit. He shifted his weight and felt, or at least thought he'd felt, the small bag in his right-hand pocket. He glanced at the small black netbook in Jeremy's hand, just over three hundred dollars. Oh yeah, if they paid well it wasn't going to take much thinking at all.

#####

Clark spent most of Sunday afternoon holed up in his room, trying to fix Jeremy's computer. The window said, "cookies". Clark looked down and snorted. Bigboobs.com; it appears his guess yesterday had been as dead on as Jeremy's. There are things that brothers, like it or not, just know about each other. He clicked on the close X and pulled out the novel he had bought the day before. There was no point in watching the computer. Between whatever virus was eating it's guts and the fact he was in safe mode it wasn't going to react any time soon. Windows for Dummies lay open beside him on the bed.

There was a knock at his door. With one quick motion, he yanked the clip on earrings off and pushed them under his butt. "It's open."

His brother opened the door and stuck his head in. "Mom said supper's ready in ten minutes."

"Okay I'll be there."

"Any luck?"

Clark nodded no. "Looks like you were right. It's fried beyond repair."

"Damn, I was hoping you'd fix it." Just as Clark raised his head to say thanks, his brother threw in, "'Cause then I could demand it back and make you use that crappy netbook."

He disappeared. I'd take the netbook any day, Clark thought ruefully. It beats no computer. If only he had the recovery disk, but Jeremy had lost it ages ago. Probably on purpose to force mom to get him something new. Serves him right to hit her on a low cash month and get stuck with a netbook.

He sighed and shut the laptop. He'd just have to wait until mom came up with the money for him to have a laptop (unlikely), he had an achievement he could use to guilt her into it (even less likely) or he could come with the money himself. I've got to call Mrs. Pirella after supper, he thought.

CHAPTER THREE

"Well here it is." Jeremy said as they pulled up in front of the split-level ranch house the next Tuesday afternoon. "You got everything? Your baby-sitting license? Your babysitters' club books?"

Clark just sighed. It had been like this for two days now, ever since he had accepted Shelley's offer. It was worth the teasing, he told himself over and over. She was willing to pay well. Seven dollars an hour, for three hours work, three times a week. That was over sixty bucks a week. At that rate, he'd have some two hundred a month. Two weeks until thanksgiving, he ticked it off in his head, four from then until Christmas. Maybe he could get himself a computer for Christmas. If not certainly sometime in January. Or maybe a lot of make-up.

"What are you waiting for?" Jeremy demanded, interrupting his reverie.

He shook his head and got out of the car.

"Now you'll have something to talk to the other girls about." His brother laughed and he was gone.

Shelley Pirella opened the door before Clark could push the door bell. She was dressed in a one piece golden dress that hung just below her knees. Tawny pantyhose ran the remaining length of her legs, which ended in heels. She was wearing dangling hoop ear rings and her make up was half done. She had foundation and blush on but there was still eye liner to be put on, and her lips were

22

still their natural dull color. Clark noticed these sorts of things, he thought, gay guys didn't.

"I am so glad you could come on such short notice," Shelley said. Then she went on needlessly, they had already discussed this on the phone. "We are going out for dinner, we will only be gone a couple of hours. But it will be a good chance for you to get to know the twins." And for you to test me, Clark thought. "If everything goes well we can work out a more permanent schedule," Shelley finished.

"Let me show you around a little bit," she said as she stood aside to let him enter. "This is the coat closet." Clark pulled off his tan coat with the fringe and hung it beside her light purple coat, a thick black leather one and two small pink ones. There were several others, mostly in feminine styles, tucked towards the back.

"This is the living room." She said, gesturing around. There was a large picture window along the outside wall. The far end of the room contained a large flat screen TV, the kind of home theater equipment that Jeremy was always moaning that he wanted and mom was always saying was too expensive. In the corner, next to it was a desk and a desk top computer. Clark looked at the computer. The monitor was bigger than their computer screen at home and a flat screen. The Pirella's were not hurting financially, that was sure.

"My computer," Shelley told him, "but you can use it. Tony hooked up a simple switch so you can change from the small monitor to the flat screen if you want to stream videos. I have a Netflix account and the girls like to watch movies that way. They have all their favorites on the list already."

"Hey it's the boy/girl," a small voice remarked from somewhere behind him. It was Britney. He knew this because she had BP emblazoned on her jumper pockets, while Holly, who was right behind her, had HP on hers.

"This is Clark." Shelley told them, "he will be babysitting you tonight."

"A boy babysitter?" Holly asked incredulous. "Will he watch Barbie Princesses with us?"

Clark just shrugged and knelt down to Holly's level. "If it will make you happy, why not?"

"But it's a Barbie movie." Britney insisted.

"Yeah, but Ken's in it, isn't he?" Clark asked. That seemed to mollify them somewhat.

Shelley led Clark through the dining room and kitchen. All three rooms formed the central single-story part of the house. The other side of the house was split leveled, they first went up the stairs. There was a single straight hallway with two doors on the left and one on the right. The communal bathroom was the first door on the left, followed by the girl's room. Opposite it on the right, was the master bedroom.

The communal bath was a pretty standard bathroom. The girls' room contained two low single beds with pink covers and two small white dressers. It was, Clark assumed, a pretty typical bedroom for a matching set of four-year-old girls.

The master bedroom was a huge affair with its own private bath. The center of the room was taking up with a king-sized poster bed with a rich pale-yellow comforter over it. Behind it on the far-left wall was the largest vanity Clark had even seen. The top was a chaotic mix, mostly Shelley's perfumes, make up, no less than three jewelry boxes and scattered throughout, male accessories as well, a crumpled tie, a man's wrist watch, a couple of cuff links.

The near wall, to his right as they entered were two doors. Shelley led him inside pointing to the first door, "private bath, just in case they both need to go at the same time, which believes me happens." The private bath was sparkling white. The wall on the right contained a sleek white toilet on a raised dais. It was separated from the bath by a low partial wall of white ceramic tile. The bath was one of those whirlpool jacuzzi style tubs. There was a narrow stand up shower stall at the back of the room. The left wall was one long counter with two sinks and an abundance of space. Lotions and scented soaps littered the counter tops.

As they left the bath Clark craned his neck to see inside the second door.

"Just my closet," Shelley remarked leading him back out of the room.

Just my closet? Clark had never seen a full walk in closet before and my god what how many clothes did she have anyway? It looked like Walmart in there. No, not Walmart, these were classy clothes, maybe a JC Penny's or some trendy mall store.

They went back down the stairs and this time took the second staircase down into the den.

"The den is more Tony's domain," Shelley remarked on the way down. Clark nodded. The rest of the house was bright, airy and painted in pastels. It had an unmistakable "women's touch" about it. The den was dark, painted in a drab sort of orange that must have been popular sometime in the seventies. It had the feel of an animal's den.

And in the middle was a man who could only be Tony Pirella. He was tall, taller than Clark at any rate. He had short wavy dark hair and deep brown eyes. His shoulders were massively broad and his forearms bulged; what Jeremy and his friends called 'big guns'. Even through his white T-shirt Clark could see well developed chest and abdominal muscles. Tony had a wide stance and stood with his arms crossed. Clark found men like Tony very intimidating.

"Tony, this is our new babysitter, Clark"

"Clark?" A glance passed between Tony and his wife. A glance that told Clark he would be the dinner conversation that night.

"Yes, Clark." She repeated.

Tony shrugged, apparently, he was used to letting his wife have her way with the kids. He held out his hand and said, "Well, welcome aboard Clark."

Clark took his hands relieved that Tony hadn't called him 'buddy'. It was then that he noticed the far wall of the den.

"Wow! Is that stuff yours?"

"Whose else would it be?" Tony laughed. "You like?"

"And how." Clark looked at the shelves that lined the one wall and the small desk that sat to one side. There were several computers here, three towers and two laptops on the shelf and one squat ugly looking thing with a monitor and keyboard next to it on the desk. There were parts too, hard drives, motherboards and lots more that Clark couldn't identify. Clark pointed to one of the towers, "4 gigs of ram?"

"Yup."

"Must run wicked fast."

"Not like Ugly Betty here." Tony pointed at the squat blank box.

Clark looked at the box. It had no markings of any kind which could only mean, "you built it yourself?" Clark asked.

"Sure, from some spare parts I happened to have laying around." Tony said. He winked conspiratorially. "It's amazing what you can have laying around when you are network manager for the right corporation."

"Whoa!" Clark said. He had never met anyone who had built their own computer. He touched the box almost reverently, "you built it yourself."

"Daddy," Holly had followed them down into the den and now ran into Tony's arms. Tony hoisted her up to eye level. "Daddy, He's going to watch Barbie Princess with us! As long as Ken's in it anyway, and you know he is."

Tony gave him a side long look. Clark just shrugged again, "If it will keep them happy."

"That's right, got to keep my princesses happy." Tony cooed and rubbed noses with his daughter. Clark found the sight of this man showing such affection for his daughter touching. Few of the men in his life were like that. He wondered momentarily if he was gay.

"Down here," Tony said sternly, "the only computer the girls need to touch is Eddy over there." He pointed to the far corner. Clark hadn't noticed the toddler sized table with a computer set at it.

"Eddy!" Britney squealed as she too came down the stairs. She dashed across to the computer and giggled the mouse. The screen came alive with over-sized icons.

"It's all educational software that Tony compiled just for them." Shelley told him. He saw a softness in her eyes as she looked at her husband, who was now squatting down next to his daughter. Those eyes mirrored his own mood.

"Well it's almost time, we got to hurry." Shelley said, turning business like again. "The girls can have mac and cheese, if you are up to that?"

"Oh sure." Clark said, thinking I can make a lot more than that. Hadn't she heard him in the grocery store talking about cornish game hens?

"And daddy needs to get dressed," she finished. Holly giggled.

"Yeah, get dressed daddy!" She commanded.

"Well, if one of my princesses says so," he replied.

#####

"In here, in here," Clark coaxed. Britney ran past him into the master bath. Shelley had been right, no sooner had Holly decided that she needed to go pee-pee and taken over the bathroom, Britney had decided she, too, needed to go, just as urgently.

Clark smiled as she disappeared with a slam of the door. This wasn't such a bad way to earn some cash. He had won the girls over easily. He had 'watched' Barbie Princesses with them on Netflix while doing his homework.

Then he made them mac and cheese. As if this feat wasn't amazing enough, he found a ginger bread man cookie cutter and made man-shaped garlic breads to go with. The girls had gnashed and chewed their men like well-trained vixens in pastel pink jumpers.

Clark sat back on the king-sized bed and listened for one of the two girls to come out. His eyes wandered to the second door, partly ajar. Curiosity got the better of him and he went to the door and stared. A line of clothes ran on either side of the closet and a shorter line ran along the back wall. A wire shelf over the hangers held boxes and boxes.

Tony had a short space at the front of the closet, dark suits mostly. Most of the closet was taken up with Shelley clothes, dresses of every description from business suit dresses to lacy cocktail dresses. Clark's mom wore mostly jeans and t-shirts, indistinguishable from male attire and often male clothes even. "They're comfortable," she would say.

Clark could sort of understand that. He understood what his mom meant at any rate, male clothes were looser fitting, they didn't pinch or force the anatomy to obey their limitations. What he didn't understand was, why did he feel so awkward in male clothes?

Clark reached out reverently to touch a silky top. What would it be like to own something like that he wondered? In his mind, when he imagined wearing such things there was no awkwardness at all. But would the reality match his imagination?

The door banged down the hall and Clark pulled back guiltily. He went into the hall. "Your pajamas are laid out for you in your room," he told Holly. Shelley and Tony would be home soon but he understood this too was a test. It was the kid's bedtime and Shelley had left pajamas out. If he didn't get them to bed on time it wouldn't be a big deal, but it would be a sign of what sort of authority he would be with the girls.

"I want to stay up until Mommy gets home." Holly whined.

"Me too," Britney whined coming out of the bathroom behind him.

Clark had learned the pointlessness of fighting things head on years ago. Being bullied does that. But there are other ways.

"You both still need to to get your pajamas on," he persisted, "then I will make hot chocolate and read from the Barbie book."

"The Barbie book!" Both girl squealed.

In the end, it was a tie. The girls managed to stay awake until their parent's arrived home, a half an hour after their bedtime. But they did so in bed, with their hot chocolates on the bedside table. Clark sat at the end of the bed, reading by the hall light. The girls were so drowsy they could barely give their mother a sleepy hello and a kiss good night before drifting off.

As he gathered the half drank cups, Clark thought he'd done well enough for his first time. He'd become their regular babysitter. He didn't care what anyone said or thought, not even Jeremy. Clark would have good money in his pocket.

"Tony is downstairs," Shelley told him. "He'll give you a ride home. It's getting nippy out there." She rummaged through her purse while she spoke. "Hmm two hours, well, more like two and half, at seven an hour that's..."

"Seventeen fifty." Clark prompted.

"Consider it a tip," she said handing over a twenty.

"Wow, thanks," he replied. Feeling almost guilty about the extra money he said, "the girls were really well behaved. They gave me no trouble."

Shelley smiled as she took the Barbie book from him. She tapped the cover, "you seem to have already discovered their weak spot. I'll talk it over with Tony and call you in a day or two about a regular schedule, if you are still interested?"

"Yeah, definitely," he said hoping he didn't sound over eager or creepy. He pocketed the money with one more "thanks," and headed down the stairs to find Tony.

Tony was in his den. His black jacket hung carelessly over the back of his chair. He sat leaned over Ugly Betty typing. Clark looked over his shoulder. The screen was black and Tony was typing in a string of strange words.

"Writing code?" Clark ventured.

"Nah, nothing that fancy," Tony yawned, "just some terminal commands. Work paged me at dinner. One of the servers has a bad disk. We are going to have to hot boot it in the morning. Thought I should back it up first, just to be safe." He turned slightly, "Shelley said you needed a ride?"

"I can walk if you are busy." Clark said. Truth was he wasn't too eager to leave. Despite not having one of his own, he loved computers and wanted to see what Tony was doing. He had never met anyone who wrote code or managed networks. He wasn't even sure what managing a network meant but it sounded cool.

"Nah," Tony said again, "that's close to a terabyte of data. It'll take forty minutes at least to back up. No point sitting and watching.

Clark didn't argue but thought otherwise. The computer scrolled out line after line of what to him was incomprehensible scripts but it was intriguing to watch.

"How much memory you got in that box?" he asked.

"Three terabytes," Tony responded.

"Holy cow!" Clark said.

Tony chuckled, "I could never justify it for myself, but it's work, you know. We got three six terabyte RAID working down there."

Clark shook his head, not fully understanding but stocking the phrases away to look up later.

"What you got at home?" Tony asked.

Clark hesitated, embarrassed. "Mom and I share an HP desktop, Pentium three, 20g hard drive, nothing special. My brother's got an Acer Aspire. He wanted a mac book but, well, it was all mom could afford right now, you know?"

"Nothing wrong with an Aspire. I got one." Tony pulled a small black netbook off the shelf. "Always carry it."

"But you've got Ugly Betty?"

"Yeah and I got three huge servers at work. But you take one off line to service it and then find out half the documentation you need is online." He grimaced, "so you learn to carry this." He waved the netbook and sat it back on the shelf.

He motioned towards the stairs and Clark went ahead of him up the stairs and to the closet. Donning his jacket Clark said, "I sort of have a ThinkPad laptop."

"Sort of?" Tony raised an eyebrow, "How does one sort of have a computer?"

"It's my brother's old one, the one the Acer replaced. Only it's got a virus or something. I have been trying to fix it, but I can't."

"Viruses can be pretty nasty," Tony agreed. "Does it boot at all?"

They walked slowly towards Tony's black Jeep. Figures a guy like this would drive the biggest, most macho vehicle he could find, Clark thought.

"It boots but runs like shit. Umm, it runs bad, I mean. Sorry."

Tony laughed, "I don't give a fuck about cussing, just don't do it around my daughters or it's..." He hitched his thumb to show that Clark would be history.

Clark nodded and continued, "anyway I have tried to clear the cookies, defrag the hard drive, reconfigure it to run for performance. I would try to restore it but my brother Jeremy lost the Windows recovery disk."

Clark climbed into the passenger seat and waited until Tony got in his side and started the engine. As they pulled out the driveway

Tony snorted. "Windows. That's half your problem right there. Windows sucks."

"Yeah," Clark agreed, trying to appear knowledgeable. "That's why Jeremy was hoping for a mac book. They don't get as many viruses and stuff."

"Not as many," Tony agreed, "but they still get them. Linux is the only way to go."

"Linux?"

"Yeah, Linux," Tony went on, watching the road, "I cut my teeth on Apache and haven't looked back."

Confused, Clark thought of his father suddenly. "Helicopters?" He asked.

Tony glanced at Clark and smiled. "Apache choppers. Yeah, that's right. Me and your dad flew together back in Desert Storm. Shame about him. Fucking tragic, in a middle of a goddamn war and we lost as many men to mechanical failure and accidents as to the enemy." He turned back, looking suddenly concerned, "I hope I didn't offend."

"No."

"Anyway, no I was thinking of the apache web servers." Tony went on, and then catching Clark's blank stare he backed up. "Okay, Linux is an operating system, there are several different systems available like Windows, Mac or Unix."

"Unix?"

"That's what most universities and big corporations use, those that don't use Linux."

"Are they related?"

"Good, you are thinking. Yeah, they're related, sort of. The guys who developed Linux based it on Unix. Both good systems. Linux is much faster, and much more stable then Windows. It's what all the serious computer geeks use."

"Cool." Clark always kind of thought of himself as a "serious computer geek". If they used Linux that was going to top his list of things to look up. "How expensive is it?"

"It's free."

"Free?" Clark wrinkled his nose, "they just give it away?"

"Yeah, Linux isn't like Windows. No company made Linux. Linux was written by a community of computer programmers. It's all part of a free and open system."

They pulled up beside Clark's house. He wished, not for the first time but for an entirely new reason, that he lived in a bigger town. This conversation was just getting going.

"Well here we are." Tony said.

Clark climbed out of the car. "Thanks for the ride," Clark said.

Tony leaned over the now empty seat. "Hey, why don't you bring that laptop next time, I'll take a look at it."

Clark felt himself smile. "Yeah, that'd be great."

CHAPTER FOUR

"So how do you like your Acer?"

"I liked my old one better." Jeremy groused.

"Tony has one and he's a pro, so they can't be that bad."

"Tony your boyfriend now?"

"F- you." Clark steamed but he shut up. Jeremy had been in a mood all weekend and it hadn't gotten any better as the week had progressed.

"Look if I was a male babysitter I'd keep my mouth shut." Jeremy groused. "If I were babysitting girls, even more so."

Clark felt smug. He knew why Jeremy was so put out. He, Clark, finally had something that Jeremy did not, a job. A job that paid well and an 'in' with a real computer expert. It was too much to pass up.

"If you ever need any help with that netbook..."

"And if I had a crush on the guy hiring me to baby sit his daughters," Jeremy almost shouted, "I'd certainly keep my damn mouth shut."

"I do not have a crush on him, you cock sucker." Clark wailed. He hated that Jeremy could push his buttons so easily.

Jeremy slammed on the brakes. "Listen buddy." Jeremy knew how much buddy bothered Clark and saved it for special occasions like this one, "I am going to tell you this once and only once, as your brother." Anything Jeremy felt compelled to say 'as his brother' could not be good. "A boy with a reputation like yours, in a school like ours, had better not be talking about any guy around school. Believe me it could be lot worse than name calling or the occasional shove. Understand?"

Jeremy stepped on the gas and they drove the rest of the short distance home in silence. Walking in the front door of their one level ranch style house Jeremy spied the new cell phone sitting on the table before Clark did.

He dropped his school bag on the table and snatched up the phone. He said, "cool mom, you got a new phone?" He held it up. It was a simple white flip phone with T-Mobile splashed across the front. He held it up to his chest and looked at their mother as she rounded the corner.

"Nope," she said, "It's for Clark." Clark peered over Jeremy's shoulder at the phone.

"But mom!" This indignity was too much for Jeremy. "I've been asking for months for my own phone. How come he gets one?"

"Because he's got a job."

"I do?" Clark said.

"Guess so," his mom smiled, taking the phone from Jeremy's shocked hands and placing it in his. "Shelley called today. She got called into work tonight for the evening shift. Tony doesn't get off until seven pm, it'll be almost nine before he's home from Des Moines. I told her I would take you to pick the girls up at four thirty from day care and then to their place."

Clark's mind calculated quickly; Four and half hours; thirty-one dollars and fifty cents. This was going to be a good evening after all. Looking at Jeremy's face he felt smug again but also glad he wouldn't be around to face his brother's mood tonight.

"This," his mother was saying, tapping the phone in his hand, "is only temporary. I need to be able to get a hold of you if you are going to be out late and Shelley might need to reach you too. It's prepaid, so don't use up the minutes, please."

"Who's he going to call?" Jeremy wondered aloud.

An angry look flashed across his mother's face and for once Clark thought that maybe she did in fact understand what it was like to be Jeremy's little brother, or anyone's little brother, when you were Clark. "Next chance we get to go to Des Moines, I'll get you on my plan. Only because it will be cheaper in the long run." This last was aimed at Jeremy.

"Anyway, good afternoon to both of you. How was school?"

"I got an A on my English Essay." Jeremy brightened visibly, recapturing some of his big brother mystique. He knew Clark hadn't done so well, Clark hadn't been able to resist venting in the car about yet another unfair grade in English. But he did not know how badly Clark had done this time and Clark hoped to keep it that way.

Dropping his bag next Jeremy's on the table he quickly extracted his essay and handed it to his mother. The title read "The Fashionista Attack on Women's Self Esteem." It was, he had thought, well written and with many sources. Granted the sources were often Internet blogs and pop songs, all of which pointed to the incredible angst that many young women felt about their self-esteem and their bodies. Across the top in bold red, was D- and the simple explanation "poor choice of topics, very inappropriate for the class room".

"I know." His mom sighed. "She called earlier."

"She's got it out for me! You read the paper, it's good."

She sighed again.

"Let's see." Jeremy grabbed the paper out of her hand. Clark groaned. "Well what do you expect? You know how she is. She don't want to believe that kids know about this stuff. You should have just written some crap about, I don't know, why sports are important, or why art is, or something like that. Why do you have to always push?" He handed the paper back to their mother and pushed his way past them towards the kitchen.

"Jeremy," their mother warned, "Look Clark, I can see both sides. It's frustrating that she won't deal with you at the level you are at but the average teenager doesn't think like this. We just have to deal with this right now."

"Why? After what the tutor said?"

After his last three D's in English mom had taken him to the Sylvan Learning Center in Des Moines. The tutor that evaluated him had read the three offending essays and declared loudly, "so this high school English teacher is upset because your son can write at a college level and she didn't teach him? What do you want me to do about that?" Since then they endured the bad grades and there was no further talk of tutoring.

"That actually wasn't why the teacher called." She paused hesitantly. "She was worried about the reference to the pro-ana movement on the web. That and you being so skinny."

"I am not anorexic!" Clark protested.

"It's because she's a cow, Mom," Jeremy put in coming back from the kitchen with an apple in one hand and granola bar in the other. "She thinks if you don't have a weight problem like her you must be anorexic. Besides Clark's more likely bulimic," he finished casually.

"Jeremy!" Mom said in exasperation.

"You've seen him," he went on gesturing, "he shuts down for days and barely eats. Then after a couple of days he makes up for by eating double portions."

She wheeled on him, "You are not helping."

She turned back to Clark, "I know, I looked at those sites with you remember? And I cautioned you about this topic. Besides I know you are not anorexic, I've seen you eat." She shook her head. "We'll talk more about it later, right now you need to grab a snack and then get whatever you need for tonight. Jeremy," Jeremy was moping at the table, obviously feeling left out. "You and I can do something special since it's just us."

Clark sighed as he sat on the king-sized bed and listened closely. It appeared the girls were at last asleep. It had not been as easy as he had thought the first time, this whole babysitting gig. His mom had warned him that the girls would test him. He hoped only that he had passed the test and they would be better behaved next time; the stinkers.

The afternoon had started badly and the evening had ended badly, but gone well most of the in between times. They had been understandably upset when it was not their mother that picked them up from day care. They cried a bit on the trip home and once they got home they turned mischievous, trying to talk Clark into about a hundred plans that he knew full well were not allowed. They hadn't given up until caught between aggravation and humor, he broke out laughing at them; "Cookie Crisp cereal for supper? I don't think so."

After that they had behaved well until bed time. Bed time involved much wailing and protesting, despite offers of reading. They knew they could not wait up until mommy came home, or even daddy, and they had had enough. It was now almost forty-five minutes after their bedtime and they had finally fallen quiet; no more shouted requests, demands for this or that toy, protestations of hunger, fear, or long trips to the bathroom, all delaying tactics.

He sat in here so he could hear them without being in their presence. Being in their presence made it too easy for them to find things to need. Here he could respond if need be or let them whine a while if it was a pointless request.

Or so he told himself. He did not sit in here because of the closet. The closet that again gaped half open, inviting him in. The closet he was pointedly ignoring.

He crept across the hall and peeked at the two forms. They were fast asleep. Who would know?

So he went back across the hall and pulled the chain on the light. He wandered for a long time, lost in thought. He idly felt the many tops, comparing them in his mind. This one was silky, this one cotton. A few he pulled out and held against him, looking in the mirror. The image that shown back at him was so incredibly normal. Why couldn't others see it?

Soon he became afraid. It was already too close to time. He didn't want Tony to arrive home and find him fingering his wife's clothes. What would the guy think?

Knowing my luck, Clark thought sourly, Tony would mistake it for lust for his wife, a normal teenage response. What's more bizarre, he thought, my desire for women's clothes or my fear that it will misinterpreted? Both, Jeremy would say. Clark wasn't so sure.

Clark heard the jeep pull up about nine. I *would have had plenty of time to try something out of the closet.* He pushed the thought away. He was sitting on the couch with his laptop (he considered it his now) open on the coffee table and Windows for Dummies and a book about debugging off of Tony's shelf (he hoped he wasn't going to get into trouble over it) on the table next to it.

He was trying to impress Tony. He had a scratch paper out of his school bag and had carefully written out what he had already tried in as much detail as possible.

Tony came through the front door and peeled his black leather jacket off his large frame. His broad shoulders sagged slightly, showing he had had a long day.

"Howdy," he greeted Clark, but thankfully left it at that. Every time they got through a greeting or conversation without buddy or kiddo being used, Clark liked the man all the more. "The rascals behave for you?"

"Yeah." Clark replied.

"Really? Usually they put the new ones through their paces the first few nights."

Clark blushed. "Yeah," he admitted sheepishly, "but they're kids right? That's to be expected."

"As long you aren't crying or running for the door I guess we are okay." Tony laughed.

The new ones? How many new ones did they have?

"I see you've brought the laptop."

"Yeah, I've been trying to get it working. I borrowed this book. I hope you don't mind?"

Tony sat on the couch next to him. He had picked up and was already engrossed in the scratch paper and made no comment on the book. After a while he nodded approvingly. "Kept a list, very methodical, very good. You need that if you are going to work with computers. But this crap," he pointed at the debugging book, "in fail safe mode is too slow. Come on, let's fix this computer."

He picked up the laptop and made for the den. Clark followed.

"I see you ran a bios post check. Great, we know the hardware is all working," Tony said. Clark beamed with pride. "Some of those viruses can permanently wreck your hard drive or even your mother board. Most don't though. They just take for freaking ever to extract. It's hours of technician's time, which is why most repair shops tell you it's junk."

"Hours?" Clark asked.

"Never fear my young padawan. We are going to take a couple of short cuts." *A Star Wars reference? Well, it still beat buddy or kiddo.*

Tony powered the laptop down as he sat it on his desk. Above the desk was a cork board with a line of USB drives hanging from clips, each was labeled with a cryptic note. They meant nothing to Clark; Fedora 9, Ubuntu 10.04, Debain mint, etc. Tony pulled one down and stuck it in the laptop's USB port. Clark looked at the spot. It said DSL repair and recovery. That meant nothing to him.

Tony powered the computer up and slipped into the bios screen. Clark followed along the best he could. Tony set it to boot from the USB drive. "You can do that?"

"Of course," Tony explained, "all these are live sticks, most Linux distros work that way. The Linux system is so small and economical that you can load it on an USB and run the whole operating system off that."

"That's awesome."

Tony winked. "Sure is, this one's called Damn Small Linux, it's one of my favorite operating systems, because there ain't nothing to it. I have that system and a couple of my own special debugging routines on this stick, see. It runs off the computer's ram not the hard drive, getting around the virus. We can search out files we want or need to save and then reformat the hard drive. After that we just reload with whatever system you want."

"I want Linux."

Tony chuckled. "Another geek in training."

The screen came up black but with a pointer for the mouse. "It's Xface desktop. Very minimal, very good if you know how to use it but not user friendly." Tony opened a drop-down menu and selected a program.

He ran through several commands and pulled up a long string of codes and writing.

"Looks like someone has been surfing for porn." Tony teased.

"It's my brother's computer." Clark said indignantly. "I just got it."

"Calm down, I am just teasing." Tony said. "Just don't let Shelley catch you looking at bigboobs.com on her computer."

Clark started to respond when he saw the mischievous smile tugging at Tony's mouth. "Heaven forbid a teenage boy would want to see big boobs."

Clark blushed furiously but kept his mouth shut and let Tony think what he would. He was not about go looking at big boobs. It wasn't that he didn't find women beautiful but he didn't need to see their boobs hanging out like Jeremy did, that was all.

"So, is there anything really important you need to save from this hard drive, other than the big boobs?"

"Jeremy said he had some vacation pictures on there and some homework but that was all. I think he already made up the assignments."

"Do you know how he labeled the vacation pictures?"

"No." Clark was embarrassed that he hadn't gotten that information from his brother.

Luckily his brother was unimaginative and they quickly found a file folder marked 'vacation' and downloaded the contents to Tony's USB stick.

"Now are you sure you don't want to save some of that porn? There's a lot on there." Tony teased one more time. Clark blushed again and shook his head, not trusting himself to speak. "Well okay, if you insist."

Moments later it was done. He had repartitioned and formatted the hard drive. He looked up at the corkboard thoughtfully. "Boy wants the power and stability of Linux, but hasn't ever used it before. Hmm." After a pause, "yeah, Ubuntu." He pulled down the USB marked Ubuntu 10.04.

"What's Ubuntu?" Clark had to ask.

"Well because Linux is an open system, anyone can change or modify it. This creates hundreds of different versions, called distros. That's short for distribution. Each has its advantages and weakness. Ubuntu is just one of many different versions of Linux but it's a good one, especially for someone like you." Before Clark could wonder what Tony meant by 'someone like you' he went on, "it's easier and more intuitive than some systems. You can learn it on the fly by using it, where as many of these systems require huge manuals to do even the basics. Also there's a thriving community online, like at Launch Pad web site and the Ubuntu forums. That means you can find help when you need it and you will. It's not a Windows world anymore."

He pushed the laptop over to Clark. It had brownish screen and a tool bar at the top and bottom. "This is the basic desktop. Let me show you a few basics and then we'll do the permanent install." He walked Clark through the three drop down menus at the top; applications for programs, places for files and system for system tools. Clark was starting to think it was rather like Windows; Open Office instead of Word, Firefox instead of Internet Explorer. There were different programs but mostly they did all the same stuff that his Windows computer did.

Then Tony showed him the Ubuntu software center. "No more loading programs from disks for you, and be careful what you try to download from the net. This is the best surest way to get new software for your computer, stuff that will run without bugs. Best of all it's all free." Hundreds of free programs available at the click of a mouse? Clark was going to spend some serious time on the software center.

He also showed Clark how to flip through the four desktops at the bottom to keep multiple projects open but separate. He showed him the terminal screen which allowed him to enter commands to run programs or update the system. Clark was quickly realizing the truth of Tony's words, this was not Windows. It was better.

After that Tony shut the laptop down again and handed it to Clark. Clark thanked him several times and then went upstairs and started packing up his stuff. He looked out the picture window and saw that it had started to sleet. Tony came up and followed his gaze.

"I'll give you a ride home," Tony said.

"I can walk home," Clark said hesitantly.

"Sure you can," Tony affirmed, "and you will." He gestured at the rain splattered windowsill, "but not tonight."

"The girls?"

"They'll be fine." Tony said, "They are sound sleepers and it won't take more than a minute or two to run you home and be back." He made a dismissive noise. "Parent's today. When I was the girl's age I would ride my trike up to the city park and play for hours with the other kids. I wouldn't come home until it was getting dark. Why do you think I came back to this tiny little town to raise my family?"

#####

Clark felt a rush of pain along his left side as he hit the lockers again. This time however he also felt a heavy weight pressing against him. A voiced hissed in his right ear, "If I had kids I wouldn't let a freaking fag like you anywhere near them."

It was John Mort, one of the football players. The comment stung. He thought about the twins, how they accepted him better than most of the kids at school. He pushed back, pushing himself a few inches from the locker.

"If you had kids," he sneered, "DHS wouldn't let you near them."

John pushed again. Clark was ready and spun, throwing both of them both off balance. John caught himself, but Clark did not hit the locker either. The two stared at each other, anger in their eyes.

"Is there a problem?" It was the deep, surly voice of the shop teacher.

"No, sir." John drawled and turned away. Amy Talba, John's girlfriend gave him a curiously sympathetic look. "Aim," John's voice came from several feet away, "you coming?"

"Yeah," she replied and turned away.

Clark blinked and looked away. Amy's tenderness was harder to deal with than John's rage. Tears threatened him. He remembered a time in elementary school, before gender became such a huge barrier, when the girls at least stood up for him, let him join them in play. He had been so sure Amy had forgotten those days years ago. Now he wasn't so sure.

Fighting tears, he made his way to his next class. Word of his new job had apparently gotten around. Jeremy's words echoed in his ears, things could get much worse.

Still it was worth it. He had a new cell phone, carefully tucked away in his coat pocket and a new computer on his vanity at home. (Clark had no intention of bringing the laptop to school. He knew it would just be another thing for the bullies to break.) He had sixty dollars in his top dresser drawer with more on the way. He would find a way to endure and some day he would out do his tormentors, leaving them in their small-town hell with their small-town lives while he left to live a real life. He just had to get through the next two years.

Clark sat in his room, a coke on his vanity and the laptop open in front of him. He had gotten the wireless code out of Jeremy that morning, after mom pointed out that while the wireless router had been Jeremy's purchase (with birthday money from Grandma) the computer it was hooked up to and the Internet signal itself were both mom's.

"But it will slow me down," Jeremy had protested.

"I ain't doing any huge downloads." Clark had argued, "it won't slow you down."

Clark was sure he would hear at supper how much slower Jeremy's netbook was now that Clark shared his signal but that didn't matter right now. He had his own laptop and he could use it in his own room. He was anxious to take it for a test drive. He planned on spending a great deal of time on the Ubuntu forums that Tony had told him about, learning how to get the most out of his new system. But the first web surf in privacy was special and he had to choose carefully.

After a long time, he opened Firefox. He was greeted with a slightly simplified version of the Google search engine that read Ubuntu. (He was not fooled by it's simplicity. Tony had told him what all computer geeks knew, anything flashy took resources. Simpler meant faster.)

Into the box he typed, "I wish I was girl"

He scanned the list. Third down his question was repeated to him. "I wish I was a girl/ is this normal?" He clicked on it.

The site was Yahoo answers. He read the question briefly. It was a paragraph long but it really boiled down to one sentence. The guy said sometimes he wished he was a girl. Was he normal?

Clark scanned the comments sections. About midway down he saw something that stopped him in his tracks.

Yoshi (7608)
You are not alone.

Suddenly Clark was crying.

#####

Clark felt the cold blast from the door as it opened. "I am sorry, work ran late." His mother was saying breathlessly. He heard her purse drop in its usual place by the door. "I didn't have time to get anything for dinner. We'll do a Casey's pizza or something...." She had her fuchsia coat halfway off. Her voice trailed off and she stood there looking at the table, her coat forgotten.

"Or something," Clark said, gesturing at the already set table. "Chicken. It will be ready in about five minutes."

"Okay," his mom said slowly, "If you don't mind me asking, what prompted this?"

"He's reaching for new levels of faggotry." Jeremy commented from the other room but without particular malice. It was hard to hate with the aroma of chicken roasting so close by.

Clark just shrugged, "I felt domestic." And it's normal for me, he thought.

"Well," his mother returned to prying her coat off, "don't let me stop you."

"Yeah," his brother said, sniffing the air as he came through the room, "this is a kind of fagginess I could live with, if you keep it quiet at school."

What am I going to do, offer to swap recipes with girls in gym? Seriously.

Jeremy stopped and gave Clark a quizzical look, perhaps

wondering why his insults had been having such little effect that last couple of weeks. Let him wonder, Clark thought to himself.

CHAPTER FIVE

Clark opened his laptop and booted up. Between working for the Pirella's and not taking it to school he hadn't had nearly as much time to spend on the laptop as he would have wished, at least not doing the stuff he really wanted. He took the laptop with him most nights he worked but kept his web surfing as neutral as possible. He spent lots of time on the Ubuntu Forums soaking up as much Linux as he could. He was learning a ton of stuff.

But he knew Tony knew more and he didn't know how tightly their network was monitored. He didn't want to risk looking up sensitive stuff over at their house. Tonight, however he was at home and in his room, where mom wouldn't be looking over his shoulder all the time.

He got online and went to Craigslist. It wasn't the fanciest forum or group but it was usually active. That's what he was looking for. Ever since finding out he wasn't alone, that others thought and felt as he did, he was craving contact. He had a name even for what he felt.

Signing into the discussion under the alias he had already created, Miss Claire, he began.

Miss Claire: Help me, I am a fifteen-year-old Transsexual girl.
Jennydoe43 :..What'cha need hon?
Miss Claire: I want to be a woman.
Jennydoe43 :..don't we all? :)!

Hearts565   ;..you came to the right place.
Miss Claire: I want to transition.
Jennydoe43 ;,,it's a process, it takes time.
Miss Claire: I know but I want to start, now
Elfgrl23   got get a therapist, letter of recommendation
etc.
Miss Claire: I see this therapist my mom takes me too. I think he

                 thinks I'm gay and can't accept that.
Elfgrl23:   I've heard that one before :(!
Jennydoe43:   Maybe it's time to get your own damn
therapist. ;)!

"It's dinner time," Jeremy called from his door way. Clark looked at the clock on his dresser. Damn, it was dinner time. He signed off and started to shut down his laptop. He felt light, serene. He had said it aloud. Okay actually he had typed it aloud, in a forum. I am a transsexual. I should have been born a girl, but I wasn't. I was never meant to be Clark. He took a deep breath and let it out.

What's more there was help; real help, not the crappy doesn't-really-help psychiatric help. He could transition. Doctors could give him hormones and testosterone blockers. Surgeons could do far more, changing that thing between his legs into something he might someday find useful. This was now his goal. A new hope had kindled inside him. He now understood his dream, the one about growing up to be a woman.

How had his four-year old mind been able to come up with that? Maybe he had been psychic or something. Maybe he had somehow absorbed knowledge in ways he wasn't consciously aware of; like he had seen a daytime talk show about a sex change but didn't remember it. But the subconscious knowledge of the show remained. However, it happened it was clear that he had known he would someday have a sex change and be a woman. Then he could look back on his life and say honestly, "I was born a boy, but now I am woman."

"Clark!" His mother's voice sounded on the stairs.

"I am coming!" He shouted back, putting the laptop up. Clark? That name would have to be the first thing to go.

Gym was Clark's least favorite class. He didn't object to physical fitness so much, in fact he had a couple of yoga DVD's that he did on a somewhat regular basis. Even the running, sports, and fitness tests they did at school weren't so terrible if you could get to them. Getting to them meant changing clothes and that meant entering the locker room.

His tormentors considered the locker room their home turf and sacred space mixed into one. Even walking in the door he was hit by a cacophony of sweat, steam, cussing and boys emitting various sub vocal noises.

"Cover yourself there is a fag in the locker room!" A voice greeted him as he nervously walked through the doors and made his way towards his locker. Several of the boys whipped towels around themselves in mock embarrassment.

He tried to ignore them. Outside the locker room he might have a snappy comeback or flip them off, but not here. He wasn't being a coward, he told himself. He was being realistic. His locker was at the very back, a long agonizing decision, but his decision none the less. It meant there were a dozen or more bodies between him and the safety of the hall. The alternative had been something close to the door but that meant changing in clear view of the majority of the guys, which made him extremely uncomfortable. He preferred to skulk at the back, take the verbal ribbing and change quickly when no one was looking.

The worst part was that the whole gym area was so far towards the back of the school. He was so far from the regular classrooms. There, at least, were a few teachers that looked out for him. The only teachers that ever came back this way were the gym teachers and the shop teacher. Ms. Gade, the women's basketball coach was rumored to be a lesbian. He didn't know but he believed she might help him if the boys decided to attack him here, if he made enough racket for her to brave the boy's locker room. Mr. Harding, the other gym teacher and Mr. Terrance, the shop teacher, were as likely to be in on the beating as to stop it.

"If he gets an erection while watching me I am going to kill him." Another jock commented to no one in particular.

"If I were a fag, I'd just kill myself and be done with it," another said.

"Fuck you!" Clark yelled, losing control despite himself. He threw his gym bag at the boy. "Fuck you! Fuck you! If you want me dead then kill me because I am never going to do it for you, you bastard. Get that through your f-ing head right now. You can hate me, you can tease me, you can f-ing kill me but I will no longer do your dirty work." Tears were streaming down his face but he didn't care. Everyone was frozen like statues; the fierceness of his anger had caught them by surprise. "I won't fucking do it. I won't hate myself, I won't be ashamed another god damn minute and I sure as hell won't f-ing kill myself for your sake."

He stormed out and down the hall, no destination in mind. His already dismal gym grade would suffer but he didn't care.

#####

"Oh my god, are you in trouble?" Christy hissed from the seat in front of him. Her short, spiked, reddish-brown hair danced as she spun her head to face him. Her brown eyes regarded him.

From this Clark gathered that the news of what had happened in the locker room had beat him back to class. He looked into her face. He wasn't sure if it was concern that motivated the question or mere curiosity. He couldn't think how this could be used against him so he nodded. "In school suspension for three days, starting tomorrow."

"In school? Could be worse." Christy said.

He nodded again. It could have been a lot worse. Mr. Harding was threatening to flunk him for the semester for having skipped out too many times. The assistant principal was pushing for full out suspension, which would stay on his school record and affect his chances at college; a dire threat since getting an education was Clark's best chance of getting out of this hell hole.

It had been a tie, with Mr. Harding and the assistant principal pushing for more serious punishment and principal Harry Reid

49

and the school counselor pushing for leniency. Clark wasn't sure which way it would have gone if his mom hadn't shown up.

"Does your mom know?" Christy was asking him.

Again he nodded, "they called her in to talk about it."

"That must have been rough." Christy commented.

Oh yeah, it had been rough, especially for Principal Reid and Mr. Harding. Mom had arrived while his fate was being decided. She had gone straight to him, ignoring the others, and asked what had happened.

As he told her the whole story her lips grew thinner and thinner, until they were the barest slit. Her face grew red and her eyes dark. He was afraid of what she would unleash when he finished but plowed on anyway. When he was done she sat silent for one minute and then, to his surprise, turned towards the principal.

Clark didn't know what he saw in her eyes but he visibly flinched. She said, very quietly, "what is being done about the boys who threatened my son."

Mr. Harding made the mistake of answering that question. "We are not here to discuss them. We are here to discuss your son, who skipped out of my class yet again today."

She turned on him. He seemed to have expected to intimidate her, or at least command her respect, but it was quickly apparent that neither was going to happen.

She stepped up nose to nose with him and said slowly, "well, I am here to discuss why my son is being harassed and bullied daily at this school and nobody seems to want to do anything about that. I am here to discuss why nobody seems to think that my son receiving a death threat is a big deal."

It had gone downhill from there. He had never seen his mom so angry. Between her talk of the school board and press, his personal balance had tipped in favor of leniency. In fact, the week of in school suspension had fallen to three days. Meanwhile there had been promises made that the boys involved would be spoken to and so would their parents. Clark had no illusions that this would do anything but piss them off even more but it was worth it to see his mom taking his side for once.

"My mom was kind of pissed," Clark told Christy.

"I am surprised you only got three days." Amy said from a couple of seats away.

"I am sure you'll miss me terribly." Sarcasm dripped from his mouth as he spoke. Amy turned away, looking hurt.

"I'll miss you." Christy said sharply, "and so will Amy."

"Sorry," he muttered.

"Not everyone hates you, you know." Christy said.

He was shocked by the sincerity in her voice. It was news to him.

#####

Clark wandered through the closet, almost defiantly. He had been here numerous times now. The girls were sound asleep, it was more than forty-five minutes before Tony would be home. He was feeling safer with this exploration. With all of his online research he was discovering that these feelings were natural, for him at least. His shame was either fading, or at least being overwhelmed by the possibility of being his true self, of being comfortable with who and what he was.

Or maybe what she was. He had been going by Claire, or Clarissa online in various forums for some time. It felt nice, comfortable. He was leaning toward the name Clarissa when he transitioned. It had more mystique than Claire.

When he transitioned; god only knew when that would be. Mom had made it crystal clear that she did not want to discuss the idea of his being transgender. Even after the incident at the school, or perhaps because of it, she was dead set against him doing anything to bring more attention on himself. She still held Philip's view, that he was a gay boy who didn't want to accept that he was gay so he concocted this fantasy of being a straight woman instead.

He hated her for that but she showed such real concern for his safety that he couldn't stay mad at her. She had cried, great big tears like when dad died, when they talked about it that night. She made him promise that he would avoid the kids who threatened him the best he could, and do everything he could to avoid drawing any further attention from them. He couldn't refuse her.

And he had done his best to do so. He had done his suspension quietly and meekly. He tried not to act overly feminine at school and he tried not to talk about those sorts of things.

But it made him angry. It made him feel restless and full of rage. On one hand, he was reading and learning that he was transgender. He was learning that it was okay for him to be this way. He was struggling, as the websites and his new online friends encouraged, to develop pride in who he was. Then he was told to stuff it all in a closet and deal with life as a man.

He ran a hand along the line of tops, rattling the hangers violently. He wanted to lash out, he wanted, he needed, some release for all his pent-up feelings, good and bad.

Then he stopped. He had time, didn't he? At first, he had visited the closet to look. Then he had worn a top, over his shirt. Last week he had taken his shirt off and put one of hers on. There was one thing he had looked at each and every time he came to the closet, one thing he had felt and longed for but never dared wear.

With quiet determination, he pulled down the black one-piece cocktail dress. He ran his hands over the silky-smooth fabric. Then he put it back and slowly began to undress.

It was everything he had hoped. He looked at himself in the full-length mirror that was attached to back of the closet door. He smiled at himself and she smiled back.

It would have to be Clarissa. Claire was simply too dowdy for this sexy little mirror girl he saw. She smiled at him coyly. She posed seductively. She was definitely a Clarissa.

Next time she would have to bring her make up, maybe that pair of pantyhose she had bought last time in Des Moines. She would need heels too. She had no clue what Shelley's size was or how she would ever find the courage to buy her own but she needed heels.

There were so many things she needed but most of all she needed to live, to stop being the mirror girl. Clark would have to step aside and let Clarissa through to the real world.

She began to imagine that. She imagined walking into school in that dress. Every one's mouth would drop. "Who is the new girl?" She'd lead the boys on and then tell them to f- off. "After the way you treat poor old Clark? No way. "

She could almost imagine Philip's reaction too. "Still think I am a gay man?" She asked the mirror and winked.

And then her face distorted as the door came open. Clarissa became Clark again and Clark came face to face with Tony.

CHAPTER SIX

Clark struggled to take a breath. A million feelings fought for his attention: Tony, the dress, his own clothes in a pile at his feet. His life, or lack thereof, flashed before him. Shame coursed up his face and turned it a ruby red.

It was over. There would be a huge scandal. No more job, no more money. He could almost imagine the look of disappointment on his mom's face. He could imagine Jeremy's smug expression. The whispers at school, "there he is, the boy who was caught in a woman's dress."

He could hear the twins asking where he went to and feel Shelley's stony silence, her stiff disapproval. Worst of all was the image of Tony, the mixture of disappointment and rage that would soon fill his whole form. The threat of violence was palpable. The image was so strong, so real, that for several moments Clark couldn't see the real Tony in front of him. The real Tony that was looking at him with an expression of mild amusement as he leaned against the door jam.

He waited patiently in that stance until Clark finally, slowly raised his eyes and met Tony's gaze.

"Hmm," he said slowly, "Shelley usually wears thigh highs with that dress." With that he turned away. One hand pointed lazily towards the dresser. "She keeps those in the top drawer." With that he was gone.

Clark stood still a long time, trying to master his breath. Slowly he peaked out of the closet. One of Tony's business jackets lay carelessly crumpled on the bed, along with a white dress shirt. Clark could hear Tony rustling around in the bathroom. The toilet flushed. The tap ran. A towel rustled loudly as he dried his hands. Then he reappeared, in a plain white wife beater and dress slacks.

"I'm sorry," was all Clark could say.

"Why?" Tony shrugged, "did you stain it?"

Clark blushed again. "No," he muttered angrily.

"Fine then." Tony said, "but why don't you get your own stuff on, so I can take you home."

Clark nodded dully and retreated to the closet.

"I never thought I'd say this to a boy." Tony called from the bedroom, "but that dress looks good on you."

Clark had just been reaching for the pile of boy clothes on the floor and nearly fell over. His heart was pounding again and his mind numbed with shock. What was going on? "She keeps them in the top drawer." It went through his head over and over. Was he being given permission to wear Shelley's things?

When he was dressed again in his own clothes he went in search of Tony. He found the man in the living room. He had pulled a T-shirt on over his wife beater. He was standing in the middle of the room with the TV remote in his hands, watching the local news. He turned when Clark came down the stairs.

"First big snowstorm of the year is rolling in," Tony said, "I hope Shelley makes it home okay. I'd better give you a ride too. It's getting wicked out there."

Clark could only nod. If Tony was going to fire Clark, tell him to stay away from the family from now on, why was he going to give him a ride home first? It had almost sounded like Tony was worried about Clark. After what had just happened, could that be? He grabbed his school bag from the couch and accepted his tan coat when Tony handed it over.

They drove home in silence. Tony didn't seem upset, but Clark couldn't trust that yet.

When they arrived at his house, Tony stopped the car and sat in silence for a minute. Here it comes, Clark thought.

"Let me tell you a story," Tony began slowly. "You know I was in the army." Clark nodded though it wasn't really a question.

"Did me good, too. Everyone should get out of their hometown and see the world. You learn things you wouldn't otherwise."

Anyway, when I was in basic we had a guy in our unit who was rumored to be gay. Don't ask, don't tell made it illegal for the sergeant to ask but it was pretty obvious. He was effeminate and the rumor said he was part of a drag show."

"I didn't care. He was a hard worker and a good mechanic. Besides it's just the way some people are, the way they are born, Kapisch?" Tony looked at Clark and Clark nodded, feeling better knowing that Tony felt that way.

"Not everyone felt that way, of course. Three redneck assholes decided they needed to teach this guy a lesson. They decided to wait up one weekend, ambush him coming back from leave and beat the shit out of him." He paused and looked out the window.

"The next morning when we all fell in for reverie, all three of the men looked like shit." Tony chuckled, "One had hamburger for a face, one had the biggest black eye I had ever seen and all three had limps."

"The gay guy, on the other hand, looked like he'd just gotten back from the spa, spotless. I tracked him down later, asked him what had happened. You know what he told me?"

He turned and looked straight at Clark. Clark returned the stare caught up in the story. "What did he say?"

"He said, if you're a sissy, you got be tough to survive."

He reached out and patted Clark's cheek affectionately, "Be tough, Clark, be tough."

Clark smiled as relief flooded him. He said. "I'll try," and as he reached for the door handle, he added, "thanks Tony."

#####

"Can I ask you something?" It was Christy. He wasn't surprised, he had figured something was up when she and Amy had sat down at his table in study hall. Nobody ever sat with him.

But that was before. Since his break down in the locker room and his now legendary speech the rumors had been running wild.

What had he really meant when he said he refused to hate what he was? Had he in fact, as many argued, tacitly admitted to being gay?

Though nobody knew it, they were also seeing the effects of his talk with Tony. He had thought about it deep into the night. Maybe Tony now thought Clark was gay, like his old army buddy. Or maybe he thought he was a cross dresser. It didn't really matter. Tony, the biggest most macho man Clark had ever met, didn't hate Clark for being feminine. That rocked Clark's world. It was good advice too; he was trying to learn to be tough. They were also seeing the effect of the mirror girl, of Clarissa. She was becoming a bigger and bigger part of Clark.

His tormentors had ramped up their verbal efforts. He was taunted more and more. They called him faggot or homo in the hall. They made lewd comments, asking him if he liked it up the ass and other crap like that. They were also making threats to beat him up or to kill him even. So far nobody had made good on any threats and physically the harassment had momentarily lessoned.

He was standing up to them, refusing to be baited. That meant refusing to confirm or deny his sexuality. It had become the question of the hour and now it would be asked.

Clark shrugged, "Go ahead."

"Well," she turned sheepish suddenly. "There this rumor that when you said that stuff in the locker room you were coming out, you know, as gay. Not that I care," she added hastily.

"Yeah," Amy put in, "and this is just between us."

He looked from one to the other and had the insane notion that they were being sincere. He thought about Amy's hurt look the other day. Part of his mind did not want to trust them. They had betrayed him, both them, in middle school. When they became part of popular clique and he had become the school freak.

Another part of his mind answered rationally, what had they really done? They had grown up and became girls. It was not their fault that Clark was not a girl. They hadn't created the concept of gender. They hadn't even created the system of cliques that ruled the school, they merely fit into it.

If someone like Tony could be cool with Clark, could these two girls still, somehow, be his friends? It was a risk, but wasn't he trying to be tough? Tough people took risks.

"I am not gay." He told them. They looked crestfallen. Strangely he felt wrong somehow. He had told the truth but he had also lied. He couldn't quite understand how that worked but he knew it was true. So he suddenly found himself making a confession.

"Well, I am not straight. That's pretty obvious, but it's not gay."

Christy crinkled her brow, "you're bisexual?"

"I am transgender. I want to be a woman."

Christy's eyes went wide.

Amy just rolled her eyes and flicked Christy with one finger. "Duh, he told us that in kindergarten."

Clark started laughing. The image came suddenly of himself at five. He was standing at the arts and craft table in the kindergarten room, drawing. Amy and Christy were there.

Five-year-old Christy held up a crude drawing of a woman wearing a tall hat with a cross on it. "When I grow up I'm going to be a nurse," she said.

Amy's drawing had a red helmet on. "I'm going to be a firefighter," the five-year-old Amy had said proudly.

Clark's drawing had long hair and a dress. "I'm going to be a woman." He said.

"You did," the sixteen-year-old Amy was insisting.

"I did," he laughed. And then all three were laughing and somehow suddenly he had two friends.

"So you seriously want to be a woman?"

"I am going to be," he asserted. "There are things that can be done."

"Like having a sex change?" Amy asked. Clark nodded.

"Wow," Christy said, "I never met a real-life transsexual before."

#####

Clark was on cloud nine for the next two periods but as he was getting ready to head home he was once again thrown against a locker and held there. He felt his face ground painfully into the metal.

"I wouldn't be looking so damn smug if I were a faggot," the voice drawled in his ear, "especially when you are living on the borrowed time." It was John Mort. His breath was thick and sweet, so close to his ears. "I am going to beat the f-ing shit out of you, faggot. You know why? Because you act like a girl, you walk like a girl, you talk like a girl, you wear your hair like a girl, you even dress like a girl."

Tony's words rang in his ears. Be tough, Clark, he said over and over, be tough. The pressure grew, as did the pain but he couldn't move. All he could manage to do was to turn his head a tiny bit. Then he caught his own reflection in a window down the hall, by the exit. He thought of the mirror girl. If he couldn't be tough, she could.

He took a deep breath and let go. With a shout, she struck out with her elbow, catching the boy across the bridge of his nose. He let go in shock and Clark/Clarissa stumbled free.

"You want a fight, fine, let's fight." John growled, he dropped into a boxing pose, his fists coming up.

Clarissa's hand shot out. She didn't even bother to make a fist. Her hand slipped inside John's fist before he could get his guard up and dealt him a stinging slap across the face.

"Oww." John shrieked. "You bast..."

Clarissa grabbed his ear lobe, pulling painfully on it and bringing his cuss to an abrupt close. She gave him an angry stare. "You forgot -- fights like a girl." She snarled. With a maniacal glee in his/her eyes, she almost casually walked his face straight into a wall.

"Teacher," a voice said quietly. But somehow it cut through both the uproar and Clark/Clarissa's anger. He let go. John rubbed his face.

"Is there a problem?" A deep male adult voice said.

"No sir." Another voice called out. Mysteriously everyone agreed. John nodded and Clark felt his head go through the same motion.

When the teacher turned away John hissed, "This ain't over." Then he turned and stalked off.

Clark turned, Clarissa subsiding somehow into a pleased silence within him. He came face to face with his brother. His brother who was grinning from ear to ear.

Jeremy broke into laughter. "How about that?" He howled excitedly, throwing one arm over Clark's shoulder. "The sissy finally learns to stand up for himself. Maybe you are one of the Holden boys after all."

"I want that one," Britney said brightly pointing at a Princess Barbie on the screen.

Clark felt a wiggle at his side. "Me too! Me too!" Holly was saying excitedly, waving a sheet of paper at him.

"Okay, okay," he told her, "just give me a minute to put it on Brit's list" He wrote Princess Barbie on the sheet in front of him and then took Holly's sheet and did the same.

"I think you two have hounded that poor boy enough for one day," Shelley Pirella said playfully from behind them.

"He don't mind one bit," Brit declared loudly.

"Yeah, Mom," Holly threw in, "he's the best babysitter ever."

Clark blushed. The truth was he didn't mind. After only three weeks he adored the girls. He glowed at their compliment. The girls had no problem just accepting him. It was not just the kids, Shelley and Tony seemed to accept him too.

He thought about the incident with John the last day of school. Why couldn't it be this easy at school? He didn't look or act any different yet the reaction was night and day. At school, he was 'acting like a faggot' but here he was 'very nurturing and kind,' Shelley's words.

"I am sure he has a lot better things to do then fill out your Christmas lists for you two." Shelley was saying now, "besides we've got to get heading if we are going to make it to Santa."

"Maybe Clark can come with us?" Holly asked.

Clark just laughed and shook his head. He followed Shelly into the other room. It was Saturday. Clark babysat for two hours in the afternoon, while Shelley caught up housework and did her charity work for the church. This Saturday was special and not because the girls were going to see Santa this evening. It was the first time he had spent with Shelley since Tony caught him cross-dressing.

"I think Clark's too big to be sitting on some old man's lap," Tony said as he came up from his den. He threw a wink in Clark's direction. Clark's pulse raced slightly, as it had every time Tony looked at him or made some reference to him. Everyone else in the household was acting normally, so Clark assumed Tony had not told Shelley about catching him in her dress. Still Clark was on edge and Tony's tendency to allude to the incident made it all the more worse. Tony seemed to be treating the whole thing as in inside joke.

"Daddy!" Holly was scolding him, "Santa's not some old guy, he's an elf."

"Oh, a fairy creature," Tony laughed, "that makes a world of difference."

Shelley handed Clark a short stack of bills, his pay for the week. "The girls are right about one thing," she said, "you really are working out well. They really like you and Tony says you've always got the place cleaned up when he gets home."

"Thanks," Clark replied. He turned to find himself almost nose to nose with Tony, who was holding a squirming girl under each arm.

"I think you're working out great, too." Tony put in and then to the girls, "okay kiss your favorite babysitter goodbye and let's get going." Each of the two girls leaned over and gave Clark a kiss on the cheek. For one second he almost thought Tony was going to give him one too but then he was turning away and setting the kids down. Clark shook his head and made for the door.

"Do you need a ride?" Shelley asked his retreating back. "We're headed out anyway."

"No thanks," he said and to himself, I need to clear my head anyway.

#####

It was the bank again. She ran for the door, terror sweeping over her frame. Heavy bodies tackled her. There was a moment of weightlessness and then a crushing blow, followed by the weight of bodies over her. Hands pressed upon her and she began to be dragged towards the vault. She fought, lashing out with her hands, seeking desk legs, chairs, any solid or solid-like objects that might slow the progress.

She was sliding along the floor. The vault was slowly approaching, the inky black interior that would swallow her. The shiny metal door was already swinging slowly shut ready to close her in for good. Her feet had passed the threshold into the darkness. The doors were closing on her. She looked up into the shiny finish and saw her own face. She screamed.

Clark woke screaming. He sat upright in his bed facing the mirror across the room. By the dim early morning light, he saw his face, her face, still etched with terror. And he understood the dream.

It wasn't his nightmare. It was hers. The vault had been slowly shutting on her and she was scared. Every day for the last four years this had been going on. When someone at school called him faggot; when mom worried about him but refused to discuss his gender identity, when his therapist suggested he accept being a boy - a gay boy, it was a small death for her. They would force that part of him into the vault and she would never see the light of day again. No wonder she was scared.

The scream must have been the only one or not as loud as he thought. Nobody was coming to check on him. Maybe he had exhausted his mom by now.

He rose and padded over to the vanity. He sat down in the dimness and stared at the mirror.

It was his face, but it was also hers. Even without makeup or any particular dress, she was with him, part of him. Maybe she was real and he was not.

Slowly he began to talk.

"I am angry but you have the wit to express it. I am intelligent but you know what to do with that intelligence. I am awkward but you have grace. I am nothing without you. I love what you can make me. I will never let them put us in that vault, I promise you."

#####

"I am not saying that Philip's a bad therapist," Clark argued. He had expected resistance to this idea, but not from Marcus. "I just need someone different."

"It's just I really like Philip," Marcus whined. "And I really don't want you to stop coming to the group."

"I won't leave the group." Clark promised. He meant it too. He would ask Philip about staying in the group even after he found a new therapist. He liked the group, especially Marcus.

"Besides," he went on, "we don't live that far apart. Once I turn sixteen I can borrow the car some time and come visit."

"That would be cool." Marcus brightened somewhat on the other end of the line.

"Don't even think about it," Clark warned Britney. She smiled mischievously, but dropped the cookie back in the cookie jar. "Maybe after supper." He called to her now retreating back.

"You babysitting?" Marcus asked.

"Yep." Mom had made good on her promise to add Clark to her regular cell phone plan. He had discovered at the next group that Marcus's mom was on the same service. That meant they were covered under the mobile to mobile. Now in the quiet moments that twins gave him, Clark often called Marcus.

They shared a lot in common. The rest of the boys in the group were in the closet. They strove valiantly to maintain their straight status at school while coping with their feelings at home and in their time away from home. A couple of the girls were "butch" and assumed to be lesbians. Two were out but the rest struggled to stay in the straight column. Marcus and Clark shared a common feature, they had failed to ever make it into the closet to begin with. While Marcus considered himself gay rather than trans, he was flaming. His gender variance, like Clark's, attracted a lot of negative attention but as he wailed in group, "there's no off switch."

"So what are you going wear tonight?" Marcus asked conspiratorially.

Clark shrugged, then realized Marcus couldn't see him. "I'm not sure. Probably the peach blouse."

"That's all?" Marcus whined, "You should try on one of the dresses, like the black one Tony caught you in."

He had told Marcus the whole story. He had also described the closet and its content in some detail. It was easier, having someone to talk to about these things. Marcus found the details very interesting. In ways, Clark thought that Marcus almost made a better friend than another trans person. He didn't understand so Clark had to explain everything but he was gay and open minded so he accepted it all.

Since being busted by Tony, Clark had not tried on the black dress again. But with Tony's implied permission he had tried on numerous other outfits in that precious hour or so he had after the twins fell asleep and before Tony got home. He was always careful to put everything back where he got it and to keep it clean. He was always back in male clothes before Tony got home. He had thought, more than once, about staying dressed until Tony got home, just to see his reaction. So far he could not find the courage to do it.

"I want something interesting," Marcus was saying on the phone. "So you can tell me how you feel."

This was part of the game. After the kids were in bed he'd head to the closet, calling Marcus on the way. He described the choices in detail and describe his reaction to wearing it. It amused Marcus and it helped Clark talk things out.

"Sorry, not tonight on either account," Clark replied. "I've got a huge paper due tomorrow. I need to get all the research and writing done tonight, so I can print it first thing in the morning. I'll wear my fav," meaning the peach blouse "but I got to work."

Clark had finished his paper about a half an hour before Tony got home that night. He thought momentarily about running up to the closet and dressing for short while, but it didn't seem worth it.

Tony found him on the couch with his laptop out, deep in thought.

"What'cha working on?"

"I can't get any of my MP3's to play on this thing. I have tried everything. I have reconfigured the ALSA mixer like ten times."

Tony laughed. "I thought you were the Linux pro now."

"I have only been using Ubuntu for a couple of months." Clark protested, "I am learning fast, but I can't do everything."

"Really?" Tony said in mock astonishment, "it seems to me like there is this new 'Miss Claire' that has been showing on the forums quite a bit. She seems to be something of a whiz and judging from her picture she seems to be wearing my wife's peach blouse."

Clark stared at him.

"Don't say you're sorry."

"You really don't care?"

"It's back in place, right? Just don't let Shelley know, she isn't as open minded as I am."

"Thanks, Tony."

"Besides, it's a good color on you."

Clark blushed, unsure how to answer.

"And you are barking up the wrong tree. It's not your computer or the sound system. MP3 stands for Media Player 3, it's a Window's format; definitely not open source. Linux purist won't have anything to do with it, so it's not pre-installed on Ubuntu. Do 'sudo apt get ubuntu restricted extras' in terminal."

Clark opened the terminal window and typed in the command Tony had given him. He loved terminal commands. It made him feel like a real programmer to be typing in strings of commands instead of working in the graphic desktop.

While Clark waited for the download to complete he looked up at Tony. "You've seen me on the forum?" He asked.

"Tony-Tux-Sudo" Tony replied with wink.

Clark rolled his eyes and muttered "geek" but he smiled as he said it. Maybe one person in thousand would get the joke. Tux was the penguin mascot for Linux. Sudo was the term for root privilege, the highest level of security on the system. Tony's icon was tuxedo wearing penguin.

Clark's forum persona was Miss Claire. He had his picture en femme - in female persona and it listed his gender as female. Did Tony know just how deep Clark's gender issues went?

"Did it work?" Tony inquired as he came back into the room with a drink in his hand.

Clark closed out the terminal and re-opened the media player.

This time his Lady Gaga CD played without a hitch.

"Oh dear," Tony teased with a dramatic sigh, "if I knew you listened to that crap I am not sure I'd have helped. I really must email you some Etta James or Roberta Flack."

"I have Roberta Flack," Clark said.

"Then there's hope for you yet." Tony said.

CHAPTER SEVEN

The front door banged open, startling Clark. It was way too early for anyone to be home. It wasn't even the girls bed time. Clark looked down at himself and his heart dropped. How was he going to explain this?

"Daddy! Daddy!" Holly squealed in the front room. Clark blew a huge sigh of relief. This was going to be embarrassing enough but it was a lot better than if Shelley had showed up. Why today of all days did someone have to arrive home early unannounced?

"Daddy!" Brit threw in and another set of feet scampered across the floor. "Guess what we did to Clark?"

Holly began to giggle uncontrollably.

"What did you do to the poor boy now?" Tony sighed dramatically. One of the things that had endeared Clark to the girls was his willingness to enter into their silly games.

Clark stepped out of the kitchen door and into the living room with his tray full of bite-sized pizzas he had made out of English Muffins. He was wearing one of Shelley's pink tops. The girls had brought it to him, along with a make-up set they had talked their mom into buying as an early Christmas present. They had brushed his hair, pulled it into pigtails and decorated his face and lips to the best of their four-year-old abilities.

"We made him a Barbie!" Brit declared proudly.

Tony snorted loudly, trying to hold in a laugh. A smile tugged at his lips.

"They thought I would make a good Barbie." Clark explained sheepishly. "I couldn't see any harm in letting them have a little fun."

"Of course not." Tony agreed with a knowing look. Clark blushed an even deeper shade, though under the layers of blush the kids had used who knew if it was even visible.

"Pizza!" Holly screamed, the experiment with Clark forgotten.

"One at a time," Clark commanded, "and sit at the coffee table so you don't make a mess everywhere."

The girls ran to him and grabbed a muffin each. They dashed to the coffee table with their prizes.

"Umm, so what brings you home so early?" Clark asked awkwardly.

"I've got some debugging to do," Tony replied lightly. "Figured I could do that from home as easily as at work. If you don't mind sticking around till the girls are in bed, then you can go home anytime."

Clark shrugged, "Okay. Umm, want a pizza? There are plenty."

"Don't mind if I do," Tony said reaching for one. Then he stepped in close, too close as far as Clark was concerned and said in a low voice, "The twins are right, you do make a good Barbie."

Before Clark could react, or even decide how he was supposed to react, Tony was gone, disappearing down into the den with two of Clark's muffin-pizzas and Brit was complaining loudly about being thirsty.

"Hold on a sec," Clark said, "I'm coming." He sat the tray on the coffee table and then sat down beside them. The tray had the plate of muffins, a teapot, three small teacups from the girls collection and a small bowl of sugar. "Chamomile." He told the girls holding up the pot.

"A tea party with real tea!" Holly gushed. "You're the best babysitter ever!" She hugged Clark's arm fiercely.

Only because those other girls were no doubt sick of tea parties and Barbie dolls by the time they took this job, Clark thought, whereas he had been banned from these simple pleasures in his childhood or teased about wanting them. I ought to spread the word on the TG forums, Clark thought, taking care of four-year-old girls that 'insist' on you playing these silly games has got to be every T-girls dream job.

An hour and half later he had them tucked into bed. He had read to them out of one of the many Barbie books the kids owned, in his best "Barbie voice" until they went to sleep, a satisfied smirk on their faces. He washed the make-up off, brushed his hair back out and returned the pink blouse, with a sigh, to Shelley's closet.

He found Tony in the kitchen. There were two bottles and a decanter on the counter. Tony was busy crushing a candy cane with a meat tenderizer.

"I saw this thing on one of those morning shows the other day," he explained, "peppermint martinis. Sounded good and I could sure use a drink after the day I've had."

Clark looked at the bottles. One was Vodka and the other Peppermint Schnapps. Tony pulled down a wide rimmed martini glass. He ran some water over the edge and sat the glass over the crushed-up candy cane. Righting the glass, now lined with candy cane fragments, he poured a measure of clear liquid into the glass. He took a sip and hmmed appreciatively.

"Want a sip?" Tony held the glass out to him.

I'm fifteen, Clark thought. Aloud he said, "I don't drink."

"Sure? It's wonderful." Tony said, "Little taste won't hurt."

Clark shook his head no, uncomfortable.

Tony shrugged, "Suit yourself." He took another long drink.

"So this guy at work," Tony said changing the subject suddenly, "kind of a big wig but he's a real idiot when it comes to computers. He brought me his laptop today. The guy spilled coffee on it or something. Instead of cleaning it off and letting it dry thoroughly, he decides to see if he's damage it. So he powers it up." Clark snorted appreciatively, stocking away this tidbit in case he ever spilled anything on his laptop. Tony went on, "He totally fried it. Arrgh. But the good news is this. He fried the whole motherboard and I had to replace the laptop but I salvaged out the hard drive. 160 GB solid state.

Clark whistled. "Wow."

"A lot more than your HP got."

"I'll say," Clark agreed.

"Want me to bring it home?" Tony asked, "we could swap it out next Saturday."

Clark's eyes bulged. "Really?"

"Sure, it's all been written off as a loss anyway, nobody would care. Just think of it as an early Christmas bonus." Tony looked up at the clock suddenly. "But I imagine you are ready to be getting home." He sat down the now empty glass and turned towards the front room. "C'mon Barbie." He said with a wink.

Clark blushed again but followed after. Was he ready to go home? Yes. No. Maybe. Tony was seriously confusing Clark. He knew about Clark but didn't care. He teased him, with comments like Barbie, but it was a different, good natured teasing.

And he offered Clark a drink. Why? It had been a test, Clark thought suddenly. He wanted to know if Clark would take a drink, or perhaps drink while on duty with the kids. It was probably a good thing he had said no. Not that he had been tempted. Clark knew that a lot of the kids, particularly the older more popular kids went to beer bashes and drank almost every weekend. He knew Jeremy had been to a few himself. Clark had no intention of ever drinking, in part because the popular kids who tormented him did it.

"Here it is." Clark said, looking at the plaque on the door.

"You really going to do this?" Marcus asked.

Clark gave him a look. "Why not? It's not half as crazy as what we got planned for later."

"I am not so sure," Marcus replied.

They were on their first official road trip together. Clark had turned sixteen the first week of January. He had passed his driving test easily and became the third driver in the family. Between his near perfect score on the driving test and his new job Clark had convinced his mother that he was old enough, responsible enough and had enough money to go shopping on his own. Besides he needed some new jeans before school began on Monday and she had to work. He had gotten permission to take the car for the entire Saturday, which torqued Jeremy off something terrible.

He had swung over to Eldora, picked up Marcus and headed for Iowa City. Shopping was only a small portion of their itinerary and even that wouldn't be exactly the kind of shopping his mom expected. He needed a couple of pairs of jeans and he told mom he'd probably spend the better part of the day pricing some computer stuff he wanted. He had found all those prices online, in case mom questioned him when he got home. He didn't know that he needed to go to that length, but it was better safe than sorry because he wasn't planning on going near a computer store.

Now they stood awkwardly in front of the office door. The hallway swarmed with traffic, like a minor pedestrian free way. Medical staff in scrubs or white uniforms strode confidently and busily from here to there. An elderly lady with a walker forced the traffic around her, like a rock in a stream. Another younger woman with a scarf on her head and a portable oxygen tank huffed by. Visitors, marked both by their street clothes and their looks of concern, made much of the traffic.

Clark looked up at the sign again. "Outpatient Child Psychiatric Services" it read. He took a deep breath and put his hand on the door.

"Will you be okay for an hour?" He asked Marcus.

"No problem," he said jingling his camera bag, which held a sizable amount of change in one of the side pockets. "I am going to back track to the vending machine. I'll be checking out all the cute male nurses. See you in an hour. Knock'em dead."

He opened the door and went in. He had discovered online, through one of the TG forums, that University of Iowa had one therapist who had a background in gender identity disorder. Her name was Elizabeth Gant and Clark was her eleven o'clock appointment.

#####

"Are you ready for some feedback?" Beth asked.

Clark nodded, fascinated. After two therapists and almost two years in therapy he had thought himself an expert. He was quickly learning that every therapist had his/her own style and they could be very different.

Dr. Edgerton's style was stiff, formal and fairly cold. Philip was friendly and warm. But both men were quiet. They asked simple, open-ended questions and waited patiently for him to open up. Clark, having no intention of opening up to either man, found the long pauses awkward. They stuck to a narrow range of "therapy related" topics. They probed his feelings, asked about suicidal thoughts and lectured about the dangers of drugs, alcohol and illicit sex. (None of which were Clark's problems, but he figured most kids his age faced these sorts of things, so they had to ask him. Like school, it was all on a script.)

Beth was nothing like that. She was loud, almost boisterous at times and very engaging. Where the other therapist had been patient, she pumped him for details. When he talked about his treatment at school, she exclaimed with outrage. She even called his gym teacher a "right bastard." He had quickly warmed to her and found himself talking about things in ways that he never would have expected.

When he spoke about Randy with Dr. Edgerton there had been an accusatory edge to it, after all the doctor had set the situation up. With Mom, there had been outrage. With Philip, it had been dismissive since Philip was already too eager to see him as a young gay man. With Elizabeth, he found himself being startling frank. "He was a pretty good kisser, you know, and I kind of liked that, but I didn't love him. He wanted to go further, but I didn't. It didn't feel right."

"Anything else?" She asked and he surprised himself again by having a ready answer.

"We met once, outside of our 'sessions' and outside of his home. He introduced me to one of his friends as "this kid I kind of know." It pissed me off."

"Because you wanted him to acknowledge the depth of your relationship?" Beth's ability to pinpoint his reasoning disturbed him slightly but it was freeing to talk about these things aloud. He had been angry, angrier than he had ever admitted, that Randy had shown him such affection in private and then snubbed him public. He had told himself that it was only coincidence that he told his mom about Randy that same week.

"Clark?" Beth was saying.

He shook his head and then nodded to her, "sure, feedback."

"You didn't come here to find out if you are transgender or not. You already know that." She began, "and you know what that means too."

Clark nodded. He had suspected it all along and his Internet research had confirmed it. "I have always felt this way, and I always will." He said.

"No amount of therapy can change that," Beth said flatly.

"But I can transition."

"Exactly," Beth agreed, "this is the real reason you came here, isn't it? Not to find out anything, not to talk about being transgender, not to work on any issues. You want me to help you transition."

He nodded.

She shrugged. "If you were an adult, that would be that."

"But I'm not."

"You're not," she agreed, "and that complicates things. You have talked to your mom about this?"

"She says I am too young, that I don't really know who I am."

"You don't feel that way."

"I was born this way. How can I be too young?" He replied vehemently.

"I understand how you feel." Beth said, "but I can understand how your mom feels too." She leaned in close, "I am on your side, Clarissa." One of the things had quickly endeared Beth to him was her first question. 'What do you want to be called?' She had used this name, not his given name, exclusively. "But transition is no simple thing. There are many considerations. Are you familiar with the Harry Benjamin Standards of Care?"

He nodded, "I've heard of them."

"I thought you might, you seem to have done a lot of research already. They are the medical standards for treating transgendered clients. They lay out what the criteria are if someone wants to transition and what sort of therapy needs to be done first. Well your first assignment, if you want to keep working with me that is, is to download them and read them."

He nodded. He definitely wanted to continue.

"When you do, you will find that ongoing counseling is one of the main requirements." Beth said. "So you might as well hunker down for the time being, it's not going to happen today. But if you stay with me I promise I will help you."

"And SRS?" Clarissa asked.

"Oh, Clarissa, it's way too early to discuss that."

#####

"You still think seeing a therapist was the crazy part?" Clarissa asked. It was definitely Clarissa. After his/her appointment with Beth they had gone to lunch and then shopping in Iowa City's downtown pedestrian mall. They had found a used clothes shop in a basement shop that sold interesting retro fashions. Marcus had bought lime green bell bottoms and an almost equally obnoxious green and yellow shirt.

Clarissa had bought a tweed skirt, white tights, a white camisole and a jacket that matched the skirt. It was, she thought, the perfect school girl's outfit. As they had shopped Clarissa had been a growing presence in his mind.

She had changed in the women's restroom at the mall. She had stood stock still in front of the restroom doors for what seemed like forever, debating in her mind. She was afraid to go into the women's room in boy clothes and equally afraid of coming out of the men's room in women's clothes. Rolling his eyes in exasperation Marcus had opened the door to the women's restroom and shouted, "Yoo Hoo!" into the bathroom. When there was no answer he gestured Clark inside and promised he would stand guard and tell anyone who approached that the toilet was out of order until Clarissa emerged.

On the way in to the mall she found a store that sold blond hair extensions that matched her hair. At first she had been slightly put out by the price but when she saw herself in the mirror she was glad she had spent the money. She had gotten two; which she attached to either side on the back of her head. Then she pulled her natural hair into a pony tail around the extensions and tied it with a band. The effect was that it appeared that she had long hair, tied in pig tails. Even without make up the transformation was almost perfect.

Now her makeup was on and they were standing outside Iowa City's one gay bar, the gay bar that advertised 'teen night' before seven on Saturdays. That worked fine for them, they both had to be home before nine and it was better than an hour drive to their respective homes.

Marcus, looking at his reflection in the glass, said, "this is going to be fun. And who knows, we might meet someone."

"Is that all you think about, sex?" Clarissa said, without malice. It had become something of a joke between them.

"Yes," Marcus said brightly, reaching for the door handle, "ladies first."

She was on the verge of getting angry when she realized she was not getting teased. She was a lady right now. She held up her head, tried to master her anxiety and stepped into the bar.

"This place is so cool." Marcus said entering behind her. They were standing in a long low room that was dominated by a stage. At the back of the stage, and scattered throughout the bar along the wall were large flat screen TV's. They were all synced together and playing the latest dance video. "To the bar" Marcus called, taking Clarissa by the arms.

"Hi ya, guys," Marcus called as he sidled up to the bar. "Two cokes."

The bartender, a butch dark-skinned woman tiredly pulled two small glasses from under the bar and filled them from a spigot. "Two dollars."

"What a rip." Marcus said under his breath, but he pulled two bills from his wallet and sat them on the counter. They found a table and sat. Clarissa turned back to check out the crowd only to discover the crowd had already came over to check out the new kids.

"Hey, hon, what's up?" A voice said at Clarissa's shoulder. She turned and looked at the girl who was talking to her. She was tall and slender, with a muscular look of an athlete. She had short close-cut hair and wore faded blue jeans and a ripped T shirt. She winked at Clarissa, "what's a girl like you doing in a place like this?"

Clarissa gave her a look, that she hoped conveyed, what the hell do you think I am doing in a place like this? She had read online that sometimes lesbians were less than welcoming towards trans women, but had not expected to face it so soon.

"OMG!" Marcus shrieked by Clarissa's side, "they think you are a lezbo."

Indeed, a small tribe of women were gathering just off the talker's shoulder, craning to check out the new girl.

"Back off Theresa," a rich, deep voice said at their other side. Clarissa turned to see a tall thin boy with olive skin and short dark hair standing at his back. The boy wore tight jeans and a skimpy women's top. His face was made up with rich blue eyeshadow and deep magenta lipstick. "I think this one belongs to us." Without waiting for a reply, he took Clarissa's arm. "We got get you made up for the show, honey." He said.

"Show? What show?" Clarissa asked.

The boy just laughed. He ushered her towards the stage.

"Teen drag show in ten minutes, Maurice," a man said as the two went by.

"We got another one, Joe." Maurice replied. Maurice paused, looking Clarissa over. "School girl, very nice. You should do Britney then." To Clarissa's blank stare he added, "Britney Spears, early stuff, Oops I Did It Again, yeah that's it."

"A drag show? I've never done a show before." Clarissa said. The truth was, she'd never even seen a drag show before, let alone been in one.

Maurice paused, taking in the new information. "Definitely Britney, then." He took her arm and started walking towards the stage again.

"Awesome show! You were the freaking best!" Marcus threw his arms around Clarissa. "She was the best, wasn't she?" Several of the girls hanging around Marcus and the bar nodded and one of the boys gave him a thumbs up.

She had been worried about ditching Marcus within minutes of their entering the bar, to be in the drag show. When her turn had come she had seen him in a large mixed group and had stopped worrying so much. Marcus had hit the ground running. Always a misfit at home, he found himself at home among this group.

She had had enough to worry about with her show anyway. The drag queens had redone her makeup. They had assured her that she had done a great job, for day to day. But the bar was dark and it had to show from the stage, so it had to be bold. Really bold. Almost clown like, she had thought thinking about the time the girls had done her face with their toy make-up set, but when Marcus showed her the pictures he took on his phone she had to agree with the queens.

She had also worried about performing. She had no clue what to do. "Just let go and do it" Maurice had said, so she tried. She listened to the music, an old Britney Spears tune as promised and just danced across the stage. The crowd had started cheering and everything else ceased. Clark was almost painfully awkward and nervous but Clarissa was a ham. She loved the attention. She had the image of the girls hamming it up for one of their parents. She hoped she didn't look that ridiculous. She couldn't help but wonder what it would be like to dance for Tony. She pushed the thought out of her mind and danced on.

"Oh, oh, oh." Marcus cried out suddenly, slapping Clarissa's chest repeatedly. "I almost forgot, there's someone you have to meet. Have to."

He said, "see you later" to his posse of new friends and pulled Clarissa towards the back of the bar. There, at a small round table, sat a middle-aged lesbian with long blond curly hair. She was a little bit on the heavy side and wore thin wire rimmed glasses. Something about her posture and appearance reminded him of his mother.

A middle-aged man in a dress shirt and slacks came up with two drinks. He sat beside the woman. She greeted him warmly and he kissed her on the cheek. Clarissa was puzzled. Wasn't this woman a lesbian? Why would a straight woman be in a bar like this? Why would Marcus want him to meet her so badly?

"Clarissa," Marcus proclaimed, "This is Jilliane. Jilliane this is Clark, I mean Clarissa, sorry."

"Clarissa." Jill held out her hand, "that's a pretty name." They shook hands and Marcus took a seat. Clarissa joined him, wondering what the big deal was.

"Jill," Marcus told him, "is a post-op transwoman."

Clarissa looked at the woman, stunned. She knew that some trans women were passable and some were not. But she had never thought that one might look so, so ordinary. His eyes widened, "you're trans?"

"Yes, and that's the best compliment you could have given me."

"Post-op?"

She nodded yes. "Had the surgery about six years ago, in Bangkok."

"Bangkok? Like Thailand?"

"Yeah, sex change capitol of the world. Best doctors, lowest prices."

"I want to know everything." Clarissa said.

Jilliane was happy to talk. Clarissa worried that she was pestering the woman but she had so many questions and no one else she could ask. If Jilliane felt pestered, she never let it show. She even suggested they go to an all-night diner nearby when the bar announced that teen night was over so they could talk longer.

"Lowest prices," Clarissa said as she slid into the booth. She looked around the diner nervously but nobody seemed to paying them any attention. Either trans people came here often or she was being read as a 'real' girl. She couldn't tell. "How low is low?" She finished.

"Five to fifteen thousand," Jilliane said, "though I wouldn't go to one of the lower end surgeons. My surgery was about ten. The whole trip clocked in under fifteen thousand and I took Doug with me." She leaned over and kissed her partner, Doug on the cheek.

"What do you have to do before they will accept you as a patient?" Clarissa asked next.

"They follow the same standards as here in the States." Jillian replied, "and the medical care is just as good. The climate and culture is the wonderful. It's such a beautiful place, I wish I could go back again."

By the time they had finished a meal Clarissa had two napkins full of keywords to look up later and was cursing that she didn't have a notepad, or better yet, her computer with her. There was so much new information to look up.

In the parking lot Clarissa found herself impulsively hugging Jilliane. "Thank you so very much!" Clarissa gushed, "It's just so incredible to meet someone who," she broke off, trying to find the right words. "Someone who is like me. Some one who has been through the whole process. I just,"

Jilliane saved Clarissa from her babbling by pulling her into a second hug.

"It's okay. I know what you mean, girl." Jillian said.

#####

"That was the best day ever!" Marcus hooted for the tenth time. Clarissa was inclined to agree or she had been inclined to agree the first six or seven times he made this statement. It was starting to get old.

"Jilliane was awesome," Clarissa put in. That had certainly been the highlight of her day, to meet a real honest to god transwoman. One that had been through transition and surgery. One that was living her life as a woman. Jill had also proven very patient, answering many questions about transition, the SRS procedure, what to expect, where she went, what it was like.

"Joey, that was my fav," Marcus said. Joey had been one of the guys at the club and was Marcus's newest love interest. They had done no more than chat briefly but with each retelling Marcus was embellishing it wildly. It was rapidly becoming love at first sight. "And you rocked the show." Marcus went on. "The lesbians, the guy at 7-11," he held up his big gulp cup, "all thought you were really a girl. You are passable, girlfriend!"

She smiled at the thought. The smile quickly faded as she saw the flashing lights in the rear view mirror. "Shit. shit, shit." She said.

Marcus paused and looked behind them. "Why are they pulling us over? We didn't do anything."

All Clarissa could say was, "shit, shit, shit."

"What's the big deal?" Marcus asked, "Mom gets pulled over all the time. Drives like a race car driver."

Clarissa's heart was racing. She had not wanted to give up being Clarissa until she absolutely had to. She could not bear the thought of going back to being simply Clark. So she had put her pants back on, but left on the top, the hair extensions and the make-up. At 7-11 it had seemed to be a fun game, to let the old man that worked there think she was a real girl.

This was a whole different matter because her ID, which the cop would definitely want to see, said Clark.

"Clarissa? You okay?" Concern showed in Marcus's voice.

She was growing pale, she knew it. She could feel herself shaking slightly. "What if he wants my ID?"

Judging from Marcus's face, he still didn't get it. "So? You've got a driver's license right?"

"Yeah, one that says Clark." She looked over at Marcus, still in his lime green pants and green and yellow shirt. The same thought was going through each of their minds; a drag queen and a flaming gay kid on an empty road at night had better hope they weren't being pulled over by some redneck cop. It could turn ugly fast.

"He can't do anything to us," Marcus said, but he didn't sound so certain.

"It would be our word against his."

"There are two of us."

"Yeah, but who do you think they would believe?" Clarissa said.

That silenced Marcus. Helpless Clarissa slowed the car and pulled onto the gravel shoulder. She fought down panic. Without slowing, the police car tore past them and raced away into the night. Marcus let out a sigh of relief, but Clarissa continued to pull to a stop, griping the wheel fiercely.

"It's okay, it's okay," Marcus repeated hypnotically as Clarissa fought to master her breathing, "He went on, he didn't stop."

"What if he had?" Clarissa said shakily, "What if it was something serious?" She knew at some level her reaction was way out of proportion to what had just occurred but she couldn't help it. "What if I had to go to jail looking like this?"

"Over a traffic stop?" Marcus said.

"I know, but what if? What if he was a redneck jerk and decided to accuse us of something worse?"

"Chillax, honey." Marcus demanded putting his hand on her shoulder. "It's okay. That's not going to happen."

"Not this time," Clarissa persisted, "but it could happen, some time."

"We are not criminals," Marcus said, "Just gay."

Clarissa gave him an irritated look.

"Okay LGBT," Marcus corrected himself. "You know what I meant."

Clarissa took a deep breath and let it out. He was right, it wasn't a felony to dress like a woman, just not very accepted. Still Marcus didn't fully get it either. He didn't understand, possibly couldn't understand how she felt. Being taken for a girl for most of the day had been an incredible joy but with it came fear. The consequences if the wrong man found out she was trans, that there was male anatomy beneath the feminine dress, could be extreme. Many if not most of the hate crimes she had read about centered on this danger.

Beth had mentioned a letter, a certified letter, from her stating the Clark was transgender and in treatment for gender identity. This letter might force the school to make some accommodations for Clark, like letting him out of gym. It might help with school and similar authorities, but she wouldn't want to trust her luck on a nearly abandoned highway. She wished she had something more solid, something that said she was in fact female. Something she could show to a cop, like an ID.

"What is up with you?" His mom's voice interrupted his reverie.

81

"Huh? What?"

"Yeah, what is up with you?" Jeremy added. At least mom's voice held some concern, not the deep cutting sarcasm. "You keep spacing off, and then getting this goofy ass grin on your face."

"Hush," mom said to his brother. She reached over and ruffled Clark's hair. "You do seem distant. Is something wrong?"

"No," he said. His mind kept going back to the day before. The conversation with Beth, shopping, the club, everything.

"You and your friend have fun yesterday?"

He nodded.

"Is he your boyfriend?" Jeremy sneered.

"No!" Clark said.

"Jeremy Holden!" His mom scolded.

"You've seen him." Jeremy said, "he's flaming."

"He's just a friend." Clark insisted. *Not my type.*

"There is nothing wrong with your brother having friends." His mom said and she looked away.

Clark sighed. He suspected his mom had been thinking the same thing as Jeremy. It seemed so obvious to both of them, and to everyone at school that he was gay.

Then he thought about the girls in the club, the waitress at the diner or the cashier at 7-11. What had been obvious to them? That he was indeed a girl. If only he could hang on to that. He thought about Clarissa, this other persona of his. He thought about the way she held herself, how she would walk, talk.

"He's gone again, into whatever gay world in his mind," Jeremy commented as he got up from the table.

"Jeremy! I don't know what's gotten into either of you today." His mother protested. He saw a look of worry cross her eyes.

She's losing us Clark thought, that's what is happening. Jeremy will graduate this spring. He's already gone anyway. He has his own mind, his own opinions. He's like our father that way, his opinions are the only ones that matter.

And me? We have always had the battle between the boy she wants me to be and the girl that I am. Now she's lost that too. I don't want to hurt her, he thought, suddenly sad, I just can't be a boy for her sake alone.

#####

"Hey, Tony," Clark started hesitantly, "I've got a question. It's okay either way," he added quickly, "but I am doing this independent study in computers for school..." He trailed off.

Shelley squinted at him. "You're a sophomore, right?"

Clark nodded.

"They let you do independent study?" She asked.

Clark nodded again. They do when you end up teaching the teacher in Freshman computer skills and he realizes that there is nothing left in his classes that you can learn Clark thought.

"Go ahead," Tony prompted.

"I was hoping I could come see your work place sometime, shadow you for part of a day or something. Mr. Hardin says I can get some time off school for it if I want."

Tony smiled, "I'll have to clear it with the boss." He paused mischievously, "Oh wait, I am the boss!" He winked and went on, "okay, when do you want to do this?"

"I'll leave you two to figure things out." Shelley said, handing Clark an envelope, his week's pay.

"Any Thursday or Friday afternoon would work for me," Clark said. "I don't have any important classes those days."

"Let's say Friday," Tony said. "And maybe we can stop somewhere for a bite on the way home."

#####

"Clark, over here," a voice hissed as he entered the study hall. He had to look around for a minute, thrown off guard. Nobody usually recognized him when he came in late.

"Over here," the voice repeated. It was Christy. She and Amy were sitting at a round table towards the back. Christy gestured towards one of the still empty seats, "here."

Too surprised to think, he went and sat down.

"How are you doing?" Amy asked.

I just nearly got tackled in the hall by your boyfriend, John, he thought bitterly but he bit it back. It wasn't her fault that her boyfriend was an ass, after all.

"Yeah it's good to see you back, are you alright?" Christy put in.

We're friends now? He wondered. Apparently, they were, there was no guile in either face.

"Were you sick?" Amy asked.

He was startled by the question. Having friends might prove awkward, he would have to explain his frequent absences from school.

Monday's issue had been simple, but not something he was ready to talk about. He had woken up and found himself physically incapable of putting on the boy jeans and T-shirt that he had to wear to school. He had laid back down on his bed and just shut down. His mom had come to get him up about four or five times. She didn't understand his feelings about his gender at all, but she knew that on the days when he shut down there was little she could do. She called him in and left him on his bed. By noon he had been able to get up (mom was gone to work) and put on some make up and gender-neutral clothes.   By supper time he was more 'appropriately' dressed and came up to supper. Jeremy had handed over Clark's homework without comment.

"Yeah I was sick," Clark replied. "I'm feeling better now, though."

"Did you see Oprah the other day?" Amy asked.

It seemed an odd question. He wasn't the type to watch Oprah, and hadn't pegged Amy as one either. He nodded no.

"The thing about Trans kids?" Christy explained. "We saw it and thought of you."

"Yeah," Amy agreed. "It was like super interesting. I have a million questions." A look of concern went across her face, "If that's okay?"

He shook his head, still mystified. Nobody had described him as interesting before.

"So when you think about yourself, do you think boy or girl?" Amy gestured helplessly with her hands, searching for the words, "you know, like how do you refer to yourself; he or she?"

The question took him off guard. He wasn't sure he was completely comfortable talking about himself. Then again he'd told them he was transgender. What did he expect? Besides he was struggling with the same concept himself. "It's funny you would ask that." He replied. "I've had to refer to myself as Clark – slash – he out habit for years but the more I am working on being out about this, the more I think of myself as she. It's weird sometimes, like there are two of us."

"That would be weird." Amy agreed.

"Wait." Christy said, "what do you mean, working on being out about this?"

"Umm," uh-oh he'd revealed too much already. Then he decided, what the hell, he was working on being out about this, wasn't he? "Yeah, I am seeing this therapist, so I can transition."

"I thought you were already seeing a shrink? At least I thought so since..." Christy left it un-said.

Clark swallowed hard and nodded. Everyone at school knew he had mental issues. His first suicide attempt had occurred in the second-floor bathroom of the middle school three years ago. Nobody except for a couple of the teachers knew the details but they all knew he'd been taken out of school for nearly a month afterwards.

"Yeah, but he's not a specialist you know? Mom's been taking me to therapist since I was fourteen."

"Was that when you?" Amy asked.

He nodded no and gave the girls his pat answer, "I didn't know fourteen-year-old boys shouldn't cry because they aren't girls."

They both broke out in giggles. It made Clark smile too.

"Girls," the study hall teacher warned. Clark looked up. "And Clark," she added.

"I think you had it right the first time," a voice said from another table. Amy stuck her tongue out in direction of the offending comment. Clark snickered. It was his own sort of strategy, defusing the comment without either confirming or denying it.

Everyone was quiet for a few moments, until the teacher turned back to her work. Then Christy leaned back in. "So this person on Oprah said that Trans people can be any sexuality, gay straight or bi. So do you know? I mean which are you attracted to, men or women?"

Clark shrugged, "Men, I guess." He certainly wasn't interested in having sex with a woman. "I mean I think so, but I am so f-ed up I can't even fantasize right."

"What do you mean?" Amy asked.

He had had this discussion with Beth too. "I like guys, okay. But I don't get all excited over two guys together. I don't want to be with a guy, as a guy, you know?"

"But you aren't a guy, right?" Christy clarified, "I mean that's what the trans things means."

"Yeah," it felt good to be affirmed, "but I have that anatomy. How do you fantasize about being a straight woman when you've got that between your legs."

"Oh my god," Amy said, "I can see how that would be awkward."

CHAPTER EIGHT

"Over here, Barbie," Tony's voice caught Clark as he came out of the restroom. He gave the man a sharp look but Tony merely winked. Clark looked both ways down the hall. It was empty. "Don't worry," Tony laughed. "We are alone as we can get. Nobody comes down here. Now if you will come this way," he ushered Clark down the hall.

"Now this," Tony went on, "Is my favorite visual statement about the advance of technology." They were deep underneath the insurance company where Tony worked. He pulled open a green metal door and ushered Clark inside.

Clark stepped into a large open room. In one corner sat four rectangular boxes with a huge fiber optics cable snaking out of each one. Tony gestured to the wide and mostly empty space of the room. "This is the main server room for the entire corporation. When it was built the 20 GB, that's twenty gigabytes," he emphasized, "servers pretty much filled this entire room. Now," he gestured towards the boxes in one corner. "Each of those servers is about 6 Terabytes. These aren't even mainframes," he made air quotes around the word mainframe, "not in the traditional sense anyway. They're just back up storage. Most of the server functions are divided up between different departmental computers."

"I thought you said you had three servers." Clark asked looking at the boxes.

Tony gave him a sharp look. "Did I?" After a moment, he

chuckled. "Here I was planning on impressing you with the memory in here," He pointed at one of the boxes. "Instead I am being impressed with the memory in here." He tapped Clark's forehead playfully. "Are all trans people so smart?"

Clark blushed but didn't answer. Just when Clark was wondering how Tony saw him and if it was safe to come out as trans to the man, Tony had left a comment on one of 'Claire's' blogs. Clark still didn't know how Tony found it. The comment had been positive. Clark figured it was Tony's way of letting him know it was okay.

Tony had led him around and shown him half a dozen smaller servers scattered throughout the corporation. Mostly though he talked and talked. Tony had a captive audience and was taking full advantage. He talked about computer security which, far from being the boring topic that most of the kids at school thought, was a fascinating game of cat and mouse with a variety of hackers, virus writers and crackers. At least it was the way Tony told it. Tony seemed to have a soft spot and grudging respect for hacking and was proving extremely knowledgeable on the subject.

In fact, it seemed like most of Tony's job or at least the part he most like to talk about was the pen test. Pen was short for penetration. In a penetration test Tony would attempt to hack his own corporation, testing various servers and programs for security flaws.

"You are right," Tony was going on, "three servers." He banged one of the boxes with his palm. "This 2-terabyte box is just sitting here. It's got some old data on it research wants to keep backed up and they won't let me decommission it, no matter how much I gripe. Nothing worse for security than an old server that's not in active use."

"That was way cool." Clark gushed as they walked through the employee parking ramp towards Tony's jeep. "I can't ever repay you."

"That's probably true," Tony joked. "How about pizza?"

Clark nodded. Mom had driven him down to Des Moines before work but Tony had offered to drive him home. Another hour or so eating pizza and no doubt talking hacking, followed by the drive home. Clark was almost looking forward to that as much as the tour.

"There's a Pizza Hut out by the mall. Mom, Jeremy and I go to sometimes on our way out of town," Clark threw in, not wanting to take Tony too much out of his way.

"I was thinking Robins," Tony said.

Robins? Clark had heard the name. It was a fancy place, he thought. Mom's last boyfriend, the lawyer, had taken her there. He wasn't sure how much money he had with him. It would be horribly embarrassing to not be able to pay for his supper after everything Tony had done for him. "Isn't Robin's pretty pricey?"

"Don't worry it's my treat," Tony said. "Consider it partial repayment for today."

"How is you taking me out to pizza repayment?" It seemed to Clark yet another favor he owed Tony, not the other way around.

Tony approached the black jeep on the passenger side and opened the rear door. He extracted an old gym bag and handed it to Clark. "Open it."

Clark slowly unzipped the top of the bag. Inside he could see shiny dark fabric and understanding came suddenly.

"It would be a great honor if Ms. Claire would join me for supper this evening." Tony said, "and more than ample repayment of any favors I might have performed in her service."

"Tony," Clark said in a quiet voice, "I don't know if this a good idea." It was perhaps the understatement of Clark's life. Tony was much older. He was married. And Claire was really a boy. Still there it was, that dress. He hadn't had the courage to wear it again since the night Tony caught him it. He had stared at it evening after evening. Now it was being offered him.

"Relax," Tony said softly, "I am not propositioning you. I just want to have a nice meal with a pretty young lady. Is that so bad?"

Was it so bad? It's just a meal. "But..."

"It's what you want." Tony said. "To be Claire. You get to be her for one evening. I get to have every man in the restaurant look at me think, wow, he must really have it going on to have such a pretty young girl on his arm. Then we leave, go home to our normal lives, no harm no foul."

Clark's heart raced. There was something in the way Tony said normal that tore at Clark. Was Tony as unhappy at home as Clark was? Wasn't this exactly what he wanted, to be treated like a woman, to be taken to a nice restaurant by a man. What a man. Tony was tall, broad, everything you could want in a man. And he was intelligent, charming, all the traits that really mattered to Clark.

There were three small problems. Okay one huge problem, Shelley and two small problems Holly and Brit. Tony was a married man. But what was Clark supposed to do? He was in Des Moines, he had no transportation of his own. He could call his mom, but that would require him to explain a lot more than he was ready to explain. Plus it could very well mean the end of his job. He really liked the girls and the money. Finally, he nodded slightly.

Tony open the passenger door for Clark. "It's going to be fun." He said, "Don't over-think it. I promise you, it'll be okay."

Tony stopped at a gas station so that Clark could change before they got to the restaurant. The gym bag contained Shelley's cocktail dress, a bra, panties and stockings. There was a pair of heels that fit reasonably well and a make-up bag. Clark marveled at Tony's perceptiveness as he dressed. Not many men would have been able to guess someone's shoe size close enough and the makeup was all in hues that Clarissa herself would have selected.

The clerk did a double take as Clarissa left the restroom, Clark's boy clothes and persona tucked away in the old gym bag. Clarissa's heart raced but she struggled to place the emotion that went with it, was she excited or scared? Tony was in the parking lot, keeping the jeep running and warm against the cold night. "There's my girl!" Tony cheered when she got in the car. "Wow, just look at you."

He seemed so genuine, so sincere that she smiled too. This is all just a lark to him, another fun game. She felt herself relax. He had said it would be okay and part of her believed it too; part of her.

It was a short but cold walk from the jeep to the restaurant, but what could she do? Clark's tan coat didn't match the outfit and was way to masculine when she was dressed like this. "You really are a girl, aren't you?" Tony muttered as he opened the door for her. She smiled and was washed suddenly in the warm light of Robin's.

The maitre de gave her a short disapproving look as they approached his podium. Keyed up and anxious Clarissa was suddenly crestfallen, sure she had been 'clocked' as the girls on the TG forums called it when someone noticed you were not really a girl.

"I have reservations for two, Tony Pirella." Tony said.

"Would you and," the maitre de paused momentarily, "your daughter prefer a table or booth?"

"Booth," Tony said as Clarissa stifled a chuckle. Obviously, the man was under no delusions that they were related, he was just couldn't resist saying something snarky about their age difference. Their age difference, not Clarissa's gender, she thought, a shot of joy shooting through her.

Once they were seated in their booth a waitress came up. "Can I get you two something to drink?" She asked.

"Some red wine," Tony answered quickly, "you?" Again he was offering alcohol. Again Clarissa demurred.

"Just an ice tea please."

Tony raised an eyebrow but didn't comment.

"Here you are," Tony said as they pulled up to Clarissa's house. It was almost ten pm. "Now that wasn't so bad, was it?"

Clarissa thought back over the evening. Tony had been a perfect gentleman throughout. They had gotten a few dark looks, mostly from middle aged women and mostly, Clarissa assumed because of the apparent age difference and whatever apparent relationship they were in. Which they were emphatically not in. It had been a friendly evening, nothing more.

And it had been fun, a lot of fun. She was called miss by all the wait staff. She had felt comfortable and in control all evening. When they stopped at another gas station so she could put on Clark's clothes again, she had taken almost as long as before. She didn't want to stop being Clarissa or Claire. In fact, on the drive home she had noticed that her mannerisms, her speech and most importantly her mind remained firmly stuck as Clarissa.

"Yeah," she said, "it really was a lot of fun. The entire day. Thank you so much Tony."

"My pleasure," he said and brushed her cheek affectionately.

As Clarissa approached the doors of her house the doubts began to assail her again. Yes, it had been fun. The pizza was incredible, Robin's had a large brick oven and it made a world of difference in the flavor. Tony had been delightful company both at his workplace while she was Clark and later at the restaurant. But that didn't stop her from feeling guilty. She could guess how Shelley would feel about their little excursion. There was also, under that, a certain amount of anger. Tony had meant this evening to be a surprise but Clarissa wish she had had some forewarning.

Clarissa turned and looked into the night. She wished she could go walk around the town for a while to clear her head but mom would surely have heard Tony's jeep and be expecting her son to be home. Besides it was a cold night. Hoping she'd gotten enough of the makeup off she turned and opened the door willing herself to be Clark again.

"How was your day?" His mom's voice greeted him from the far room as he entered the house.

"It was good."

"You're late getting home." Clark looked at the clock. His mom was already in her pajama's but didn't seem mad.

Clark just rolled his eyes. "Tony," he said.

"I figured it was okay because you were with an adult," she said, "but when you said you were stopping for pizza..."

"Tony had to go to Robin's," Clark said dismissively.

"That's a pretty ritzy place," his mom said.

"They're loaded." He hadn't gotten a straight answer from Tony on his salary but he knew it was in the six-digit range. Tony was also high enough in the corporation to get stock options on a regular basis.

They talked for a while about his day and Clark quickly warmed to the subject of Tony's job and the stories of computer hacking the older man had shared. It beat thinking about the evening's activities. Tony had Clark convinced it had been an innocent game. Talking to his mom forced him to reevaluate the evening from an adult's perspective and it didn't look very innocent suddenly.

#####

"How can you eat that and be so skinny?" Amy commented.

Clark looked at the candy bar in his hands thinking this was going to be another awkward friends moment, having to explain his idiosyncrasy. Like how he shut down on Saturday evening and didn't get up or eat all day Sunday or Monday. Now he was making up for it by being ravenous on Tuesday.

"Amy!" Christy hissed sharply. Clark looked up as the two exchanged a dark look. They were in final period study hall, which due to how small their school was, was held in the cafeteria. Which meant they could have snacks. Amy had a small container of baby carrots. Tom, Christy's boyfriend had a pop in front of him and Christy an ice tea. Clark was wolfing down his second candy bar.

"I'm sorry," Amy said, "I get kind of bitchy when I'm on a diet."

"Why do you need to diet?" He asked.

"I'm fat," she insisted.

"You are not," Christy replied with a worried look. Clark's eyes widened with surprise and understanding.

"My life's not perfect, you know." Amy said in a low quiet voice.

"I'm sorry," Clark said. He wasn't sure what else to say. An image of Amy bending forward played through his mind, the vertebrae on her back showing through her blouse. Amy staring at herself in the mirror and repeating, "I'm fat, I'm fat." The homemade lunches of raw veggies and salads. He held her gaze softly and the words "anorexia" rose in his mind. She seemed to nod slightly, as though acknowledging word too.

Then Christy snorted suddenly and the moment was broken. "What?" Tom asked.

"No question about Clark's gender," she muttered and Amy giggled.

"What?" Tom persisted, "what just happened?"

Amy looked at Clark mischievously and said, "boys are so

oblivious sometimes."

Christy had told Tom about Clark's admission. She claimed that he was okay with it. So far Clark and Tom hadn't spoken to each other about it but he seemed comfortable enough that the girls would ask questions or make comments in his presence. So far no rumors had spread around the school, so Clark figured the three must be trustworthy.

"Boys and girls communicate differently," Christy explained, "with girls there are more nonverbal clues. There's more than what we say going on. A look can convey an entire message."

"But why not just say it?" Tom asked.

"Because sometimes you don't want to say it," Clark said glancing at Amy. Then he glanced down at the candy bar and wondered suddenly if the girls knew more about him and about his depression than he had said. Probably. He looked at Amy shrugged sheepishly. She gave him a warm smile.

"I don't get it," Tom said shaking his head.

"Clark does though," Christy laughed. Clark felt a smile well up inside him, the first genuine smile that had crossed his face in a long time. Usually it was the other way around. Usually he was stuck in a group of boys and he was the outsider that didn't get what was really going on.

Tom shook his head, "Whatever." He said, "you know what else I don't get? English." He pulled out a short stack of papers stapled together. "Last time I wrote my book report the day before it was due and I got an A. This time I put a ton of work in and barely pulled a B minus."

"I got an A," Christy said.

"As usual," Amy threw in, "all I got was a lousy C plus. How did you do Clark?"

It was going to be another awkward friends moment, he realized. "I got another perfect Daa." He said.

"Daa?" Tom echoed, "Like a D? But you're like the smartest kid in school."

Clark blushed, "Daa," He explained, "D slash A." He pulled out two separate papers. "You see I take this correspondence course through DMACC." DMACC was the Des Moines Area Community College.

"You take a correspondence course at college?" Amy gasped. "And you are taking independent study in computers? It must be true about you being a genius."

Clark shrugged dismissively. "I've got to take the correspondence course." He said, "Cause Mrs. Turlow is out to get me. I know, I know," he went on shuffling the papers across to them. "Everyone who gets bad grades says that, but look, they're the same report exactly."

It was his book report. "Even Cowgirls get the Blues," Christy read, "funny title for a book."

Midway down the first page on both copies one sentence was underlined. The sentence read; The lesbianism of the cowgirls has less to do with their real sexuality and seems to be a metaphor for the feminist movement of the time period. Mrs. Turlow's copy said in the margins, "Lesbians? Is this really an appropriate subject for a school book report?" Mrs. Tyler, his correspondence instructor had written simply, "great insight."

The most telling difference however was on the second page. Clark had written a paragraph about why he was drawn to this book and what emotional connection it had for him. It was the main character, Sissy Hankshaw that he could identify with the most, he said. Her deformity set her apart from everyone else, made her different from the people around her. Clark felt like that too. He felt different from everyone around him.

Mrs. Turlow's comments began with a line of red "??? You identify with someone who's got enormous thumbs? I don't get it." Mrs. Tyler's comments on the other hand, had nearly made him cry when he read it the first time.

She said, "Clark, I have only met you in person once but I totally get what you are saying. You are truly a unique individual and I can tell from your writing that the other kids in rural Iowa don't understand you. But consider this, Sissy's deformity and difference is also the source of her freedom and her beauty. There will always be those who will hate you for being different, but there will also be those who will love you for it. I for one am proud to be in the second category. Keep up the good work."

Christy whistled as she read it. "Wow, that's really high praise Clark."

"You got like a photographic memory or something?" Tom asked glancing over the two papers and the two disparate grades, D minus and A plus.

"No," Clark said shrugging slightly.

He felt a presence at his side and looked up to see his brother standing there. "No, Clark don't have a perfect memory." He said sarcastically, "he only scored 98 percent on reading retention."

Looking up into his brother's face he had the sudden impression that his brother might be bragging about him. His brother quickly dashed that by adding, "It's like that Sh*t My Dad Says book," he laughed, "Nobody says you aren't smart. They say other stuff, but not that." One of the seniors standing next to Jeremy snorted.

"Anyway," Jeremy went on, "Basketball practice is canceled on account of there's a storm coming in later this evening, so as soon as the bell rings I am heading for home." As if on cue the bell rang.

Clark understood he was being offered a ride. "Great," he said, "if you could just drop me at the Pirella's."

"The Pirella's?" Amy asked. Her eyebrow rose quizzically. There was something else behind her eyes that Clark could not read.

He looked at Christy and back at Amy. "Yeah," he said slowly, "I baby sit for them."

Christy and Amy exchanged a look. A look that unfortunately this time Clark could not read.

CHAPTER NINE

Clarissa slowed as she approached the small-town park. She sighed and pulled her stocking cap down over her ears and zipped her tan coat the last couple of inches up. The days were getting warm but the nights were still bitterly cold. She was not ready to go home yet.

She sat down on a swing. The wind blew as though trying to push her. She knew she could not stay long but she needed to clear her head before going home and becoming Clark again.

Or was she already Clark? She had his tan coat on and his hat and gloves. She had just come from his job but she was wearing a pink shirt. She had spent most of the evening thinking and feeling more like Clarissa. That was the problem. Her two personas were colliding.

Tony! She sighed. She was in over her head and she knew it. But how had she gotten here?

The entire week had been tumultuous. It had started over the weekend. Clark's last therapy session with Philip had been one of their most contentious. When it was over, Philip had surprised Clark by saying it was their best session so far.

Clark had come out to Philip as transgender. On a surface level Philip was accepting. He even said that a lot of what Clark had said in the past, things like how he liked boys romantically but didn't think he was gay, made a lot more sense from the perspective of gender.

The problem was that Clark wasn't looking for a superficial "I

97

accept you identifying as Trans". He was looking for real world help. He wanted, no needed, to transition. Philip had copped out. First he said he didn't know anything about transition. Then he felt Clark should wait, that he needed to form an adult identity before making permanent changes.

It was so frustrating. He had known he should have been a girl since he was four. All of the research he had done online said that was normal, most people like him knew from a young age. Yet the professionals in his life kept telling him he had to wait until he was an adult. What was he waiting for?

He had nearly fought with his mom as well. He had called her into the session with Philip and told her as well but she agreed with the counselor. He was too young to know. She had added that it would only make things harder for him at school.

At HyVee a woman was selling pink shirts that said "fight like a girl" across the front. It was a cancer awareness fund-raiser. Clark and his mom had nearly had another fight about the shirt. She had given him that look, the one that said "you know it will only lead to trouble."

Not wanting to hear another round of excuses he had used his own cash to buy the shirt. This small victory made up in some small way for what happened in the therapist's office. When he thought about it later it felt good and right that he'd bought it himself. Nobody could deny it was his.

Monday he had overheard Jeremy complaining to his friend Dylan about Clark's laptop. It wasn't fair, Jeremy groused. He had been planning to talk their mother into buying him a Mac Book with her tax return this spring by offering to give Clark his netbook. Now Clark's laptop was running so well that he didn't need Jeremy's netbook. Worse still Clark instilled some different operating system that Jeremy did not know how to use, so he couldn't demand his old laptop back in exchange for the netbook either.

If Jeremy expected sympathy he was quickly disappointed. Dylan laughed. When Dylan spied Clark out of the corner of his eyes he turned on him and practically begged Clark to help him with his laptop. "It's runny all wonky," Dylan said.

Clark eyed him suspiciously. Dylan was not among the Clark's tormentors but he was no friend either. Then Dylan had offered to pay and Clark decided he was not averse to taking the boy's money.

These two victories, totally unrelated to each other, had forced his worlds to collide. How could a pink shirt and wonky computer create so much havoc?

The pink shirt had set in his dresser until Thursday. He wasn't about to wear such a thing to school. His mom was certainly right about that leading to trouble. He had nowhere to wear it except the Pirella's. The girls would love it, they did love it. Tony didn't seem to mind. (And now he wished Tony did mind, at least a little.) If Shelley every found out he could play it off as charity. She did a ton of charity work herself. She couldn't complain.

So he wore the shirt, his coat zipped up tight so neither his mom or Marcy, the girl's daycare provider, would see it. The girls were ecstatic. They twisted his hair into pigtails. They also felt compelled to show off their best kung fu moves to demonstrate how they would 'fight like a girl'. It had been quite the sight.

Then Tony came home. He had taken to doing this more and more often. He would arrive right around, or just before, the girls' bedtime. He would have some ready excuse about work he needed to do from home on Ugly Betty. Once the girls were in bed he would be upstairs again, getting himself a drink and wanting to talk.

Sometimes he wanted to talk shop. He would talk about computer security, complain about his day or just share some new hack with Clark. He brought stuff too. Sometimes it was something he had salvaged off another computer, like the hard drive they had installed on Clark's laptop. Another time it was computer manuals they were replacing. More than once he had brought Clark a USB drive with "some interesting subroutines" on it. What Tony found interesting, Clark found shocking. He was slowly amassing a collection of sophisticated hacking tools, sniffer programs, password crackers and even a copy of the dreaded DDoS program that hackers used to shut down websites.

"Are you teaching me security or hacking?" Clark had asked once.

Tony had laughed the question off. "They are one and the same," He said. "You can't protect a system if you don't know how attacks are done."

Then there were nights when Tony did not want to talk shop. Nights when he asked pointed questions about something Clark had said on one of his private blogs. These were complicated nights. Tony followed everything that Clark did whether it was Clark, Claire or Clarissa. That alone was intimidating.

But Tony seemed to accept Clark/Clarissa. He was very smart and an adult. He made an great sounding board. Who else could he talk about these thing with? Marcus was cool but he was often immature. He had trouble understanding how Clark's gender identity was more complicated then his own sexual identity. Tony was more level headed and perceptive.

The problem was that discussing transsexuality with Tony brought Clarissa to the surface. And Tony made Clarissa weak in the knees. He would compliment "Claire" on an outfit and Clarissa would catch herself blushing fiercely.

But nothing like tonight. Tonight, Tony had arrived just as she was setting out a plate of sugar cookies and tea for the girl's bedtime snack. Tony had kicked off his shoes and set on the floor in front of the coffee table, right beside Clarissa. She still had the pigtails in and the almost clownish Barbie makeup the girls had put on her.

"Look what we did daddy!" Brit declared proudly.

"It's our most beautiful Barbie creation yet." Holly piped in.

"Indeed," Tony agreed, "you've made a really beautiful Barbie alright."

Clarissa blushed fiercely and looked away. The girls went right on enjoying their cookies and talking about their day. Tony went right on flirting, flirting with Clarissa. Flirting; there was no other word for it. The girls were to young to get it, too young to realize that teenage boys did not wear pink or let little girls braid their hair. They were too young to realize that grown men like Tony did not tell teenage boys they were beautiful or special.

After cookies and tea Clarissa shooed the girls up to bed. She heard Tony heading down the stairs into the den and blew a sigh of relief. When the girls were settled she took her hair out of the braids and washed off the make-up.

She thought about calling down into the den that she needed to go early and would he mind, but Tony was already back upstairs in the kitchen as she came down. He made a comment as she came down the stairs about "Miss Claire and her little pink shirt" and Clarissa knew that he wasn't going to talk shop tonight.

She thought suddenly of Dylan's laptop. Maybe she could steer the conversation to safer waters. "Umm, this kid at school wanted me to fix his laptop," she said. "It's been running a little wonky."

"Wonky?" Tony raised one eyebrow.

"His word, not mine," Clarissa said hastily. "Actually it's got a couple of viruses, more than a couple really. You've talked about removing them before."

"Of course," Tony agreed. "It's boring work but not hard. You got this laptop with you I presume?"

Relieved Clarissa had gone into the living room and sat on the couch. She pulled the laptop out of her school bag. She meant to take it into the kitchen but Tony followed her into the living room and sat down on the couch next to her, right next to her.

People sat beside each other on couches all the time, part of her mind protested. The wind blew the swing and Clarissa shivered. It hadn't felt innocent. She would have probably convinced herself it was innocent except for the kiss.

It had happened while he was teaching her to spot and delete virus files.

"Oh that shouldn't be there," she had said, spotting an out of place file name. "That's a virus right?"

"We'll make a virus hunter out of you yet, Barbie," he hooted and kissed her on the cheek. "Now get it."

She flushed. She stared hard at the screen. She deleted the file. Inside her mind was screaming. He kissed her. It was an act too bold to be written off. She could not explain it with Tony is a nice guy that accepts me as I am. This could only be Tony is a guy who sees me as a girl.

Clarissa felt a million feelings were warring inside her. She was thrilled to be seen as a girl. She was excited that it was a guy like Tony but terrified too. Unaccountably there was anger. Anger at Tony for creating so much awkwardness. Anger at herself for having a crush on Tony. Anger at the world. Why couldn't the first man to accept her be someone more her age and available?

When she thought of Shelley there was fear and guilt. Shelly must never find out. Clarissa would have to keep what happened a secret. That was okay, she was used to keeping secrets. Her whole life up to the last few months had been one long secret. But this felt like a heavier, darker secret.

She rose and retrieved her bag. As she walked away from the swing and towards home she felt the phone shift in her coat pocket. Marcus, she thought suddenly. Maybe I don't have to keep this completely secret. The thought warmed her, if only marginally.

#####

"Ping-a-pong!" A boy's voice sang out in the hall.

Only one person in the entire school even came close to Clark when it came to teasing and abuse. Her name was Vong. She was the only South East Asian in the school, the daughter of Laotian refugees. She was overweight, not obese, but definitely plump, and she had thick buck teeth that her parents could not afford to fix. Her nick names were many and none were nice. She was Bunny Vong because of her teeth, Very Vong because of her weight and often, ping-a-pong just to be mean. The boy who had used this name had also knocked the books in her arm up in the air and then ran off singing his cruel song.

Clark had never paid much attention to Vong before. Until his recent encounters with Amy and Christy he had mistakenly assumed no one in the school liked him much. He and Vong had had classes together and she seemed nice enough. The boys who tormented Clark were mostly a few hyper masculine jocks. They ignored Vong. It was the juvenile kids that taunted her. They mostly ignored Clark. Why would either one of them risk coming to the attention of a new group of bullies by reaching out to each other?

He was also afraid to approach girls for fear that they would think he was sexually interested in them. Besides he had never had any reason to pay much attention to Vong, until now. That was before he found out that South East Asia was home to the "sex change capital of the world".

He picked up a notebook off the floor and held it out to her. "Sowasdee."

She looked at him with a mixture of surprise and suspicion. He realized suddenly that she too simply assumed no one liked her. It made him sad.

"Sowasdee," he repeated. "It's Thai for hello, but it's similar to Lao, I am told." Actually, he had read online that both languages were mutually intelligible. He hoped it was true.

"Yeah," she agreed reluctantly, "it means hello in Lao too."

There was an awkward pause, so Clark pushed on. "I am doing a project for geography about Thailand. I think it's such an interesting language, Thai."

"My family is Thai," Vong said.

"Really, I thought you were Lao?"

She brightened slightly. "We are, we're Thai Dom." She explained, "We're from Lao, but we are ethnically Thai."

"That's interesting. I would love to learn some Thai. I was even thinking of asking to do an independent study course in Thai. So much cooler than Spanish," he pulled a face.

"Spanish is my worst subject," she agreed. "Both my parents speak Thai at home. Mom's English isn't good." She hesitated and then shrugged, "I could help you, if you want."

"You're kind of distant lately," His mom said.

Clark just looked at her. What was he supposed to say to that? He made a mental list of conversations he and his mother would not be having right now: Mom, every day the part of me that's a girl is getting stronger and the part of me that's a boy is happily withering away? No. Mom, this guy kissed me and I really liked it.

No. Mom, I met this Lao girl who is going to help me learn Thai because that's where they do sex changes. No. Mom, Marcus and I have this plan to create some fake ID's if we can come up with the right stuff. No.

"I'm fine," he said.

She sighed. "School going okay?"

"It's okay." Amy, Christy, Vong; friends, everyone else, still hating him.

"Work?"

"It's good." The twins loved him now. Tony had kissed him. Shelley? He didn't think about her more than he could help.

"Anything you want to talk about?" She was getting desperate to make him open up.

"Not really, you?"

"No, I guess not." She sighed and let it go.

"I just don't know," Clarissa shook her head. She watched her hair move in the mirror. The extensions were great, but she wished she could grow her real hair long instead. Well it was sort of Clarkish Clarissa again. She and Marcus were in his room. She had thrown a light peach top (she had managed to find one that matched her favorite item from Shelley's closet on their last trip to Iowa City), her hair extensions and some make up in her bag before getting mom to drive her over to her friend's house for the afternoon. Now that she had changed and put some make up on she looked more like a girl, a flat chested girl with narrow hips and boy jeans. She sighed. "Do you think my jaw is too square to pass?" She asked Marcus.

He snorted and replied, "no. You are going to ruin my reputation. People are going to think I am hanging out with a girl. They might even think we are dating." Marcus protested playfully

She had stuck her tongue out at him and continued to put her make up on. Only once she was done did she pull out her laptop and show him what she had done so far.

"That's awesome." Marcus exclaimed.

She was glad he appreciated it. It had taken hours of work with a graphics program. She had taken a picture of her mother's driver's license. Then she had painstakingly set up an image to match the boxes but with her, and then Marcus' information. The seal in the background had caused all sorts of issues but she had finally gotten it to look mostly right.

Mostly, that was the problem. They might be able to pass these ID's in a dimly lit bar or to a cashier that didn't pay much attention. If they could find the right thing to print them on, that was. They currently had a half dozen pieces of plastic out, trying to find the right thickness and consistency.

"This is about right." Marcus said, holding up an empty game case and an exacto-knife. He had his real ID next to him. Clarissa inspected the square of white plastic. It was looking like a likely experiment at any rate. If only it would take the ink from the printer.

She sighed, "yeah, it will probably work."

"Then why did you sigh?"

"This whole idea," she said. "It'll work, for you. We can make something believable enough to get into a bar or buy smokes, whatever. It's not going to work for me."

"Why?" Marcus inquired, "Don't you want to get into the gay bar on a regular night?"

"Not really."

What Clarissa wanted was something more solid, something that would pass a more substantial inspection. Something she could show a cop if need be. She had not forgotten almost being pulled over.

Something more was starting to occur to her. If the cops pulled her over, they might run the license. So it not only had to look right, there had to be something in the computer system about it too. Was that even possible?

The more she had researched the more complicated the idea became but also the more appealing. What if she could manufacture a whole identity for Clarissa? What if she had all the necessary legal documents and stuff?

She was sixteen. It would be two years before she was a legal adult and could tell Beth she wanted to transition and not need her mom's permission. Two years might not seem like much to Beth, or to her mom, but they were not being forced to wear the wrong clothes every single day. They were not forced to spend six hours out of their day at a school where they were harassed, beaten and threatened. They didn't have to stare in the mirror and know that male hormones were working, giving her more facial hair and making her more masculine looking every day. They didn't live under the weight of knowing their life was on hold, unable to even start living until they were able to transition. Any short cut would be worth the effort.

But how? She didn't have the skill to even begin making a fake identity. She knew someone who did though. Only two questions bothered her. What would Tony want in return? And would she be willing to pay?

"Hear that faggot? Ping-a-pong's going to protect you." Clark gasped for breath, blood running down his nose where he had hit the side of the school building.

He used his hands to push, giving him a little space between himself and the brick wall. He could hear Vong screaming curses at John but there were two other football players between her and them. Besides she as much a victim of their bullying as he was. "Fuck you." He spat out.

John grabbed him by his hair and pulled his head back, ready to slam it into the brick wall again. He strove to hold himself back but he had little illusions about his ability to stop his head from hitting the wall again.

"Let him go!" A voice yelled. Amy was striding across the school parking lot towards them.

"Stay out of this Aim," John growled. "The faggots got to learn he can't walk around like he owns the freaking school. And he can't be walking his new girlfriend home." He spat towards Vong as he said it.

Faggot means gay, Clark thought bitterly, why would a gay boy have a girlfriend? He kept it to himself. Pointing out this faulty logic was what had brought on the beating to begin with.

"John Mort, that boy has never done a damn thing to you, nor has Vong. Why must you torment them so?" Amy was sounding a bit like his mother.

"I said stay out of it." John growled. Clark's head went back again.

Amy was having none of it. She stepped in closer and pointed a finger at John. She was shaking slightly but she did not back down. "You let him go or I swear it's over."

They were locked in a triangle for a long moment while John's gaze passed back and forth between him and Amy. John's eyes went, very briefly, towards his friends as well. He's wondering if she'll really do it, Clark thought and what his friends will say if she does. Then Clark was shoved roughly away. "Fine," John said dismissively. "He's not worth my time anyway."

Clark used his shirt, which was pretty well ruined anyway, to dab at his bloody nose. He watched the retreating backs of the football players with a hateful malice. His eyes fell on Amy's blond hair and the feelings were more conflicted. Sure, she had saved him but why did she even date that ass? As the group rounded the corner of the school, Amy looked back and their eyes met. She paused and for an instant it looked like she was going to come back. Then her head cocked, as though someone had called for her. She shot him an apologetic look and disappeared around the corner.

"Wow." Vong said at his side, "I always thought I had it tough, just getting teased."

He knelt and picked up his pack. "Let's go."

CHAPTER TEN

"I hate to ruin a good thing," Vong started. They were sitting on her bed, a gaudily decorated elephant statue and a Buddha statue laying between them, "I mean it's nice of you to talk to me, or pretend to be my friend..."

"I am your friend."

She paused, looking at him. "Why are you really here? I mean, I know you aren't interested in me." She looked at him hopefully as she said it, as if he might contradict her. He held his face impassive, not wanting to send the wrong message. She went on, "I mean even if it weren't for your reputation you haven't given me any reason to think..."

"Can't we just be friends?" Clark said, "why does there have to be more to it?"

"And all this interest in Thai culture all of a sudden?"

"I am interested in it," he insisted, "I want to go there someday. Serious." He looked away and bit his lower lip. The truth had worked before. He glanced back at Vong, trying to judge what her reaction was going to be. "It's where they do sex changes, you know."

He glanced at her again. Her eyes narrowed slightly, "you want to have a sex change?"

"No." He said, "I need to. I can't stand my life as it is."

"Wow!" Vong said. She paused and added, "kind of makes sense, but still, wow."

Clark watched as she bit her lower lip and thought. She didn't seem to be angry or upset, just really thoughtful.

"I have a cousin who is gay," Vong started after some time. Clark was about to protest but she went on, "Dad told me it was his karma. We all have a karma. It's like fate but it's based on our actions in a previous life. It's just part of who we are and we have to learn to accept it. That's a huge part of our culture, learning to accept our karma. My cousin's karma is that he's gay. My karma is that I am fat and ugly. Yours is this."

Relief flooded Clark. "So what, John's karma is that he's an ass?" He quipped. "and you're not fat and you're not ugly. You just need braces, that's all. Besides you and I have something in common."

"What's that?"

"Both our problems can be treated with a little surgery."

She giggled.

"Seriously, imagine it, I get my sex change," Clark said

"I get a nip and tuck, and braces," Vong threw in.

"And then we come back to school, the cutest two girls there. All the guys want to date us, but we tell them 'f- you, you didn't give us the time of day before'. And then we find cute boyfriends and leave this place for good." Clark had never said anything like this before, but it was making Vong laugh so he kept it up, describing how cute the two of them would be someday, how the boys would chase them. He acted the parts out, gesturing and using different voices for them and for the boys, like when he told the girls a story. She nearly fell of the bed laughing.

"You're so funny," she told him, "and nice."

He blushed, unsure how to answer. There was a long pause where neither one said anything. "Clark?"

"Yeah."

"How do they do it? Do you know?"

He did, sort of. So he told her as much as he knew about transition and about the surgery.

Afterwards she leaped to her feet and skipped out of the room. She came back holding something close to her bosom. "I can't help you with surgery but I can help you with this." She held out a little round plastic pill dispenser and a piece of paper. "My parents insisted on getting me on the pill. They don't want me to get pregnant until after I go to college." She shrugged. "It's not exactly my biggest problem, in case you haven't noticed." She held out the piece of paper and said, "look the brochure they gave me says the whole premise is using female hormones to trick your body into thinking it's already pregnant. Anyway, hormones are hormones, right? These should work?"

He took the pamphlet and read it. He shrugged. "I guess so."

She pressed the pill dispenser into his hands. "Somebody might as well get some real use out of them. And I can help you learn Thai," she went on. She lay back on her bed.

He lay down next to her and put her outstretched hand in his. "I don't know how I can ever repay you."

"Today when those boys attacked you," she started slowly. "It was because you were with me. Yet you never denied being my friend. That's huge, Clark, huge."

She thought he had been beat up because he was her friend? He shook his head. He had assumed that her presence had been nothing more than a pretext. If she hadn't been there he would have been beaten for something else. Glancing over he saw that she was serious. In the end it didn't matter, he decided. What mattered was that fear of the bullies had kept both of them from reaching out and he was going make sure that stopped now. "I would never deny a friend."

She giggled. "I always wished I was friends with one of the cool kids."

Clark rolled his eyes. "I am so not one of the cool kids."

"Yeah?" She replied, "Amy Talba stood up for you."

Clark froze and considered that. Before he could decide how he felt about that Vong was talking again and on a different subject. "I was an outsider from the day we moved into town."

Clark scrunched his brow. "That was third grade?"

Vong nodded. "I would watch Amy, Christy and you play. I would come home and imagine Amy was my friend. We'd play dress up, do our hair or put on make-up. All those silly girly things."

Clark glanced for one second at the dresser on the far side of the room. From his vantage, he could see a hair brush, some ties, a perfume bottle and an assortment of small containers that appeared to be make up. Not letting go of her hand he rolled to his feet, dragging her with. "Well, come on then, what are you waiting for?" He laughed.

#####

"Why do you have three laptops in your locker?" Christy asked conversationally as Clark took his books out for study hall.

He shrugged, "I do some computer work." Word had gotten around that he had a knack for fixing computers and his side business was blossoming.

"Oh my God!" Amy said, "maybe you can help me." Clark looked at Amy. He had been mad at her for a couple of days after the incident with her boyfriend John, but then had decided to forgive her. After all she had intervened on his behalf. When he thought about her and John, he thought about his own conflict feelings about Tony, and wondered if he had any right to judge. Maybe love was just like that, maybe some men were assholes and some women just loved them anyway.

"With what?" He asked.

"My dad is so going to kill me." She went on, "it's like the third time it's happened."

"What?" Christy put in exasperated.

"I spilled something on the keyboard." Amy said.

"Bring it," Clark said.

"Only I can't really pay." She said.

"Maybe we can work something out." He said.

"You want my old netbook? It's an Asus Ee Pc. It's not great but it works, sort of."

"How can a computer sort of work?" Christy asked.

"Lots of ways." Clark told her.

"It was a little slow but otherwise worked good until I tried to upgrade to Windows Vista. It couldn't hack it." Amy explained. "So dad got me a ThinkPad. Only I have spilled stuff on the keyboard like three times and now a bunch of keys get stuck."

"Probably needs a new keyboard."

"Can you do that?"

"You think you are the only one in this school who has spilled something on their keyboard?" He asked. He pointed at one of the computers in his locker. "Terry Mullen took his to a kegger, the idiot." He leaned in conspiratorially, "Was surfing porn too." Amy giggled.

"How do you know that?" Christy asked.

"Didn't clear his history or delete his cookies." Clark said.

"How much does a keyboard cost?" Amy asked.

"I'll have to look it up online." He said, "but I am thinking less than an Asus. Even with the work I think that's more than a fair trade."

"Even if the Asus doesn't work well?"

He nodded. He wasn't about to explain that once he wiped Windows and put on Ubuntu it would probably run like new.

Christy's boyfriend, Tom walked up. "You guys ready?"

"I think so," Amy replied. Clark shut his locker and nodded.

They headed to study hall, Amy on his right and Christy and Tom on his left. A group of jocks walked past the other direction, Ben at their lead. Clark felt suddenly awkward, like a spot light had been turned on him. Ben's brow was furled and dark but he gave no other sign as he passed. Clark looked down at his light blue T-shirt and blue jeans. Very neutral, he thought, what had he done now?

Amy glanced once in his direction and motioned him to keep up. He shrugged off the thought and hurried after them.

In study hall Christy and Tom both pulled out their math books and bent their heads together to drill each other for their upcoming test. Clark opened a laptop, Jake's. He pushed the button and watched briefly while it did not boot. He hit the F12 key and got nothing. He inspected the led lights on the edge of machine. He shut with a snap, mumbling, "hardware problem."

Amy was sitting across from him, not looking at anything in particular. She had her English book out but it was unopened.

Clark shoved the laptop back in his bag. "I can't fix it here," he groused looking for his Kindle.

"I have to use the bathroom," Amy announced. She gave Clark a sharp look and a nod in the direction of the restrooms. Clark raised his eyebrow quizzically but she was up and gone across the cafeteria, stopping briefly beside the room monitor.

Clark set there for a couple of minutes. Then he too got up, mumbling that he too had to go.

He rounded the corner, out of sight of the study hall and towards the men's restroom. He had never been in that particular men's room. He had one bathroom towards the front of the school that he would use if absolutely necessary but he preferred to hold it till he got home if possible.

This hall ran the length of the gym. On the opposite side were music, home economics and art. At the far end the hall T-boned on the locker rooms and the back door. This whole end of the school scared the crap out of him. The danger of being trapped down here by the jocks and other haters haunted him.

Inside the restroom he could hear voices talking. He lurked outside, by the water fountain, not needing or daring to go in.

Amy was lurking too, just inside the door to the women's restroom, keeping watch for him. She stepped out quickly and grabbed his arm. She started down the long hall. "Thanks," she said quietly, "I just need to step out a few minutes."

As they headed for the back doors comprehension caught up with him. "Cheerleaders skip class?"

She gave him a sharp look. There was an edge in her voice when she spoke, "You think you are the only one who hates this place?"

No, he thought, I know Vong hates it too. But Amy? She was the most popular girl in the school and she was beautiful. How could she hate this place?

Out loud he said, "I'm sorry, I just didn't realize you could. Won't they kick you off the team or something?"

"No," she said with surprising bitterness, "when you're popular they make allowances."

Clark snorted.

"It's not the great thing you think," she went on as they pushed through the back door and out behind the school. Amy stopped and looked carefully around a corner. "Okay coast is clear, over here." She bolted for the greenhouses where the advanced biology class worked in warmer months. As Clark followed he saw a small group of hoods, poor kids with poor grades and few prospects. They came to school only because they had to. They spent much of their time ditching class and smoking behind the building. Today they were huddled up against the building against the cold wind.

He followed Amy around the greenhouse and suddenly they were out of the wind and into the sun. Despite the fact that it was winter and neither had coats, it was tolerably warm here.

"I discovered this place last fall. It's nice and warm here even in the winter. It's also out of sight of the school."

The greenhouse was edged with a raised flower bed composed of cinder blocks. Amy crouched down and sat on top of one of the blocks. Clark followed suit. They sat in silence for a long time, Amy lost in thought and Clark unsure what to say.

"The thing about being popular is," Amy began slowly, "it's a trap. Everyone's always watching you, expecting you to act a certain way or talk a certain way. Then when you're sick of it and you think you've found the way out, they make some allowances so you can stay stuck."

She stopped again and stared off into space. "You're so brave, Clark."

"Yeah right," he replied sarcastically. "How am I brave?"

"You are who you are. Everyone else at this school are such phonies. They pretend their lives are so happy, so good. They do what's expected and what's worse they pretend that's what they wanted to do anyway."

"Are you okay, Amy?"

"No," she replied in a small voice. "I try to be, but I'm not."

"What's wrong?"

Crying now, she rolled up the sleeve on her sweater and showed him the spider web of thin red lines. One had a gauze taped over it and was obviously fairly fresh.

"Why?" Stunned, it was all he could think to say, though it sounded wrong even as it came out of his mouth.

"You don't have to be transgender to hate yourself. Some of us manage that anyway."

He sat there, numb with shock until she went on, "I've done terrible things, Clark, terrible things." She broke off and spat out, "Men!" She wrapped her arms around her knees, hugging herself into a tight little ball.

A cold suspicion washed over him. "Were you," he hesitated not sure if he should use the word, "raped?"

"No," she said, "not exactly. In ways, it was worse. I did it willingly." She wiped her tears on her sweater and shivered violently. "It was about three years ago. He, he made me feel so good sometimes. He was so nice and sweet at first. He was, older, a lot older and I really thought he liked me. The things we did, they made me feel so good at the time, but then later I would feel so bad, so guilty."

Clark covered his mouth. He knew that feeling too well.

"It lasted a few months and then I told him we had to quit. He got mad but I stuck to my guns. I thought it was over, but it wasn't. Ever since I can't shake it. I started dieting because I thought maybe then boys my age would like me. It got compulsive, like I just had to keep dieting. It made me feel in control. When I don't I start to have these feelings, anger, rage, sadness. I get to feeling so angry I have to, have to," she broke off.

"Hurt yourself?"

She nodded.

"You know what the worst part is?" She said after a long time. "I keep making the same decisions." She snorted derisively. "You think I don't know what John's like? He's an ass, just like..."

Curiosity burned in Clark's mind but he knew he couldn't ask. It was too personal. Was it a family member? It often was, he thought he read that somewhere. An uncle or something. Or maybe it was a teacher. No matter who it was, it could ruin Amy's reputation if it got out.

"Thank you for coming out here." She said after a long while. "I thought," she paused, "I just thought you'd understand somehow."

Without saying a thing, he pulled up the sleeve on his sweater.

"Jesus!" She said grabbing his arm and inspecting the two long faded lines that ran up his left forearm.

"What?" He pulled his arm back hurt. "You've got more."

"This way hurts," she said running her finger across her arm. "That way will kill you."

"Isn't that the point?"

"I remember junior high," she said slowly, "something happened. They'd never tell us anything of course, but you were gone for almost a month."

Clark nodded. "Second story bathroom, I broke the mirror. That's the short one here. I did the other at home, with a razor blade." He shrugged, "That was over summer break, the same year."

"Clark," she said softly, a scared look in her eyes that brought tears to his eyes.

"I don't feel that way now." He said looking away.

"Please, don't," was all she said.

They both shivered. "It's getting cold," Amy said looking at her phone, "and it's almost time for school to let out."

They stood and Amy hugged him suddenly. He was shocked by the gesture. At first, he felt uncomfortable, unsure what this gesture was meant to convey. Was she coming on to him? Then she lay her head on his shoulder and it occurred to him that he had seen Amy do this a hundred times, with Christy or one of the other girls. It was just affection. He melted into her embrace realizing he had never allowed himself any physical affection with anyone.

After a long time she broke the hug and said, "thanks, I feel better."

"Me too," he said. Mysteriously it was true.

"Pink. Why am I not surprised?" Tony teased looking at the little netbook.

It was Amy's old Asuss EE Pc. It was way more than a fair trade.

Clarissa like the little pink machine enough to have almost considered making it her primary computer, except it had a lot less storage. Besides she needed a dedicated machine for certain slightly illicit acts and this was perfect.

"Alright, pinky," Tony continued and sat down next to Clarissa. (It was Clarissa now almost always, especially when Tony was in the room.) "What are we going to hack tonight?"

"I was wondering about setting up IP addresses, how to change them and stuff. Remember what you told me the other day about being able to make a computer look like it's from a different place or that it's a different computer?"

"You aren't doing any illegal hacking, are you?" Tony teased.

"No." She said. She was. Setting up Clarissa's legal identity required a few important steps outside the law. It was only prudent to do these steps from a computer that had never been owned by 'Clark' and couldn't be traced to her former life in any way.

He laughed. "You know even if you never do an illegal hack, it's good to know them." Was this another one of Tony's tacit approvals? "Any serious security expert spends lots of time studying hackers. You can't protect yourself if you don't know how an attack can be done."

That made sense. So this wasn't his approval. Oh well, he'd teach and she'd learn. Then when she got home she'd do it again, changing the IP address on this machine yet again so that even Tony wouldn't be able to trace it.

They sat at the kitchen table with their heads bent together for nearly an hour. If she hadn't been so intent on what he was teaching her it would have been incredibly distracting. Changing IP addresses turned out to be ridiculously easy, as was sending an email that was essentially untraceable. Child's play, Tony had declared and promptly began showing Clarissa other tricks, ones that were neither child's play nor were they in any within the bounds of legitimate hacking. He had shown her how to create a shadow web using a laptops wireless network. "This is how hackers share information in repressive regimes like Iran" Tony explained as though it were likely that Clarissa would find herself in Iran needing an Internet connection that wasn't monitored by authorities. Then he began to show Clarissa how to create a dummy server on a computer without the owner's knowledge or consent.

"See," he said sliding his laptop around so she could see the screen. "Now type in your command."

Clarissa took over his currently unprotected remote desktop and began entering commands. She watched as Tony's computer responded, but not as she expected. "I got you trapped." Tony explained, "it looks like you are on this laptop." He pointed at his computer, "but it's only a small portion of my computer. I could use this at work to catch a hacker or to feed him useless information. He'd think he was getting the goods."

"Or," Clarissa said catching on, "you could set it up so they enter certain data and think it's being published to the web but actually something completely different shows up if someone access it from the public server."

"You are going to be a top-notch hacker someday," Tony said and Clarissa beamed at the compliment, "but not tonight."

Clarissa looked at the clock. It was eight thirty. The twins were safely tucked in bed and it was a half an hour until Clarissa's usual time to go home. Of course, when Tony showed early, like he had tonight, it was always anyone's guess when he would decide it was time for her to go home. Tonight, it looked to be early.

Clarissa was a little bummed, especially since it was friendly computer expert Tony tonight, not pushy let's talk about Claire and make you feel uncomfortable Tony.

Tony closed his laptop and looked at Clarissa long enough to make her squirm. "So I've thought over your little problem." He said slowly and Clarissa froze. "Actually, I did a little more than think, I talk to a couple of sources and..."

Clarissa stared at him, about to burst. Her "little problem" could only mean one thing. She had broken down and told Tony about almost being pulled over in women's clothes. She had asked if there was some way for her to have an ID that would pass a computer search. What had he found?

"I got you a little something." He ended suddenly, "upstairs, in the bedroom."

The bedroom? Clarissa blood ran cold, but her curiosity got the better of her. There was no point in asking. She paused at the foot of the steps, trembling.

"Go on," Tony prodded her. Slowly she climbed the stairs and went to the bedroom.

She shook as she looked at the two packages on the bed. A manila envelope sat on top of a garment box. The manila envelope had written on it in felt tip ink, "Clarissa Holden". The garment box bore the imprint of Victoria Secrets.

"I thought the birth of a woman," Tony said quietly from the doorway, "especially one as beautiful as you, deserved some commemoration."

Clarissa slid the envelope aside and looked at the box. She ran her hands over it. Slowly she opened it. The outfit within was black, lacy and far too revealing, but thankfully not quite lingerie. It seemed to designed after the cocktail dress, but Clarissa couldn't imagine such a dress would be appropriate for public. "Tony," she said in a small hard voice, "I don't think I can,"

He stepped across the room and cut her off with his finger, "I just want to see it, once. I want to see the look on your face when you realize what a beautiful creature you are. I want to be the first to tell you are beautiful, to make you feel like a woman. I promise, I would never force you do something you didn't want." He seemed so sincere suddenly.

He just wants to see me in the outfit, she thought. The outfit he bought me. That was fair, wasn't it? He promised. Her eyes fell on the envelope. She swallowed hard and nodded quietly not daring to look at him. She heard his feet retreat down the hall and then down the stair.

She took a long time changing and then applying her make up out of Shelley's vast collection. Part of her was scared about what was happening, part of her, she had to admit, wanted to look her best. The gulf between those two emotions threatened to swallow her.

I want Tony to like me. I want him to see me as a woman. I want him to tell me I am beautiful. God, I just want him.

But what about Shelley? What about the twins; who slept innocent in the next room. She didn't want to ruin their family or destroy their lives. Why did Tony put her in this situation? Was he like the others, like Clark, Amy, and Vong? Did he feel trapped too, trapped in this small town and hating his life, wanting a way out? Was it that simple? Or did he simply want Clarissa? She couldn't tell.

When she finally worked up the courage to go back downstairs Tony was sitting on the couch in the living room, a drink in his hand. BBC world news was playing on the TV but he didn't seem to be paying attention. She watched him from the top of the stairs briefly before padding down barefoot. He caught the sound and turned his head her way. "You'll make a good girl, Miss Claire," he said teasingly, "You already know how to make a guy wait."

"Sorry, I was just putting on some make up." She trailed off. She stepped off the stairs and out of the shadow.

He whistled softly, "I take it back, it was worth the wait." He approached her slowly, cautiously. Her heart hammered in her chest. Part of her wanted to bolt, to run back up the stairs. One hand reached out and brushed her hair away from her face. She blushed and looked down.

Damn, I wish I had my extensions, Clarissa thought briefly. Then he put his face almost against hers and kissed her softly on the lips, driving all other thoughts away.

He stopped kissing her but stayed close, nuzzling her with his nose. "You are so special," he whispered, "you know that don't you? You are so beautiful, so unique, so different and so wonderful." They kissed again, this time Clarissa returned the kiss fully, their tongues probing each other tentatively. She couldn't believe this was really happening. When he pulled back this time he said, "a guy could fall for a girl like you, you know."

Clarissa stood still, conflicted. Why did the one dream that came true have to be the one she should have never wished for? All the reasons she shouldn't be doing this swam through her head, holding her fast. "Tony... I..."

He put his finger over her lips. "You don't need to explain anything to me. I know. I'm an old, married man. You can do much better. But you've given me great joy, Claire, just in this." He kissed her again softly.

Then Clarissa heard one of the twins cough quietly in her sleep and it broke the spell. A cold guilt fell over her. "Tony," she cried softly, "I can't." She pulled back, backing into the wall

"I know," he said.

She looked down, unable to meet his gaze. "I should go," she said leaden.

"If you wish." It was clear that if she wanted to stay, he would not object either. Fearful that she might change her mind, she quickly climbed the stairs and changed back into her regular clothes.

When she came back down he was watching some news show. She had the outfit back in the box and the envelope in her hands. She gathered her bag and said quietly, "thank you," holding the envelope up. She could find no other words. Not waiting for his acknowledgement, she turned and walked out the door.

It was past midnight before Clark went down to bed. He had ran downstairs immediately to hide the box and envelope before his mom saw them. Then he had come back up and taken a shower. He let the water run over his naked body, slumping down against the back of the shower shivering. He felt dirty and no amount of scrubbing seemed to help. Finally, his mom called at the door to ask if he was okay. He caught the scared tone in her voice and knew she was afraid that he was cutting his wrist again.

He climbed out quickly and told her he was okay. He even went so far as to wear only a T-shirt when he left the bathroom so she could see his arms and know he was okay.

Sleep still far away, he sat down at his vanity and pulled out the envelope and opened it. He dumped the contents on the vanity. There was a birth certificate and a social security card. He didn't know how Tony had done it but he had. Clark was now also Clarissa Holden, an eighteen-year-old girl. He would need a lot more than these two documents but he could handle the rest.

He went to his bed and lay down, staring at the wall. He was not sure when he finally fell asleep.

CHAPTER ELEVEN

"I." Clark slammed into the wall. "Didn't." He hit the wall again, "Ask." and again, "What, was going on." John was shoving Clark, hard, into the wall to accent each word. "I told you to stay the F-away from my girl."

Clark's ribs and back ached from the force with which he was being slammed into the wall. John punctuated his sentence with a quick hard slap to Clark's face. Clark hit the wall again and fell with a crash. John kneed him, catching him the stomach and making him curl in pain. Half of the boys in Clark's gym class, many of them John's friends, watch on without intervening as John leaned over. He dragged Clark back up. Clark stood shakily. "If we have to repeat this conversation," he said slowly, "I am going to F-ing kill you, you hear?"

"John Mort!" Mr. Harding's voice rose over the crowd easily, "get you ass in the locker and get changed out. Now!"

John let Clark go and he slumped to the floor. John stalked off and the crowd of boys quickly followed.

Finally, it was only Clark and Mr. Harding. Mr. Harding eyed him coldly. Mom and Principal Reid had made a plan for this sort of situation. The teacher was supposed to send anyone harassing or threatening Clark to the principal immediately and then send Clark to the guidance counselor. His mom was to be notified promptly and they would all meet to deal with the situation. If Mr. Harding hadn't been at that meeting, it would be easy to assume he hadn't gotten the memo.

"Clark," he said without moving to help Clark up, "you too. Get in there and get changed out, class in five minutes."

"But," Clark sputtered, tasting blood as he did so. There was no way he was going into that den of boys, to give John a second chance.

"Clark," Mr. Harding interrupted, "we've had this conversation before. One more unexcused absences and I will have to flunk you for the semester." With that he turned and disappeared into the gym.

Clark climbed painfully to his feet, his stomach still aching. He stalked past the gym, past the boy's locker room and out the back door.

######

"I am just worried about you," his mom persisted. "Why is that a terrible thing?"

"It's not." Clark snapped, "but I keep telling you I'm fine."

"You say that, but I can see something is going on with you. You're changing."

"It's called growing up."

"It's not growing up." She corrected him, "when you ditch school."

"You know why."

"Yes," she said, "and I understand. I told you I am going to meet with the principal again tomorrow and so help me god he's going to take this off your record and start dealing with the situation. I am with you on that one. But there's more going on and you know it."

He sat motionless in the chair, not answering. His mind was on Tony. In the cold light of day, it seemed so crazy but also so natural. Tony understood he was a girl on the inside. And once you make that jump was is it so strange that a straight man might be interested in that girl?

"This is what I am talking about." His mother's voice interrupted him. "I can see something is bothering you. Why won't you talk about it? What's wrong?"

"My whole life has been something wrong." He barked. "From the time I came home from kindergarten crying, my life has always been about something being wrong and about us talking about it." *And now something was right, why fight it?* "I don't want to talk about all the things wrong with me."

She sighed. She did that a lot these last few months. "I don't want to imply that every thing's wrong. In ways, you are doing so much better this year at school and you've got that job. You've really shown a huge amount of responsibility. I am so proud of you, you know that. You are growing up to be quite a young man."

No, I am not. Three times he had tried to bring up the whole trans issue. Three times she had told him he was too young, too naïve to know. Each of the three times she implied that he was gay. She didn't say it out right, he assumed because a gay son was only marginally better than a trans daughter. But she referred to Philip which implied that she thought his theory was correct.

After a short pause, and no acknowledgement from him, she pushed on, "I also know some of the problems that are going on. I know about a lot of the stuff that has happened at school. Your brother does talk to me and he cares for you, in his own way." Clark snorted, "I know you've gotten beat up several times this month."

"Yeah, I think I've set a record for beatings or something." This was his way of reminding her that kids had been picking on him and beating on him since grade school.

"I've even talked to the school about it, but they don't seem to be able to do anything." She was almost in tears. "They say they don't have record of a lot of the incidents, or no teacher saw it, or whatever excuse they can use. When I confront them with evidence they act like that was one isolated incident. I am about ready to go to the board, if that will help."

"I will survive," he said. Then he thought of Gloria Gaynor and thought, god that was a cliché thing to say.

He turned and stared at her, startled by her expression. Could it be that she had doubts, that she thought he might not survive high school?

"It's not fair!" She burst out. "It's just not fair. You shouldn't have to survive! I shouldn't have to send my son to school and wonder if he's going to come home black and blue, or if his psyche will make it through intact." Tears ran down her cheeks.

"It's not that bad, mom." He said pleading trying to calm her. He did not want to see her this upset. "Sure, they pick on me, but who cares? You know why it's getting so much worse? I don't care anymore, that's why. They can't hurt me. They can't make me cry or carry on like they used to and it's driving them nuts."

His mom looked at him and he saw uncertainty in her face.

"Seriously mom, I am so over those bastards." He went on. "Like you said, I have a job and some responsibility. I can see what life will be like when I don't have them bothering me and it won't be near as bad." *And when I don't have you dictating who I am.* "Heck, Mom, I even have some friends now." He was thinking of Vong, Amy, Christy and especially Marcus. People who knew about him and liked him anyway.

"Is there a special friend?"

What was she asking him? Special friend? Who, Vong? She couldn't possibly be thinking of Amy or Christy, neither had so much as set foot in his house. Vong had stopped by briefly the other day to see him and give him her next month supply of birth control pills. He shook his head no, "if you mean am I dating? No."

"So, you and Marcus aren't...experimenting?"

"Mom! Ewww."

"I am just asking. I mean, I don't know, Clark." She grabbed a tissue and wiped her eyes. She went on, "I just don't know what to think or say to you these days. And I mean Marcus is gay, isn't he?"

"Yes, but I am not. I am transgender." He hadn't meant to start that debate but there it was out of his mouth before he could stop himself.

"What is that supposed to mean, Clark?"

"You know exactly what that means." He almost shouted. "We've been discussing it in one way or another since I was four! I am a girl, on the inside. I just want the outside to match."

"We are not going to discuss any .... anything like that right now.

And you're changing the subject anyway. Gay, transgender, what's really the difference? All I asked was; is there someone special in your life? I am not trying to judge you or change you. I am just curious. Is that wrong?" She eyed him defensively.

"How can there be someone special?" He said. "I can't date someone as a girl because I am not a girl, not physically. I can't date someone as a boy because I am not a boy, not psychologically."

She threw her arms up. "You have a one-track mind, you know that?"

"You are the one who wants to talk." He shot back.

"Look it's not like I'd love you any less if it turns out you are...transgender, or whatever." This was news to him. "You are my son and I love you no matter what. But Philip says we should wait, that's it probably just a phase you are going through."

"Beth doesn't agree."

"Now whose Beth?"

Now, he realized, he was in for it. There was nothing to do but come clean. "The last time I went to Iowa City," he said slowly, "I got my own therapist."

"Your own therapist?"

"Yes, Mom, one I choose. One who specializes in gender issues. She is fully licensed and accredited," he assured her, "in fact she works for the university."

"And you made an appointment on your own and went to see her?" His mother seemed incredulous.

"And she says I meet every single criteria for gender identity disorder. That I am transgender and that I would qualify for transition, if you would agree." Or I turn eighteen, he thought. Or maybe even had an ID that said I was eighteen.

"I can't believe you would do something like that, Clark," she scolded him. "Go behind my back like that. I want to know who this Beth is, where she works and I want to talk to her."

"Fine," he said. At least they would have a real sit down conversation about this issue with someone who was on his side. "I have her card."

######

"OMG!" Marcus exclaimed, "this is so cool."

"No, it's not." Clarissa replied. "It's creepy and weird. Or cool possibly," she admitted sheepishly. "But whatever it is, I've got to decide what to do and quick."

He was talking to Marcus on the phone. It was eight thirty and he had already gotten the twins to bed. He was sitting on the couch. Tony had so far not shown up early like he had been doing a lot lately. Waiting for him to show and trying to figure out how she was going to deal with it were driving her crazy. Finally, in desperation, she had called Marcus and confesses what had happened between them.

"Some big beefy straight guy wants to swing for you and you don't think it's cool?"

Clarissa sighed, she needed to talk so she would just have to put up with Marcus's attitude. "It's hardly that simple," she said. "He's old, married and a perv." But he was also cool, sophisticated and her friend.

"I know," Marcus said, "I am just teasing. But for the record I have never had a straight guy of any age want me to pose in anything for them. I am like way jealous."

"He's married, Marcus," she said ignoring his comments. "This could ruin his family. I can't help but feel like this is all my fault. If he hadn't caught me that one time none of this would have happened."

"Whoa, right there," Marcus said. "Yeah, you're a hot little drag queen but I don't think that made him a perv."

Clarissa rolled her eyes at the drag queen comment. "I know," she went on, "but I still end up feeling guilty every time I think about it."

"Because you think too much. If you want to have an affair, go for it. If not, say no."

Have an affair? Clarissa hadn't thought about it like that. "An affair? Like sex? I couldn't."

"It's not that hard," Marcus assured her.

"Yes, it is," she corrected him, "at least for me it is. Besides what about the girls?" Or Shelley, for that matter, but she was having a hard time saying that name aloud.

"Don't tell them." Marcus replied, "I am sure Tony won't."

"Plus, this isn't about sex, Marcus."

"Oh? He bought you a sexy outfit and he kissed you. I think this is about sex to him." Marcus replied. Leave it to Marcus to cut right to the heart of the matter.

"Well, it's not for me." She replied curtly, "I have to consider the family."

"Whose family?" Marcus said.

Mine, she thought and then she stopped. Hers? It wasn't her family, it was Tony's family, Shelley's family, the girl's family. She was the babysitter, nothing more.

She remembered one of the first days that Tony had come early, while she was having bed time tea with the kids. She saw herself sitting on the floor with the girls drinking tea. Tony with his shoes off sitting next to her, talking about his day. The girls eating sugar cookies and chatting excitedly to their daddy. How peaceful it had been, how satisfying.

It was something she would never have. Science could do incredible things. She had seen pictures online of before and after transition. Heck for that matter she could look in the mirror and know that as long as she managed to transition soon, before testosterone had permanently marked her appearance, the results would be nearly perfect. She had even seen pictures online of "down there" after the surgery. She knew that if she could someday afford it, and she must, it would look completely natural.

But no one could put a uterus in her. She would never have children. She might become a woman but she would never be a mother, not a biological one anyway.

"Are you okay?" Marcus asked and Clarissa realized she hadn't said anything in a long time.

"Just when you think your life can't get any more complicated."

"What now?"

"Look I admit, I've got feelings for Tony and I know that's totally inappropriate," she said. "And I think he has feelings for me,"

"Which is even more inappropriate."

"And the way he shows it is very inappropriate," Clarissa groused. "But god, someday to have a man like that and two beautiful little girls." She trailed off lost in thought.

Marcus blew a raspberry, "Please, let's not get lost in some chick fantasy now."

Clarissa smiled into the phone, pulled back to reality. "Oh, shut up." She said playfully. Then she heard Tony's jeep pull up and said, "I've got to go, he's here."

"Good luck," Marcus said on the other end of the line, "and call me if there's any juicy gossip."

She felt better for having talked to Marcus about things, but she still had no clue how to deal the man who was probably walking up the front steps right now. She stood quickly. She didn't know whether to be relieved or upset that she was caught in her "male" clothes, if the light blue sweater and blue jean combination actually qualified as male or not. The sweater would have gotten her grief at school but it wasn't drag either.

She grabbed her bag and started putting her books away, as much to be doing something so she would not have to face Tony as he came in the door. "In a hurry tonight, Ms. Claire?" He asked from behind her.

"It's after nine," she said sheepishly. "I figured it's time anyway."

She turned and he stepped in closer. "We've got a couple of hours..." He said, "if you want to stay and talk awhile, or something."

A couple of hours before Shelley gets home, Clarissa finished in her mind, her blood turning cold. There it was. Tony's tacit admission that whatever was going on had to be hidden from Shelley. Because it was wrong.

"I'm sorry," she muttered, "but I can't." She fumbled for an excuse, "Mom will be up, she'll be worried if I don't get home soon."

"Did I scare you the other night?" He asked putting his arms around her shoulders, "I didn't mean to."

His touch distracted her, made her blush. "No, no," she

stammered, "I just,"

He leaned in close and whispered in her ear, "I just want to help you Claire."

"I know," she said, "and I thank you for being so accepting, but I can't..."

"Can't what?" He said, "What have I asked you to do?"

"Nothing," her voice sounded small and distant.

"That's right, nothing. I have kept your confidence. I let you dress in my wife's clothes, I even helped you by giving you stuff to wear." Ice reached for Clarissa's heart as she heard the implied threat in his voice. "All I want in return is to be your friend, to spend some time together."

She fought against panic. One word, one casual mention and he could undo everything. If Shelley knew Clarissa had worn even one article of clothing out of her closet, heck if she even knew that Clarissa existed under the exterior she knew as Clark, it would be the end. She'd never see the kids again. She'd lose her job, her money. If word got out beyond this house why she'd been let go, Clark's miserable life would get a whole lot more miserable.

Not to mention that if Tony turned on her she'd lose the best friend she had ever found. He was bright, articulate, handsome and he accepted her as a woman. If she could just somehow force the ghost of Shelley from her mind it could be so easy to fall for Tony.

She relaxed against him. With her head buried within his massive shoulder she gave the tiniest of nods. "Just not tonight Tony." She whispered, "I'll stay and talk, I want to, but not tonight. I've got too much going on."

"Of course, dear," he replied magnanimously, "of course."

#######

Clarissa woke in a cold sweat. It had been the dream again. At least she hadn't screamed, at least she didn't think she had screamed. She listened quietly for a minute and there was no sound of movement upstairs. She hadn't screamed or maybe her mom had just given up.

She looked around the room, starting to feel a chill from the sweat. The room was ghostly in the limited light coming through her window. The digital display on her clock shone five thirty.

Shit. She had over an hour before she had to start getting up for school. She should lay back down, but she already knew that sleep would not come again.

The dream was getting worse; not outwardly, she rarely screamed now, but emotionally. Now that she understood what it meant she didn't see the darkness of the vault as much as she felt it. Felt the walls closing in on her, felt her life slipping away. She could feel the bone crushing depression that would haunt Clark without her in his life. She had read enough online about transgender youths, about their high suicide rate. She didn't feel that way right now, but she understood just how easy those thoughts could get started.

The hardest part was that now that she understood the dream, the vault haunted her waking life as well. Every time she argued with her mom the hope of transition seemed to take one step back. The small light it provided dimmed that much more, the darkness threatening her. Every time she was taunted at school, or where ever, she lashed out, feeling the hands on her dragging her towards the darkness. She thought she was going to crack.

She climbed out of bed, the sweat drying on her. She walked over to the vanity and sat down. She would have to take a shower this morning anyway, so she might as well be washing make up off with the sweat. It might make her feel better.

And as if she didn't have enough on her plate, now there was Tony. What was she going to do? Talking to Marcus had helped but there wasn't anything he could do. And there nobody else Clarissa could talk to. Who would possibly understand?

She felt like she was drowning in a pool of Tony. Her feelings were too conflicted to follow. They flitted back and forth across her soul. He was nice, he was handsome and he loved her. Or he was a snake and a perv and wanted to use her. If he would just stop pushing her, keeping her so off balance then she could see what he was and what she truly felt. Why couldn't he give her some space?

Then there was Shelley and the kids. She knew that doing anything with Tony would be wrong because of them. She knew that it wasn't fair to them. But when was life ever fair? Her being born with a boy's body wasn't fair. It would hurt Shelley, but people did stuff to hurt Clarissa every day and no one seemed to give a damn. If it were just Tony and Shelley that might be it. But Clarissa couldn't hurt the kids like that. It tore at her to even think about it.

All these thoughts circled and collided around one central theme, Tony liked her as a girl. This was the horrible shameful crime that she must hide, to be liked as a girl. The harassment at school, the fear he saw in his mom's eyes when he talked about transition, the disapproval in the eyes of women like Shelley, all centered around this one crime. How dare you let someone like you?

Why couldn't the rest of the world take a hint from Tony? Why couldn't they let her be who she really was? Her experience in the club and with Tony had taught her that if she was given a chance she could play the role perfectly. It was such a simple elegant solution. As a boy she was unbearably awkward, for herself and for the people she had to interact with. As a girl she was poised and graceful.

But they wouldn't allow that option. The bullies at the school had made it painfully clear that the effeminate boy that was Clark would forever have their scorn. Mom had made it perfectly clear that she would have to remain that boy as long as she lived at home. Beth, kind as she was, had copped out on her, refusing to do more than talk about transition until either her mom was on board or Clarissa turned eighteen.

Eighteen was two freaking years away. She didn't know how she could last that long.

What if she didn't have to wait? What if she could become Clarissa right now? She paused and sat down the brush she had been twirling idly for several minutes. She closed up the blush and set it back in the right-hand drawer. She looked at herself in the mirror.

An idea was forming in the back of her mind, an image of her getting out of this town, getting out of this life. She pushed the drawer shut and turned to the other side of the vanity, pulling her laptop out and opening it before her. A wild plan was forming in her head. It would require a lot more than a birth certificate and a social security card... It would require Clarissa to have a real legal identity. Driver's licenses, high school diploma, medical records, she ticked off the items in her mind, imagining how she might obtain each.

######

Clarissa hoped the clerk didn't notice her palms sweating as she passed the piece of paper over. It was a master piece, much better than the ID's she and Marcus had made. Tony had really come through, despite the cost. Or so she hoped. She hoped the certificate was not just a really good fake. Now here was the real test.

"You've never had a state issued ID?"

"Nope," Clarissa lied, "Mom didn't want me to take driver's ed. She's kind of dysfunctional and Dad skipped out a long time ago."

She had more. She had concocted a whole long and slightly sad story of a childhood of neglect and living on the edge of the system to go along with the fake birth certificate she had just handed over. Now that she was eighteen and in charge of her own life she intended to go legit. She wanted to go to community college and she had faked school transcripts to back her story up. But she didn't need it. The clerk simply shrugged, turned to his computer and started typing. "Current address?" He asked.

It was over in a matter of minutes, and as the first seriously illegal thing Clarissa had ever done, it was strangely anti-climactic. She was told to sit in front of the camera and they snapped a quick picture. She went to sit with Marcus while they printed her new driver's license, Clarissa's.

This was only the first step but it was an important one. If you wanted to sneak into a bar while under-aged, like Marcus did, all you needed was an ID card that would pass a simple inspection. She wanted to do something drastically different.

She wasn't sure if she was going to go through with the plan or not, but she was dead serious about having it as an option. She wanted to be able to run away and take up living somewhere else, as a girl. She would need to be able to support herself somehow, find a place to live and find a doctor who could help her transition. That meant convincing a lot of people who would do more than just look at her driver's license for a minute. They would attempt to verify it with the authorities. That meant those record had to exist.

And in modern American society it all hinged on the social security administration. If they bought her birth certificate and her a social security number then she could get a legit ID. One that would convince a doctor that she could sign a consent for herself.

Marcus was waiting for her on the cold plastic seats. She sat down next to him on the bench and started shaking with post adrenaline jitters. "How'd it go?" He asked.

"Okay, I think." Clarissa said. "I mean I passed the test easy enough." Now let's see if Tony passes his test. She dropped her voice to a whisper, "if the birth certificate and social security number are in the system like they are supposed to be, they'll be calling my name and handing me a new legit ID any minute."

They had rehearsed things the entire way down to Des Moines. "The secret," she had told him with more confidence than she felt, "is to lie as little as possible." And that's how she had planned it. Her name was to be Clarissa Holden, close enough to her real name. Her year of birth had been rolled back to make her eighteen but her date of birth was her own. "So it rolls off my tongue naturally," she said.

Marcus had whined about the age a bit. "Why eighteen? Twenty-one and you can drink and get into bars."

"Twenty-one is too obvious." She had insisted. "I can't pass as twenty-one anyway. Even eighteen is a stretch, but that's at least believable."

She took a few deep breathes to control the shaking and gave him the thumbs up. "I didn't even need most of the story we rehearsed. He just took my info and filled out the application."

"So, what is next?"

"The post office," she said.

"You gonna mail something?" He asked.

"I want to apply for a passport." She said.

"Why, you going somewhere?"

"No," she said, "but it's another test and I want as much documentation as possible."

Her mind had already thought beyond that. She would begin to build a new identity from scratch, faking as little as possible as she went. A short trip to Kirkwood Community College and, she felt reasonably certain, she could pass her GED exam. Then she could go to work or college as Clarissa.

"I meant, what's next today?" Marcus interrupted. He had already endured an entire morning of discussion about this. It was not, as he had pointed out, his plan.

"Oh, yeah. There's this club called the Garden. They have a teen show this afternoon."

"Now that's more like it," he enthused.

CHAPTER TWELVE

Clark slowed as he rounded the corner. He hadn't exactly been hurrying, but the town was too small for him to take long. Marcy, who provided daycare for the girls during the day and then dropped them off at home for Clark would mad if she had to wait too long. It wasn't Marcy's familiar Honda Civic in the driveway. It was Shelley's Ford Fit.

He stared at it in surprise. He had been dreading today and as conflicted as he was about Shelley he was kind of glad she was here. Thursday night he had promised Tony he would stay late, just not that night. Saturday Shelley was there. Tony dropped several hints that he was anxious to talk to "Ms. Claire." Clark was starting to feel extremely uncomfortable with where things were going. But he still hadn't figured out any solution. He could hope it was "good Tony" who wanted to talk computers or he could try once again to make an excuse.

He had almost thought of quitting but there were so many problems with that solution too. For one thing, the thought of leaving the girls filled him with an almost painful sadness. Then there was Tony's implied threat. If Tony let his wife know that Clark had been cross dressing in her clothes it would be over for Clark. Clark had no idea if it was serious or not, but he knew he would be a nervous wreck trying to play chicken with a man like that. And he'd be out of good paying job.

Maybe Shelley had been canceled for work. It happened, or so she had said once. It didn't happen often and he'd not seen this before. Still it would a relief to be able to go home.

As he opened the door he saw the twins sitting on the couch, eyes wide and full of tears. They huddled almost meekly together. The TV was playing their favorite Barbie Princess movie but they weren't watching.

Clark went to them immediately, sitting on the coffee table to face them. "What's wrong?" He asked.

They both gave a nervous glance towards the stairs. There was the sound of activity up there somewhere. "Mommy's mad." Britney whispered.

"And sad," Holly added, "she's been crying."

He reached over and patted their cheeks, remembering suddenly the first night he had babysat them. How the two wore their initials on their jumpers and that was the only way he could tell them apart. Now they seemed as different to him as any two random kids off the street.

"I'm sure it will be okay," he told them though in his heart he felt a sense of foreboding. "I'm going to check on her, okay?"

They nodded seriously.

Nervously he climbed the stairs. He called Shelley's name softly and went into the master bedroom. It was empty but he could hear Shelley rustling around in her closet. On the bed a garment box lay open and a suitcase lay open further down. Dread filled him as he looked into the garment box. It was lingerie, skimpy and pink.

"It's not my size." Shelley's voice said behind him, her voice deadpan, "or my style."

Clark nodded, his mouth dry. He could guess whose size it was.

Shelley was a mess. Her hair was disheveled and her mascara had run halfway down her face. "I can put up with a lot, because he's a good provider and a good father. But there are limits, Clark, there are limits."

"It was one thing when," she paused and went on, "when I could pretend it was them. It's been going on since the girls were born, you know. We've had to have babysitters, mostly teenage girls. And he has this effect on girls, believe me I know that. So, I thought, it's them, they're throwing themselves at my husband and he's too weak to resist. I really believed that Clark." She was insistent, wanting him to believe. He stood mute and numb with shock.

"I thought, if he was away from the temptations, maybe things would go back to the way things were. Maybe I'd be the center of his world again." She sat on the bed stared off into space. Not knowing what else to do, Clark went into the bathroom and found a washcloth. He ran the tap until it was warm and got the washcloth damp.

"They'll kick me out for sure." She was saying as he came back, "all of them. I know it. But they've got to understand, I can't live like this."

He had no idea who they were, or what she going to be kicked out of, so he didn't answer. He took the wash cloth very gently to her face, wiping away the mascara lines.

"Oh, Clark," she said, reaching up and putting her hand on his cheek. "You are such a sweet boy. You know that? You are so wonderful with the girls. You'll never be like him. You'll make a great father and you'll never hurt your family the way he does."

Clark closed his eyes, not trusting himself to speak. He bit back on the bile that was threatening to leave his throat. Too many feelings fought for his attention. He couldn't keep track of them all. He would never be a man like Tony because he would never be a man. *I will be a woman before anyone stops calling me a boy.*

He wanted to run and hide. Guilt held him in place. He wanted to fall into her lap and confess what he had done. He had led Tony astray yet again. *If only I hadn't wore that dress that one night, if Tony hadn't come home and found me like that, none of this would have happened.*

There was something else, gnawing at his stomach and tearing a new empty space inside him. Tony had done this with other girls. It was like a red-hot blade twisting through his gut, other girls. There had been other girls.

He couldn't say anything, so he just kept washing. Finally, he licked his dry lips and said, "if you need anything from me, I can watch the kids whenever. Just tell me." In that moment he felt it too, he would atone for whatever fault was his by standing by

Shelley and the girls. It wasn't much, but it was all he could offer.

She nodded. "The girls will really miss you, Clark. They love you more than any of the others."

Miss me? "Are you?" He let it hang in the air.

"Leaving?" She nodded. "Yes, I am going to stay with my uncle and his wife in Wisconsin. It's best that way. I told work I am taking family leave. I don't know if we'll be back or not, but I need some time away." She stood again and returned to packing.

"I'll give you a reference if you want." She said not looking at him, "and your full week's pay of course. This is all such short notice. It really is the only fair thing."

He too turned away, unable to face her. Tears were threatening him and he didn't want her to see or wonder why he was taking this so hard. "Can I help?"

"Could you get the girl's stuff together? Just an overnight bag with some clothes, some of their favorite toys. I can't take much."

He nodded again, not trusting himself to speak and left without looking at her. He packed one large suitcase full of the girls' clothes. Then he filled each of their Hello Kitty backpacks, backpacks that he had bought them for Christmas, with their most important toys. Suck it up, he told himself as he finished, at least until you get home, you can't let them see you cry like this.

He scooped the two back packs under one arm. Shelley met him the hallway. He pocketed the money she offered without counting it or commenting. She hugged him and he stood there passively, unable to return the hug. Momentarily spent of emotion he made for the stairs. Downstairs he handed the bags over to the girls, who were still sitting on the couch with the deer in the headlights look plastered on their tiny faces.

"Are we leaving?" Holly whispered.

"Just for a while." Clark answered, "like a vacation."

"Is daddy coming?" Brit asked.

"I don't think so," Clark said, not wanting to be the one breaking that news but not wanting to lie either.

"Are you coming?" Holly asked.

Clark smiled a wan smile. "I wish I could, I love you too so much."

"We love you too." They both said together. He hugged them fiercely for a long time, tears threatening to return. He smiled at them and brushed both cheeks gently, "you girls be good for your mom." He turned and fled the house for good.

"Home already?" His mom said when he came in the door. He nodded dully.

"Are you okay?" She asked, her voice full of concern.

He shook his head again. "No, mom it's not me. She, um Shelley had to go to Wisconsin or something, some sort of family stuff."

"Is it serious?" She asked.

He shrugged.

"You seem pretty upset."

"I just worry about the girls, you know."

"Clark!" She said sharply. Then her expression softened and she touched his cheek, "It's sweet the way you dote on those girls. But seriously, they are with their mother. I think they'll be fine."

If only she knew what was really going on she wouldn't be so sure, he thought.

"I'm not feeling that well anyway." He shrugged dismissively as he said it. "I think I'll go lay down a while."

He lay on his bed and stared at the blank wall. All he could think was why Tony? Why did you have to push? Now you've gone and ruined it for all of us.

######

"I ran into Gladys at the supermarket today," Kelly said as she handed over a dish of mashed potatoes. "She said Shelley Pirella took the kids and left."

Clark nodded as he took the plate. For the last three days, he had been running on autopilot and for the most part had avoided thinking about the Pirellas. He started to hand the dish of potatoes over to his brother when his mom spoke again, "Clark?"

"What?"

"Aren't you going to take anything?"

He glanced down at his empty plate. "Oh sure," he said putting a spoonful of potato on his plate.

141

"I am starting to worry about you." She said.

"I'm just not hungry." He mumbled.

"You have hardly ate anything for days now. You need to start eating."

He made a show of putting gravy on the mash potato and toying with the mass with his spoon. He even took a bite. It was bland and tasteless in his mouth.

"Anyway, Gladys says she left Tony." She looked at him for confirmation.

"Yeah she's gone."

"I'm sorry Clark, I didn't realize. That's why you've been so down, isn't it?"

He shrugged. "Yeah, mostly."

"I know how much that job meant to you."

He closed his eyes and nodded, trying to push the feelings down. He had spent the better part of the last three days trying desperately not to feel anything. Now his mother was going to undo all his work.

Luckily, he had his brother to save him, "poor kid, no job, no money, no reason to have that cell phone..." Jeremy commented.

"Jeremy!" His mom snapped. "I don't suppose you know what is going on?"

"No, mom," he lied, "I have no idea."

No idea it had been going on for years, that is. No idea that he was only one in a long line of girls, baby sitters and god knows who else that had crossed that man's path. He wanted to hate them all. He wanted to look down and despised them for falling for Tony's lines and seductions. At the same time, he wanted to count himself apart from all of them. He had an excuse. Tony had been the first person to ever show him that kind of attention. The first guy that ever liked him, as a girl. Of course, he had fallen for it, but what about them? What excuse did they have?

"I miss," he started without realizing he was talking. He caught himself and went on, "the kids, you know. They were kind of fun." Had he almost revealed himself? Had he almost said he missed Tony? He did miss Tony. That was the crazy part, he missed him terribly, almost as much as he hated him.

"You must miss Tony too." His mom said. Clark nearly jumped out of his skin. Did she know? Or suspect? He looked at her but her expression was innocent. "It always sounded like you really admired him. I think maybe you have found your calling with all that computer stuff."

He nodded slowly. "I do miss Tony," he admitted as frustrated tears threatened him again. He couldn't break down in front of them. "But you know..."

"What?"

"Nothing," he amended. "Can I be excused?"

"No," his mom said sharply, "You haven't eaten. Seriously, Clark, are you okay?"

He looked down at the small pile of mash potato on his plate and reached for a bowl of corn. The corn had no more taste than the potatoes but he forced himself to chew and swallow mechanically until his mother was content that he had eaten.

######

"Well I say good riddance to the two-timing bastard." Marcus said. Marcus was the one person Clarissa had told about Tony, and therefor the only person she could vent to now.

"But..." Clarissa couldn't bring herself to say it.

She didn't need to, Marcus guessed dead on. "But it was different with us." He mimicked, "he's going to show up one of these days and tell you how he didn't really love all those other girls, not like he loves you."

"It was different." She said sullenly.

"Because you are a trannie." Again, Marcus nailed it. "Sorry girlfriend, wrong on both counts. Face it, you're a hottie in a dress. For a guy like Tony, that's all that matters."

"He accepted me."

"Because he wanted something." Marcus replied.

"I thought he was different from other guys."

Marcus just snorted. "Hornier maybe."

"You told me to go for it." She snapped back.

"Yeah, but I didn't tell you to get attached. Geez, he's married.

That didn't bother you. Why do the other girls?"

She shrugged and rolled over on her bed. "I don't know but it does." She said. She did know, she just didn't want to go through it all aloud. It bothered her because she had thought that her relationship with Tony was special. She had thought some unique and wonderful spark had grown between the two of them, something neither had experienced before or would again. To find out that she was only one in a long list of girls he had flirted with, toyed with, groped and possibly had sex with, that was too much.

But under the pain and rage was a certain sense of satisfaction at, for once, being grouped with the girls. She had at last found one man, one man in all the world, who viewed her, totally and completely as a girl. Now that man was gone from her forever.

"I think I am falling apart."

CHAPTER THIRTEEN

"I am so scared." Kelly admitted in to the phone. Her chest loosened slightly, saying it aloud had that effect. "I don't know what's gotten into him."

"Tell me what's going on," Philip said on the other end of the line, his voice smooth and unflappable, always the professional.

"That's just it," Kelly moaned, "I don't know what's going on. He's been acting strangely for a couple of weeks now. I know he's really upset about something but when I try to ask I always get the same response."

"Which is?" Phillip asked.

"Nothing. I ask what's going on, he says 'nothing.' I ask what he's upset about and it's 'nothing.'"

"He's never been very communicative with me," Philip reminded her.

"I know, and he's been shutting down with me lately too. But I thought we were getting along better. Now he's just completely shut down. He spends hours in his room by himself, either on his computer or just lying there depressed. When he does go somewhere, like to his friend Marcus's, he's so secretive about everything."

There was a long pause. "Do you have any reason to believe he's suicidal?"

Kelly paused almost as long. "I just don't know. He's never said anything about that, but I've never seen him this depressed before, not even," she trailed off.

"Not even when?" Phillip persisted.

"Not even back when he was suicidal." She finished finally. "There's more, I've found out recently that he's been going to Iowa City with this Marcus and they've been going to a gay club." It had come out as part of their conversation about his trips to Iowa City. She hadn't mentioned Beth to Philip and didn't see any reason to. He was still, in her mind, her son's primary therapist. "Do you think he might be doing drugs?"

"I'll be honest, the gay bar scene has a reputation for party drugs. But that hardly means your son is falling into that. I don't know about Iowa City, but here in Des Moines one of the gay bars has a teen night. It's ran very respectably, the bar is closed so there's no chance of under-age drinking, and adults watch the scene very carefully. If this was Chicago or San Francisco, I'd be more worried. But I don't think there's a huge drug scene in the local gay community."

"That doesn't mean he's not using," he went on. "Some of the stuff you are telling me fits; sudden behavior changes, secretive behaviors, depression. But your son's never shown an interest in drugs before. I think I would have picked up on that."

Kelly sighed. "That's a relief. What do you think is going on?"

"I have no idea." Philip admitted. "Could it have anything to do with the job?"

Kelly had told him about Clark losing his baby-sitting job. "I wouldn't think so," Kelly said. "I mean he was really bummed about losing the work but it's only a job, right?"

"Yeah but you indicated that he was really attached to the girls and to this man, Tony."

"Maybe. His whole face would light up when he talked about them or Tony, but still I can't imagine that's all there is going on."

Now it was Philip's turn to sigh. "The fact that you can't tell me if he's suicidal or not really bothers me. I think you need to find out what's going on, even if you have to push. Can you do that?"

"I'll try." She said.

"You know the number if you need me. Don't hesitate to call."

######

Clarissa lay on her bed. In the past she had had good days and bad days. Now she had feverish days and dead days. Last night she had worked feverishly on her computer for six straight hours, wolfing down supper without a single comment to her mother or Jeremy. Then immediately disappearing into her room again.

Today was a dead day. The total absurdity of her plan hit her midday at school. She had barely been able to drag herself through the rest of the day. Both Amy and Vong had commented nervously on her absent stare. Now she was home, laying on her bed, thinking.

In the right-hand drawer of her vanity was a growing stack of papers in a neat manila folder; Clarissa's identity. About a quarter of them were fakes. About a quarter of them were real. The rest were somewhere in between, real papers based on fakes, fakes based on real things.

The birth certificate, a fake. The social security card, real with a real number that showed in the system but based on the fake birth certificate. The GED was real, Clarissa had aced the test easily.

Beth had been preparing Clark a letter to use with the school board. She had hoped to relieve at least part of her suffering by forcing the school to acknowledge his gender variance. Their goals hadn't been high, let him opt out of PE or at least not change in a room full of boys, allow him to grow his hair longer than the school's policy stated.

Her signature and the notaries seal had been scanned in the computer and lifted from the document. Now he had another letter, where Beth unwittingly approved Clarissa for both hormones and when appropriate, surgery.

There was still a lot she needed. But what was the point? Right now, she could walk away from this town, this life. She could go from being a sixteen-year-old boy to being an eighteen-year-old woman. She had a few clothes and she knew she could pass.

But there was one big thing she didn't have, money. She had a small sum left over from the baby-sitting gig and some from her side line in computer repair. As long as she stayed where she was, it was a lot. Just shy of three hundred dollars bought a lot of CD's, computer stuff and make up. By teen standards she was loaded.

Outside of this small town she would need a lot more dough than that. To set up a new life would cost ten times that. Even if she stayed in the cheapest hotels she could find, that wouldn't last more than a couple of weeks. Then there was first and last month rent on a permanent place. And that was only short term. She wanted to transition and that cost money. How much could an eighteen-year-old girl with a GED and no job experience make? Not nearly enough.

It was pointless. Running away just wasn't a serious option after all. All she could do was lay here, stare at the wall and hope to die.

Her phone beeped. Marcus texting to check up on her, unless her mom had gotten so desperate she was now texting 'are you okay?' She pulled the phone out and found she didn't recognize the number. She flipped it open and opened the message:

Can we talk?
T.

She stared at it a long time. She didn't have to guess who T was. It a gutsy move to contact at her at all. Shelley had left town and not spoken to anyone since as far as Clark knew. That didn't stop rumors from running wild, and with Tony being who he was, cheating had come up time and time again. Several people had asked Clark point blank if he saw any evidence that Tony had been cheating. It pissed Clarissa off because nobody had the decency to even suspect the one person who actually had an opportunity. It was a sign of just how conflicted her feelings had become. She was intensely angry with Tony for what he did, how it had ruined everything for everyone involved, Tony included. At the same time she longed for the slightest hint of acknowledgement that she was worthy of his attention.

Now he was texting her. Why? While she was angry that she was being totally overlooked as a woman, she was equally afraid of the truth getting out. How long would it take, if Tony tried to keep up his 'friendship' with the effeminate boy without the pretext of the job, before townspeople to started suspecting?

A small part of her wanted to believe that he was going to tell her how much he loved her, how he planned to divorce Shelley and wait until Clarissa was eighteen and legal to continue their relationship. Unfortunately, in the days since her discovery she had gone over in her mind every moment she had spent with the man. In the harsh light of day she could see his little seductions and flirting for what they were. All the little tests he gave; they had been tests after all but not the kind of tests she had thought. When he offered her alcohol, he wasn't trying to see if she was a wholesome influence on the girls, he was trying to see if he could ply her with alcohol.

What really pissed her off was just how well he had succeeded. Clarissa had no doubt presented a unique challenge but he had found all her weaknesses. She had passed the obvious tests, like when she turned down the alcohol. But now she could see clearly all those other tests, the ones she had failed. She had allowed him to shower her with gifts. Computer parts, technical manuals, software; maybe not traditional lover's gifts but she hadn't blinked at accepting all of them. There were compliments galore too, some about his skills with the computer, but increasingly compliments about "Ms. Claire".

Worse still were the little traps he set for her. The 'permission' to use his wife's closet. It never even crossed her mind that he could use that to blackmail her, to keep her quiet. But he had.

He was not her knight in shining armor, he was as sexual predator. He manipulated women, no girls, into having sex with him. Underneath the warmth, Tony was a cold bastard.

Even as her mind spit out all of these accusations and ideas her heart kept singing a different tune. He was nice to her, he accepted her in a way that no one else did. He got the whole gender thing, she was a girl on the inside. What was so bad about that?

What if Tony had been like Clark, or Amy, or any of the others? What if he was trapped in a life he hated, unable to find a way out? If she could just ask him the right questions she could find out.

Now he was giving her the chance. She typed into the phone:

Sure
C.

"Clark, we need to talk."

His mom's voice was serious, serious enough to drag him out of his head and into the present. "Can't it wait Mom? I've got stuff to do."

"No, it can't."

He sighed and folded his light spring jacket over his arms. He followed her meekly into the living room. A motley assortment of people were waiting for him. His grandfather was stretched out in the big recliner looking nervous and uncomfortable. The pastor from the Lutheran Church they nominally belonged to and went to about twice a year, was sitting on the couch next to his brother and his brother's current girlfriend. They were watching Vong, who was watching them back. His mother stood in the middle of room, her eyes wide with concern and her face looking nervous. She took a deep breath and began,

"Clark, we all love you but we're concerned..."

"What the hell, Mom?" Clark exploded, "This is an intervention!"

"Clark," she started desperately, "it's not what you think."

"I am not an alcoholic mom! I am not a druggie!"

"I know, I know."

"No!" His grandfather put in, "Clark, we don't know that. All we know is that you have been acting funny and you won't tell your mother what's going." He sat back in his chair, apparently feeling he had contributed his share to the proceedings.

"I am not accusing you of anything," his mom said, "but I am your mother and I need to know what's going on with you right now."

For a second he was tempted to tell her. To yell in her face that he needed to go to see his male lover, who was a thirty-five-year-old married man who had fucked about a billion other girls before he came along. To yell that he was a sixteen-year-old transsexual that was beaten almost daily at school and so tormented that running away and creating a fake identity was the most rational solution he could find. Instead he just stared at her, angrier than he'd ever been before.

"And I keep telling you," he said through clenched teeth, "that nothing is going on. Why can't you accept that?"

"Because it sure doesn't seem like nothing is going on."

"I am sorry," he said acidly, "but there is nothing to tell." With that he turned and stormed out of the house.

He fumed as he marched through the gathering dusk. He pulled his coat on against the chilly night air. It wasn't until almost five blocks later, as he was coming towards the Kum and Go on the edge of town that he slowed down.

How could she have accused him of being on drugs? It was bad enough that she had so little idea what was going on with him. It wasn't like he wasn't willing to talk about his gender. It was just that she was so unwilling to accept that this was really what was going on. And she was unwilling to understand what it meant for him.

He was so lost in thought that he didn't even notice the Camaro parked by the side of the Kum and Go or the guys leaning against the hood drinking Cokes and watching him. Not until it was too late to avoid them.

"Well, well," John said. He was usually the one who initiated these sorts of things, "look who we have here, the faggot himself"

Clark pulled his coat tighter about him and started towards the Kum and Go, but he knew they were already too close. He pressed closer to the building, but in two strides John and his friends were there as well, two in front of him and two behind.

John put his arm up against the faded brick wall, "going somewhere, faggot?"

"Yeah," it was Randy Dermont, a linebacker on the football team, one of John's closest friends and one of Clark's worst tormentors. "We've been wanting to have a talk with you outside of school for a while now."

He stood with his back against the wall, staring at them defiantly, refusing to speak.

"This faggotry has got to stop." John said.

"We ain't against gays or nothing," Randy said, "but you can't go on flaunting it in our face, forcing your lifestyle down our throats. It ain't natural."

This was too much. "How am I flaunting anything?" He snapped. He had almost said, my lifestyle, but that was stupid. It wasn't a lifestyle. It was his life.

"How? How?" The question seemed to enrage John, "I'll tell you how." He brushed Clark's hair brusquely, "with your faggot hairdo and with crap like this," he pulled on Clark's spring coat. It was a light purple. "I mean really. And the way you walk, the way you talk, everything about you."

It's not my fault that I walk a certain way or talk a certain way. He kept it to himself however. The boys were leaning in closer and looking angry. He was starting to get really scared.

"So, what are we going to do about this?" John asked him.

"We could beat him up," a voice said, not so helpfully from behind Randy.

"We've done that plenty." Randy said, "and it don't do any good."

"I say we cut his hair off," said the voice behind John.

He looked at Randy. The big guys eyes were dilated wide, his nostrils flared. There was a hint of something almost sadistic in his eyes. Clark realized suddenly Randy was excited by this. "I say," he said very slowly. "We give him exactly what he wants. What all the little faggots want." Clark's mouth was dry. He had a suspicion what Randy was suggesting. He wanted to ask, but he didn't want to know either. "You'd like that, wouldn't you?" Clark veins ran ice. "If all four of us bent you over my Camaro, right here in the parking lot, one after the other."

He was trying to edge away from Randy and he was desperately trying to keep from looking at him. He didn't want to see his face, to know how serious he was about raping Clark. He looked instead at John.

To his immense relief John was looking uncomfortable with the conversation too. Then his eyes hardened. "I say we just kill him."

He felt Randy's hand on his chest, groping. "Got put him in place first, make him squeal like the little girl he's always wanted to be. Then cut off all his fucking hair. Then kill him." Randy's breath was on his neck and Clark knew he was being serious.

The honk of a car interrupted them. It was a black Jeep Grand Cherokee. Clark used the moments distraction to push roughly through the four boys and dash toward the sound.

He risked a quick look back as he slammed the door. The boys lurked against the wall of the Kum and Go, staring at him malevolently. He shuddered, unable to doubt the sincerity of their threats.

"Is something wrong?" Tony asked.

Clark softened briefly towards the older man. He shook his head no. "Just my life, but that's nothing new." He risked a quick glance at Tony. *Will he help or add to my problems?* "Just drive."

Tony pulled out and drove. They drove through town randomly for some time. They sat in an uncomfortable silence, neither knowing how to begin the conversation. Finally, Clark blurted out, "she found some lingerie. Not intended for her."

Tony nodded. "She's staying with her uncle. Old coot doesn't like me. That's why she went there. Her mom," Tony went on, bragging, "loves me, thinks I am an F-ing saint or something. She'd tell Shelley to come back like a good girl."

"Like she did the last time?" Clark said on a hunch.

"They're good Catholics." He replied, "and they know its a woman's duty to put up with her husband's flaws."

Clark felt a tear slide down her cheek. Her heart felt like it was being ripped out of her chest. *You wanted to know. Now you know.*

"It never meant anything to you, did it?" He asked.

Tony seemed to notice that he had let something slip. "How can you say that Claire?" He protested. "You're not like-"

"Not like the others?"

Tony sat still, an impassive silence between them.

"How many others?" Clark persisted, "How many were there?"

"They were nothing like you," Tony said, trying to throw her off his tracks. "And nothing like what we'll have when Shelley comes back and things go back to normal."

"When is that ever going to happen, Tony?"

"This will all blow over, Claire, just wait and see." He replied, something slick and oily in his voice, "and it will blow over even faster after you tell her that the package was yours and she realizes this was all a big mistake."

Clark's mouth fell open, flabbergasted. "What?"

"It's no big deal," Tony persisted, "just tell her you bought it for your girlfriend and were storing it at our place because you didn't want your mom to find it."

"I don't have a girlfriend."

"Shelley don't know that," Tony said like he was speaking to a child.

"I can't just lie to her."

"Once she's back I'll convince her to re-hire you." He went on, "it won't be hard, she really likes you, and the girls do to. Then you get your job back, and your Tony." He flashed a smile and wink as he said it. Clark stared in stony silence. "Come on, we had fun, didn't we?" He reached out and touched her cheek.

Clark blushed and looked away. They had had fun, lots of it. But that didn't change how wrong this was. "I can't lie to her," he repeated. Besides that wouldn't work anyway because I saw the package, he thought. I can't go back now and say, oh by the way, that was my lingerie for this girlfriend I have. She'd never buy it.

"I am disappointed in you, Claire," Tony went on, "I thought you enjoyed our games. Besides you have to realize she's going to figure out those panties were yours eventually." His tone had changed abruptly.

Clark started momentarily. Was Tony threatening to expose them both? Would he take it that far?

"She's going to find out that you were cross dressing in her house with her clothes, sooner or later." He went on, "and then it's only a matter of looking and she'll know that you were buying things online with her computer."

Clark stared as the enormity of what Tony was suggesting

became clear. Tony had bought those gifts on Shelley's computer and done it in a way that would implicate Clark if it ever came out. He really was a bastard.

"Stop the car!" He said suddenly, "Stop the F-ing car!" He grabbed for the door handle and had the door open before Tony had the jeep completely stopped.

"Come on Claire, let's discuss this," Tony called to the open door. Claire was already disappearing into the night. Tony cussed suddenly.

Clarissa awoke, if indeed she had ever been asleep, with a spider web of bright lines flowing through her mind. Each node had a string of numbers associated with it but she could not grasp the meaning. She struggled for greater consciousness and comprehension.

She had come home from her meeting with Tony to find the crew gone but her mom still up crying. They had had a long emotional conversation and Clarissa had promised that she was not on drugs, (which it turned out was not what her mother thought anyway) nor was she was not considering killing herself or doing anything rash. (That last bit was a white lie. She wasn't going to kill herself but something rash? Rash was the only hope she had left.)

Afterwards she had gone downstairs to her bedroom and collapsed, staring at the wall. Always that same blank spot, her life was about to be condensed to that spot. It was just a matter of time before Tony made good on his threat and Clarissa would be revealed. Shelley would buy it and come home but Clarissa would not be welcome in that house again. And it would only take a couple of muttered hints for the rumors to get started and soon the entire town and school would know his secret.

Not that it mattered. It was hardly secret and it was only a matter of time before the boys caught him out of school again. Somewhere out of sight where they could make good on their promise. He only hoped they did kill him. His mental state was fragile enough. Could he survive being a rape survivor on top of it? He would rather be dead than in the looney bin for the rest of his life.

In times like these most people saw their lives flash before their eyes. Not Clark. His mind, as though it was already in the looney bin, wanted to replay one and only one inane piece of his life, a brief conversation in the lower levels of Tony's work.

"I thought you said you had three servers." Clark asked looking at the boxes.

Tony gave him a sharp look. "Did I?" After a moment he chuckled, "here I was planning on impressing you with the memory in here," He pointed at one of the boxes, "instead I am being impressed with the memory in here." He tapped Clark's forehead playfully.

Comprehension dawned on her suddenly. Clarissa sat bolt upright in bed. She climbed on top of her bed and peered out the window. It was dark, late at night. Feeling foolish she looked instead at the clock. It was one am. Time enough.

She dressed quickly, pulling on the darkest blue sweater she could find in her drawer. It was one of many typically boy styled clothes that periodically showed up in his drawers courtesy of his mom, who would then complain when Clarissa never wore it.

Next, she unplugged the pink netbook and climbed back on the bed. The window was tiny, a basement window only. It was not meant for egress but years ago Clarissa had used it to sneak out anyway, pressing herself flat to wiggle through. Though taller now, she was still thin. She pushed the netbook out ahead of her and wiggled through.

Though spring, it was still cold at night. She wished she had grabbed a heavier coat but she didn't dare go back. She'd just have to deal.

She ran quietly through the shadows, avoiding the more lighted streets despite the barrenness of the hour. Along the way she thought over everything she had read, or that Tony had said, about hacking.

Hacking, according to Kevin Mitner famed hacker and author, was an opportunist's game. The best attack was to find an old server, no longer used and therefor no longer as heavily guarded but still plugged into the system. Once it was hacked it could be used to send a trusted signal to other computers within the system.

Tony had unwittingly handed Clarissa the keys to the kingdom. "This 2 terrabyte box is just sitting here. It's got some old data on it research wants to keep backed up and they won't let me decommission it, no matter how much I gripe. Nothing worse for security than an old server that's not in active use."

If the aptitude tests were correct, there was a ninety-eighty percent chance that Clarissa could remember the direct IP to an old server at Tony's work. From there it would be easy to send a trusted request to one of the other servers, servers that in turn had a trusted link into Ugly Betty.

She reached the school and ran around towards the back. What she was doing had two huge risks associated with it. There was the immediate risk of being out at a time like this. Kids who were receiving death threats had best not be caught out alone late at night.

There was long term risk with doing any sort of hacking of this level, a risk that drove her out despite the danger. She was not going to be foolish enough to do this on her mother's Wi-Fi signal. It had to be through a much harder to trace location, like a public hotspot.

Behind the greenhouse, in Amy's spot, it was a little warmer. It was still cold and would be colder still after he had sat awhile. But she could pick up a signal from the school's open Wi-Fi from here. It wasn't much but it was stable.

She opened the netbook and quickly booted up. For a long time, she forgot about the cold, lost in a haze of code and protocols. Hacking, again according to Kevin Mitner, is often less about computers and more about social engineering. Hackers cultivate friendships with people in a targeted company and use every hint dropped to target their attacks.

Without intending it, Clarissa had done a great deal of social engineering on Tony. He came home tired because they were so back logged on security patches. Hitting old servers and software they hadn't patched recently she quickly found holes she could exploit. Tony sometimes griped about executives by name, people who didn't understand computer security or password safety. When she saw those names turn up in files she hit them hard. In less than half an hour she had access to almost the entire system. But she still didn't have a clue how to find Ugly Betty.

She stuck her hands in her sweater to warm them and thought. There had to be a way. He backed up a lot of the work's info on Ugly Betty, those would be huge files. Her hands were out again typing madly, trying to keep up with her brain. Suddenly like magic it appeared; a list of huge file transfers to a computer outside the system. She'd found Ugly Betty.

Finding Tony's personal computer was only half the battle. She still had to crack it and that wouldn't be easy. Worse, she had to do it quickly. It would have been an impossible task but she had a secret weapon.

She spoke aloud, the cold air hurting her lungs slightly. "Tony, I'm better than you."

She didn't need to crack the entire system. All she needed was one set of directories, the one with whatever personal incriminating evidence he had on her. Finding that one hidden directory would be a challenge. She had been secretly writing a program for just such an occasion. She called it her "Un-Search Engine." It scanned the entire disk but instead of looking for items it selectively filtered them out. By selectively eliminating common and innocuous files, it became easier to search for hidden files.

First she copied and pasted the entire transfer protocol into her Un-Search Engine. That eliminated the work files Tony had backed up and more than three quarters of the directories were gone from her results. There were still hundreds of directories and sub-directories. It would take hours to search them all. She started typing madly, entering names of common Linux programs and sub-routines. Program files and files associated with the operating system disappeared. It was becoming a much more manageable list with each new "un-search".

Then she spied it. Tony's Trophies it was called. She snorted. It was so typical. A sexual predator had to keep some sort of souvenir of his exploits. Tony wasn't half as exceptional as he thought. But it was password protected and Tony's password wouldn't be easily cracked. His weakness was that he was not only arrogant, she thought, but proud of how arrogant he was.

Then in a moment of blind intuition she typed in Tonyis1arrogantb@st@rd. The screen went blank and for a split moment she thought she had goofed and sprung some sort of trap. Then a display ran across the screen, "Yes I am" and she was in. She threw her hands in the air.

There were five folders. They were listed in alphabetic order; Amy, Brenda, Claire, Debra and The Rabbit Hole. He stared at the names. Logic would dictate that he go to Claire, find out what Tony actually had on her. Instead his mouse drifted over Amy.

"I've done terrible things, Clark, terrible things." Amy broke off and spat out, "Men!"

Her hands shaking, Clarissa clicked on the folder. Amy stared up at her, a younger more innocent Amy. There were pictures, many pictures. They were mostly innocent at first but they grew bolder, more risqué. Towards the end of the collection many were lewd, pornographic even. The face had grown less innocent, the smiles clearly forced.

Then came the movies. She clicked on the first one. She quickly realized something was wrong. Amy was not posing for the camera. She was undressing, apparently unaware that there was a camera there.

A sense of fear and violation coursed through Clarissa. She frantically clicked out of the movie and the folder, opening her own instead. There were far fewer pictures, mostly innocent ones that Tony had snapped to help her out with her online profiles; her smiling in make-up and a peach blouse, her in her pink T-shirt with her hair in braids. Then there was a movie clip. She opened it, already knowing what it would contain. He had filmed her with a hidden camera putting on that black outfit. There was another clip of her coming down the stairs. In both clips Tony himself was safely absent. He could claim at any time that he had set those cameras up because he had a suspicion about Clark and say, "look

I caught him wearing lingerie when he was baby-sitting our kids."

The final folder had him flummoxed slightly. The Rabbit Hole? Was that supposed to be an Alice in Wonderland reference? The folder contained a single text document. It in turn contained a series of names and numbers that meant nothing to Clarissa.

Once again, she stuck her hands into her sweater. She closed her eyes and let her mind wander. She knew the answer was there somewhere. Alice in Wonderland seemed too obvious. Besides it gave no clue as to what this file really was. In the Matrix one character had said something about going down the rabbit hole. But she'd read about rabbit holes somewhere else if she could just remember. She'd seen the term in fantasy books. Medieval kings often had small tunnels hidden in their castles, so they and their families could escape if necessary. It was called the rabbit hole.

This file was Tony's escape route? How? Credit Suisse, Zurcher Kantonalbank, Schweizerische Nationalbank; they are Swiss bank accounts, Clarissa thought. Suddenly the numbers made sense too, account numbers and balances. It totaled nearly one hundred thousand U.S. dollars.

How much would it take to start a new life?

She became aware that she was shivering. The darkness was deepening now. She had heard the term "darkest before the dawn" but never experienced it before. She glanced at the computer screen and saw it was nearly four in the morning. The battery light was red and she had maybe another twenty minutes. Twenty minutes to figure out what to do.

The bastard had stolen her innocence. Nothing would ever bring that back. But she could get even to the tune of a hundred thousand dollars.

But he had taken from others as well. It was right here where she was sitting that Amy had shown her arms, the lines of cuts. That pain was Tony's doing.

She had no idea if he had copied any of her pictures onto Shelley's computer yet or if he had spread any of his lies. She also had no idea how quickly he would detect her intrusion or what his reaction would be. She would have to act fast and assume the worst. She couldn't afford any other course of action.

In the end, it wouldn't matter. Even without evidence it was Tony's word against Clarissa's. She had no doubt how that would turn out. Everyone in this town were eager to think the worst of her. Even the rumor of what had happened in that house would bring John and Randy down on her worse than ever.

But she had to do something and not just for her sake. She had to act for Amy, for the other two girls. It felt like a line in the sand. If she wanted to be counted as a girl she had to stand with them. She had to show her loyalty in a big sort of way.

She quickly copied the entire directory onto her hard drive and then deleted it from Ugly Betty. There was no way she was going to leave those pictures for him, not the pictures of her, or of Amy or any girl for that matter. As for the money, it was probably illegally gotten anyway. Right now, she figured he owed her that much.

When it was done and she started to shut off the netbook, fear stole over her. When would Tony discover what she had done? What would he do? She couldn't win. Playing keep away with a man like Tony was playing with fire. She'd get burned for sure.

What would a real hacker do in a desperate situation like this? She smiled as the answer rushed through her. "If you can't win the game; change the game." She whispered to herself. She wouldn't dodge Tony or John either. She'd leave them in her dust.

Later, when questioned, the janitor would recall having seen a figure with blond hair in a blue sweater leaving the school grounds as he arrived early that morning. He couldn't rightly recall if it was a boy or a girl but he did recall that they moved slowly, as if stiff from the cold.

CHAPTER FOURTEEN

"I gotta go, mom." Clarissa said, ignoring the bowl of cereal that her mother was trying to thrust on her.

"But you need to eat, hon. To keep your strength up."

Acting on impulse, Clarissa hugged her. "You to Mom."

She looked at her son Clark skeptically, like he was acting weird again. Well, he is, Clarissa thought, she doesn't know this is goodbye, she can't know. And she won't see that this isn't her son anymore either.

"Eat," Clarissa clarified, "and keep your strength up, mom."

"I will," a mystified Kelly Holden responded.

"But I still gotta go," Clarissa went on, "I got Vong's computer." She patted the overstuffed messenger bag at her side, which did not have Vong's computer in it. "I am going to drop it off and then her parents are giving us a ride to school."

"I didn't know she had a computer?"

"She doesn't yet. I got an old broken one and fixed it for her." Leave it to Mom to be nosy today of all days. "And now I need to hurry."

She rushed off across the lawn and down the street. She had only twenty minutes and a lot to do. This was the riskiest part of the entire plan. Too many people knew her here and might remember seeing her.

Gay boys ran away in the middle of the night. Transgender girls didn't. If she were caught hitch hiking by the boys she would end up dead in a cornfield. If a trucker picked her up, she'd end up raped and dumped at a truck stop or rest stop along the interstate, for the next trucker to do the same. Clarissa wasn't just any transgender however, she was a smart transgender with almost a hundred thousand dollars in a Swiss account.

Two laptops and her envelope of documents were in her messenger bag. It also had two outfits, all she could really fit, her hair extensions, some makeup, her kindle and an Ipod. These things represented everything that really mattered to her.

At the Amoco station on the edge of town he bought a Red Bull and asked the bored attendant for the bathroom key. Less than five minutes later she came out makeup on and hair extensions in. She left the key in the nob for the attendant to find later.

Eighteen minutes after she had left the house, a tall skinny blond girl with her hair in pigtails sat on the bench outside the local country inn suites. When the bus pulled in a few minutes later, it looked as though she had just checked out. She bought a ticket under the name 'Kelly Holden' paying cash. It was traceable, way too traceable. She would get off and get a new ticket in Des Moines, one that wouldn't be.

She took one last glance back at the town she was leaving. She smiled at the driver and climbed on board. She sat in her seat and put an ear bud to one ear. She turned on her Ipod to listen to Marcus's most recent gift, a cut of "small town boy" from the Queer as Folk soundtrack. As the music started and the bus rolled out she felt it was the perfect song for the occasion.

As the bus rolled out of town she removed a pink laptop from her bag, opened it up and started typing furiously.

#######

Kelly Holden had come home from work angry. In fact, she had fumed for more than half the day. Now, as she looked into the gathering dusk, she was starting to worry.

Clark had played hooky from school. The school had called about eleven. He was 'sick' so often that the call was almost perfunctory. "Did you forget to call him in?"

She hadn't. He had left that morning for Vong's or so he said.

But he never went there. She had called Vong's mother as soon as she got off work to see if the two of them had gone off somewhere together. It seemed a long shot on a number of counts but it was all she had. Vong had gone to school and hadn't seen Clark at all that day.

The first thing she did when she got home was to check his room. It was empty and for some reason it filled her with foreboding. Jeremy hadn't seen Clark at school either. He had shrugged it off. He assumed Clark had made it halfway to school and turned around. That happened often enough as well. He was surprised to discover that Clark was not curled up in bed.

Kelly had even called Marcus. Marcus said he hadn't seen or heard from Clark that day. Kelly wasn't entirely sure she trusted the boy. If Clark had played hooky and ran off for the day, Marcus was the most likely accomplice. But Marcus was at home, she'd called the land line. That seemed to punch holes in her theory.

And that was pretty much the extent of places that Clark might be. Since he had lost the job at the Pirella's, this was the sum total of Clark's world; school, home, Vong, Marcus. Where could he be? It was now seven thirty. She'd been home for two hours, ready to give him the lecture of his life when he showed up. Now she was ready to cry.

She picked up her cell phone for the hundredth time. She fought the impulse to call his. It was sitting on the kitchen table. Jeremy had suggested calling it and they had heard the ringing. It had been under his pillow. That had only increased her foreboding.

She stared at the time readout on her phone and wondered about calling the cops. She looked at the door again. At eight she'd call them, she decided.

She paced the hall. Jeremy sat at the kitchen table. His homework was out but he didn't seem to be making any progress. The fact that he had not finished and gone to sack out on the couch and watch TV was the only sign he gave that he too was worried.

She forced herself to sit at the table opposite him only to immediately get up again and go into the kitchen. She heard a car pull around the corner and rushed to the window. A black Jeep was pulling into the driveway.

She felt a rush of relief as she recognized the jeep as Tony's. Perhaps he knew something. Perhaps Clark was with him, some computer thing she had forgotten about. She half expected to see Clark climb out of the passenger's side but it was only Tony that approached the door.

She opened before he knocked. He looked a little taken aback but then recovered quickly.

"Hello, Mrs. Holden," he said, "I was wondering if I could talk to Clark for a moment?"

Kelly felt crestfallen. She had been so sure he was coming with information about her son. "He's not with you?" She asked.

"No," he answered. "Why would he be with me?"

"Umm, I guess I'm not sure." Kelly said nonplussed, "I," suddenly she felt very uncomfortable and very afraid.

"I take it then he's not here?" Tony said.

"Umm, no." She replied, not sure how much to divulge.

"Well tell him it's very important that I talk to him, immediately, Kapisch?" Tony said and he turned to walk away.

"Excuse me," Kelly asked his retreating back, "is something going on? What do you need to talk to him about?"

"Just tell him to call me," Tony replied without turning back, "it's important."

Her sense of foreboding had risen to a sense of panic. Screw eight o'clock. She looked at her phone and hit 911.

The dispatcher took the report and sent a deputy around. The deputy took her report and told her not to worry too much. Clark would turn up soon. He said he'd check around but they couldn't do anything official until forty-eight hours had elapsed.

He called back about ten. He'd let the other officer know about the disappearance. He'd asked around a few places. Nobody had seen anyone by Clark's definition and nothing unusual had happened that evening.

Tony poured himself a rather larger than necessary amount of

Southern Comfort. In company he preferred mixed drinks, usually vodka based drinks or martinis. When he was alone and in a foul mood there could be nothing but whiskey and Coke. And he was alone and in a foul mood.

Tony had a simple philosophy; what's mine is mine, what's yours is yours. He didn't care how others lived their lives or what they did with their stuff. All he cared about was his stuff and his stuff was supposed to stay right here. He jabbed his thick finger into the coffee table to demonstrate where his stuff should be.

By his stuff he meant his family, Shelley and his girls. Shelley was old now, no longer new and sparkly, but still she was his. He had spent years cultivating his relationship (or as he saw it, his ownership) with that woman. She was his. She had no right to run off and ditch him, even less right to take the girls with her. If she wanted a divorce, fine, he could live with that. If she thought she'd take his girls from him she was going to be in for a shock. He'd sic every lawyer he could find on her and they would have the custody battle of the century.

But right now he had other stuff to worry about. His newest project, that little bitch Claire. She was his too and she should be right here. Seduction was an old game for Tony. He had practiced it since high school and throughout college. He had had more girls in his younger years than most men had in their whole lives.

After he married Shelley and "settled down" he discovered he missed the chase, the seduction. So being a practical man he took it up again on the side. He had had a couple of affairs at work but found that women his age expected too much. They wanted relationships.

Then just when he began to despair the girls were born and with the girls came babysitters. Suddenly he had an endless procession of cute young things who were too naive to expect anything of him.

Claire perhaps had been a mistake. Tony stopped and took another slug of whiskey. Because she was really a boy? He thought about the first time when he had walked in on Claire in his wife's cocktail dress; the long lean legs, the blond hair, the shy, scared eyes. He knew that second he wanted to see more of this creature. No, he had no problem with the fact that Claire was really a boy.

The problem had been with how smart that boy had been and how obsessed with computers. He gave each of his projects what they wanted most, attention. With the other girls that had meant feigning interest in inane conversation, listening to them drone on about their social standing at school, or worse still, their feelings.

Claire had been different, she wanted intellectually stimulating conversations. Whether it was computers or her gender identity, she asked sharp questions and wanted real dialogue. That made her dangerous. He had sensed the danger early on. He knew that he was starting to want her not just as a project, a toy to seduce, but as a friend. It was dangerous game, but Tony liked danger.

What he didn't like was losing. He had only 'lost' in his mind once. James McMillan had gotten the pretty girl, the girl Tony had his heart set on, to go to the prom with him. James was now living in some low rent apartments in Des Moines. When James's parents died Tony had bought their house, the best in town, just to show the world that he had, in the end, trumped poor old James. That was how much he hated losing.

Since then he hadn't lost much. He got the girls he wanted and when he was ready to settle down he got the wife he wanted. When that didn't satisfy, he went back to getting the girls he wanted. He got the job he wanted, with the office he wanted. He wasn't exactly rich, but he pretty much had the money he wanted when he wanted it. His job gave him a finger in a huge number of corporate pies so if he decided he needed more he was certain he could get that too.

Then Claire had to go and take what was his. His trophies, his pictures of the other girls and his rabbit hole. The money wasn't half as important as the pictures were. They were his trophies. He counted out his reasons on thick, drunken fingers. They were his means of controlling the girls. They were his means of incriminating Claire if need be. Most importantly, they could be used to incriminate him. They had to be gotten back.

He looked at his smartphone. It was almost one in the morning.

Obviously, Claire was not calling tonight. Tony had other means of forcing the issue but for now he would bide his time.

Vong took a deep breath before approaching the table. Amy Talba and Christy Henderson were way out of her league socially. Christy seemed nice enough, but Vong knew not to push her luck. But they all three had something in common, Clark.

"Hey guys," she said as she stood over the table where they were studying. The two girls looked up.

"Yes," the girls smiled what Vong interpreted as the 'being nice to the ugly people' smile.

"Um, you guys are friends with Clark too, right?"

"Yeah." It was Amy that responded and she responded automatically. She went up a notch in Vong's mind because she hadn't hesitated to acknowledge that friendship. Hell, Vong thought twice before acknowledging being friends with Clark. After all he had taken at least one beating over it and she had been teased about her "new boyfriend." It didn't really bother Vong, who was teased all the time anyway but surely Amy and Christy would be afraid to bring teasing on themselves, wouldn't they?

"He's not at school today." Vong said.

"He's often sick." Christy said. This was pretty common knowledge but also the point of Vong's foray into the social A club.

She sat down hurriedly. "I know, but I think this is different. He wasn't here yesterday and last night his mom called me, asking if I had seen him."

"Really?" Amy asked, "why?"

"Well I guess he claimed he was bringing me a computer." Vong said, "but he never came to my place. Then he wasn't at school and then his mom said he never came home. I called this morning, and she hasn't seen him all night either. I'm worried."

"Do you think somebody did something to him?" Christy asked Amy.

"I don't think so. The guys don't like him much, but it's all talk." Amy replied, "could he have been kidnapped or something?"

"Or ran away?" Christy said, "that would make more sense."

"What about that Tony guy?" This was Vong's theory. Vong had seen Tony Pirella once or twice around town and had come to the conclusion that he looked like a gangster.

"I doubt that." Amy said.

"I still say that him running away makes the most sense," Christy said, "your boyfriend and his friends tease him so bad, I'd run away."

"I've told him to knock it off a hundred times." Amy said sourly, "but he won't listen."

"If John's driven Clark away, I won't ever forgive him." Vong said stubbornly. She looked fearfully at Amy.

To her surprise Amy said, "me either."

######

Clarissa knocked on the door and waited. A boy opened the door a crack and peered out suspiciously. "Who is it?" The boy asked.

Clarissa paused, almost tripping over the name, "Melissa Holdenfield."

The door opened to admit her into a small apartment living room. The boy went over to a large machine, where another man in his early twenties was working on a laptop. Three college boys sat on a couch talking quietly. A female of about the same age sat on a recliner nearby, listening to them.

"What's wrong with it?" The middle boy said, gesturing at the Iowa Hawkeye's T-shirt he was wearing.

"Dude," the boy to his right said, "We are supposed to be from Arkansas. That's where the machine is from," he gestured at the other two men, "that's what our fakes are going to say. Why would someone from Arkansas be wearing a Hawkeye's T-shirt?"

"Because I knew I was going to go to Iowa." The boy replied.

Clarissa found a kitchen chair and had a seat. She was exhausted. It had been fun, at first, to play the spy and have so many aliases, but it got tiresome quick. She had been Kelly Holden from Grundy Center to Des Moines. It was a foolish alias; it would be seen through as soon as the authorities started looking for Clark.

But that couldn't be helped. She had needed a name to get the bus ticket. She needed to put as much time and distance between herself and Grundy Center before using Clarissa.

Des Moines had been a blur. She had found the public library was thankfully only a few blocks from the bus station. She had spent the entire morning there working on her laptop. She had set up an internet bank account for Clarissa with a portion of the money from Tony's Swiss account. She sat up a couple of numbered accounts of her own at one of the Swiss banks, so she could move the money out of his grasp.

The bank account had required her to first find the nearest post office and set up a P.O. box as a dummy address. Her new credit card would come in a couple of days. Until then she needed to survive off of what cash she had.

She had discovered in her earlier research about running away that there were cheap hotels in Des Moines that took cash. They were mostly down town and mostly catered to the homeless population. That option, quite frankly, terrified Clarissa.

The rest of the downtown hotels tended to be pricey and only took credit. So instead she found a hotel further out. She had grabbed a bus schedule at the library and rode down to the south side and checked in for the night. She couldn't afford to stay until her card came, but she didn't want to stay in Des Moines anyway. She had other business.

She wired almost two thousand in cash to a bank in Iowa City. Then she activated an online persona she had created in hopes of going to college in cognito. It wasn't as complete as the Clarissa identity but she could perhaps get a few days of subsidized housing out of it. She bought a pre-paid phone at a Walgreens on her way out to the hotel. She called the admissions department at the University of Iowa saying she would be in town the next day and could she tour the place? They were quite agreeable and even set her up in temporary student housing for the night.

It was late afternoon by the time she checked into the hotel. She had been awake for over twenty four hours and she was exhausted. She barely managed to stay awake long enough to eat the room service meal she ordered.

The next morning, she bought a ticket from Des Moines to Iowa City in cash under the name Claire Holly. She had arrived in Iowa City and had been greeted by a U of I recruiter as Melissa Holdenfield, a seventeen-year-old girl from Omaha Nebraska. A girl whose fake high school records made her a great candidate for a full ride scholarship next year. She got a tour around campus, which she didn't need, and a place to stay the night, which she did.

She had spent the afternoon, when she had supposedly been reading the many pamphlets the recruiter gave her, loading visa check cards into another bank account. She had gotten her cash from the bank and purchased ten visa check cards at the mall in downtown Iowa City. It was a slow process, but she needed a thousand dollars or so on a credit card that couldn't be traced to either Clark or Clarissa. Melissa had enough of a legal existence to do that, barely.

Now she had two weeks and two more destinations before leaving for good. She needed a couple more identities. She didn't have the time to create them, but they didn't have to be foolproof and thankfully there were the good old boys at Rho Epsilon.

The fraternity had somehow come into possession of a driver's license printing machine. They had hacked it with a laptop and taken it from its home in Arkansas on a cross country trip. It was a trip that was earning them thousands selling fake ID's. She had learned about it online and made an appointment.

CHAPTER FIFTEEN

Sheriff Gaskell took off his wide brimmed hat as he entered Kelly's house. A sense of foreboding had filled her the moment she had seen him pull into the driveway.

"Have you found something?" It was eight thirty in the morning. Kelly had called into to work. There was no way she could handle it in the state she was in. Clark had not come home again last night and she was beside herself.

"No, nothing," he said. "I'm just here to, well, bend the rules a bit I guess. I saw your car and I thought, we are supposed to wait forty-eight hours from your report but really, it's been forty-eight hours since anyone has seen your boy. If he ain't back, I can get my boys investigating."

"Thank you." She gushed.

"We start with the worst possibility, even though it's the most unlikely." The sheriff said, settling himself at the kitchen table and pulling out a notebook. "Anyone threaten your son recently?"

"Some of the kids at school." Kelly answered.

"Do you know their names?" He asked.

She shook her head. "No."

"It's a far reach. Besides, it'll be easy to check. Your son disappeared during the day, so we can check attendance records and know if anyone else was out that day. I'll put one of the boys on it. Anyone else?"

She shook her head and then said slowly, "well he didn't ever threaten him, but I couldn't help thinking, could this have anything to do with the Pirellas?"

"Do you have any reason to suspect Tony was involved?" The sheriff asked. He apparently knew enough local gossip to know that Shelley and the kids were out of the picture for now.

"Not really," Kelly admitted, "but Tony stopped by last night asking for Clark. He wouldn't say what he wanted but he said it was important. And..." she trailed off.

"And what?" The sheriff prompted.

"I don't know but Clark has been acting odd lately and I can't help but think it all started about the time Shelley left town. At first I thought it was just losing the job but it seemed like he was too upset for it to just be about a job."

The sheriff nodded thoughtfully. "It won't hurt to have a deputy stop by and ask some questions there. Any other theories?"

"Could he have been abducted?" She asked.

"Non-family abductions are pretty rare," the sheriff said. "Plus, it was broad daylight. If it was something like that I am sure someone would have seen something. It's a small community, word will get around that he is gone and people will start coming forward."

She nodded dully.

"Now let's deal with the more likely issue. Has he said anything to make you think he might run away?"

"He has been acting a little funny lately, but we had a huge talk just yesterday and he promised he wasn't planning to do something rash."

"Why did you ask him that?" He asked.

"What do you mean?" Kelly said.

"Why did you ask him not to do anything rash?" The sheriff persisted, "what did you think he was going to do?"

"I don't know." She replied, "he'd been acting oddly, like I said, and I thought maybe he was..." the word died on her lips. Her heart started racing suddenly and she felt herself go pale.

"Ma'am," the sheriff said, his voice full of concern, "are you okay?"

She wasn't sure she would ever be okay again. "I thought maybe he was suicidal." It was barely a whisper.

The sheriff's face was impassive. "I'll let the fire department know and we'll run a standard search." He reached out and put his hand on hers, "we'll treat it as a possibility, but hope for the best. Usually suicidal people leave a note or contact someone before attempting. Let's continue to assume he's alive, okay?"

She nodded dully.

"If he has run away, where do you think he might go?" He asked.

"I don't have any idea." She replied.

"Any friends, family, that sort of thing?" He asked.

She gave him Marcus's number but said she'd already called and he wasn't there. The Sheriff promised to drive over and check it out in person. He also took down names and phone numbers for anyone that might know where Clark was or might have any information where he might have gone, or even know something about Clark that would help the police guess where he might have gone. It was a short list. She gave them Vong's number too. Those two, Philip, Elizabeth; as far as she knew pretty much the sum total of her son's existence.

"Now here's the thing," the sheriff said as he stood to go. "My deputies have made some preliminary inquiries." He paused, as if searching for the words. "It seems your son had something of a reputation around town." She felt her blood chill. "Now kids like that often run away. And when they do, they don't run for family or friends. They head for a big city, one with a community, you know."

"What are you saying?" Her eyes narrowed suspiciously.

"I am saying that the best chance we have of finding your son is for me to make sure there isn't any indication that he's hiding out locally. Then I can get someone with a broader jurisdiction involved, like the FBI."

#######

"So the little faggot is actually gone? Like gone gone?" Randy mused.

"That's what the rumor is," John said. "It's been a couple of days since he's been in school."

"Do think he's really ran away though?" One of the guys asked.

John just shrugged, "I for one, don't care. I'm glad he's gone."

"Think we scared him off?" Randy asked.

Again John shrugged.

"And what exactly is that supposed to mean?" A shrill voice asked at his back. John turned slowly to face his girlfriend's wrath.

"John Mort!" Amy screamed. "You will explain what you meant by 'scared him off,' now."

"Nothing."

"Nothing?"

Unfortunately for John, Randy was ready to talk. "We just explained to him how we felt about his constantly throwing his sexuality in our faces."

She rounded on Randy. "Did you hurt him?" She demanded, "did you?"

"No," John answered, "we never laid a finger on him, not that it's any of your business."

"We just told him what he had coming." Randy said.

"You did threaten him then?"

"Why are you always defending him?" John sneered. "He's just some fag."

"He's a really sweet person who wouldn't hurt a soul. If you've driven him off I'll..."

"You'll what?" John was mad now too. "So, we laid down the law with a little fag. We told him if he didn't cut his hair, we would. We told him if he kept acting all flaming around here, somebody would kill him. We never said we'd do it."

"You did threaten him."

"Is he your boyfriend, or am I?" John demanded.

"Neither!" She said turning on her heels and storming off.

"Humpfh." Randy said at her retreating back, "she ain't serious. She'll be back. She always is." John, watching her walk away, wondered if that was true.

Jeremy approached his mother. "Still no sign of him?"

She merely nodded. She was sitting in the recliner that grandpa usually used when he came over. She was just sitting there.

"Can I get you anything?" He felt protective suddenly.

She nodded no again. Then she seemed to come to herself. "The sheriff came by this morning. Took the report and started an investigation."

"He's really gone?" He asked.

She nodded.

"What do they think happened?" He asked.

"They think he ran away." She said.

"They don't think he was... you know."

"Murdered? Kidnapped?" Both thoughts had crossed his mind, and obviously his mother's as well. "No." She answered. "They are investigating as though those are possibilities but they don't think so."

"How can they know?"

She merely shrugged.

"Did they say where they think he's ran away to?" This was always the sticking point with the running away theory, his brother didn't have anywhere to go.

"They think he ran away to a 'big city' where there's a 'community'."

"What sort of community?" He asked.

"A gay community," she answered, "apparently that is what everyone thinks of my son."

The doorbell rang. Jeremy stood back as his mother went to answer it. Standing on the front step of their house was a pale faced blond girl with tears running down her cheeks.

"Mrs. Holden?" Amy said, "I think I know why your son ran away."

######

"Kelly, Jeremy," Sheriff Gaskell said by way of introduction, "This is officer Rod."

Officer Rod was tall and broad. He had a sharp chin and a hooked nose. His hair was dark and cut in buzz cut. His eyes were dark and menacing.

"Officer Rod's a really nice guy once you get to know him," the sheriff assured them. "He's been my point man on this investigation." He paused reflectively, "Steve's got a talent for certain kinds of interviews. I thought he'd work perfectly for this job."

"Talent?" Jeremy wondered aloud. Officer Rod scowled and let out a low hum of disapproval. Jeremy quailed and took a step back. To both his and Kelly's surprise the sheriff laughed and Officer Rod gave them a lopsided grin.

"Yeah," he said, "the boys were rather eager to spill the beans. They ratted each other out in record time." He scowled again and took a step towards Jeremy, "you know that statement alone could be taken as verbal harassment in the first degree..." He growled. He gave another lopsided grin at Jeremy's look of horror. Then he turned more serious and turned towards Kelly.

"They didn't do anything to your son, ma'am."

"We already pretty much knew that," the sheriff said. "They were all in school at that time."

"But they did threaten him. All four boys threatened to cut his hair off. One threatened to kill him and another threatened to rape him."

Kelly stared at him, mouth open. After several minutes shock began to give way to anger. "Who were they?" She said angrily.

"Now settle down ma'am. We can't reveal that right now."

"Are they being charged?" She demanded.

"Not at the present." Seeing the dangerous look in her eyes, the sheriff hurried on, "we are waiting for our investigation to be complete and then we will let the District Attorney decide about charges. For right now we know that the girl's story checks out, your son was threatened and that's probably why he fled."

"It happened Tuesday night, at the Kum and Go. The night before he left," Steve said.

The night of the intervention, she realized. He had stormed out. When he came back they had talked, but he hadn't mentioned being threatened.

"That's the night we had the big thing," Jeremy said.

"What thing?" The sheriff interjected.

"The... intervention thing, or whatever, when mom was worried he was going to kill himself." Jeremy said.

"We talked afterwards," Kelly said hurriedly, "he didn't say anything about threats. He just promised to try harder not to get into trouble and assured me he wasn't suicidal."

"Don't blame yourself, ma'am. And don't worry. I am sure none of the kids had anything direct to do with his disappearance. And I put the fear of god into them about the threats. When we find your son, he'll have no more trouble from those boys," he assured her.

Kelly turned on him angrily. "That's what the school kept telling me! It's not that serious. They didn't mean it. We have talked to them. It never changed a thing!" She glared at the sheriff.

Officer Rod grinned maliciously. "I talked to the school too," he said, "I think you will find them a tad more helpful in the future."

Kelly still felt angry but raging at the police would not get her son back safely. She bit back her anger and shrugged helplessly. "What do we do now?" She felt close to tears but bit them back.

"We have looked into most of the local leads at this point. We can't find any evidence of foul play or anything like that," the sheriff said. "I've had the volunteer fire department out all day doing searches of any likely place, but they haven't turned anything up either, thankfully."

"Has anyone talked to Tony?" Kelly asked, thinking of the strange conversation she had with the man.

Officer Rod nodded. "He's a tough cookie, that one," he said with grudging respect. He sat heavily into one of the kitchen chairs. "Good poker face. He said he doesn't know anything at all about Clark's disappearance."

"You think otherwise?" The sheriff asked.

"Not sure, sir. He's hard to read but there's something going on there. The incident at the Kum and Go? Clark ran and got into a black Jeep Grand Cherokee. All four boys were consistent on that point."

"Tony drives a jeep," Kelley said. Clark hadn't mentioned Tony either that night she thought to herself.

"That alone makes him a person of interest in this case." Officer

Rod said.

"If it's his jeep," the sheriff put in.

Officer Rod nodded and went on, "I would upgrade that to primary suspect except for the fact that you saw Clark after he spoke with Tony. Tony claims he was surprised to find the boy was gone but I don't trust him."

"Why is that?" The sheriff wanted to know.

"He was dropping these hints but I can't tell if he was trying to tell me something about Clark, or trying to set up his own case for the divorce court."

"How are they related?" Kelly wondered.

"For one thing, he mentioned that he didn't think the discovery on their assets looked right. He made it clear that he couldn't pin point any particular item of value missing, said his wife had lots of jewelry and sometimes kept more cash around then he liked."

"He thinks my son stole from him?" Kelly asked.

"That's the funny thing. He made it clear that he couldn't pin point anything that would hold up in court and that he doesn't want to press charges or anything. Said he kind of likes the kid, you know." It was a fair impression. "He just thought we ought to know that maybe Clark has some assets. Thinks we need to 'think broader'."

"What does that mean?" The sheriff wondered.

"I asked," Steve went on, "he meant the kid might have money for bus fare, hotels, etc. And that we might not be looking for someone hitch hiking, that kind of thing."

Kelly much preferred to think of her son riding a bus somewhere then hitch hiking but she wanted him home more than anything else.

"Anything else?" The sheriff asked Officer Rod.

"Yeah, and this one burned my ass. I tried to get him to tell me why he wanted to talk to Clark the night after he went missing. He told me it was none of my business." Steve scowled. "He mentioned he's doing an investigation too. I read him the riot act. I told him it was our business if we thought it was. He wouldn't back down. He said it had to do with work or something and wanted us, can you believe this? He wanted us to give him access to Clark's computer. He thinks he can track the boy down if we do."

"Mr. Rod, sir?" Jeremy interrupted nervously.

"Yes, son." He turned to Jeremy.

"My brother used to talk a lot about computers and about Tony. Clark was the smartest person I ever met and he learned a ton about computers in no time from this Tony. If he says he can track Clark, he might be able to." Jeremy said.

"Well he isn't getting any cooperation from us until we understand his part in Clark's disappearance." The sheriff groused. "And he's still our official person of interest. As far as finding your boy, I think this case is out of my hands. Mrs. Holden I'd bet my life your son is out of this vicinity. I think our best chance of finding him is to turn it over to the FBI missing person's bureau, first thing tomorrow morning."

######

The phone rang at eight thirty the next morning. Kelly had called in from work again. Her boss said he understood and told her to take the rest of week if she needed to. She grabbed for the phone. "Hello, this Kelly Holden speaking."

"Kelly, this is Agent Ronald Hodgekins, FBI. I am assigned your son's case and thought I would call and introduce myself."

"Thank you. It's nice to know this isn't sitting on somebody desk for days." Kelly said.

"Oh no, the quicker we can start looking the better our chances of finding him. I had them fax over their entire investigation and I have read through it."

"Do you have any thoughts?" Kelly asked.

"I tend to agree with the sheriff. I think your son's heading for one of the big cities. If I had to guess, I'd put money on San Francisco." He replied.

It infuriated her that everyone saw Clark's 'reputation' and made assumptions. "You know, my son always denied being gay, whatever people thought." She said defensively. *Didn't I make the same assumption?*

"Yes ma'am" Agent Hodgekins agreed, though it was obvious he didn't believe her. "But he was in therapy over identity issues, and according to his therapist he crossed dressed at least occasionally."

Kelly felt shocked to hear it said aloud. Then she felt chagrined. *I knew that,* she told herself, *why does it shock me that someone else knows?*

"If I were a teenage boy with identity issues who crossed dressed, I'd head for good old San Fran. 47% of homeless teens are LGBT. They tend to end up in large cities."

"LGBT?"

"Lesbian, Gay, Bisexual and Transgender." He explained. "They end up in large cities mostly, ones with reputations for having a community."

"Transgender," she said shakily. She had never heard it put together like that.

"What?"

"Transgender, my son said he thought he was transgender. He wanted to, to transition, or something, to take hormones and have some crazy surgery. I told him no. I said he was too young."

Oh my god, she thought suddenly, I'm the reason he ran. It wasn't the threats. It was me. Me and my refusal to even discuss that. Tears threatened to overwhelm her.

"Mrs. Holden?"

"Please, it's Kelly."

"Kelly?"

For a moment she couldn't answer, panic was clawing at her chest and tears were flowing. Finally, she managed to get out, "yes?"

"I am going to find your boy." His tone was calm and reassuring. He sounded confident and in control.

She took a deep breath and let it out. The tears receded momentarily. "Thank you," she said weakly.

"In fact, I have a question for you." He said.

"Shoot."

"Did you go to Des Moines, Iowa by bus on the morning your son disappeared?"

"No why?" She asked puzzled.

"Because someone named Kelly Holden did. And I am guessing it was your son."

"He's in Des Moines?"

"He was."

"Should I go there?" Hope rose in her chest. She could see herself speeding down the interstate towards her son.

"No. That was three days ago now. He could be anywhere. I've ran checks and found no Kelly Holden leaving Des Moines or checking into any hotels but he could have easily switched aliases. I've alerted the local authorities with your son's description and information. I've also talked to a couple of local youth shelters. I made it clear that he's in no danger if he returns, but their help is voluntary and often they don't volunteer. Still we will keep trying, but I doubt he stayed."

"Why not, it's as good of a place as any, isn't it?"

"Not really. It is cold in Iowa. For a homeless kid that's an important factor. There's some gay community but not much. Your boy will want a larger community."

"My son's not..."

"I know, but the trans community tends to go along with the gay community. And a big trans community spells safety for a kid like yours, plus other perks like black market hormones. Let's be realistic here, if your kids half the computer whiz the report makes him out to be, he's no doubt met other people like him online. He's probably got a place lined up where he can stay."

"I hope you're right Agent Hodgekins, I hope he's safe somewhere. What are the odds that you can find him?"

"It's not the dark ages and the FBI have a lot of resources the locals don't."

"You seem to have made progress already." She agreed hoping he was right.

"His love of computers will be his undoing. I'll talk to the attorneys and see if I can subpoena Mrs. Gant, the therapist in Iowa City. She can't legally violate confidentiality without that, but she sounded concerned when I called her this morning. I think she'll cooperate. And I am going to track this Tony character down.

He should have the IP addresses for Clark's computer on his router. If he can come up with those numbers, I am sure we'll find Clark sooner or later. Also if you could look around at home and call back with any email addresses, online profile names, anything he might have used, we'll watch the web for him. If need be I have a couple of computer experts on tap at the U of I. I can see about sending the boys around to look at your computer for themselves."

######

Kelley sat at her computer, intent on following Agent Hodgekin's advice as quickly as possible. She knew Clark was particular about his passwords and she had little hope of being able to access any of his online profiles, but she would try like his life depended on it. Who knew, maybe it did? The fact that someone had bought a bus ticket in her name was a huge relief. She should call the sheriff with that tidbit immediately. He could call off the searches and the dredging of the lake. Clark had left town alive under his own power.

Out of habit she opened her email. She shook her head angrily, she was supposed to be looking for information on Clark. Then she spied it, an email with the words "hey mom" in the subject line. She didn't recognize the address.

She opened the email and read it quickly.

Hey mom,

I saw the news last night, that they were searching local parks and stuff for my body. I am alive and well, so don't worry.

I can't say much right now except that things have gotten too complicated for me. There are too many things going on right now and I don't know what to do about most of them. There's one thing I do know I need to do so I'll start there.

Don't look for me. Just know I am alive and well. I love you very much. I know this is hurting you and I am sorry for that. Please don't hate me. I will be in contact later.

* * *

Clark

Kelly sat at the desk and cried with relief and guilt for so long that the screen went to sleep. She bumped the mouse to bring it back and typed a long rambling reply, telling her son that she loved him and if he would please come home they could work everything out.

Within moments of hitting the send button her reply came back with a notification that the address in question did not exist. She gave a snort of frustration. "Figures," she grumbled, "that boy is too smart for his own good."

######

"So, look," Tom cleared his throat and set down his Ipad, "it says here that National Mortgage Company announced today that it was hit by a cyber-attack. The article goes on to say that the attackers did not get into any sensitive information and," he leaned forward and emphasized his words carefully. "It seemed to be a targeted attack aimed at one employee inside the corporation."

Vong stared at him blankly. She had never been invited to sit with the A crowd at lunch before. But now Amy was making a huge point to diss John and the whole A crowd table by sitting with, of all people, Vong. Christy and Tom had come along for a ride. Vong wondered if this was the sort of conversations they usually had?

Apparently not, as Christy and Amy exchanged a puzzled look. "Now that Clark's gone I think your boyfriend is trying out for the geek spot." Amy teased.

Tom gave her an annoyed look. "Don't you get it?"

"Umm, no," Christy said.

"National Mortgage Company?"

The two girls exchanged another blank glance. "We don't get it, sorry," Amy groused.

"Tony's company, right?"

"Tony," Vong scowled, "I still say he had something to do with Clark's leaving."

"I told you, John and Randy threatened him." Amy said with a dark look towards the A table.

Vong wasn't sure that this was the end of the story and apparently Tom didn't either.

"I would run if those goons were after me too," Tom said, "and I am on the football team with them. But I think there is more to this. Don't you think it's a little suspicious? Tony and Shelley split, their babysitter, who happens to be a computer whiz, disappears and suddenly Tony's company is announcing it got hacked?"

"Why would Clark want to hack Tony's work?" Christy asked.

"I don't know but remember what the article said, it was directed at one certain employee. What if Tony was that employee?"

"Why not just hack Tony's computer?" Christy asked. Amy blanched slightly and looked away.

"It doesn't work that way," Tom said irritably, lining up salt and pepper shakers to demonstrate as he talked. "Tony's computer is protected right?" He tapped a salt shaker to indicate it was Tony's computer. "So, you hack into his work and find one computer not protected." He tapped a pepper shaker. "Then you use that computer to send a signal to the server." He tapped Christy's tray, "Which allows it because it thinks it's this guy," he tapped the pepper again, "and it sends a signal to Tony's home computer which appears to be from the server, so it's allowed."

Christy stared at him. "You are trying out for the geek spot," she said. Vong giggled.

"How do you know all this?" Amy asked.

"Umm, Clark told me," Tom said in exasperation, "while you two were teasing me for missing all the underlying emotional crap I was actually hearing what he was saying."

"When he got to talking computers," Amy admitted sheepishly, "my eyes kind of glazed over."

Tom had one ally at least. "I'll bet it's related," Vong said. "I'll bet Tony's involved somehow. He's a bad character, that Tony."

Christy nodded politely. Amy paled slightly and looked away.

######

Clarissa fidgeted nervously as she sat on the hard-backed chair.

185

This was it. She looked around the federal office building. This was the true litmus test. If she made it through this hurdle her identity was as secure as possible. Her palms were slick with sweat and she rubbed them on her jeans. If she made it...

"Clarissa Holden?"

Clarissa smiled at the clerk. It was a thrill to hear her own name called, especially here. She made her way towards the desk. "Yes," she said brightly.

The clerk gave her a 'how dare you be so chipper' sort of look and tiredly handed her a small blue booklet.

She took it and opened it up. There was her picture, and her name. Clarissa Holden, United States Citizen.

"You must be going somewhere awful nice," the clerk commented enviously.

"Oh yeah," she replied, tucking the passport book into her purse, "trip of a lifetime."

She began to shake with relief. She turned and left quickly, hoping the clerk hadn't noticed.

CHAPTER SIXTEEN

Maybe I should start a new diet, Amy thought as she stared at the rail thin girl on the screen, something vegan this time, maybe raw foods. That was better than trying to cut portion size or restrict calories, wasn't it?

She knew she shouldn't be thinking this way. She had promised her mom and her therapist that she was going to start trying to learn to love her fat hideous self just the way it was. She wasn't sure how that was supposed to work but she had promised; no more diets.

Her eyes darted to her left arm, exposed as it never was at school. She pulled her eyes back to the computer screen. *Better to be looking at Pro-ana sites then that.*

She'd been in therapy awhile now and she knew the lingo. She was feeling out of control, in a big way. These feelings were triggers, triggers that made her want to starve herself or cut herself. The problem was that knowing this and being able to do something about it seemed to be two different things.

She had dumped John. The fact that she had dumped him, instead of the other way around was probably the only reason the break up hadn't sent her instantly into a spiral of cutting and starving. Still she didn't have someone to validate her anymore, to tell her she was beautiful and worthy of attention. John was like Tony in that way, he said all the right words. At least as long as you were playing his game.

She knew she shouldn't need that kind of validation, but she did. She had friends and that helped. It helped to talk to people that weren't interested her sexually. Christy had been a great support for years. Then Clark came back into her life after years of being closed off. It had felt nice. She remembered they had been good friends when they were young. It was sad how a handful of people had driven them apart and convinced him that everyone hated him.

They had talked, opened up about the issues that had kept them apart and she had felt better. Then he had left. As if this weren't enough suddenly everyone wanted to talk about Tony. The one name she hoped to never hear again. She could feel the darkness threatening her, it was only a matter of time before she would have to do something, cut or starve. Which was worse?

Then she noticed the corner tab. It read Facebook (1). She switched tabs and saw she had an instant message. Christy checking on her or John trying to get her back she thought sourly. At the bottom right hand side she saw "Clark". She froze. Clark? Clark who never used his Facebook. Clark who had been missing for close to a week.

"Amy," the message read, "I have something for you. Only I need something more secure than FB. Please give me an email."

She quickly typed in her gmail and waited. Then she noticed in the fine print, sent from mobile device. That made no sense, Clark didn't have a smartphone.

What could he possibly want? To tell her why he left? Where he was? She couldn't imagine that she would be the one he would turn to. Why not just call home? Or turn to Vong, he was closer to her than to Amy, at least Amy had thought so. It was hard to tell with him, he could be so closed down sometimes.

It was my boyfriend that drove him away, she thought guiltily, maybe he hates me now. Maybe that's what he wants to tell me. She could almost hear her therapist lecturing about negative assumptions, but she couldn't help it.

She didn't have long to wait, luckily. She opened up gmail and there was a message and an attachment.

* * *

Dear Amy,

I have a gift for you. I am afraid you won't like a big chunk of it but I didn't know what else to do. I have spent the last two days sitting in a hotel room staring at the walls. I know what comes next for me, but there was this one thing I couldn't leave without dealing with and I couldn't decide how to deal with it. Part of me says I should have handed this over to the authorities. It would be the right thing to do. Another part of me wanted to destroy this, just hit the delete button and forget about it.

I couldn't do either because in the end, this is yours. You need to know about it and you need to decide what to do with it. I took these from Tony's computer. There are three other files, mine included. There was money too, numbered international bank accounts. I suspect how the money was obtained and it's not his either.

So there you have it, there are four members of Tony's club. We each have one fourth of the money and all the pics and video that belong to us. We each can decide; destroy the evidence and take the money, or turn it over to the authorities and see what they do to Tony. I am sorry to put the burden on you but at least this way you have the satisfaction of knowing those pics aren't out there anymore.

As for me, I have a plan for my share of the money. As for my pics and my story, if you squeal on Tony, I'll send them to back you up. I'll even testify if I can do so safely.

Thank you for the friendship you've shown me the last few months. I have been in a very dark place but you made it bearable.

I have had the smallest glimpse of what you've been through. I have found my escape and I hope you do too. Until then please, take care of yourself and be stronger than that bastard.

Your friend,
Clark/Clarissa

With a dreadful certainty, Amy opened the attachment.
######
The chair was a red mushroomed-shaped cushion. The girl that sat on it wore bright blue stockings, a denim skirt and a yellow top. The laptop she was typing on was pink. Above this rainbow presentation was a sign that read, "Naruto International Airport" and "Welcome to Japan" in English and presumably, the same in Kanji characters.

Clarissa looked up and sighed. She stared at the laptop for a long time. She was feeling sentimental. She couldn't afford to be sentimental. They would catch her if she was sentimental. She stuck a USB flash drive in the side port and rebooted. Five minutes later it was done, the computer was as blank as the day it came out of the factory.

She got up and sat it down on the bench nearby. She hoisted her messenger bag, much lighter now. Overhead she heard, "Delta flight 153, to Bangkok, boarding in ten minutes." With one last look at the laptop she turned and walked away.
######
"Thank you for calling me so promptly." Agent Hodgekins said. "And you're absolutely right, now we know he's okay, at least he was when he sent that email. It also confirms our theory that he's ran away. That has to be a huge relief."

"To know my son's not dead in a ditch somewhere?" Kelly replied shakily. "Hell, yes." She rarely cussed. It felt strange but good to let it out now. "He's alive and well. I am very relieved." She sat down the notepad she had been toying with and then immediately picked it up again.

"I imagine a little pissed as well." He said

"That he's put me through all of this? Yeah, honestly," she replied, "but I am pissed at a lot of people right now, the kids that threatened him, the school that ignored it all, the therapist that led him on and told him about transition and all that."

"He'd have found out about that online anyway. I wouldn't waste too much time being mad at Dr. Wilson." Agent Hodgekins said, "what do you make of the email?"

"I thought that was your department?" Kelly responded.

He laughed. "Yeah, but I want your point of view first."

"I don't know what to make of it. It's so vague. If the guys threatened to kill him, I understand his being afraid, why not just say that? I have read it and read it but I still don't understand what's so complicated?"

"I don't know," Agent Hodgekins replied. "My guess would be that he's trying to protect you. That's common enough. He doesn't know that you know about the death threats and he's not going tell you either."

"What do you think he's planning?" Kelly asked, "he said he knew what he had to do, but what? What does that mean?"

"I think he's talking about transition," Agent Hodgekins said. "I am even more convinced that he's headed for San Fran, or somewhere similar. He's gotten some information about where he can get female hormones or something like that."

"Isn't that dangerous?" She said alarmed.

"Yes and no." Agent Hodgekins answered, "I talked over that possibility with Dr. Wilson at some length. It's risky from a medical standpoint to do hormones without medical supervision. But I am a cop and compared to running away without a plan and ending up on the street, I'd say it's relatively safe. Hormones take months to build up in the system and we'll find him before then."

"You seem pretty confident."

"The email is a great sign."

"It means he's safe right now, but other than that it doesn't mean much, does it?" Kelly asked.

"Yes, it does," he corrected her, "the fact that he's willing to communicate is huge. He might have some money now, or someone to bum off of. It won't last long and the life of a run-away isn't comfortable. If he ends up on the streets, or in a shelter, there's a good chance he'll call when the money runs out and want to come home on his own."

"You think so?"

"Oh yeah, the kids you see on TV, the ones that end up drug addicts or prostitutes, come from broken homes mostly. They have no choice. Clark's got a nice comfortable bed waiting if he'll man up to where he is. That's got be tempting and will get more so as his money runs out."

"I hope so."

"Besides, I told you, his love of technology will be his undoing. Forward that email to me like I asked and we'll know exactly where he sent it from. Every communication he makes will give him away. And Tony's being super cooperative about giving us those numbers to start searching for his laptop."

There was something about the way Agent Hodgekins said 'super cooperative' that made her wonder what was going on that she didn't know about. She still thought that Tony Pirella had some involvement in her son's disappearance but she couldn't understand what. "Why would Tony care?"

"Well he says he took a shine to the boy." He said, "but I don't think that's all there is too it. He wants to talk to Clark about something. He won't say what."

"Do you have ideas?" Kelly asked.

"Well it wouldn't be a big stretch to think maybe Clark took some money from the Pirella's to fund this whole get away."

"You think my son stole?" Kelly asked sharply. "Clark is not a thief!"

"Maybe not normally," Agent Hodgekins said quickly, "but if he felt it was his life at stake, it would be easy to bend the rules. Besides Tony's hinted to something like that but he says he doesn't want to make a report because he can't really prove anything. It appears Shelley isn't talking to him either, so he has no way to confirm what she took and what she didn't."

The truth was that Agent Hodgekins was not even sure it was money that Tony was concerned about. He had his own suspicions. He did not tell Kelly that he already had discovered one of Clark's online names on his own; Miss Claire. He had shown Tony a picture of Miss Claire and said simply, "I wonder who took this picture?" Tony had blanched. He recovered quickly and explained that he had taken the picture to help out the boy, who had some gender issues. Hodgekins immediately suspected there was more going on. On a hunch, he asked if Shelley knew about Clark's cross dressing. Tony danced around the question. Hodgekins couldn't push the issue, he had no proof, and Tony knew he didn't. But it had shaken the perv. Hodgekins had the guy by the balls and wasn't about to let up until he had Clark and his mother reunited. Tony was a top notched computer security expert, and Hodgekins intended to milk that resource for all it was worth.

#######

"So, where do you think he's gone?" Christy wondered aloud. Amy didn't have to ask who she was talking about, it had been the subject of conversation on and off for the last week. Amy shrugged irritably as if to say, "I still don't know."

A gun went off and a group of runners took off down the track. They watched them go from the sidelines. Amy went back to her stretching. Christy and Amy ran the relays which weren't for another several heats.

"I don't have a clue," Amy said. "People keep saying San Francisco, because that's where all the gay people are but I think that's too cliché for Clark. Besides he is trans, not gay, right?"

"Well they aren't that far apart," Christy said, "but I agree, he won't do the expected."

"I miss him." Amy said.

"Me too," Christy agreed. "He was fun to talk to."

"You must be talking about Clark," a voice interrupted. The owner of the voice was a slender boy with mid length dirty blond hair hanging down in his face. He had on tight boy's jeans, a pink polo T-shirt and bright yellow sneakers. He stood with his weight on one leg, and other hip jutted out.

"Fag." One of boys muttered as he went by. The boy made a sarcastic "o" face and put his hand to his mouth as though he were scandalized.

"Don't talk to my girlfriend," John said as he went by.

"I am not your girlfriend, convict!" Amy shouted hotly at his back. It hadn't gone anywhere, but the police had filed preliminary charges against both John and Randy for verbal harassment.

"Whatever," he replied. He fully expected that they would make up any day now. The belief was being tested sorely with each passing day.

"What makes you think we are talking about Clark?" Christy asked the boy.

"Well," he said ticking things off on his hand, "you said San Francisco, you said he wouldn't do the expected, both of which sound like Clark. Besides I recognize the two of you from a picture he had on his phone."

"You're a friend of his too?" Amy asked

"Marcus," the boy said, putting his hand on his chest. "I don't normally go for sports, they make you sweaty. I don't do away meets either, but I volunteered to be water boy for today because I thought I might find you two or that Asian chick." He sat down next to them and said, "I miss him too."

"How did you know him?" Amy asked.

"We were in a group for LGBT youths together." Marcus said. "I am gay."

"Were you and him..." Christy asked suddenly, "boyfriends?"

"Eww." Marcus replied, "not a chance. We both like the same thing," he explained matter of factly, "tough guys." Amy giggled.

Christy's eyes went wide. "Clark and Tony?" She asked. Amy looked away, uncomfortable.

"No." He replied, "well sort of, it didn't go anywhere. I would have. Clark was too romantic. You didn't know?"

"No. Spill." Christie said.

Marcus was glad to, "Clark, or perhaps I should say Clarissa, dressed for the old perv more than once, but they never, you know. I kept telling her to go for it, how often do you get a chance to score with a guy like Tony? He's built like a brick house."

"OMG!" Amy said laughing uncomfortably, "you are like, so out there."

Marcus smiled sheepishly. "Out is my middle name."

"Tony knew Clark cross dressed?" Christy asked, stunned.

"Yeah."

"So," Christy said, "since you seem to know so much, where's he's going?"

Marcus moaned, "I don't know. He just up and left. I got an email from him saying he was okay but he didn't want to say where he was in case they came looking."

"Do you think they will? Come looking for you that is?" Christy asked.

"They already have!" He said throwing his arms in the air. "The police took a report the day he went missing, and I got a call from the FBI."

"The FBI called you?" Amy had never met anyone who had been directly contacted by the FBI.

"Yeah." Marcus puffed up, happy to be the center of attention, "I didn't tell them anything, because I don't know that much anyway. But I do know this," he leaned in conspiratorially, "he had a plan."

"A plan?" Christy asked.

"Oh yeah, this isn't some random run-away sort of thing. We made these fake ID's. Mine was crap but I didn't care. It got me into the gay bar in Iowa City, and that's all I really care about. But Clark was obsessed with getting everything perfect. He wanted to be able to run away and completely assume this new identity as Clarissa. He had everything; birth certificate, social security card, everything. He even made me go with him to Kirkwood community college so he could take the GED in drag."

"This is so cool." Amy enthused. "It's like a spy thriller. Plus, I hate the notion of Clark trying to live on the streets somewhere. I hope he is living as Clarissa somewhere, safe and sound."

"He's probably setting up a computer shop as we speak." Christy added.

"He was certainly one of a kind." Amy said.

######

"I have some really good news, some not so good news, and

some really bad news." Agent Hodgekins said by way of greeting.

"Please, go ahead," Kelly said. It had been only two days since she had forwarded Clark's email. She must have read the email a half million times, trying to decipher anything more out of it. She had been to work once, but she was so distracted that her boss sent her home. She had been hoping to hear something, anything, from Clark or from the FBI.

"The good news is that we have had a rather remarkable break. You know Clark made the news?" Kelly had been interviewed by one of the local news stations and they had ran about a minute and half on Clark's disappearance. "We got a lead. A couple of college boys in Iowa City saw something interesting. They called saying that they were unsure if this meant anything or not but they had seen this young girl who looked like she could have been that boy's twin sister."

"So?" Kelly asked.

"It's time to be honest, Kelly. You know your son was a cross dresser. I have found an online profile for him too, under the name Claire. The boys saw this girl at, well it's somewhat dubious how they saw him at all, but there was a black-market ID ring through Iowa City recently and this girl was there."

"A black-market ID ring? What do you mean?"

"They were making fake ID's for college students," he explained. "It's illegal and we do our best to shut those sorts of things down, but the demand is high. This group was using a stolen machine to manufacture driver's licenses."

But none of that's important. What's important is this. This girl who looked a lot like the boy they had seen in the news was there getting a couple of fake ID's. That was the first thing that made them notice her." He said. "The other things that stood out to the boys was that she kept feeding the ID people some really specific information. She was obsessed with having the right numbers, dates, etc."

"And this is a break because?" Kelly said, still not following what he was saying.

"We've been looking for the wrong gender, for starters. We have sent out hundreds of APB's to other agencies and local authorities based on your son's school picture and description. That isn't going to lead anywhere if he's going around in drag."

"Surely they'll see through that."

"I take it you haven't seen your son in drag."

"What does that mean?" She groused.

"Well let's just assume that they won't see through it and if he's got an ID that says he's female, he'll be completely off our radar if we don't recognize that fact and address it accordingly."

"Okay fine, I'll take your word for it, what else? How will this help find him?"

"We got some names. That will be a huge help. I am already realizing your kid isn't no ordinary run away."

"Just now?" She chided him.

"I am not referring to the gender thing, Kelly, I am referring to your kid being smarter than a whip."

That caught her off guard. "Yes, he is."

"The first alias the boys gave was Melissa. That was the girl's supposed real name. It seems that a Melissa Hollyfield had spent the day being shown around the university and had even spent the night in student housing, as a potential scholarship candidate. At least she was a candidate until it turned out her records were fake. She's since disappeared anyway."

"Now they gave me at least one other good solid alias, Claire Holden. We are currently searching for that name. There was another Melissa, with a different last name, but they couldn't remember what. Still it's something to go on."

Kelly's head was spinning with the news that her son was not only impersonating a girl, and doing it successfully, but was impersonating multiple girls and creating fake identifications for them too.

"You said something about bad news?" She asked, pressing on.

"The not so good news, yeah, that email, the address was hidden"

"Hidden?" She echoed.

"It can be done. I talked with Tony and he sheepishly admitted that he might have told Clark how to do that."

"He told my son how to hide his email address?" Kelly asked archly.

"Oh, that's only the beginning. Apparently, Clark was something of a protégé. Tony 'might have' mentioned a dozen of hacks and tricks on the computer. It's going to make finding Clark a bit more of a challenge."

"What does that mean?" Kelly asked. Her head was spinning and she sat down heavily in her chair.

"That means it's more important than ever to keep Tony under thumb and helping our cyber guys."

"And how exactly are you keeping Tony under thumb?" She asked sharply, suspicions rising in her.

"Honestly?" He paused awhile, picking his words carefully, "while we have no reason to believe that anything inappropriate occurred, we know that Tony was aware of your son's crossdressing."

"And?"

"That's it. But let's just say a thirty-five-year-old man letting a sixteen-year-old boy crossdress in his house could lead to rumors."

"That my son was his lover?"

"Like I said, we have no evidence that that was the case. Tony says he took pity on the boy at first, and that they became friends when he figured out the kid was smart and liked computers. He taught him a bunch of stuff, stuff that will now make him a lot harder to track."

"How do you know he was aware of the cross dressing? Should I be worried about what happened over there?" Kelly persisted.

"Honestly, I can't say." Agent Hodgekins said, "Here's what we have. I found a Facebook page for Miss Claire. It's obviously your son. The pictures are pretty harmless, by the way, nothing revealing. The thing is, he obviously didn't take those pictures himself and it's obvious that some are inside the Pirella's house."

"Tony's admitted that he might have taken some pictures, to humor the kid. He says nothing else happened. I couldn't say anything more without talking to Clark or Tony's wife. If she knew what was going on, it was probably harmless but if she didn't just talking to her would be enough to trash Tony's reputation in the community. I strongly suspect that is why he's being so helpful right now. As far as Clark goes, I will ask him about it, when I find him."

"If Tony did something to my son, I'll have his hide," Kelly said vehemently.

"You and me both," Agent Hodgekins assured her, "but remember I said there was some really bad news too."

"What?" Her heart leaped in her throat.

"Well Tony's got at least one legitimate reason for wanting to talk to Clark so bad." Agent Hodgekins said.

"What's that?"

There was a pause. "It seems your boy has been named as a person of interest in the recent cyber-attack on Tony's employer."

"What?"

"They think he did it but they don't have any real evidence to make him a suspect."

"But why would Clark hack into Tony's corporation? That makes no sense."

"Without knowing the details of the attack, it's hard to say. And they aren't releasing that information yet."

"Not even to the FBI?" Kelly was incredulous.

"Oh no," Agent Hodgekins corrected her, "the FBI cybercrime department is involved already but they aren't releasing anything publicly, or to us down here in missing persons."

######

"We're with the FBI." Eric said again.

"Newly deputized." Terry added.

The two were, Kelly had already decided, two of the strangest people she had ever met. Eric Stallon had long dark hair, which hung loosely down either shoulder. The effect wasn't either feminine or 'hippy', he merely looked like he couldn't be bothered to get a haircut. He wore a black t-shirt that said, "Today is not a good day to die, how's next Tuesday?" It rode up his belly. He wasn't obese, but he was definitely overweight, and carried most of it around his gut.

His partner Terry MacMillon was short and thin. He had nondescript shaggy brown hair and John Lennon spectacles. He wore dirty blue jeans, a faded flannel shirt and t-shirt. His t-shirt had a long mathematical equation across the front and under it, "yes, actually it is rocket science."

Eric's android smartphone buzzed again. He touched it nervously and it went silent. It had been this way since they had arrived. One or the other's phone was constantly buzzing with texts, calls or something. Kelly would have written them both off as shiftless homeless beggars if it weren't for the rather nice Toyota Prius they had arrived in, the obvious expense of their phones, the constant attention these phones seem to require and not to mention the badges they had shown her.

"You are with the FBI?" She said again. They looked nothing like what she thought an FBI agent should look like.

"Newly deputized." Terry said again.

"Doesn't it take years of training to be in the FBI?"

"It takes a minimum of four years in criminal studies, plus police academy, plus the FBI's own academy." Eric told her.

"But sometimes they bend the rules a little." Terry smiled.

"But it takes nine months, two weeks and three days to learn everything you need to know to circumvent the FBI," Eric said brightly. "At least if you are Claire."

This conversation was getting more and more confusing. "You said something about the university?" Kelly asked, "and who is Claire?"

"University of Iowa, Computer programming department," Eric said. "We've been consulted,"

"And deputized," Terry added. He seemed enormously excited about this fact.

"To help find Claire." Eric finished.

"Claire?" She repeated again.

"Your son Clark." As soon as Eric said it Kelly felt chagrined. That was one of the alias Clark had been using.

"Yeah, all this time I thought Tony as holding out on us because his new protégé was a cute girl. I'd have never thought she'd turn out to be a boy." Terry said.

"You guys know my son?"

"Yes and no." Eric said, "we talked online, but never met."

"What did you talk about?" Kelly asked.

"Computers." The two men said together and then exchanged a look that said, 'what else would anyone talk about?'

"And now the FBI wants you two to find him." Kelly persisted.

"I thought the proper etiquette for Transgender people was 'she'" Eric said to Terry.

"Yes," Terry replied, "but maybe mom doesn't know."

"I'm in the room." Kelly said.

"Maybe she didn't know Claire was trans?" Eric went on as though she had not spoken, "you didn't."

"Like you did?" Terry shot back, "You totally thought she was a girl."

"I only saw pictures. I remain confident that if I had met her in person, I would have known." Eric continued.

"Oh, and I suppose you knew that Shelly Tondall at IT&T used to be a boy?" Terry countered.

"No," Eric said amenably, "I did not know that. That's Shelly from the conference?" Terry nodded. "Okay I concede, it is possible that I would not have known."

"I knew my son was transgender," Kelly said irritated. "What's the point?"

The two men looked at her and then at each other blankly for a moment. "Point? No point. We don't care that your son's gender identity." Eric said.

"We're more interested in her brain." Terry affirmed.

"And the FBI asked you to help because?" Kelly asked.

"They can't find her...him...Claire...Clark," Eric said.

"And you can?" Kelly asked.

"We've got a better shot than the feds, that's for sure." Terry said.

"But I thought they could find him. I mean they said they could track that email."

"They tried," Eric said.

"The ping came from inside the house," Terry said.

She just looked at him blankly.

"You know, the classic cult horror movie line?" Terry explained. "The call came from inside the house?"

"I think we need to back up," Eric told him. "They tried to track it. Every contact on the web is first initiated by a ping. It's a little subroutine that checks to make sure the line is open and the receiving port is operating. So we tracked the ping on that email and it came from your computer."

"What? He sent the email from my computer?" She looked around as if Clark might materialize from thin air.

Terry snorted. "A couple of the idiots in the FBI suggested that. They had a theory that she's hiding out locally and sneaking into the house." He snorted again to show how stupid he thought that idea was.

"So what's your theory?" Kelly asked.

"We don't have one." Eric told her, "yet. We need to look at your computer, which is why we are here."

#######

"Go on," Amy said to Christy, "I'll catch up."

Christy shot her a quick are-you-okay look and followed Tom down the hall. Amy lingered a moment watching them leave. Then she backtracked towards the girl with shaggy dishwater blond hair and western styled blouse, Debra Halloway. Debra was in their grade but the two had barely spoken in the two years they had shared the high school. It wasn't that Amy had anything against her, they just had nothing in common. Now she thought maybe they did.

"Debra?"

Debra startled and got a scared look in her eyes. "Umm yeah?"

"Can I talk to you about something?"

Debra gave her a suspicious look. So many in the A crowd were cliquish and stuck up. Was that her reputation too? "What about?"

Amy took a deep breath. This was the moment of truth. "Umm, an email."

Debra blanched and Amy knew she had guessed correctly. She put a hand on Debra's shoulder. The girl looked like she was about to cry. She started backing away. "What sort of email?" she asked warily.

Amy held her gaze, "you know what I'm talking about. I got one too." Understanding passed through Debra's eyes.

"What's there to talk about?"

"I want to know who the other girl is," Amy said, "For one thing."

"Other girl?"

"And I want to discuss what we're going to do about him." Amy said.

"Tony?" It was barely a whisper.

"No, Clark." Amy said sharply.

"Clark? The boy who ran away? How is he involved?"

"What did your letter say?" Amy asked suddenly. Debra blushed. "I know what was in the attachment, or I can guess," Amy told her, "the letter?"

"Not much. Just that they were mine and I should do what I thought was right. That and there's money too. There was no name or anything." She looked at Amy for confirmation, "what's this got to do with Clark?"

"You don't know?" Amy asked. She went on, "it was Clark, he was the last babysitter. He's..." She paused. Debra obviously didn't know about Clark. Would Clark want it known that he too had been one of Tony's victims? She felt suddenly reluctant. "He's the one who found our stuff. Now he's gone and I just heard today that the FBI is looking for him."

Debra's eyes went wide, "the FBI?"

"Yes," Amy stared at her intensely, "and there are only four people who know the truth, you, me, Clark and one other person. We've got to find that other person and the three of us have to help Clark."

CHAPTER SEVENTEEN

"Ms. Holden?"

Clarissa stood and bowed to the older Asian man. He raised an eyebrow, but didn't comment. She knew however, that she had scored a point on etiquette. He bowed back and then stood aside.

She entered his office, sat on the indicated seat and waited for him to go back to his side of the desk and sit down. He was, like most Thai people she had met, of an indeterminate age, anywhere from late thirties to high fifties. His dark hair was cut short and wavy. He wore wire rimmed glasses and had a smooth brown face. He favored her with a warm but serious look.

"Ms. Holden," He said. She fought the impulse to correct him with her first name. The books she had read about Thailand made it clear that formal etiquette was expected in work relationships. She would remain Ms. Holden for as long as she worked here. "Your credentials are quite impeccable." This was an overstatement, she had forged those credentials very carefully. They were good enough for the kind of job she was seeking, but not so high she couldn't meet them once she had the job. Or so she hoped.

"Thank you Mr. Prachong," she replied. Then she added impulsively, "Cap Kun Ka." It meant thank you.

"Kun Poo die passa Thai?" He replied, *do you speak Thai?*

"Nit noi." *A little bit.*

He nodded and went on in English, "good, at Hathon

204

International School we pride ourselves on top notched Western style education, with English proficiency as a focus. But the position we are currently hiring for is lower level education, with eight-year-old girls. Their command of English is not the best, obviously. Some Thai proficiency will serve you well."

He picked up his papers and shuffled them. "So, you are wanting a short-term contract – one quarter – or six weeks, why? Someone like you we might pick up on a more permanent basis."

Clarissa had already prepared her cover story, "That would be a great honor, Sir. But I am taking a semester off college for this experience. My parents would not approve of me staying longer."

"You plan to teach when you get home?"

"I am studying primary education," she lied. "With an emphasis on English as a second language. Even one quarter at Hathon will be quite a good point on my resume."

"The pay is not great," he said slowly.

"The pay is sufficient. It is not the primary reason for seeking the job."

"The experience," he provided.

Actually, she was looking forward to the experience, through the anxiety. She really had no idea how she would feel about trying to teach a class room of eight-year-old Thai girls to speak English. But that was not the reason for taking the job either.

She needed to earn enough to support herself for a few weeks while she hunted for a surgeon. She needed to turn her tourist visa into a work visa or leave the country in thirty days. More importantly she needed to stay off the radar. Surely the authorities would eventually crack the line of aliases and fake identities she had left behind, she had no illusions about that.

This was her last line of defense. When they found out about Clarissa, they'd find the passport and the airline ticket. That would bring them as far as Thailand.

Here, hopefully, official help would end. The Thai government was a quagmire of bureaucracy. There would be no quick computer search. Her short stay had already confirmed that. She had showed the same paperwork to a half dozen people and it was always copied by Xerox. So far, she had managed to avoid scanning anything since leaving immigration.

The State Department would still search, no doubt. At best, they'd be searching for a run-away boy. At worst, they'd have caught on to her identity issues, and be looking for a Transwoman, or Kathoey as they were called in Thailand. But in either case they'd be looking for a tourist. Hathon was in Northern Bangkok, close enough to search on her days off, but off the beaten track for tourists. Or so she hoped.

She studied Mr. Prachong and said, "it will be the experience of a lifetime, I am sure."

"Ubuntu, configured to look like Windows." Eric said as he booted up Kelly's computer. The last few minutes had done nothing to change her opinion that these were the oddest two men she had ever met.

"Yeah, my friend Judith forwarded me this news clip on Facebook," she began, "well I thought it was from Judith..."

"So you clicked the link." Terry provided.

"And poof, Windows went down in blaze of malware," Eric finished.

"Yes." She said sheepishly. "I was going to try system restore, but Clark said, well, he said he didn't trust me with Windows anymore. But he sat this up so that it looks like Windows and mostly it works the same."

Eric laughed. Terry patted her knee affectionately. "Don't feel bad," he said, "I did the same thing to my mother."

"The mystery widens then," Eric said.

"Why?" Kelly asked.

Terry answered, "we have been assuming one of two fairly common windows hacks. He could have written the email before he left and used a remote desktop hack to send it. Which we will be able to tell shortly."

"Or he could have used a bot." Eric said, "my theory. But that's a virus type that usually only lives on Windows."

"James," Terry said to Eric, "raised another interesting possibility last night. If Claire, I mean Clark, knew she was running, she could have written the email on this computer and set a timer to send it on a given date."

"She's meticulous, but not that meticulous." Eric replied. "If she set it up to send on a certain date it would have defaulted to 2400 hours; not midmorning."

"She could have set a more specific time." Terry replied, "and I think she is that meticulous."

"Exactly how well do you know my son." She asked suspiciously.

"Thousands of people get on the various computer forums every day." Eric replied, without taking his eyes off the screen. "We both see thousands of different screen names, pictures and icons."

"But of those thousands," Terry said, "one in a hundred ask intelligent questions."

"And one in a thousand ask really good questions," Eric finished.

"When the same screen name shows up again and again," Terry said, "and they ask consistently good questions again and again, we take notice."

"Claire was asking stuff way past her level. A lot of people are aware of her disappearance and are looking for her."

"What sort of people?" Kelly had the sudden image of mobsters chasing her son.

"No one you need to worry about." Terry laughed, "though I heard MIT is offering a full ride scholarship if she can repeat the Melissa stunt."

"What Melissa stunt?" Kelly asked.

"Melissa Hollyfield? She spent one day being wooed by our own university and spent the night in student housing." Eric said.

"What's so amazing about that?" Kelly asked.

"In itself, nothing. I got a look at the school records. They were good but forgeries in the world of photoshop is old news. The part that has MIT hopping is that she had a full set of records online too, when the university checked. The dean of admissions considers himself a geek." The look on Terry's face showed what he thought about that subject, "he bookmarked the records for verifications purposes."

"Thing is," Eric said, "that the school didn't have those records. In fact, no one else can find them." The two men had obviously worked together for years and easily completed each other's thoughts.

Kelly shook her head, "I am sorry I am not that computer literate. What's so amazing about faking school records. Shouldn't that be punished?"

"The amazing part is this, when the dean of admissions sits at his computer and enters this URL he gets a complete set of records. When I sit at my computer and enter the same URL I don't. That's a pretty sophisticated hack."

"As far as punishment goes," Terry said, "the computer world takes a pretty practical approach. The ones smart enough to do hacks like that, need to be rewarded with big cushy security job, preventing the next hacker from actually doing damage with a similar hack."

"Damn it," Eric exclaimed, "how can two smart people be so dumb?"

"What's wrong?" Terry asked.

"Ping bot. Really simple too. We missed the freaking obvious." He shook his head and turned to Kelly. "Okay, I told you earlier what a ping is right?"

"To check the connection thingy." Terry patted her knee again encouragingly to her blank look.

"A bot is a little subroutine that listens for and transmits information. It's mostly used in the malware world to steal personal information. It infects the system like a virus, but then instead of affecting the computer it just passively sits there, at least until the right info goes by. Say you get online and buy something with a credit card. The bot reads your credit card numbers and forwards them to the bot owner."

"Or it reads your email addresses and spams all your friends, like poor Judith did." Terry added.

"This bot isn't nearly so malicious as that." Eric said. "It waits for certain encrypted information to come along, presumably the encrypted version of your email, and then un-encrypts it and sends it back to the server, thus making it look like the email came from your home computer. What had us tricked was that Linux is supposedly immune to bots like this."

"Is that no longer the case?" Terry asked, looking worried.

"I would say that's still the case. This is such a simple trick." He turned again to Kelly. He seemed to relish the teacher role. "A lot of people mistakenly believe the lack of Linux viruses is because there aren't many Linux users, so it's not worth hacker's time to write malicious code for that platform. In fact much of the security is built into Linux at many levels."

"Having hundreds of geeks and programmers on your development teams, and in your community, helps." Terry put in.

"Yes, in Ubuntu for instance one of the simplest and best lines of defense is the sudo, or root user. To make any change to the system you have to enter your password. That eliminates the vast majority of viruses. They can't automatically install, like in Windows."

"I wish Microsoft would, just once," Terry moaned, "say screw ease of use and fix that hole once and for all."

"So we were assuming that in order for this to be a bot, Claire had to work around that issue somehow." Eric said, "but we missed the obvious, she was sitting right here with the password."

"Umm," Kelly said a thought percolating up through her mind suddenly.

"Umm, what?" Eric asked concerned by the tone in her voice.

"Well it occurs to me that Clark, Claire to you, had a side line fixing computers for some of the kids at school and even some of their parent's too."

Eric sighed. "So this encrypted signal pings back to a local server, of course. We go there, show our badges and run a ping on that signal..."

"And it pings to some high school kid's laptop..." Terry said.

"And so forth and so on." Eric finished. "Any idea how many computers he might have worked on in say, the last few months?"

Kelly shrugged helplessly shaking her head.

######

Harry Gelt took off his glasses and rubbed his eyes tiredly.

Putting his glasses back on he stared across his desk at Tony Pirella. Harry considered himself a good judge of character and right now every alarm he had was ringing incessantly.

He had met Tony once before, about three years ago. National Mortgage Company had hired him to track down an ex-employee they suspected of embezzlement. They had plenty of digital evidence to back up their case. They had a strong suspicion about one particular individual. All they needed was one single scrap of physical evidence to tie the virtual crime to the real-world person and they could go the FBI.

He had followed the retiree, who lived in Florida, for three full months. Finally, he followed him on a short vacation in the Caribbean and got one picture of him entering an international bank, a bank where the missing money had been traced too. It was enough to give the FBI probable cause and they did the rest. That one case had earned him a tidy bonus. Not to mention he had gotten to spend three months of a particularly nasty Iowa winter in Florida.

He sighed and looked down at the paperwork in front of him. Two pictures stared up at him. They could have been brother and sister. A somber effeminate boy gazed moodily against a professional matte background. Next to him a shy smiling girl looked through a simple web camera shot, a partial view of a clock on the wall the only indication where that picture was taken.

Harry Gelt was a private detective, an old-fashioned PI at that. Many thought his line of work was antiquated and useless in the days of the Internet but in fact he had found his own specific place in it. He picked up the two pictures and said, "okay, I'm not trying to be dense here, but let's run through this whole thing again." He said. Tony sat impassively and nodded slightly. "You want me to find this boy," he held up the first picture. "Who might be going around as this girl," he held up the second picture. Tony nodded.

"This picture," Harry Gelt said slowly holding up the girl's picture, "was taken inside your house, was it not?" Tony had already stated this.

"Yes," Tony said again, "he was our babysitter."

"And you were aware of his cross dressing?"

"I knew he had some gender issues, yeah." Tony replied. Harry's alarms went ping, ping, ping.

"And you had no problems with this?" Harry asked.

"So he wears one of my wife's shirts now and then? I'm an enlightened man, Harry," Tony explained, "I figure if he's trans-" Tony paused slightly, "whatever, that's fine with me. I don't believe in stereotypes. Did you know most pedophiles are straight men? Yeah, so I figure if I know what this boy's thing is, it makes him more trustworthy around my girls, right?"

That pause was just a little too contrived, Harry thought, he knows a heck of a lot more about this boy's identity than he's letting on. And I am the last person he needs to be lecturing on stereotypes. It had never come up in what was strictly a work relationship but Harry was, he liked to joke, queerer than a three-dollar bill.

"Alright, let's move on," Harry said out loud. "So this boy takes something off your computer and uses it to hack the corporation you work for? No, no, he hacks the corporation you work for to get something off your computer? Money? And some 'sensitive' information?"

Tony nodded again.

"And this sensitive information?"

"It's under a nondisclosure contract." Tony supplied.

Bullshit, Harry thought, you think I am stupid? If that's the case why not slide a nondisclosure contract across my desk and put me in the loop? Again, the alarms were going ping, ping, ping.

Harry opened the file and glanced over the information he had already read through twice. Some aspects of this case were certainly legitimate. Tony's 'nest egg', a numbered international account was indeed empty. The soon to be ex-wife seemed a more logical suspect for that and who knows if it would even be a crime in that case.

The National Mortgage Company had been hacked. It showed all the hallmarks of being a very sophisticated hack at that. The odd part was that the hack had gone straight through their system.

The hacker hadn't even tested their ability to hit sensitive information within the corporation's system. It had been solely and obviously aimed at one thing, getting into Tony's personal computer. Why?

Still, National Mortgage took these sorts of things very seriously. It added another important type of legitimacy to the case. National Mortgage was hiring him to do this investigation, not Tony. Harry could have whatever suspicions he wanted to about this one man, but in the end he reported to the corporation not the man. That didn't mean he wouldn't continue to drill Tony for a while.

"So this was a pretty complicated hack," Harry said, "especially for a sixteen year old boy."

"He was good with computers," Tony said, "damn good."

"And he had some help?"

"I don't know what you mean," Tony said.

"Somebody had been teaching him for a while." Harry prompted.

Tony blushed, "yeah, I was showing him some stuff about security. He said he wanted to go into computers when he was older. I didn't see any harm in giving him a few pointers."

"A few pointers?" Harry replied, "and taught him some hacks, as well?"

"Well, you got to know how an attack is done to stop it."

"And maybe a few programs, sophisticated hacking programs?"

"Training tools, only, I had no idea he would actually use them." Tony said, spreading his hands in feigned innocence.

And yet again the alarms went ping, ping, ping. Tony's protégé had turned on him, that much was clear to Harry, but why? And what had he taken?

"One more question," Harry said. "Why are you wasting your money on this? From what you've said he's ran away and the FBI missing persons are already looking for him. Why not just wait for them to find him?"

"Because they won't," Tony answered, "those idiots, they'll look through their freaking databases for Clark. They'll expect him to make some simple mistake like registering for something in his given name or showing someone his driver's license."

"But he's too smart for that," Harry replied. Tony nodded. "Because you taught him too well," Harry finished. Tony shrugged. Harry went on, "you must think a lot of yourself Mr. Pirella."

Tony snorted, "if I'd been half as smart as that kid at her age..."

It was, Harry's intuition told him, the first genuine thing the man had said. He gave a mild snort. Her, he thought, that slip shows just how familiar you are with this kid's gender identity problems.

"Clark is smart about some things," Tony went on, "smart about computers, but dumb about people,"

He trusted you. And he had some reason for wanting to get away from you.

"The FBI won't find him surfing the net in their office, and my people won't either. Someone's got to go out there, beat the pavement and look. It's the only way he'll be found."

Harry signed the bottom of the contract quickly and with a flourish. Tony visibly relaxed as Harry handed the form over. This was Harry specialty. Harry found people. He did it the old-fashioned way, he used intuition and hunches and most importantly, he went looking.

And when I find this boy, he thought as he watched Tony leaving his office, I'm going to have a lot of questions before I bring any report back.

######

Dear Clark,

I was so happy to hear from you, to know that you are safe for right now. I hope wherever you are you are always safe. I hope you are being careful. I wish so much that I could see you right now and know that everything is okay. I miss you terribly. Please come home.

But maybe you don't think it's safe here. I understand that now, better than ever. The police have interviewed the boys that threatened you. They claim to have "put the fear of god" into them and promise they won't cause you any trouble in the future.

* * *

I won't make that promise. That's a big part of the problem, the reason you had to run away, isn't it? Too many times I have told you to come talk to me, that'd I'd keep you safe, but I couldn't. Too many times I told you to go to your teachers, or to the principal and they would keep your safe. They either couldn't or didn't.

I have been reading online and talking to people too. I have talked to one of the regional directors for PFLAG. They have dealt with bullying like this many times. I talked to someone at the Iowa Safe Schools group too. They said having a Gay Straight Alliance is one of the best things to reduce bullying. I have talked to the school board about that. I would gladly be a chaperon or advisor, or whatever. They weren't thrilled about the idea, but they are willing, if you come back.

Another idea that has been growing on me is moving. Other schools aren't so bad. Jeremy graduates this year anyway so it might be good timing after that. I talked to my lawyer friend Gerald about that. (I know he isn't your favorite person, but he's a nice guy if you give him the chance.) He is willing to help us if we want to move. He'll help us get settled in Des Moines.

Speaking of Gerald, I don't know if you know this or not, but Tony has accused you of hacking into his computer, and into his corporation. I don't know what to think, I don't believe you would have done such a thing, but they claim they have evidence. I for one have a terrible feeling about Tony. I don't know what happened between him and Shelley or you and that family. I want you to know that I don't believe what they say, and Gerald doesn't either. If you come back he'll be your lawyer and help you anyway he can. But he can't help you if you don't come home. Please, come home.

As far as the whole "transgender" thing, I promise to try harder on that front, if you come home. I was and am so afraid for you. I worried that trying to be transgender here and now would only make it harder for you, only make it more dangerous. Now I see that was wrong too. I've been in contact with a group called PFLAG, Parents and Friends of Lesbians and Gays. They have put me in contact with other parents of kids struggling with their identity like you are. If you come home I am sure we can work this all out.

I also want to say I am proud of you. I don't mean for what you have done either. I don't know what to think about this. I am still trying to figure that out.

But through this I have met some of lives you have touched. I met Amy, Christy, Vong and Marcus. They all miss you. You have made a real difference in their lives. I have met two very strange guys from the University of Iowa. They gave me this email, they said they thought you were still using it. They said to identify themselves as Darktater101 and Puppymaster, whatever those names mean. They know you as Miss Claire from some of the Internet forums. They seem to really respect you. They both think you have a future in computers, if you come back.

I love you, Clark. Please email me again when you can, and please, please come home.

Your mother,
Kelly

Her cell phone rang in her purse. Kelly dug for it, but not as frantically as she had say three weeks ago. Then every time the phone rang she was sure it him, or was Agent Hodgekins saying they'd found him. But Clark had been gone for nearly a month now. She got the occasional email, always the same, assuring her he was safe and working things out, and would be more forthcoming soon. But no details.

She would forward the emails to Agent Hodgekins. He would

forward them to Eric and Terry. They would call and say something like, "They are pinging off dozens of servers. No way to trace it." Sadly, that would be that. Even Hodgekins constant assurances were wearing thin. She was starting to think they'd never find Clark.

She finally found the phone and looked at the number. It was Agent Hodgekins. She belatedly hurried to answer.

"Hello, Kelly?"

"Yes, Agent Hodgekins, I am sorry I didn't realize it was you calling."

"No problem. Any new contact?"

"No, the last email was last week. Your guys can't track that one either, I take it?"

"No luck, but I have good news. We got a trace on the laptop. Our own cyber guys pulled that one off, I should say, not the university geeks." He sounded proud. "They kept dismissing it as a dead end. And... I was right. San Fran. The signal originated from a coffee shop."

"What should I do?" She had an image of rushing through to the airport to fly out there.

"Nothing, just relax." He replied. "I talked to a youth worker I know out there. She's going to hang out at that coffee shop. She does that a lot anyway, it's in one of the student areas where a lot of run aways end up. She's got his description, and her description, so either way Clark's presenting she should be able to identify him."

"A youth worker?" She asked.

"We aren't going to send the cops to nab him, not if we can help it, or he's in danger. We want to initiate gentle contact, see if we can get him to come home voluntarily."

"That's what I want, too." She said hastily.

"And that's hopefully what we will get." He said.

She closed her eyes as she turned her phone off and silently prayed.

CHAPTER EIGHTEEN

"You are really quite lucky." Dr. Parn was saying. He would have reminded Clarissa of her boss except that his mannerisms were so different. They were both middle aged Thai men with short wavy hair. They both had that ageless look that the Thai people seemed to have mastered. They both dressed like conservative American business men, in suit and tie.

The similarities ended there. Dr. Parn was happy go lucky and laid back. He smiled easily and insisted on addressing Clarissa informally. He laughed easily and often. As he led her back to his office, she had noticed that he had ditched his dress shoes for a pair of slippers with gold fish embroidered on them. The slippers held no surprise for Clarissa, Thai people rarely wore regular shoes inside, it bordered on rude to do so, but the colorful nature of these pieces of footwear made fun of the austere suit.

"To transition so young." Dr. Parn went on, "the results will be quite excellent."

He thought her so young at nineteen. What would he have thought had he known the truth, that she was not yet seventeen?

"Yes, sir," she replied.

"Your parents accept this?" He asked.

"Yes, sir." Her mother was going to go through the roof.

"How much longer do you have at the school?"

"Three weeks, sir."

"You will need at least six weeks off. SRS is fairly major surgery," he said. "We won't be able to do anything sooner than the end of the semester, obviously."

"Obviously," she agreed.

"We got your approval letter and it looks good. The only problem is that you haven't had a preoperative physical."

"I can get one here?"

"Of course, I'll have the driver take you to a clinic this afternoon where they can do the labs and a chest Xray. I'll do the rest as part of the exam today."

"That would be wonderful."

"Now what can I tell you about the procedure itself?"

She shrugged, "I think we've been over this already." She had talked via email and on the phone with both the doctor and his staff. Clarissa had made a "wish list" of surgeons almost as soon as she learned the surgery existed and Dr. Parn had been top of the list. To discover he was not only close at hand but had openings in his schedule was an amazing coincidence. They had been in contact almost weekly for the last three weeks, since she had arrived in Thailand.

"We are planning a simple reassignment surgery. No breast augmentation, you can always do that later if you like, but you're wise to wait and see what the hormones do, at your age you may not need it. No facial feminization surgery, you definitely don't need that."

Clarissa beamed at the compliment. She would need some electrolysis for the few patches of facial hair, but she didn't want to have the extensive facial reconstruction that some trans-women went through. The reassignment she definitely wanted. "How long will it take?"

"SRS only?" He said musing, "the surgery itself will be about six hours or so. You'll be in the hospital for about five days. During that whole time, you will be pretty much on bed rest. I doubt you'll want to move much anyway, but it's critical that we give that skin graft time to take in the new place.

"On the fifth day, we take the stent out. Then you leave the hospital. Our staff will take you to the hotel, you are staying in our hotel?"

The doctor had an agreement with a hotel named Baan Siri, peaceful house. She had agreed to stay there. It meant she got a reduced rate. More importantly she would get visits from his nurses daily.

"You need to stay there for a couple of weeks at least. It depends, are you going back to teaching, or back to America?"

"Back to America." As the words came out of her mouth, Clarissa's heart quailed. It was her intention to return home, but to what? Her mother had indicated that she was willing to work things out and that gave Clarissa hope. But she had been monitoring the local news online and she knew she was in deep trouble over the hacking of National Mortgage and Tony. Eventually she was going to have to face the music and she did not relish the thought.

"Then it should be a month before you travel that far. If you were staying in Thailand I would say you could return to the school's housing, but not back to work for another six weeks."

She chuckled to herself. Returning to the school might prove awkward. They didn't know she was transgender there. She had confessed this secret to only one teacher, the British School marm who had taken her in and taught her the ropes. She had promised to keep Clarissa's secret as long as necessary. It didn't matter. The place had served it's purpose. She had enough money left for the surgery, the aftercare and then the return flight home, with a little to spare.

Kelly and Gerald shared a look as there was a knock at the door. Kelly sat her coffee down and went to answer the door.

A man in his late forties, early fifties stood on her doorstep. He was dressed in a brown suit and had wired rimmed glasses. "Hello, my name is Harry Gelt and I am a private investigator. I would like to talk to you about your son Clark."

Kelly rolled her eyes. "Wait a minute, I am starting to get this down." Kelly said. "You met my son, as a girl of course, in some online chat room for private investigating and now you would like to help find him?"

Harry had thought this case was odd before, now he knew it was without a doubt the strangest case he had ever worked on. He wondered suddenly if he had been wise to take it up at all.

Kelly meanwhile was going on, "why does it suddenly seem like everyone knows my son except me?   My son lives with me for seventeen years and I can't get him to open up about how his day went but some guy named darthtater knows every freaking detail."

"Ma'am." He interrupted her, "I have no idea what you are talking about. I have never met your son and I certainly don't know anyone called darth tater."

Kelly stopped and regarded him levelly. "Perhaps we should talk," she decided suddenly, realizing he was serious. She ushered him inside.

"I should tell you for the record," Harry said as he came in the front room and settled himself in an easy chair. "That I have been contracted by National Mortgage Company to find the whereabouts of your son."

"National Mortgage Company?" A tall thin man with gray at his temples came out of the kitchen with two glasses of coffee. "Interesting. I think Clark's lawyer should be present in that case." Gerald said with a smile.

"Really this is an informal..." Harry began, not wanting to put off his investigation or get lawyers involved this early.

"It's okay," Kelly Holden told him, "this is Gerald and he is my son's lawyer."

How often do you have coffee with your son's lawyer, Mrs. Holden?

"As you wish," Harry conceded.

"Why has National Mortgage Company hired you to find my son, Mr. Gelt?" Kelly asked.

"They simply wish to know where he is."

"Really," Gerald said, "It wouldn't have anything to do with their baseless accusations that Clark hacked their system and stole something from one of their employees?"

"It might," he conceded.

"Shouldn't they go to the authorities with that sort of thing? If they have any real evidence that is. And shouldn't it be the responsibility of the authorities to find Clark, not some private investigator?" Gerald went on.

"If I may be blunt?" Harry said.

"By all means." Gerald replied.

"Whether or not these accusations are baseless depends on how Clark answers certain questions and whether or not his location and activities can be connected to certain online activities. National Mortgage Company can neither dismiss these accusations nor turn them over to the proper authorities as you suggest without finding out more about Clark's location and activity.

"Secondly, certain people within National Mortgage Company,"

"Meaning Tony," Kelly threw in.

"Do not have particular confidence in the ability of the authorities to find your son." Harry went on, "which is why they consulted me."

"What happened in that house, Mr. Gelt?" Kelly asked sharply over Gerald's nodded objection, "What happened between my son and Mr. Tony Pirella? What was taken that has him so hot?"

Harry paused. It was a sticking point for him, but he wasn't about to admit it yet. "Other than a pile of money?" He asked innocently.

"Has anyone spoken with Mrs. Pirella?" Gerald asked, "She is as likely of a suspect and since they were married she may have legal right to any funds she took."

"I am not privy to that aspect of the investigation." Harry said. "I am merely supposed to find out everything I can about the location of Clark Holden and," he emphasized his words carefully, "report back to National Mortgage Company."

"Well, I don't think we can help you with that," Gerald said.

Harry stood, "I really didn't expect so. I really just wanted to introduce myself. I will be in and out of town doing my own investigative work." He paused and added, "Mrs. Holden, I am not your enemy. I have no preconceived notions of Clark's guilt or innocence. If I find evidence clearing him, I'll be the first to call Mortgage National, or the FBI for that matter. And regardless of his guilt or innocence, I would like to see your son home safely."

As Kelly watched Gerald usher the man out she wondered, can I believe him? He seemed sincere but there were too many unanswered questions and her son's safety rode on those answers. She sighed and let it go. She did trust Agent Hodgekins. He said he would find her son. She would just have to wait for him to come through on his promise.

######

"I've been hearing rumors that the underclassmen's social order is having some sort of shake up," Brenda Oleson said derisively, her eyes going from Debra to Amy and back. Debra was sitting on Amy's bed. She looked more disheveled and anxious than usual. Amy sat her desk, cool and collected, she hoped. "But really has it gone this far?" Amy scowled. Just because Debra and her weren't close didn't mean she felt she was above Debra in some mysterious "social order" but arguing with Brenda wouldn't help matters right now.

"Enough," Amy said. Debra was already practically in tears, and Brenda's assault wasn't helping. "We asked you here to talk about something serious."

Brenda raised her eyebrows as if to say, it better be. She sat heavily on the bed opposite Debra.

Amy took a deep breath and plunged on. "We both received an anonymous email a few weeks back, and we are pretty sure you did too."

"Ooh, are we a spy club now?" Brenda joked sourly.

"You know what I am talking about." Amy said.

"I am not sure I even care what you're talking about," Brenda answered.

"You don't care what that bastard did to us?" Debra almost wailed.

"What I am supposed to be all weepy and emo cause some old man thought I was a hottie?" Brenda sneered, "F- that. I am supposed to be ashamed because he bought me a ton of pretty things, took pictures of me, told me I was beautiful?"

"He abused us," Amy snapped.

"Oh cry me a river," Brenda went on. "The only difference between Tony and any one of the high school boys you or I have dated is the quality of the gifts. I wish I still had that job."

"I suppose you liked how he held those pictures over your head anytime you said no, huh?" Amy answered hotly, "How he insinuated that it would be you who took the rap if it ever got out."

"How it was you that took the rap," Debra added, "you got fired, just like I did. You got fired 'cause of him."

They had scored a hit, but Brenda scoffed, "so what, what I am supposed to do about it?"

"For one thing," Debra said, "thank Clark."

"The little fag who ran away?" Brenda said.

"He's my friend," Amy fumed.

Brenda gave her a cross look, "whatever. He's a freak. I don't care if he's gone and I am not afraid to say it."

"Clark's the one who sent those pictures." Debra said.

"What? He's got the pictures now?" A worried look crossed Brenda's face.

"No, we do," Amy assured her, "Clark hacked Tony's computer and got them. He sent us the originals."

"We're free, because of him," Debra said, "we don't have to go through life worrying that Tony will reveal that to the world."

Amy looked away uncomfortably. It was true, but she was about to ask the girls to do exactly what they most feared, reveal what had happened.

"So fine, if I ever see the little freak again," Amy glared at her but bit her tongue, "I'll thank him." Brenda conceded, "so what's the deal with the money? Is that legit?"

Debra shrugged. "I think so."

"Clark divided it up, he says Tony got it illegally anyway and maybe it'll be at least a partial payment for what he did." Amy said.

"You know what?" Brenda said, "I still don't care. I did what I did. It's not like I haven't slept with other guys."

"But Tony used you," Debra said, ticking it off, "he used you, took pictures, blackmailed you to stay quiet about it, sold you out when his wife started to suspect, made it out to be all your fault, he dumped you and then he replaced you," She snapped her fingers, "just like that."

Brenda laughed, "he may have replaced you two, but he didn't replace me." She smiled a wicked, triumphant smile.

Forgive me Clark, Amy thought. *Wherever you are, forgive me.* "He did too."

Comprehension dawned on Brenda's face. "That bastard!" She cried, "With the freak?"

The term angered Amy and she bolted to her feet. "He's not a freak!" She shook her head fighting to control her anger and then went on, "I don't know what happened, okay? I don't know how far it went with Clark. I think Clark was smarter than any of us because he got out before it got bad. But I do know Tony tried with him too. And you know why? Because it never had anything to do with love, or how beautiful you were, or how lonely Tony was. It was about control and manipulation. It was about Tony taking what he wanted from each of us. That's all it was ever about!"

Brenda folded her face into her hands defeated. "Fine, you win," she said through a muffled cry. "It sucked royally when Shelley accosted me and he sat there and said I had thrown myself at him. He had pictures on his damn phone, but he'd rigged them somehow so it looked like I had texted them to him. He said he didn't know what to do about it. Then when Shelley looked away the bastard gave me this cold smile, like you know she'll never believe a word you say. It sucked. It felt like I had been kicked in the gut, okay? Is that what you wanted to hear?"

Amy paused and let Brenda get herself together. Then she said, "they're looking for Clark. The FBI, some insurance company, there's even a freaking private eye going around town asking tons of questions. Do you know what happens when they find him?"

Both girls nodded no.

"Twenty, thirty years maybe," she said, "in jail."

"They can't do that," Debra said.

"Oh yes they can! Hacking a major corporation? Theft, Fraud, god knows what else they can find and throw at him. What do you think would happen to a boy like Clark in jail?"

Brenda made a disparaging sound.

"Is that any way to thank him for what he did for us?"

"So what are we supposed to do?" Brenda asked.

"We can go to the authorities," she said, "tell the truth."

Debra blanched. Brenda said, "I thought you said we were free now. Now you want us to go tell the freaking world?" Her expression was defiant but there was fear in her eyes.

"If they know why he did it, what he took," Amy persisted, "then Tony will be in trouble, not Clark. We all know how Tony turns things against you, we can't let him do it again. We can't let Clark take the fall, not after what he did for us."

Brenda looked suspiciously at Amy and Debra was on the verge of hyperventilating. Amy knew this was going to be a hard sell, but she had to convince them. Clark's life depended on it.

#######

The cellphone vibrated from where Kelly had left it on the table. She looked over distractedly. She had been baking for the first time in months. For three days now she had been riding a wave of hope. They knew where Clark was, San Francisco. She could almost see him sitting at a coffee shop, a youth worker asking if she could join him.

"Agent Hodgekins," Kelly said as she answered the phone, "I hope you have good news for me." She felt happy, even jovial. It was better than she'd felt in several weeks, actually, since Clark left. The feeling had been growing all week. Any day Agent Hodgekins would call and tell her that Clark was on his way home.

"I've got some bad news actually." He said.

"Has something happened to Clark?"

"No, not that bad thankfully." Agent Hodgekins replied quickly, "we made contact, but it turns out to be a dead end."

"You made contact with Clark?"

"Nope, my friend, the youth worker, just called, she made contact with a Miranda Shuester at the coffee shop."

"Another alias?"

"Another woman entirely, a student at San Francisco State. It seems she bought a new laptop off ebay a month ago. The seller went by the name Claire, and guess what, the shipping address was Iowa City, Iowa. The time period matched perfectly too. He sold the computer off while he was in Iowa City."

She felt crushed. Where was he?

"I'm stymied to be honest. I don't know what to do now. I was so sure he'd keep a hold of that computer from what everyone said about your son and I was so sure your son would head to San Francisco."

"What if he had another computer?" Kelly asked. She seemed to recall him sometimes using a small pink netbook.

"Do you think he did?"

"Maybe. He fixed a lot of computers for kids at school. He was always coming home with stuff someone had given him. I think most of them went back to their original owner after he took care of them, but I know he sometimes worked in trade, took old computers. He would fix them up and then gave them to friends or sold them. I remember him giving Marcus a computer once, and that last day his excuse for leaving early was that he was giving an old computer to his friend Vong. Right after he left I thought that was just a cover story for leaving early and having an overstuffed bag but what if he really did have an extra computer? And he ditched the one he figured you'd trace?

"That's an interesting theory. You wouldn't happen to be able to give me information on that computer?"

"No, it's just a theory. I don't even know for sure he had one."

Agent Hodgekins sighed.

"What do we do now?" Kelly asked.

"I am not really sure. I can send the boys around again to see if they can lift the trace numbers on any possible other computers through your computer's router. I don't know if that will give us anything useful to go on, but the boys will find it fun."

She figured by 'the boys' he meant Eric and Terry or Darthtater. At least this time she could brace herself for their onslaught.

"Aside from that, there isn't a lot we can do without more to go on. We have pretty much automated the search for his legal name and the three alias we know about. If they show up in any federal database we will know." He paused. "There is something else you should know and I don't like telling you this anymore than you are going to like hearing it. I've gotten pretty attached to this case. Listening to all these people talk about Clark has given me an enormous respect for your son. He's got a real future, if we find him and bring him home. On the street, it's another story."

Kelly was left with a vague sense of dread. Her world was shrinking, constricting into a tight ball of anxiety. What did he think this would be hard for her to hear? Then it came.

"I've spent an enormous number of man hours on this case already and we have a large caseload. I am getting pressure about keeping my perspective."

"Meaning?"

"Meaning I can still spend my spare time checking the databases, but he won't approve more field investigators or consultants, or taking other agent's time, etc. Plus, I have got to focus on new cases coming in more."

"So, the FBI has done all it can, and now they're closing the case?"

"Not closing it." He replied carefully, "just well, re-prioritizing it. I promise, I am still personally dedicated to doing what it takes to find your son."

"With no leads and around your other responsibilities?" Her voice sounded leaden.

"I am sorry, I know it's hard. I wish there was something more we could do."

Like pound the pavement? She thought about the man that had come by last week, the PI. What was his name? Harry something. She still had his card. He said he would listen to Clark's side before turning him over to National Mortgage. But could she trust him? Did she have another choice?

She heard her own voice saying, "I understand." She didn't want to understand. She wanted to rage at him. Her son was out there, god knows where and he wanted to talk about keeping perspective? "You've done so much already and there are so many runaways." So many that were never found, never seen again. Other that were found but not before they had lived through horrible traumas. She was not going to let that happen to her son.

As soon as she hung up the phone she found the card in her purse and called Harry Gelt.

"This is Kelly Holden," she said. "I really shouldn't be talking to you but," she stopped and stammered, "but your right, the FBI isn't going to find my son. Just please promise me you'll give him a chance to explain. I am sure he didn't mean to do anything wrong."

She spoke for nearly an hour straight. She told him everything from the initial disappearance to her latest talk with Agent Hodgekins. Harry Gelt listened patiently, asking questions when necessary, but mostly just letting her tell the story in her own long, rambling way.

When she finally finished he paused so long that she had to ask if he was still there.

"Yeah, I'm here. For starters, I have to say it's pretty remarkable that the FBI has done as much as they have already. Usually if they know a kid's not in immediate danger they don't do much at all. Like Agent Hodgekins indicated they have a huge caseload."

"This case has been burning in the back of my mind. I have been trying to figure out what I can add, what I have that neither the FBI or the computer guys have. I have a thought about that.

"The FBI is giving this lots of attention, but they are still treating it as a simple run-away situation. Kids who run away are focused on getting away from something, the destination is an afterthought. And the computer geeks are focused on how he's hiding from the increasingly omnipresent computer databases. That's still the wrong focus."

"Here's how I know Tony, or perhaps I should say how Tony knew me. I did some work for his corporation a few years back. It should have been a simple embezzlement case, but they couldn't find the guy and they couldn't connect him to the funds. The FBI wouldn't get involved until there was some solid evidence to go on, which means they had to find the guy. That was my job, to find the guy and provide one tangible bit of evidence that he was connected to the crime."

"There is an important similarity here. Clark isn't running away in the traditional sense; that is he's not focused on what he's running from. He's forward focused, on where he wants to go and what he wants to do."

"And do you have any idea where that is?" Kelly asked.

"None whatsoever," he said, "but I have an intuitive hunch that the more important question is who he wants to be. Figure out who he wants to be and the rest will follow. I've an idea on that score too."

"Go ahead."

"I can see the logic behind his aliases. He's figured out that he passes pretty well as a girl, and that makes it easy to avoid the obvious things, like being identified as the boy that was on the news or on some missing child poster. The names he has chosen are pretty telling too. He seems to stick close to his real name. That's smart because it's easier to bluff. You can react naturally to someone calling you something that's close to the name you've had for years. He varies the name in minor ways, to confuse a computer search, but still make it easy on his own memory; Claire Holden, Kelly Holden, Claire Hollow, Melissa Hollyfield; these are the ones we know.

"Claire, he used online a lot, so that's a natural. Melissa seems out of place until you take into account that many friends have said he favored the name Clarissa for his drag persona. Clarissa, Melissa." He sounded the names out slowly. "Now do you see what's missing?"

"No."

"Clarissa. He used it extensively before leaving, but it hasn't shown up in any of his aliases."

"So?" Kelly wasn't following.

"My hunch is that this name was special to him. He has been saving it for something. Using weaker aliases for the early running part, but I am willing to bet money he'll use Clarissa whenever he gets where he's going."

"So what do we do?"

"Just drop that hint on Agent Hodgekins. And let me know what falls out."

######

"Everybody dance now!" The computer at Clarissa's back blared the English dance hit suddenly. She smiled. Around her twenty-three eight-year-old Thai girls leaped to their feet and began to wiggle and giggle like maniacs.

Which they were, Clarissa had decided some weeks ago. Still they had grown on her. At first, she hated teaching. She had felt lost and confused. She was in way over her head and she knew just enough to realize that. By the end of her third day at the Hathon International School she had broken down in tears.

Bridget, a fifty something math teacher from Britain, had found her huddled in the teacher's lounge. Clarissa expected a lecture, but instead the heavy woman sat down and put her arm around Clarissa's shoulders.

"Teaching is not for the faint of heart, honey."

"I don't know if I can do this."

"We all thought that at first. You'll do okay."

They'd sat for a long while so Clarissa could pull herself together. When she had finally dried her eyes, Bridget caught her eye and told her what Clarissa still thought of as the secret to life. "They're rough, the wee ones, but here's a tip for you. Never let an eight-year-old get bored."

Which is why every half hour Clarissa's computer blared two and half minutes of some American dance classic. Two and half minutes of guilt free wiggling made the other twenty-seven and half minutes fly by. It wasn't the only trick she had picked up either.

As the music stopped the girls obediently returned to their seats. They watched her expectantly. She pulled out a bright scarf she had bought the last weekend from a street vendor outside Wat Pho, one of her rare tourist outings, and carefully covered something on her desk. It was a simple ballpoint pen, but this was the other big secret of teaching that she'd learned, it's all about showmanship. She held it aloft and with a dramatic flair, yanked the scarf away.

There was a momentary pause and then one girl called out in English, "Pen, Ms. Clarissa."

"Correct Ms. Sri." She replied. The girl beamed and stuck her tongue out at her neighbor Tair as Clarissa turned away.

Yeah, she was getting the hang of teaching.

######

Kelly opened the door. The man on the other side was stocky and well built. He wore a nondescript brown suit and a tie. He had sandy brown hair that was cleanly cut and he was clean shaven. When he moved she caught the flash of a badge at his belt. She had never met the man but recognized his voice the second he opened his mouth to say, "Kelly Holden?"

"Agent Hodgekins?"

He held out his hand. "It's wonderful to finally meet you in person." She shook his hand hesitantly and stood aside so he could come in.

"To what do I owe this visit?" She asked not bothering to hide her irritation. "I thought you had 're-prioritized' my son's case."

"Things change," he said evasively, "priorities change." He went into the dining room and sat at the table. "Have a seat, we need to talk about something."

"What is going on? Has something new come up? Is Clark okay?"

"Clark is, well we don't have any news on Clark, I am sorry to say. However, finding him is definitely a higher priority now. The other half of the FBI is looking for him too now."

"What other half?"

"Well not half, they are the majority. Look, it's like this, my department is missing persons. We tend to be nice guys, trying to reunite broken families, that sort of thing. I ran that alias you gave us the other day."

Two days ago, she thought, and now this? That was some hunch. Harry Gelt went up a notch in her estimation.

"It was a hit, a big one. Clarissa Holden is far more than an alias. It's a complete legal identity, one that belongs to real a person, with history and documentation to back it up, except for two small facts."

"Which are?"

"Clarissa has only been active for about six months and all her pictures match your son."

"What does all this have to do with the 'other half of the FBI?'"

He wiped his brow to show how hard he'd been working. "Missing persons tends to play pretty loose with the law, considering that we are the FBI after all. Finding kids is our focus. Lying to a bus driver about your name, or in this case, your gender, is dishonest but not illegal. Buying fake ID's is a misdemeanor, but we could probably overlook that, or sweep it under the rug if it got your son back safe and sound. Even the trick with school records could be written off."

"But this Clarissa identity gets into some pretty high-level fraud. She's got a social security number, for Christ's sake, a driver's license, a GED and most worrisome, a passport."

"A passport?"

"That's got some big wigs jumping. Homeland Security is threatening to claim jurisprudence in this matter. The State Department's called me, the State Department! I have spent all morning arguing with my boss, the boys from criminal, everyone. I am trying to convince everyone to keep it a missing persons case and work under the assumption that his only intention was to escape his situation here. So far, they've kept me on the case, which is a good sign. But they see this as probable cause in the hacking case, so there's a criminal prosecutor on the case too now. It's not going be easy for Clark when we find him I am afraid."

Kelly blanched. She stared at the agent in horror.

"I don't know how much law you know," Agent Hodgekins went on, "but intention is extremely important in fraud cases. If it turns out that Clark took money that wasn't his to take, or had some malicious purpose for what he did, he could be looking at some serious criminal charges. The fact that he's a minor gives us a lot more leeway than we would otherwise have, but we have got to find the boy, find out what he's been up to and soon."

"Do you think Clarissa is the identity he's been using?" Kelly said, "can you track that?"

"Well that's the other thing I thought I should come tell you in person. I said he had a passport that said Clarissa. It's been used."

"Used?"

"That passport, and presumably Clark, left Minneapolis Airport on an international flight."

"To where?"

"Asia, we can't do better than that yet but we will be able to soon. We have applied for a warrant to get the flight records. But here's the hitch, it took Clark a mere two weeks to get from here to Des Moines, to Iowa City, back to Des Moines and then on to Minneapolis and off. That was five weeks ago now. We are way behind him. It's going to take some time to get back on his trail. It's just bureaucratic red tape I promise, and I will let you know as soon as I know anything."

"Where did my son get the money to travel overseas?" Kelly asked.

Agent Hodgekins shrugged.

"Tony?" Kelly supplied.

"We assume so."

"Where would he have gone?"

Agent Hodgekins shrugged, "that was supposed to be my question."

######

Amy shuffled blearily down the hallway. She had not been sleeping well lately. She had just gotten to sleep when her dad had woken her. It must be nearly midnight. Just figures, how my weeks going, she groused to herself. She had barely managed to convince the other two girls not to destroy the evidence of Tony's crimes and go on a huge spending spree. Neither had agreed to go to the cops, yet. If Brenda agreed she was pretty sure Debra would too, but Brenda was going to be hard to convince. To make matters worse she had called Mrs. Holden to see if she had any news and the woman had broken down over the phone. The FBI had just filed fraud charges. If found Clark was going to jail.

"Visitor for you," her dad said with an obvious look of displeasure. Who would show up at this time of night?

Brenda stood on the doorsteps, haggard and obviously drunk.

No wonder her dad looked at her that way. "Hey," Brenda said breezily.

Amy stepped outside and hugged herself against the cold, "Hey, Brenda. What's up?"

"Nothing much, just wanted to talk," Brenda replied looking away.

"About what?"

Still looking away she said, "I slept with Ben tonight."

"And you thought you'd stop by and tell me?" Amy replied, her voice thick with sarcasm.

"The whole time," Brenda went on as though she hadn't heard. "The whole time I kept seeing his face, feeling his hands, hearing his voice." She didn't have to explain who he was. She looked at Amy suddenly. "I thought when I got that email, got those pictures in my hands, it would be over. I would be free. But I am not." A tear slid across her cheek.

"You'll never be free," Amy voiced a thought that had been growing in her mind over the last few weeks, "You'll never be free until we are all honest about what happened."

"I'm scared," Brenda admitted.

"I am too," Amy said. They both stared off in the distance for a long time. Then Amy said, "I've got the name of this lawyer, the one that's representing Clark. I thought he'd be a good place to start. I'd like it if Debra and you went too. We don't have to decide about the authorities yet, just find out what this lawyer says, you know."

Still crying, Brenda nodded.

#######

Tony waited impatiently as the elevator climbed to the highest floor. Being called to the board room first thing in the morning was typically not a good sign. He hoped that something had come through on the investigation, but if that was the case one of his people would have sent him a text before he arrived.

The board room opened to admit him as soon as he approached. He looked around the table and saw the majority of the board seats taken. That was also not a good sign. He took a deep breath and willed himself to relax. Whatever it was he would find out soon enough.

Herman Fitts, CEO greeted him grimly, "Tony Pirella, I am sorry to call you up here like this." No good to see you? Tony thought, really worried now. "It seems our hacker has hit again." Herman said.

Tony stopped startled. Claire had dared try again? "What?" He sputtered in shock, "we closed those security holes. I can't imagine how it happened again. I'll get my boys on it right away."

"That won't be necessary," Mr. Fitts told him, "I have already talked with David."

They talked to David? Why would they go to my second in command? Shouldn't they have come to me? Anger flared.

"She didn't take anything this time either." Mr. Fitts said.

She? Had Claire revealed herself?

"In fact, this time she left us a little something." He went on turning towards the huge computer screen at the front of the board room. He clicked a remote and the screen came alive. "I am sure you are able to read a graph, Mr. Pirella?"

Tony stared at the screen but said nothing.

"Are you able to understand the significance of this particular graph, Mr. Pirella?" The voice had taken on an icy tone.

Tony said nothing.

Mr. Fitts used the pointer to point at the bottom of the graph. "These marks show major decisions we have made as a corporation over the last ten years." He went on, "this line shows how the markets reacted to those decisions. This line here is your own portfolio if I am not mistaken?"

It was all going to come out in disclosure which was now inevitable. Tony knew better than to try to lie his way out of this one. He licked his lips, "yes sir, I believe it is."

"Insider trading is a serious crime, Mr. Pirella," Mr. Fitts said slowly. "And it seems this graph has somehow also ended up in the hands of the FCC."

Tony swallowed hard and said nothing.

"As CEO it is my job to protect the interests of National

Mortgage Company." He paused and looked at Tony, "I think you know what comes next."

Tony nodded.

"You are relieved of your duties and placed on administrative leave until after the investigation is complete."

Tony turned to find two security officers standing behind him. They were from a private contract outfit, men he did not know. It was an added precaution and a statement that spoke louder than words. They would not allow in-house security to walk him out. He unclenched his fists slowly, unable to remember clenching them in first place. He sat his face to a mask and nodded that he was ready to go.

Gerald hummed to himself pleasantly as he stirred his morning coffee. He was happy. He felt more than a little guilty about this fact. A boy was missing, a boy he knew and cared about, on the run from the law and facing serious charges should he be found, and Gerald was happy. He couldn't help it.

He had dated Kelly Holden a few years back. He had instantly felt a connection and was sure he had found his soulmate at last. He was sure she felt the same way. Unfortunately, she was a widow and a single mom. Her two kids were not ready for a "replacement dad" as Clark had called him. She had broken it off with him. It was heartbreakingly ironic that he was drawn to her devotion, the very trait that led to their break up.

When he saw the news report that Clark had gone missing he had called, to offer a helping hand to a friend, or so he told himself. He and Kelly had talked and the connection was still there. When it came out a few days later that Clark might be in legal trouble, Gerald had leaped at the chance to get involved. He felt like he was taking advantage of the situation, but being back in Kelly's life was making him enormously happy.

"What business does this fine Saturday morning bring us?" He asked his secretary. Some light office work, he thought, a couple of drop ins maybe and then up to 'check on' Kelly this afternoon.

"You've got three walk-ins waiting in your office," his secretary responded. The look on her face told him it was not a typical walk-in.

"What do they want?"

She shrugged. "They'll only talk to you."

Three pale faced teen-age girls were waiting nervously in his office. One looked like she had been crying for some time, and the other two looked like they were close to joining her. He started to greet them glibly, but seeing their expressions he set his face into a more somber mood. He could see they were in trouble. He tried to project an air of calm and trustworthiness.

He raised a hand for silence, though none had spoken. "Before we begin I think it would be advisable if you each gave me something, anything will do, even a penny." He reached in his drawer and pulled out three sheets of paper, "and I'll have you sign this form. That way you are all officially my clients and anything you say is privileged." Normally he wouldn't go through this until after he'd heard their story, but he wanted these girls to understand they could tell him anything.

The girl in the middle, who seemed to be the leader, took three one dollar bills out of her purse and handed them each one. They signed their sheets and slid them back with a dollar each.

He gathered up the sheets, ignoring the money for now. He stood and turned to put them in his file cabinet. With his back to the girls he said, "so what brings you to my office today?"

Without preamble or warning one of the girls blurted out, "Tony Pirella sexually abused us, all of us."

He dropped the papers on the floor. Not bothering to fetch them he turned back towards the girl. It was youngest one that had spoken, the chubby one with the dark blond hair, the one that had been crying. She looked at him fearfully, searching for any sign of judgment. He willed his face to be impassive, accepting.

The skinny blond in the middle said, "she's right. And he tried to abuse Clark too. That's why Clark left."

Gerald took one step back towards his desk and sat heavily in his chair. "You have evidence of this?"

Amy nodded and pulled out her laptop. "This is what Clark

hacked into Tony's computer to find. This is what he took." She turned the screen towards him, not bothering to wipe her tears.

######

Shelley Pirella reached for a tissue. It had become a habit in the past few weeks. She cried every day, often two or three times. Her uncle and his wife were being saints, taking care of the girls and giving her space even though they couldn't understand what she was going through.

Not that they were unsympathetic. They understood how heart wrenching the whole idea of divorce was to her. It was the personal trial of faith they couldn't understand. She felt as if God himself had slapped her in the face. Everything she had held sacred, everything she just knew had been right had now been shown wrong. She couldn't find any way to reconcile things.

She had believed Tony. Time and again he had made it sound like the girls had come on to him, but he had rebuked them. Even when that last girl had texted, texted him scantily clad pictures, he had come to Shelley.

If it had been just one girl that came forward she would probably still believe him, choosing to believe the girl had some sort of sour grapes. But it had been three, three girls with consistent stories. Since they had started asking around there was plenty of corroborating evidence. Other girls had quit because they were scared of Tony. One girl, Brenda, had bragged to friends. One had confessed to a therapist.

Most damming were the pictures and videos. Pictures that Clark had found. Clark, who instead of ending the problems had become somehow, another one of Tony's girls. She could not seem to convey to her aunt, who was far more open minded than most in her family or to the counselor her aunt took her to, just how much that had shaken her entire world view. Tony, her straight husband and that effeminate boy; it was inconceivable to her.

The whole idea that the sweet endearing young man could have been a gay cross dresser, at his age, was astounding. She had tried once to talk to her aunt about it. Her aunt had said, as though it were the most obvious thing in the world, "well, some people are just born that way."

The girls had come forward, they said, to protect Clark. But then again Shelley had been trying to protect Clark too, in her own way, when she hired him. Little did she know she was unwittingly introducing him to the worst monster of all, her husband.

"Can we please stop now?" She asked the FBI agent across from her in the drab conference room. He glanced at his partner who was standing by the door. His partner nodded and the agent stopped the video clip that was playing. It was one of a dozen or more hidden web cameras that Tony had used to catch the girls undressing. She shuddered. How could she have misjudged him so terribly?

"You knew nothing about this?" The agent asked.

"Mrs. Pirella knew nothing of her husband's activities," her lawyer, her uncle's lawyer really, said on her behalf. "In fact, she too was duped by his lies, he used material from this pornographic collection to make it look like the girls were coming on to him."

"Mrs. Pirella?" The agent said.

Shelley nodded.

Her lawyer said, a note of irritation in his voice, "she's given a full deposition at my office and we have forwarded a written copy. I fail to see why you are subjecting her to this cross examination."

The agents ignored him. "And the money that Clark stole from Tony? The hacking of Tony's personal computer? Did you know about either of those things?"

An image came into her mind of the bright boy who had been so tender with her girls. How tightly he had hugged them that last day, how close he had been to tears. She could not reconcile that image with what she knew about the gay lifestyle. It was too much. A million sins swam around her and threatened to engulf her; Tony's betrayal, her own audacity at divorcing him, Clark's sexuality. What was one sin against the hundreds that had occurred in that house?

"My client was not," her lawyer began.

"That last day," she said suddenly, touching the lawyers arm, "I said...I asked Clark to help me. I did, I said I knew something was going on, I suspected," she broke off and shook her head. "I asked him to help me," she said in a sudden fit of inspiration, "and he helped me. That computer was in my house and I as good as gave him permission to look and see what was on it. That money, it's our money, not just his."

"What are you saying, Mrs. Pirella?" The agent asked. "Did you tell him to hack into Tony's computer?"

The lawyer gave her a warning look. She ignored it and said. "I didn't in so many words, but I did ask him to help me find out what Tony was up to. So, in a way I gave him permission. It's not hacking if I gave him permission." She shrugged, "it's more like computer repair, right?"

She didn't know why it was so important but in that instant, she knew she didn't want Clark to take all the heat for this. Maybe it was because she couldn't reconcile the sweet boy she had known with the computer hacking/cross-dressing run away wanted by the FBI. Or maybe it was because Tony wanted Clark caught and tried. And Shelley wanted to hurt Tony any way she could.

The agents and her lawyer were looking at each other uncertainly. "No, I am afraid that breaking a password is illegal, even with a wife's consent."

Her lawyer, catching her mood, said. "True but that money is indeed as much Mrs. Pirella's as it is Tony's at least until a divorce court finds otherwise. At least half of it should be hers, and the boy kept only one fourth. I think she would indeed have grounds to have some say on whether or not charges should be filed."

The agents exchanged another set of looks. One made a soft noise of frustration.

As the lawyer ushered Shelley Pirella out of the conference room, a District Attorney in a dark blue suit entered. He had been listening to their entire exchange from behind a tinted glass window in the next room.

"What just happened?" One of the agents asked. "Does she really have a say?"

"No," the DA said emphatically as he sat down. He put his head in his hands, "but if she wants to stake her claim on the money or refuse to cooperate with our investigation she can tie this whole thing up in courts for months." He rubbed his temples. "God, this case is going to turn my hair gray."

#####

"Do you think they will ever find him?"

It was Jeremy who asked the question. He looked up briefly from his mashed potatoes and at the adult's around the table and then went back to eating.

They all exchanged looks. It was two weeks from the day that Agent Hodgekins had arrived on the Holden's doorstep. They had talked daily on the phone but tonight's supper was Agent Hodgekins second time in the Holden's house.

Gerald Butler coughed nervously. "I am sure the State Department is doing all it can."

The State Department, Jeremy thought, it wasn't the FBI looking for his brother anymore, it was the State Department. The FBI didn't have jurisdiction where Clark had gone.

Gerald was here as Clark's lawyer, but Jeremy thought he seemed quite pleased to be having supper with Kelly again. Both boys had hated Gerald when mom dated him, Clark for the simple fact that Gerald used his least favorite word, 'buddy.' Jeremy on grounds that no one could replace his dad. Three years older, and on the cusp of manhood, he saw Gerald in a different light now. He was a good man. He made Mom happy and he seemed enamored of her. She deserved that.

"I sincerely hope so." Agent Hodgekins said without any real hope in his voice.

"How big is Bangkok?" Jeremy asked.

Bangkok, Thailand, Clark had boarded a flight at Minneapolis, stopped over in Tokyo Japan and then flown on to Thailand. He had been given a six-month work Visa and then promptly disappeared into what by Iowa standards was an incredibly huge city.

"Eight million people, give or take. Six hundred and some square miles," Gerald said. The number was too abstract to mean much to

Jeremy.

"The computer boys explained it to me this way," Agent Hodgekins put in, "If you put Bangkok where Des Moines, Iowa is on a map, Grundy Center would still be within the city limits." Jeremy's mouth fell open, trying to comprehend a city that size.

"Yeah but how many Americans are there?" Kelly said, grasping after any ray of hope.

"Twenty-five million American's go overseas every year." Agent Hodgekins said around a bite of pork chop. "Thailand is a pretty popular destination, but I don't know the exact numbers. I do know that we are at the tail end of their tourist season. The State Department estimates several thousand Americans currently in South East Asia. That's a lot of people but it's possible they'll find him."

"If he's still in Bangkok," Jeremy said, "I mean he's given you the slip before."

"Jeremy!" His mom scolded him, "you say that like it's cool or something."

"It is, isn't it? I never pegged Clark for the international man of mystery. But he's like a spy or something." Jeremy said. He missed Clark at times. He had always secretly admired Clark's intelligence. Now he admired his daring as well.

Agent Hodgekins chuckled. "I have to admit the boy is on to something. As much as I would like to see your son reunited with you guys, part of me wants to see him give the State Department the slip. It would make me feel better about how he gave me the slip."

"How likely is it that they'll find him?" Gerald asked.

Agent Hodgekins shrugged, "If they are looking as hard as they say, they'll find him, at least if he's in a tourist area. But I think he's gone to ground somewhere."

"Because of the emails?"

"Yeah, I think there's a significant pattern now of when they come."

"So?" Jeremy said.

"So, he's not traveling," Gerald said, "I think it makes sense.

They come about once a week, at roughly the same time. The time conversion for Thailand would be about five pm Friday afternoon. He's got a routine."

"But he'll run out of money," Kelly said, "and then what?" She both looked forward to the day that his funds ran out and he had to come home, and feared what it would be like, trapped in a foreign country with no money.

"Not soon I should say," Gerald said. "I looked up the currency rates. At thirty bahts to a dollar, Clark's pretty rich by their standards."

"Suppose they force the issue?" Jeremy said, "by freezing his assets. That's what the State Department said it would do, right?"

"I hope not. It would be hard on the boy, trapped in a foreign country where he doesn't speak the language and has no money," Gerald said. Kelly glowed. Jeremy understood that Gerald really did care about Clark's well-being. Yeah, he could live with this guy in Mom's life. "Besides they can't." Gerald went on, "They'd need either the local authorities to agree or interpol to get involved. Now that Tony's confessed, it's not likely to happen."

Tony had cracked as soon as it came out that Clark had went overseas. His lawyers had been working overtime, using the fact that Tony had been helping the FBI track Clark for a while to plea bargain a half a dozen charges down to something more manageable. The allegations of sexual contact with a minor loomed heavily over the entire situation, and Tony's fate was uncertain.

"I don't think they'll do that anyway," Agent Hodgekins put in, "the whole case is in such confusion. Given the abuse allegations, the girl's testimony and their evidence. Clark's hacking in to Tony's computer may have been justifiable, even if technically illegal."

"I'll certainly make sure the prosecutor thinks twice before pressing any charges," Gerald growled. Kelly touched his arm, smiling.

"The fed's case is in even worse shambles. They are fighting over jurisdiction, The FCC, The FBI and the State Department all want part of the case. They don't want to touch the abuse portion, which leaves them the theft of the money. But no one can decide whose money it was or should have been. The FCC wants to freeze the assets and go after Tony for insider trading. Shelley Pirella is insisting that part of that money is hers. She is just as adamant that she had no intention of pressing charges."

"We are just going to have to wait him out." Gerald said bringing the conversation back to Clark. "He keeps referring to having something he has to do. I think he's smart enough not to be doing something stupid. Hopefully he'll figure out whatever it is he's trying to figure out and come home."

"I hope so," Kelly said. "I don't know how much more of this I can take."

"What do you think it is he's doing or planning?" Jeremy asked.

"That's the million-dollar question." Gerald replied.

"I'll say this," Agent Hodgekins said, "I'll bet when we find out, it'll surprise us all."

CHAPTER NINETEEN

As Gerald cleared the table and Kelly brewed the men some coffee, Jeremy went to the computer in the den to check his facebook. He noticed something that made him call for his mother, "Mom, there's an email for you, from Clark!"

"But it's not," she replied. She broke off and rushed to the den.

"So much for the pattern," Agent Hodgekins muttered.

"What's it say?" Gerald asked.

Jeremy rose quickly so his mom could sit. She opened the email and read it aloud.

Dear Mom,

This is the last email I am going to be able to write for a while. I don't want you to worry however, I will be in safe hands and well cared for. If you don't hear from me again just know that I love you very much and I am sorry for any pain I have caused you.

I should be able to email you again in about a week and half. At that time I will be able to be more open with you. I would like very much to come home again. I miss you. I even miss Jeremy, if you can believe that. :) I am tired and lonely.

The truth is my entire life has been one long lie. I never intended to lie or to fool anyone. I just want to be me, to live as myself in as honest and open way as I can. For some reason, this is harder for me than for most people. For a long time, people made assumptions about me that were not true. It made me feel dishonest and guilty. For the last three months, I have lived more honestly in many ways, but I have done so through dishonest means. I know there will be a price to pay, and I will come home and pay it.

Tell Gerald that I accept his services as my lawyer. He can tell the FBI, the State Department and even Homeland Security that I will tell them everything. I will explain exactly what I did and why. He can make whatever plea bargain or defense he thinks will get me the best deal legally and I will cooperate. I have prepared another email that covers most of what I did and why. I will send that shortly to his email address.

As far as your two questions, I cannot answer fully. You say the State Department has tracked me to Thailand. I won't confirm or deny whether I am still there. I promise in a couple of weeks I can be more forthcoming.

As far as Tony goes, we did kiss. It went no further. I don't want to get into the whole story here. Suffice it to say I loved Tony for a time or at least I thought I did. What it was for Tony, I now understand was something very different. What he did to the other girls certainly does not qualify as love. I have no illusions left that I was any different in his book. We never went farther than kissing, though I think it would have eventually led to more.

He did use me but I used him too. I will not apologize to you or anyone for taking the pictures from him, they were never his. But I took money. I have heard that the girls came clean in the end. I will add what few pictures there are of me and add my testimony to their case. The girls gave the money to the authorities, while I took my portion and ran. So I guess they are better than me, but I was desperate. I don't know how anyone will judge me, but I will testify honestly about everything.

I love you.

Your daughter/son
Clarissa

#####

Clarissa tapped the keys nervously as she watched the laptop power down. She had just put the finishing touches on three emails. Two she had sent. One to her mother and one to her mother's friend Gerald who was now Clarissa's lawyer. A third she had not sent but set to be sent in a couple of days, just in case. In contained everything she had been doing and why, as well as a heartfelt goodbye. Hopefully she would wake up, get online and stop that email but you never knew.

As she shut the laptop screen her hands began to shake. She took a deep breath. She had to be strong just a few more minutes. Her hands continued to shake so hard she almost dropped the computer.

Another hand reached out, touching hers. She looked over at the older woman sitting next to her. Her name was Marie and she was French. She was a middle-aged woman with long dishwater blond hair and a kindly face. She reminded Clarissa of her mother, only Marie was transgender. She had just had her SRS surgery with Dr. Parn a few weeks ago. Marie and her partner Oliver had extended their stay in Thailand by a couple of days just to be here now with Clarissa.

It almost made Clarissa cry when she thought about it. That this woman, who shared one small link with her, that they were both transgender, had stayed just so Clarissa would not be alone on this day, was overwhelming to her. Marie sat next to her on the waiting room bench. Oliver, a short man with dark hair and an easygoing smile, read a French newspaper in a nearby chair.

Marie took the computer from Clarissa's shaking hands and placed it by her side. She held Clarissa's hand and said in a thick

French accent, "it will be okay."

A Thai nurse in green surgical scrubs approached them. "Ms. Holden, we are ready for you," she said in almost flawless English.

Marie gave her hand a gentle squeeze. "We will be here when you wake up."

Clarissa gave her a pale faced nod and a quiet but sincere "thank you" and stood. Later Clarissa would only recall bits and pieces of that morning, as though it had been a dream. Her anxiety peaked as she followed the nurse down the hall to the surgery suites. In the changing room, she saw her reflection in a mirror as she undressed. The male body that confronted her steeled her resolve to move forward. Then the nurses were helping her into a gown, leading her into the surgery suite itself. There was a pricking as the IV was inserted. Finally, where she should have been waking from the dream she instead heard the anesthesiologist say in a thick accent, "it's sleepy time Ms. Holden" and the world went black.

#####

"Kelly, it's going to be okay." Agent Hodgekins was saying. Kelly kept crying.

"Listen to him," Gerald coaxed.

"Yeah, mom," Jeremy added.

She knew she was being hysterical. But she couldn't get the email out of her head. It had come sometime while they ate. That was not his usual time. It would have been about eight thirty in the morning there. But it wasn't just the timing it was also the tone of the message. It had such a note of finality to it. "He's going to do something, something big and dangerous, and soon," she said, holding Gerald's hand tightly as he stroked her back.

"We don't know that for sure. He said within the next two weeks. The State Department will have found him before then. They are getting so close," Agent Hodgekins said. "Think about it. They have found out which branch of Kasikorn National Bank all of his activity is coming from. They know he's still in Bangkok, and have it down to one district. It's just a matter of time now."

One line kept coming back to haunt her over and over. She repeated it quietly to herself "if you don't hear from me again just know that I love you very much." That meant there was a chance that he wasn't going to come back, ever. She couldn't stand that thought.

There was a knock at the door. Jeremy got up and went to answer. He came back moments later. "Mom, there's a guy here to see you, says his name is Harry."

"That's the private eye," she said absently. "Let him in."

"What private eye?" Agent Hodgekins asked suspiciously.

"The one National Mortgage hired," Gerald said.

"And you've been sharing information with him?" Agent Hodgekins asked.

"He's the one that figured out Clark was using the name Clarissa." Kelly said in Harry's defense.

"What are you doing here?" Agent Hodgekins demanded angrily of Harry as he entered the den.

He regarded the FBI agent levelly. "Actually, I just stopped by to let Mrs. Holden know that I am defecting." He said.

"Defecting?" Kelly asked. She looked at him blankly, still too overwhelmed by Clark's email to comprehend what he was saying.

"I recently discovered something interesting about this case," he went on mildly. "It seems that Mortgage National did not in fact hire me, Tony did."

"Tony?" Agent Hodgekins said.

"He gave me a contract on company letterhead, but the money he fronted was his. He was hoping to find Clark and get those pictures back before anyone official got a hold of the boy. I thought for a while about writing off the whole thing as bad business deal but then a couple of things occurred to me."

"Such as?" Agent Hodgekins asked suspiciously.

"Well, the money's been fronted already and given his current legal predicament I figure Tony's not likely to come back looking for it. Besides I have put so much work in already." He turned to Kelly, "I am pretty sure I know where your son is and what he's doing." She hadn't talked to him since the passport had come to light. He had no idea what a storm his revelation had made.

"We already know where he is," Agent Hodgekins bristled.

"Please," Gerald said, "let's hear him out."

"So I take it Clarissa has come to light?"

"Yes," was all Gerald said.

Harry waited a moment, and when no further explanation was forthcoming he went on. "I have two questions first. They might seem random at first, but I assure you they are both vital and pertinent."

"I am the family's lawyer," Gerald said, "I will decide if it wise to answer, but by all means ask away."

"First, this Lao girl, Vong; is she Hmnong or Taidom?"

"What?"

"Her ethnicity; Hmong or Taidom?"

"Is that really pertinent?"

"Very much so," Harry said. "Would someone please call her and ask? It really is important."

"Okay." Gerald said slowly and motioned to Jeremy. Jeremy went to find Kelly's cell phone.

"Your other question?"

"Several terms keep coming up in regard to your son." He aimed this question at Kelly. "I have heard him described as a gay youth, a cross dresser and as gender variant. Have you heard the term transgender?"

"Yes," Kelly answered automatically without even looking towards Gerald, "Clark defined himself as transgender. Why?"

"He's in Thailand, that's why. He's going to have a sex change." Harry answered. Agent Hodgekins did a double take. Gerald swallowed hard.

"Show him the last email," Agent Hodgekins said. He seemed to have made his mind up about Harry and quickly filled him in on everything that had gone on the last two weeks while Kelly went and printed off the email.

Harry read the email silently and didn't speak for a long time. Everyone stared at him in anticipation. "I think I need to go to Thailand, as soon as possible," he said.

"Hey," Jeremy interrupted, "Vong said she's Taidom."

Harry took his glasses off and sighed. "I was afraid of that."

He turned to Agent Hodgekins. "You realize the State Department has no chance of finding the kid."

Agent Hodgekins shrugged. "And you think you have a better chance?"

"Maybe at least I am not hampered by inaccurate assumptions. That's been the problem all along, everyone has been working with inaccurate assumptions. It's like I told Kelly. We have assumed that like most kids, Clarissa would be running away from her situation here, not running towards something else. That's not the case.

"The State Department is making two completely false assumptions. They are looking for a gay kid. They won't be finding one. Thailand has a different culture. There are gay people in Thailand of course but there are also a lot of trans people there. They call them Kathoey. There are similarities between the two, like there are here in this country but there are important differences too. If you go looking or asking around in gay bars, or gay areas of town, you won't find a trans-person."

"Bangkok's a big place," Gerald said. "That could make all the difference."

"Well and the Vong thing complicates the matter even more." Harry said.

"Because?"

"Taidom means black Thai. They live in Lao, but are ethnically related to Thai people. They speak a very similar language. If Clarissa made a special point to befriend a Taidom person, and as I understand it, did several class projects on the culture and language then we have to assume she has a working knowledge of both. She will most likely have found a place outside the tourist areas. We are going to have to widen the scope of our search to include practically all of Bangkok."

"Um, can I ask a question?" Jeremy said.

"Sure kid," Harry said as he turned towards Jeremy.

"Why do you keep saying Clarissa? I mean I know he used that as an alias, but..."

"Kid, if I don't get my happy butt to Thailand and find your brother in the next few days, you are going to have to get used to using Clarissa too."

He turned towards Agent Hodgekins. "Well, we can play this one of two ways. You can start out by pointing out things like I am civilian and interfering with an official investigation. You can point out that there is a huge conflict of interest with Tony paying for me to find Clarissa, etc. And then I can point out things like you have no jurisdiction in Thailand." He paused and then smiled. "Or we could start out with me pointing out that I have a generous expense account, generous enough to add another ticket."

Agent Hodgekins smiled back, "well I do have some paid time off that I am due."

"Ever been to Thailand?" Harry asked.

"Nope," Agent Hodgekins replied, or rather Ron since he was technically off duty. His boss had approved his leave of absence, because he had so much paid time off built up it would have been hard to refuse. And because Agent Hodgekins had such a good track record his boss had done him one other huge favor, he had refused to ask where Ron was going. "But I went to England last year, thankfully." Kelly Holden had wanted to come as well, but she didn't have a passport and there was no time for her to get one.

"You?" Ron asked.

"Yeah, love that place." Harry said, "I try to go at least every second or third year. Beautiful climate, beautiful country and beautiful people."

"What do you make of this kid?" Ron asked suddenly.

Harry sighed, "I don't know. It's a wild story that is for sure."

"No doubt!" Ron agreed. "There's something about the whole thing. I mean he's broken a ton of rules, not just rules, laws. And the whole trans thing, I encounter it a lot at work, I mean they make up an inordinate proportion of the runaways but I have never really thought about it like this before."

"What do you mean?"

"Well it's most theoretical, in the other cases. We hear there is some kid who ran away. We search and we find them in San Fran, New York, L.A. one of those sorts of places. As you are closing the files you read somewhere that they were making a paltry living as a drag queen or are HIV positive because of sex trade. You see some note in their file about gender identity issues or being gay and you think, that is why they ran away."

"This is the first time I have set down and interviewed local authorities, friends, family. I always thought, why would a kid leave a nice comfortable middle-class home to live on the street? I understand the ones that run from broken homes, or drug addicted parents, or abuse. But why would anyone think that living in a city like New York on the street is better than living in a nice comfortable house in the suburbs? I mean really, can't you accept a couple years in the closet?" He paused and said, "But then I read the report about the kind of harassment Clark was facing at school. I don't know, maybe I would have run too."

"He's just kid, you know." Harry said, "you and I think, sixteen is just a couple of years until adulthood. Then he can move where ever, get a job, even do this transition if that's what he wants. Just wait it out, you say. But when you are sixteen, it's a whole different world. Two years can be a long time."

They found their seats on the plane. It was a Delta Airbus, nonstop from Minneapolis to Tokyo, probably the same plane Clarissa had taken three months before.

"I don't know about that." Ron commented.

Harry looked away and said quietly, "I ran away, long time ago."

"Serious?" Ron said.

Harry nodded, "yeah, I'm gay. I knew since, well, since I was too young to know what gay meant. I just knew I was different. I can remember being nine or ten and seeing these guys dancing on TV, out in the street in all sorts of strange get up. It was a news report about a pride event. I was sitting in the Jefferson Café, in Jefferson, Iowa. The news was running on a little color TV way up in the corner. I couldn't hear what the newscaster was saying, but I could hear what the men in the café were saying."

He paused and took a breath. "It wasn't pretty. They were complaining about those 'homos' in New York City. I knew some how they were talking about me."

"Nineteen eighty-two, I am fifteen years old. I have known that I was gay for five years. I dated this girl anyway, figured I had to, this being rural Iowa. There was an incident a couple of towns over. There was a boy about my age. He had a reputation for being a 'queer.' He supposedly came on to the star quarterback. The quarterback and his friends cornered the boy in a cornfield and beat him with baseball bats. They left him for dead in a ditch. A trucker found him and brought him to Greene County Hospital, just two blocks from my house. He was in a coma, expected to die." The story came slowly, in staccato bursts.

"I saw the writing on the wall. Nobody had threatened me but I knew I could never let anyone know I was gay. I knew I could never reach out to another guy, show anyone even the slightest trace of what I felt on the inside. I didn't know if I could do it. Three years is a long time when you are fifteen and full of hormones. So, I got the hell out of dodge."

"Just like that?" Ron asked, enthralled.

"Just like that." Harry replied. "I emptied my piggy bank. I had been mowing lawns and doing odd jobs. I had a small nest egg. It wasn't much but things were cheaper back then. I remember stopping in front of the hospital, I wanted to go in and say something to the kid but I was scared. Besides, he was in a coma. I got on the bus and headed for New York."

"Did you make it?" Ron asked.

"No, probably a good thing too." Harry answered. "This was the early eighties, and the AIDS epidemic was looming on the horizon. If I had made it to New York, I would probably be dead now. No, I made it as far Columbia, Ohio. There I ran out of bus money and stopped. I found out that Columbia had a thriving gay community and I stayed. I got damn lucky too. I hooked up with a guy about my age. We were both strapping young lads. He was street smart and landed us gigs bouncing at, of all places, a strip club. Owner knew we were gay, that was a big part of it, he trusted us around the girls."

"How long did you stay?" Ron asked.

"Almost twenty years. I got my GED and went to school for

criminal justice. I had planned to become a cop. That didn't work out and I fell into the private investigation field. I have been there ever since. I moved back to Iowa after my mom got cancer to help take care of her in her dying years. I have thought about going back but it's been almost five years now and I haven't gotten around to it. I guess I am hitting the age where you get comfortable where you are and don't like to move around. That is the long, sad story of Harry Gelt PI."

"Wow," Ron said, "that's pretty amazing."

Ron pulled the files out of his briefcase. Harry looked over and asked, "Okay, my turn. What do you think of this kid? Clark/Clarissa, whatever, I mean trans thing aside, what do you think of this kid?"

Ron shrugged. "What do you mean?"

"I haven't had as much time or access to as much of this case that you have had, but there's something different about it." He said. "The more I think about it the more I realize, it's the kid."

"He's dang smart," Ron said. "I wish I had half that much brains. And he's dedicated."

"You can say that again," Harry replied. "I've met transgender people before. They all feel that dedicated, you know, they'll sit there and insist that this is the way they are and what they want."

"You doubt them?"

"No, it's not that. It's just, they'll sit there and feel this. They will get pissed if someone tells them they can't be how they feel, or they'll get sad or upset. A lot of them are pissed at the world for being the way they are. But this kid... I got a feeling when anyone told him no, he would quietly say okay, get up, cross that person off some internal list and find another way; just like that."

Ron laughed. "That pretty much sums this whole case in a nutshell. The kid's got gumption, as my dad would say."

"And there it is again." Harry said gesturing at Ron. "I knew something was out of place when Tony came to me with his story. I saw through his bullshit from the start. I'd have told you the instant I saw him that Tony is a selfish, opportunistic bastard. But why did he want Clark found? Especially when it became clear that he understood he could never again be in Clark's life? It just didn't jibe with what I saw, or thought I saw, in Tony. It wasn't until just now that I figured out what it was, when I saw your expression."

"My expression?"

"Yeah, what gives with you? You are an FBI agent. Clark has done far more than bend a few rules. He's broken some pretty major federal laws. You should be after blood."

"Aww, he's just a kid. Besides there are plenty of mitigating factors, like the threats and stuff. Besides I work in Missing Persons. We are supposed to find these kids, not hunt and destroy."

"Those are just excuses. Face it, you like the kid. No, more than that, you admire him."

Ron paused and then agreed. "Yeah, there is something about him...her." He was holding up one of the pictures of Claire that had been printed and put in the file. It was hard to look at the skinny smiling blond and say he.

"It's more than that." Harry pressed, "he's got, gumption, was it? But he's got more than that. He's got a dream. It's not a dream you or I share, or even fully understand, but it's a dream. On the one hand, he's a scared teenage runaway. We are looking for him to stop him. On the other hand, he's the underdog, running for his dream. You can't help but want to root for him in some way. That's what didn't fit with Tony, and that's what doesn't fit with you, those computer geeks, Kelly, the kids at school or even the rest of the damn FBI."

"All right, you win." Ron said, raising his hands in surrender. "You're right on the money. No one says it, but we are all thinking the same thing. If I had pursued my dreams with half the intelligence and commitment that this one kid has shown, I'd... well I would have anything I wanted by now.

"Whatever happens next," Ron went on, "it's been a fantastic ride. I hope, I don't know what I hope. I hope he's okay of course. I hope I can tell his mom, he's okay. But beyond that I don't know. That's the one big sticking point. You're right, I want him to win. I just don't know what winning is."

CHAPTER TWENTY

"Baan Siri?" Ron asked.

"A hunch," Harry answered. "I could have picked somewhere closer to Boy Soi but I think is better."

"What's Boy Soi?"

"Soi means road." Harry explained, "Boy Soi or boy road, is where a lot of the gay bars and Kathoey hangouts are. It's very popular with a certain type of tourist, if you catch my drift."

"Kathoey is the local name for trans, right?"

Harry nodded.

"It would be the obvious place to go looking for Clark. I am sure the State Department would recommend that."

Ron read off some of the addresses the State Department had provided for them to start their search. They would meet with a local State Department official in the morning to go over the list and look at some maps.

"Bingo," Harry said as Ron read the list, "all of them right along Boy Soi. We are going to avoid that area like the plague."

"Because Clark would," Ron said, agreeing.

"Baan Siri is a bit off the beaten path, but it's a good location to start looking. Quite a few ex-patriots stay in the area, so Clark could blend in easily. I also googled and downloaded some info on the top doctors in the region. There were quite a few hits nearby. I suspect they'll recognize those pictures right off."

"You're probably right, your hunches have an uncanny way of

working out," Ron said. "I think we are here."

The taxi rolled off the street suddenly. The Baan Siri was set back off the road, almost invisible at first glance. The building was six or seven stories high, with a small garden in the front. A Buddhist shrine, which Ron would soon learn was typical, was placed prominently in the front of the building. They drove past a water fountain, up a circle drive and under an awning, where the taxi stopped. A guard stepped out and opened the door for Ron, who climbed out.

Another taxi pulled in behind them. Clark had arrived three and half months ago, Ron thought, towards the beginning of tourist season. Now tourist season was ending but the hotel was still busy. Harry had explained that even a five-star resort like Baan Siri ran under forty dollars a day in U.S. dollars. Clark's twenty-five thousand would have dwindled somewhat getting to Thailand but the remainder would go a long way here.

The lobby of the Baan Siri had the look of a hotel that must have been majestic, fifty years ago. The brass fixtures had been polished until they gleamed, the tile floor was clean and then wood rich and recently varnished, but nothing could hide the fact that hotel was not what it once had been. Still to Ron, who had never stayed anywhere fancier than Comfort Inns, it looked every bit the part of a five-star hotel. This was one of two hotels that catered to medical tourist, people who came to have various surgeries done. It was even recommended by a couple of the top plastic surgeons, so Ron wasn't too surprised to look into the hotel's restaurant and see a woman with a slightly too masculine face sitting at one of the tables. What happened next would continue to surprise him even years later when he thought about it.

"Do you have your room already?" A Thai woman was saying behind him. He turned. Two Thai women were helping a third, young American woman, into the hotel. They had apparently been in the taxi behind him and Harry.

"Yes," the American woman said. "I checked in last week."

"We should head up to your room then." The second Thai woman said.

"I want to see if I can ask a quick favor at the front desk first," the American woman said.

The Thai women were smartly dressed in American style clothes. In the U.S. the slacks and dress shirts would have been dubbed 'business casual'. The woman in between them was young, very young, wearing a T-shirt and a knee length skirt. One of the Thai women was holding a catheter bag, and the end of it ran up under the girl's skirt.

It was the face that had caught Ron's attention. She approached, her gait shuffling as though she were weak. She was saying to the nurse, "I want to see if I can give the staff some money and have someone run down to 7-11." 7-11 was obsequious in Thailand, and Ron had noticed one just down the road from the hotel on the way in. "And get me an international calling card. I know I am not supposed to walk far yet but I want to call home."

Ron was already reaching for the phone in his back pocket as he stepped in front of them. He said, "you can use mine, I think you're mother Kelly would very much like to talk to you, Clarissa."

Clarissa just stared at him dumbly. Harry walked up, apparently nonplussed by the sudden turn of events and said "well, so much for searching all over Thailand." He shrugged. "And I was sort of looking forward to it." He held out his hand. Still not comprehending, Clarissa took it. "Hello, my name is Harry Gelt PI, this is my travel companion and partner, Ronald Hodgekins, FBI. We came to look for you Clark, or should I say Clarissa?"

"Clarissa," she replied defiantly. "You're with the FBI?" she asked warily. She glanced around as though calculating her odds. Then a look of pain crossed her face and her shoulder's slumped in defeat. "You're here to arrest me, aren't you?"

"Ronald is on vacation." Harry said, "we don't want to ruin that. Maybe in a week or two."

Clarissa was looking at him, trying to judge if he was being serious or not.

"I am with the FBI." Ron said. "Missing Persons. My job is to see you safely home to your mother. Not to arrest you."

"I want that," Clarissa said. "I will cooperate." She held out her hands like she expected one of them to handcuff her right there.

"Once you've recovered, you mean." Harry corrected, taking her by the elbow. "We are not here as your enemies. Let's you get up to your room and settled in, you are as pale as a ghost."

"I didn't know the surgery would be so hard." Clarissa admitted, looking for a moment like the frightened teen she was.

"It will be okay now." One of the Thai women said, "it takes time to recover."

They rode the elevator up together. Harry had returned to the front desk, explained to the man working there that Clarissa was someone they knew and could they please be on the same floor. As luck would have it, there was a room just across the hall. Tomorrow they would notify the State Department that Clark, now Clarissa, had been found. Who knows what they would decide to do, but for tonight there seemed to be little reason to think she would be able to run again even if she wanted to.

The ride passed in silence, everyone lost in their own thoughts. Clarissa took short shuffling steps, and the walk down the hall took considerably longer than Ron expected. As they reached the door to Clarissa's room, Ron joked lightly, "well, I have had enough surprises for one day. I don't think my heart could take another one."

"Uh-oh," one of the Thai nurses said slyly and winked. She opened the door.

A chorus of "Surprise!" came echoing out at them. Of course, in the thick Thai accents it was often "supplies" "sue prize" or even "soup flies".

Clarissa cautiously and curiously peeked into her room. The wall was covered in a bright banner with Thai and English characters on it, saying, "Get well soon". A large section of the room was now taken up with posters with bright simple drawings and butchered English well wishes. A large clump of Thai girls, maybe eight or nine years old sat on the floor, held in place by the watchful eye of an elderly western school marm.

The woman favored them with a cool smile and said, in an Irish accent, "well, the wee ones wanted to see their favorite teacher one last time. What was I to do?"

Clarissa gave the older woman a hug. This was the unspoken signal for the kids to leap up and rush her as well. With the older lady holding her upright, they braced for the under aged onslaught together. "Clarissa!" The children chanted happily.

"We're glad you're okay," one of the girls said.

"I wish you could come back and teach us more," another said.

Kelly's phone rang. She looked at the display. It was agent Ronald Hodgekins. She did the calculation in her head, eight am here would mean it would be eight pm in Thailand. If the flight had gone according to schedule, they would have landed around one or two and checked into the hotel by four. He should now be settling, and letting her know they had made it safely.

"Hello, Agent Hodgekins."

There was a long pause. She was on the verge of asking if he was okay when she heard the quiet voice. "Mom?"

"Clark?" She gasped, taken aback.

"Yeah, it's me."

A million questions went through her mind. Why was he calling her now? And why did the phone show Hodgekin's number? Was this his latest hack? Where was he? What was he doing?

Before she could decide which question to ask first he spoke again. "Mom?"

"Yes."

"I love you."

She felt tears threatening to overwhelm her. "Oh, Clark, I love you too."

"I am sorry. I am so sorry for everything I have put you through."

She could hear the sincerity and intensity in his voice. He wanted her to believe and understand. She couldn't get mad at him yet and yet she couldn't quite forgive him just yet. "Oh, Clark," was all she could say as the tears began to flow. Then she said. "Why, Clark, why did you leave like that?"

"I am sorry Mom. I know you love me but you don't understand.

Maybe you just can't, not really, unless you've lived it. I didn't mean to hurt you, I just had to..."

"Did you?" She interrupted nervously. She didn't want to say it out loud, but she had to know.

"Yeah," he replied, "I was so scared Mom." She could hear his voice break and knew he too was crying. "I wanted you to be there so bad, to hold my hand. I wish it could have been like that. That's my only regret, Mom, that I couldn't have you there."

Without hesitating, she replied, "me too. If it had to happen I wish I could have been there. And Clark, I am sorry too. I am sorry I didn't understand how bad it was for you at school. I am sorry I didn't understand how bad it was," she broke off trying to find the right words, "to be how you are."

"It's not your fault Mom."

"No, I am your mother." She said still crying, "I should have been there for you. I should have protected you."

"That day you talked back to the gym teacher," Clarissa said, chuckling through her tears, "that was awesome Mom! You did everything you could. Besides it wasn't the school situation." It was Clarissa's turn to struggle for the words, "Tony, the job, you said you were so proud of me for having that job and I blew it by..."

"Clark!" Kelly said sharply, "you did not blow it! He was a predator! He tried to make you do something terrible. You can't blame yourself for things he did."

"I went along," Clarissa said quietly, "at first."

"And you stopped when you saw where it was leading." She countered, "we are going to have a long talk about the how someday soon but you have got to know you were absolutely right to stop him."

They talked a short while longer. Clarissa asked about Jeremy, the rest of the family and how things were going at home. Kelly could tell he was tired. There was a short pause and then Agent Hodgekins' voice came on, "my turn."

In the background, she could hear Harry's voice as well. "No, it's time for you to rest. You've had a very busy day. You can talk more tomorrow, when you are feeling better, hun."

"So you found him already? That was quick." She said still stunned.

"A total shocker," Agent Hodgekins said with a laugh. "By some cosmic coincidence we booked the same hotel. Harry hadn't even checked us in when this young American girl walks up to me and asks if I would help her buy a calling card so she could call home to her mother."

"Girl?"

"Yeah," he said turning serious, "five days ago. They did it at Piyavate Hospital, about three miles from here. A doctor Parn. The nurses say it went very well. Clarissa, Clark, is frazzled. She's been on the run for months now. She's been incredibly strong and self-reliant for the entire time. Still she's only seventeen and it takes its toll. I think all she wants now is to come home and be mothered for a while." Kelly's chest ached in sympathy. She wished more than anything that she had been able to go along, that she was there to hold her son right then, to be his mother.

"I've got to tell you something else." Agent Hodgekins went on. He sounded, incongruously, like a proud father rather than a policeman who had just nabbed his suspect. "Do you know what she was doing here in Thailand?"

"Having a sex change?"

"No, I mean where she was hiding."

"Where?"

He laughed. "She was teaching English at an international school. We brought her up to her room and found a dozen little Thai girls waiting in her room. They got one of the staff to let them in. They had balloons and banners and the works. She made a real impression."

"Yeah, Clark's like that. He makes an impression wherever he goes." She laughed, "I suppose I should say wherever *she* goes. I guess I am just going to have to get used to that, like it or not."

They talked for a while longer, about Clark's surgery, his job and his future when he came home. Gerald had already been discussing a possible plea bargain with the authorities. To her surprise the feds were being a lot easier to work with than the local authorities. The federal prosecutor had assured her that if he, she, she corrected herself mentally, cooperated fully with their investigation, they would probably drop most of the charges. "If he shows us the holes that he used, it will be more than worth it. We can plug them before someone truly malicious, like a terrorist uses them to get into the country," the man had said.

Clarissa had already written a detailed letter about Tony and their hacking. If the case had not been hopelessly quagmired before it definitely was now. The most obvious and worst charge against Clarissa was the fake passport and identity, major fraud in the eyes of the law. But those documents had come from Tony, which made him an accessory at very least. Most of the hacking programs and tools had come from him as well, and the entire case against Clarissa was hopelessly intertwined with the sexual abuse case against Tony. Gerald felt that was for the best. Now the federal prosecutor's best chance of nailing Tony lay in getting Clarissa's full cooperation and testimony.

Faking school records fell under the jurisdiction of the local courts, and the local prosecutors didn't have the same attitude at all. Still Gerald felt confident that a judge would take the situation into account, and the fact that Clark was still a minor would limit any permanent damage.

The job in Thailand struck Kelly as classic Clark. The moment he did something so totally reckless and irresponsible, he did something so responsible too. Like going behind her back to go to Iowa City and then finding his own therapist. She could never make heads or tails of it.

She sat down in her chair, and realized that for the moment it didn't matter. All that mattered is that he was safe. As the realization hit her, she began to cry again, tears of relief. Her son was safe.

#####

Vong walked slowly towards her locker. She heard one of the boys snicker behind her back. She didn't know what had been said but it didn't bother her as much as it used to. She didn't have a boyfriend, or even that many friends, but she knew that not everyone hated her.

First there had been Clark. He'd been really nice to her. It might have started with an ulterior motive, but he had turned into a real friend. She would have thought that after he left she'd be miserable but it hadn't quite worked that way.

For a short time after he left, she was the center of attention. She knew more about him than almost anyone, so everyone came to her for gossip. She'd actually talked to Amy and Christy, two of the most popular girls in the school, and they were nice to her. She'd met Clark's gay friend, Marcus and her had exchanged phone numbers.

None of this prepared her to have Amy walk up to her in the hallway.

"Hey, Vong, did you hear?" She said, leaning against the locker next to Vong's smiling.

"Hear what?" Vong asked.

"They found him." Amy said, "well sort of..."

"They found Clark? Wow. Wait, sort of?"

"They found *her*," Amy said, "his mom called me. She said she tried to call you too, but you were gone for the weekend."

"I was at the Tai festival in Des Moines." Vong said.

"She told me that he was in Thailand." Amy went on.

"He had the surgery?" Vong asked in surprise.

"You knew about that?"

"Well, not exactly," Vong said, "but we talked about the surgery and how they do it a lot in Thailand. That was part of the reason he was so interested in Thai culture and learning my language. He knew he wanted to go to Thailand someday and have the surgery."

"I'm confused, aren't you Lao?"

She was surprised that Amy knew even this much about her. "Lao and Thai are similar, similar enough that we can understand each other. But how did he get the money? I mean that's why I didn't even think of him going to Thailand."

"His mom didn't really say." Amy said quickly, "she just wanted us to know that he was safe. At first, I don't think she was planning on telling me the rest of it, but then she said we would find out soon enough. We might as well be prepared."

"Will he be back soon?" Vong asked.

Amy shook her head no. "She said it would be almost a month before he can travel. If she can get her passport she might go over there. Even once he gets back she's not sure he'll come back to school right away, or even any time this school year."

Vong giggled, "you mean, she."

Amy laughed too, "Yeah I guess you are right. That's going to take some getting used to. Wow, I know a real transsexual. Who would have expected that in a small town like this?"

"What are we supposed to call him now?" Vong asked.

"Clarissa," Amy said.

The hot wet Thai air hit Kelly like a wet blanket as she stepped out of Bangkok International Airport. She stared up into the deepening twilight. The sky was overcast.

"It's like a sauna." Gerald said at her side.

How am I ever going repay him? Kelly thought as she looked at the man at her side. He had signed on to help her find her son early on, giving hours of his time to the effort. Then as events unfolded he became Clark's, now Clarissa's, lawyer without once asking for more than a token payment to seal the contract. Then out of the blue he all but insisted on buying her a flight to Thailand to see her son. Part of her hated taking charity, but she couldn't have managed the last few months without him. And she needed to get to her son. Besides it was nice to have him back in her life. Out loud she said, teasingly, "maybe next time you should change out of your suit before we land." She tugged at the cuff of his gray suit as she said it.

"Well, I am here to represent Clarissa," he replied stiffly, "I should look the part. Besides the hotel will be air conditioned, I hope." He pointed suddenly, "look"

A young Thai woman was holding a sign saying, "Kelly Holden". They went towards the woman.

Kelly tried to remember the many pointers about Thai etiquette that Clarissa kept trying to explain to her over skype during the last few conversations they had. Luckily the woman stuck her hand out American style for Kelly to shake.

"I am May-Eee," she said, pronouncing her name slowly, "I am with the U.S. Embassy. I will be your's and Clarissa's liaison with the State Department."

Meie talked rapidly and gregariously as she led them out onto the street, into a waiting cab and most of the way to the hotel. Gerald listened politely and made comments now and then. Kelly was too distracted to follow most of the conversation. She caught that Meie was in fact an American of Thai descent, but not much else.

Kelly remained distracted, looking but not able to keep her eyes or attention on the passing buildings and cities until they pulled into the hotel's circle drive. There she saw something through the picture window that covered most of the lobby that she could focus on, her son. He was wearing a white T-shirt that said, "I love Thailand" and a long flowing skirt. His blond hair had grown a couple of inches and clearly crossed the line from gender ambiguous to feminine, but she would know her son anywhere. To his left was the familiar forms of Harry and Ron. To his right was a young Thai woman and an elderly white man. They were talking animatedly.

Then as she stepped out of the taxi she saw him do something she hadn't seen in years. He smiled. His whole face lit up, like when he was small. He grabbed the closest person, who happened to be Harry and pointed at her.

Then she was through the doors, tears streaming down her face as she ran to her son. He took a couple of quick shuffling steps as well and they were hugging.

"I don't know how I am ever going to repay you," Kelly commented for what seemed the hundredth time.

Gerald took her hand in his and smiled, "there's no need really, it's been my pleasure."

Gerald looked around the crowded market and quickly spotted the bright blond hair and long flowing skirt of Kelly's new daughter/son. As if on command Clarissa spun in their direction. She smiled and held up a light blue button-down silk shirt with floral prints. "You should buy him this," she said to her mother, "that's how you should repay him." She held the shirt up to Gerald's chest. "Definitely."

"That color does suit him," Kelly remarked, "it really brings out the blue of his eyes."

"Do I get a say?" Gerald asked.

"You are in the tropics now, pops," Clarissa told him, "it's time you started dressing like it."

Gerald had ditched his suit after the first day's formalities were concluded. Still sweat stood out on his temples and he shrugged uncomfortably. Perhaps it was time to ditch the heavyweight cotton T shirts for more local wear. "I suppose then I have no choice but to concede," he sighed dramatically.

He saw the playful smiles that passed between the two and felt a surge of joy. He was pleased with this new dynamic. Before he would try to engage Clark in the simplest of conversations only to be rebuffed time and again by the surly teenage boy. Now he schooled himself carefully to refer to her as Clarissa and sometimes "young lady." In turn, she referred to him as 'pops', a title he hoped fervently Kelly would allow him to gain for real someday.

He caught a tiny twinge in Clarissa's eye as she handed the shirt to her mother. "We'll get this shirt," he said with mock severity, "but then I think it's time to get this young lady back to the hotel. We can't be over taxing her."

Clarissa gave a wan smile. "Yeah, maybe," she conceded, "that canal ride was awesome though. Thanks." She turned towards Meie, who smiled as well.

Clarissa was technically in custody, but with Meie and Agent Hodgekins sharing the responsibility, it never seemed like it. Meie took one of Clarissa's arms and started leading her towards the road. Gerald took her other side. Kelly paid for the shirt and then joined them as they made it to the road.

"I've got a little present for you two as well," Clarissa said with a mischievous smile. "When we get back to the hotel."

"You shouldn't be taxing yourself," Kelly said sternly, "and you are not to be spending any more of that money either."

"Don't worry on either account," Clarissa said. "I've talked Mike, that old guy from New Zealand, into giving you both dance lessons in ballroom tonight."

A look of panic crossed Kelly's eyes.

Gerald put his free arm around her, "I don't think we can argue with her in this state," he said with a sly smile. "We'll just have to tough it out."

#####

Kelly ran her fingers through the blond-haired kid that lay with her head on Kelly's shoulder. My daughter Clarissa, she thought, will I ever get used to that? Or will I always be stumbling over Clark?

She should be sleeping like Clarissa, or like Gerald who was snoring lightly in the seat on her other side. But Kelly couldn't get comfortable in the cramped airplane seat. Right now she didn't care, she was content to sit and stroke Clarissa's hair, to know she was safe after months of worry.

She was so similar and so different at the same time. Physically it was still her son Clark. The part that the surgeon had "fixed" was not something she had seen since he was old enough to dress himself and she was certainly not ready to see what had been done. Her hair was a few inches longer and she had it layered in a very feminine cut now. None of this prevented her from seeing Clarissa as her son Clark, though everyone else seemed to accept Clarissa's femininity as a given. Harry had told her that she had too many years invested in seeing him as Clark. Perhaps he was right.

Psychologically there seemed to be an enormous gulf between Clark and Clarissa, as if they were two separate people. But that's not entirely right either, she thought, it was as though the last five years of Clark's life had been wiped clean, for better or worse. Clarissa was a lot more like the bubbly bright pre-teen Clark then the surly depressed teenager she had known for the last five years. The perpetual scowl had been replaced with a face that reflected every emotion she felt. She didn't slouch but instead bounced with impatience anytime she was still. One word answers had given way to long conversations. She loved to tease, especially the men. She referred to Gerald as "pops" and Ron and Harry as her "uncles."

But not all the changes had been for the better. When a man answered her teasing too boldly she got a wary look in her eye that reminded Kelly of the close brush Clarissa had had with Tony. The last five years had left their mark as well. Clarissa could dissolve into tears in a heartbeat, like when Amy accidentally let it slip that the boys around school still referred to he as Clark and he and still used the same old tired insults. There were times when she could turn petulant and whiny. Kelly would just stop and wonder, how can the kid who orchestrated a hack on a major corporation, faked an entire identity and managed to flee halfway across the world be so freaking immature?

"She's going through a huge life change right now," Gerald had said by way of explanation, "it's like a second adolescents."

"Oh my god!" Kelly replied, "we barely made it through the first one. What's this one going to be like?"

Harry, on the other hand, had more experience with transsexuals and a more biological explanation. "She's not producing testosterone anymore," he said, "and she's not on estrogen. Her hormones are completely out of whack. Get her on estrogen before she drives herself, or you, nuts."

Clarissa had been totally shocked when she had brought that up. "We should get you to a doctor as soon as possible when we get home," Kelly said over dinner the night before their return flight.

"I'm healing okay," Clarissa had replied. "And I don't really care for Dr. Shoemaker."

"I know, but maybe Dr. Gant can help us find someone who has experience with this sort of thing, you know, the hormones and stuff."

"You are on board with that now?" Clarissa said shocked.

"No," Kelly replied. "well, yes, I mean it's not like you have given us any choice."

"What your mother means," Gerald said coming to her rescue, "is that she's worried about your long-term health. Since you no longer have male hormones, it is in your best interest to start female hormones soon, if that's still what you wish."

The sleeping form on her shoulder began to move, interrupting her reverie. Clarissa yawned and stretched. Kelly looked into her child's face. It was pale and wan. "Are you okay?" She asked.

Clarissa nodded, "I'm fine."

"I have your pain pills in my purse if you need one," Kelly said.

"No," Clarissa shook her head, "I'm not in pain. I'm just," she paused, "worried, I guess. I mean I ran halfway around the freaking world to escape my problems. Now I am flying right back to face them plus a whole lot more."

It'll be okay, died on her lips. She had said that too many times before and it wasn't true. "It'll be different this time." She said. "You are different, I am different. We'll find solutions, I promise."

"Everything okay?" Gerald murmured sleepily at her other side.

Gerald, the man who had given her so much the last few months and expected nothing in return, well almost nothing. He had finally told her as they walked through the street outside the hotel one night, what he wanted.

"You keep saying you can't repay me," he said putting his hand in hers, "the only repayment I would want or accept is for you to answer one question truthfully." For one second she was scared he was going to 'pop the big one' but instead he went on, "four years ago you told me we had to break it off because you were not ready for a serious relationship, or more to the point, your kids were not ready for you to be in a serious relationship. You said that was the only obstacle to us. Given how things have changed and the fact that I am now on relatively good terms with both your kids, is there any further obstacles to us?"

He had left it at that and so far she hadn't answered. She leaned over close to him and said, "Nothing."

"Hmm?"

"That's my answer, there is nothing in the way of us being in a serious relationship, if you still wish it."

He smiled sleepily. "I was hoping you'd say that," he said reaching for her free hand.

#####

Clarissa stared down the ramp and swallowed hard.

"Now that's a bit of overkill, don't you think?" Harry said following her line of sight. At the bottom of the ramp waiting for them was a short balding man in a dark suit flanked by two massively muscled law enforcement personnel. They were wearing gray t-shirts with the Marshall's logo emblazoned on the chest and black dress slacks. At their belts they had badges, firearms and handcuffs. "Two U.S. Marshals and a senior FBI agent for one teenage transsexual?"

Clarissa looked to her other side and saw that her mom's mouth was in a tight worried line. Gerald at least, appeared unflappable, "it's a show of force. They are trying to make a point of exerting their authority. The fact that you eluded them for so long has certainly pissed off some of the agents." He turned towards her, "be respectful, but don't be afraid of them. Whatever you've done wrong, you've never been violent and you are surrendering peacefully. They have no right to use any sort of force."

Drawing from his strength, Clarissa squared her shoulders and walked down to the waiting men. "Clark Holden," the balding man began, "You are under arrest for the following crimes, fraud..."

#####

Amy bounced impatiently in her seat, trying to see over heads of the crowd to keep her eye on the door. It had been rumored for nearly a week that he, no she, would be here today. It made sense after all, Amy thought as she glanced around the high school gymnasium. It was her brother's graduation. Of course, she would want to be present.

Still no one seemed to know for sure. Clark/Clarissa's whereabouts had remained almost as mysterious as when she was missing. Her arrest at Minneapolis International Airport had briefly made the national news. What else would one suspect? The story had everything for the prurient interests of a jaded TV audience. Miss Claire, infamous hacker turns out to be a gender variant boy. (See flashed across the screen two pictures, one is Clark's school picture, the other of him in a school girl's outfit. The backdrop appears to be a club. Amy suspected Marcus at first but Marcus told her they took the picture from a promotional poster for the teen show.) As if this twist isn't enough, there's Tony. (Flash another picture of the day they arrested him for sexual conduct with a minor. He looks seedy and malicious in that picture, the perfect villain.) Add in for good measure the fact that Miss Claire had revealed that Tony had other girls. (Someone on the case has leaked pictures. Faces are covered because the girls are minors and the pictures are artfully cropped to be decent. Amy knows it's her picture though.) She had seen this clip a hundred times. She fast forwards through most of it now, stopping at the final image, a slender ambiguous teenager wedged between two beefy federal marshals. Clarissa looks terrified but determined.

Amy knows from having talked to Jeremy and once to Clarissa on the phone that she was arraigned at the courthouse but never held in jail. She knows that Clarissa has been to the FBI headquarters in Chicago and testified in front of the cybercrime department no less than twice. She's given a deposition locally in Tony's case and in Shelley's divorce case. She was arraigned in a county courthouse in Southern Iowa somewhere, where she hacked a school computer and faked some school records. She knew they'd been home too, but they kept a very low profile. Not everyone was accepting of what she'd done and there had been hate mail. Clarissa had not returned to school, nor did she intend to this year.

Maybe I should have asked her to fake my school records, Amy thought sourly. With her own testimony against Tony and that whole scandal, she had not been doing well in school. Coming clean was worth it, she told herself fiercely, I am doing better in therapy and I haven't cut in nearly a month.

Then she caught sight of a tall thin man with gray at his temple, Clarissa's lawyer Gerald. He had been kind and caring when the girls had gone to him. He had worked hard to keep their names private and had called personally to apologize when the pictures were leaked, even though he had nothing to do with it. She had not seen him personally since that first day.

Why was he here now? Behind him was Kelly Holden and then

a familiar form, Clark, now Clarissa in a gender-neutral shirt and blue jeans. All eyes turned towards the door and a hush fell over the crowd. There were many disapproving looks and more than a few muttered comments.

Amy ignored all of them, leaping to her feet. She waved frantically for Clarissa's attention. Clarissa smiled and waved back. Amy caught a flash of white and looked up into the opposite side of the gymnasium. She laughed and pointed. Vong had made a handcrafted sign on white poster board. It said, "Welcome Home Clarissa!"

#####

Amy saw the familiar and not so familiar form as she approached the house. The hair was longer, past shoulder length now. The outline of the face was the same, but the box she was carrying pressed against a bust line that hadn't been there. As she turned to put the box in the van Amy thought that maybe the hips were rounder but she couldn't be sure. Then Kelly's voice came out of the house. The figure paused and cocked her head to one side and put her weight on one leg, with the other jutted out. It was a pose that was typically feminine and typically Clark. Only it was Clarissa now.

"Howdy, stranger." She said. The figure turned and favored her with a shy smile.

"Hey, Amy."

"How are you, Clarissa." She was careful to use the correct name and worried that she would screw up and use the wrong pronoun without meaning to.

"Good." Clarissa answered and then winced slightly, "still a bit sore, at times." She corrected, "but really, good."

They stood awkwardly for a minute, Amy wanting to move closer but not sure but not sure if she should. Then Clarissa sat down the box she was holding and held out her arms. Amy moved into the hug quickly. She squeezed her friend tightly, tears threatening her and whispered, "thank you, thank you for everything. So the surgery went okay?" She asked when they finally broke the hug. They had talked on the phone a couple of times, and it seemed a silly thing to ask as soon as it left her mouth.

"Yeah, it went by the book," Clarissa replied. "And I am healing okay."

"How was Thailand?"

"Great. You gotta go some day if you can. It's beautiful." Clarissa said, leaning against the van. Her mom's voice came at them again, requesting help. Her mom's face made a brief appearance as well.

"Hi, Amy," she said and to Clarissa she added. "Take a break and visit, I'll get Jeremy to help me."

"How's it going with?" Amy nodded towards the door.

"She's adjusting. It's not like she didn't know I was transgender. She's pretty sore about the way I went about things. Once she got over being glad I was safe I heard about it for about four or five days straight." Clarissa rolled her eyes.

"She went over too, didn't she?" Amy asked.

"Yeah she got her passport and was able to come for the last week and half and she was able to come home with me. I am glad too, traveling was pretty hard and it was nice to have some help."

"I'll bet."

"Still, I think Thailand cooled her jets." Clarissa laughed, "It's hard to be mad for very long over there. We did some sight-seeing, nothing fancy, but we saw some beautiful temples and took a ride on the canals. The last three days we were there, the rainy season started. It poured and poured. All we did was sit in the hotel and talk. It was nice. It was the first time in a long time that I have been able to be really honest with her and I think that went a long way towards us being okay again."

"She's your mother, she has to love you," Amy assured Clarissa. "How did the doctor take it when he found out you were a minor?"

"He was a little upset. One of the nurses was really pissed. Nuch, my favorite nurse, just said "mai phen rai" and went on with her care."

"Mai Phen..." Amy sounded the words out.

"Rai, it means, no big deal. It's sort of the way they deal with everything over there. That's what I loved about it. If I stumbled and bumped into someone in the mall, I'd say I was sorry and they'd be like "mai phen rai." We'd bow and walk away happy. Around here they'd give you a dirty stare or something. A taxi driver gets cut off and instead of laying on the horn, he shrugs and says mai phen rai. Like I said, it's hard to stay mad long in Thailand."

Amy chuckled, "Sound wonderful. Can I send Mrs. Gade?" Mrs. Gade coached the cheer leading team. Then Amy turned serious, "and the authorities? Are you going to jail?"

Clarissa just shrugged, "doesn't sound like it. Gerald had already made a pretty good plea bargain on my behalf. He's good at what he does. He's argued it wouldn't serve societies interest to lock me up. I'll have to do probation and community service, but I am okay with that. I had to talk to about a dozen different people from a dozen different organizations. At the FBI I thought I would be in a little room with a couple of hard core interrogators, like you see in the movies. Instead it was in a conference room and I had to give a two-hour presentation about what I did and how.

"It was kind of funny," Clarissa chuckled. "The guys were all from the cybercrime department and were computer geeks. Some of the guys wrote their various screen names on their name badges, guys I knew online. It was weird to meet them in person, but not half as weird as realizing the people who had been chasing me were the same ones that had inadvertently shown me how to do it all. I think maybe that's why they went so easy on me."

"You must be so smart." Amy said.

"Naw, I mean I know I am pretty smart, but I'm no genius. If I was a genius I'd have realized how stupid it was to run away. I'm seventeen, I could have had my surgery in another year anyway, and it would have been legal and the freaking FBI wouldn't have been chasing me."

They both laughed.

"Anyway, it was all simple stuff, stuff they had mostly taught me. I just used it in a new way, and used a combination of hi tech and low-tech stuff. Like the ID thing. I faked the birth certificate, but the rest was all footwork. I went to the DMV and got a license. I really did go to Kirkwood community college and take the GED exam."

"Not a genius?" Amy said with arched eyebrows. "Sixteen and you took the GED?"

"You could pass it." Clarissa said dismissively. "Anyway, the FBI, State Department and Homeland Security took my little lecture and said that evened things up a bit. As far as they are concerned I have revealed some significant holes in their security, so I really did them a service. Not to mention that with my cooperation and testimony, their case against Tony is pretty airtight."

"That's pretty cool of them."

"The locals haven't been quite so agreeable but they are coming around." She chuckled, "Darthtater talked the school into dropping the charges against me for hacking their system."

"How?" Amy asked.

"By pointing out that I used known security holes in the Windows operating system. He casually suggested that since they were known holes, they should consider suing Microsoft about the breach. It was a nuisance suit, but Microsoft bought them out with an offer of several computers for their computer lab."

"Still I have to face charges for tampering with public records. Gerald's going to be my lawyer, and he's pretty confident that the judge will be lenient. I am a minor and I didn't use it for any malicious purpose. Also it's a nonviolent offense, so I shouldn't have to do time."

"And the money?"

"Not much was left after the surgery, a few thousand. I gave it to Shelley's lawyer. She doesn't want to see me but she did stand up for me for some reason." Clarissa said.

"That's too bad, I know how you liked those girls. What do you think about Tony?" Amy said.

"I don't know. Part of me wants to see him pay the full price for what he did, to you and those other girls in particular. But part of me is glad they made the deal. He's still going to jail, he'll still be on the sex offender's registry when he comes out, and this way we don't have to go to trial."

Amy blew a sigh, "I know I was seriously freaking about that. Facing him on the stand?" She shuddered. "Besides they are still after him over the insider trading crap, so he's likely to get a few years more added on to his time. Yeah, I think it's enough. I am just happy to finally be done with it."

"What about the other girls?" Clarissa asked.

Amy rolled her eyes, "Brenda's pissed because she didn't get to keep the money, and then she wanted to sell her pictures to the Enquirer for a million dollars but her parents won't agree. I think Debra's doing better though. We've been doing some workouts together. Don't worry, I am not overdoing it this time, I'm helping her get in shape and she's helping me not to overdo it.

"We all owe you a huge debt of gratitude," Amy went on. "We could have spent our whole lives knowing that those pictures were out there, over our heads. That he could show back up at any time and be like, do this or else. Now we're free."

"You ended up exposing those pictures anyway," Clarissa said, "and that helped me stay free, so I think we're even."

"So what now?" Amy asked.

"Mom's moving us to Des Moines." Clarissa gestured at the half-filled van. "Says she only stayed in this town for us. It was Dad's hometown not hers. So with Jeremy graduating and the fact I haven't exactly had a stellar connection at school or around town, it's time to move on."

"I'll miss you." Amy said sadly.

"I'll miss you too." Clarissa said. She led Amy to the porch and they sat down beside each other on the steps. "It's too bad, I finally made friends at school and I got to say goodbye." Clarissa bumped Amy's shoulder playfully, "but one of us still has a driver's license. I expect a visit or two."

Amy smiled and nodded. "Definitely, but you really should get out if you can. I mean some of the people that didn't like you before are even worse now. I wish you could stay, but if I were you I wouldn't go near that school again."

"Mom feels, and I agree, that it will be easier to start over as Clarissa, with new students." Clarissa said. "They don't even have to know about Clark. However, if I want to be out, she found a place on the northwest side of Des Moines. The school, Roosevelt, has a good GSA."

"GSA?"

"Gay Straight Alliance." Clarissa explained. "It's a club for gay kids. According to some research my mom found, having an active GSA in a school is one of the best indicators that there won't be as much harassment."

"She really loves you, you know that, to move just for your sake."

Clarissa leaned in conspiratorially. "That's what she says, but I think Gerald having a practice there and a house a few blocks away might be a big part of it."

"Are they going to get married?" Amy asked.

"I don't know." Clarissa shrugged, "but I've only got one more year of school and I will be out of the house too. It's time for her to find someone for herself. She deserves that. He's a really good guy."

"Amen to that," Amy put in. "He was very kind to us. You and I know how bad men can be. You find a good one, hang on to him!"

Clarissa laughed. "Yeah, I wish I could have seen that before, when they were dating the first time. I was kind of a shit to him."

"You were in a dark place then," Amy said. Then she changed the subject, "how is Jeremy handling all this?"

"I can tell he's still a little uncomfortable about the gender stuff." Clarissa said, "but I think he'll adjust. He is happy to have me back and he's always going on about the hacking stuff and how smart he thinks I am. Then he'll call me something like La Femme Clarissa, international person of mystery."

"Brothers," Amy said rolling her eyes, "they have funny ways of saying they love you."

"Yeah, that's how I try to take it anymore." Clarissa said.

Kelly came out and sat on the porch next to the two of them. "We are almost done packing this load. We need to run it down to Des Moines. We'll probably stop for pizza on the way. You want to come?" She said to Amy.

"I'd love that," Amy replied, the two rose and followed Kelly into the house.

CHAPTER TWENTY-ONE

Rachel's writing explores diverse social topics and characters. She takes on LGBT issues and coming of age in her YA novels. Her writing has been described as engaging and thought provoking by critics and fans.

She also writes science fiction and fantasy under her initials R. J. Eliason. Her writing can be found wherever books are sold online.

DISCLAIMER

There is one simple rule for the writing process. As a writer you take everything you know, pour it into a blender and hit puree. Then you pour the thick gooey mass onto the page.

Sometimes family and friends may read a piece of fiction and recognize one tiny piece of something on a page (it may be a piece of a conversation or a description) and mistakenly assume the piece glued next to it must somehow also relate to them as well. That is simply not the case. All of the characters in this book are either directly or indirectly based on people I know, but all those people have been through the blender. Because one character has the body or the face of a man I knew briefly does not mean that he has the same personality.

People have asked me if this book is autobiographical. I reply no, but it has been cathartic. I was not 'out' about my gender identity when I was in high school and did not face even a fraction of the harassment that Clark/Clarissa does. However I experienced similar situations. Growing up in a small town in a time period before the Internet I definitely experienced the isolation that my character feels. No, this is not autobiographical but it was very cathartic.

Finally for the sake of authenticity, most of the places mentioned in this book are in fact real places. The people that inhabit those spaces and the events that occur there are entirely fictitious. The town of Grundy Center was convenient, close enough to both Des Moines and Iowa City for the action set in those cities, far enough to give the sense of isolation. I do not mean to imply that Grundy Center is any worse, or any better, than any other town in Iowa.

In short, this is a work of fiction and any resemblance to real peoples places or events is entirely coincidental.

47579233R00159

Made in the USA
Columbia, SC
02 January 2019